Withdrawn Stock
Dorset Libraries

By Roopa Farooki

THE GOOD CHILDREN

ROOPA FAROOKI

TINDER
PRESS

First published in Great Britain in 2014
by TINDER PRESS
An imprint of HEADLINE PUBLISHING GROUP

1

Cataloguing in Publication Data is available from the British Library

ISBN 978 0 7553 8342 9 (Hardback)
ISBN 978 0 7553 8343 6 (Trade Paperback)

Typeset in Sabon by Avon DataSet Ltd, Bidford-on-Avon,
Warwickshire

Printed and bound in Great Britain by Clays Ltd, St Ives plc

HEADLINE PUBLISHING GROUP

An Hachette UK Company
338 Euston Road
London NW1 3BH

www.tinderpress.co.uk
www.headline.co.uk
www.hachette.co.uk

For my mother, who made me believe that everything is possible.
For my children, who show me every day that this is true.

We sit in the dark
And we sit in the cold
We're obedient kids
We do what we're told
It's good to be good
So we do what we're told

Professor Sully Saddeq
Collaborators – How Good People Do Bad Things

It suits you when you say no . . . I should try saying
it more often. It's a powerful little word.

Dr Jakie Saddeq, British GP and aid worker

PART 1

GOOD SONS, GOOD DAUGHTERS, 1938–1961

Chapter One

Sully

I'M SULAMAN SADDEQ, AND I'M SITTING IN A CLEAN WHITE ROOM, thinking about the decisions we make. It seems to me that our decisions are so terrible, so tragic, it's better to believe we're not the ones who make them at all. That we have no choice. I've just worked this out, here in my chair. A script at my right hand. A machine on my left. I'll blame someone else. Blame him. Blame her.

I raise my hand towards the machine, and pause. There's a sobbing man on the other side of the wall. The doors are closed. I can't see him. But I can hear him. He sounds like he's in agony. He's banging on the wall now. 'Let me out! It's my heart,' he yells. 'It's troubling me, I'm telling you! Let me out!'

I look into the blank wall like it's a mirror. I'm smooth and sinless. Bleached like a bone on a beach. There's no blood on my hands. It feels like there's no blood in my whole damned body. Like I'm good and I'm dead. Like this white room is as close to heaven as I could ever get, and now that I'm in heaven, they'll never let me leave.

'The experiment requires that you continue,' says the white coat. 'Go on, please.' I know that he's more than a white coat. He's called James, but tells his friends and colleagues to call him Jim. It's how he introduced himself to me. I'm Jim-Just-Jim. He has blue eyes, a cheap haircut and good shoes. I know that he's keen to please his boss. Our boss, I should say. The professor. Because I'm working for the man too, for four dollars an hour, plus fifty cents for gas. This is New Haven, Connecticut, this is 1960, and in this town, at this time, four dollars is great money for an hour's work. I walked here, so the gas money is a bonus.

'He said he wants to leave,' I say weakly.

'Go on, please,' the white coat says again. I'm meant to pull the next switch. They're the cheap black switches that can be bought in any local hardware shop. Along the line of switches, laid out in neat military ranks, there's a label marked Mild Shock, and further along, one for DANGER, and beyond that, at 450 volts, is an ominous, anonymous XXX. I suppose a skull and crossbones would be too obvious. You're meant to guess, but you're not meant to know. I know. I'm in on the dirty little secret. I'm in on the joke.

'It is absolutely essential that you continue,' says the white coat, moving smoothly to the next prompt, acknowledging my hesitation, my hand still hanging in the air. As though I'm a child in need of a little nudge to do the right thing. His words are like an arm around my shoulders.

I do what I'm told. I'm shaking a little, and have to swallow back a hysterical laugh. I tell myself I'm not to blame, not any more than the machine. I'm just doing what I'm told. It's only a memory test. An experiment. And the man gave the wrong answer, so he gets buzzed. He's a volunteer. He's getting paid for this too. The hairs on his forearms were damped down with the sponge. The electrodes moistly attached. I didn't see this. It happened behind the wall. I touch the switch, and it's smooth under the pad of my finger. It's easy. I don't see the shock. I don't feel the shock. The electricity is as invisible and clean as poisonous gas. Carbon monoxide filling a car with sleep.

And in a faraway world, on the other side of the wall, someone screams.

The man doesn't answer any more, but the white coat reminds me that silence is a wrong answer too. The man said he had a heart condition. It's possible that he's dead. But I still do what I'm told. I keep asking the questions on my script. I'm good and he's dead. I pull the switches all the way to DANGER. I'm flying now, to the end of the line. The last switch sets me free. XXX. I'm good and I'm dead. It's over. I'm free.

4

We sit in the campus cafeteria afterwards, with cups of coffee and plates of greasy food, and the other two want to huddle up and talk about the sad little play we put on. To dissect our performances. Like new med students performing post-mortems. Cutting up one donated body after another. Skulls gifted from the thoughtful dead like theatre props.

Jim is worried he sounded too casual, not professional or stern enough. He's worried that he was meant to wear an ambiguous grey coat for today's trial, not a white one, and that the boss will find out. He tells a long and tedious story about what happened to the grey coat, something to do with his wife and a miracle detergent. He laughs at the end, as though he's just shared a hilarious anecdote, and I realise that he was boasting a little, about his I-Love-Lucy life and his ditzy, charming wife.

Danny, the screaming man, thinks he hammed it up too much; he thinks he needs to do it better on the next recording, or the volunteers will get suspicious. He's worried about the script change from our boss; he doesn't think he should be shouting about a heart condition. It feels wrong. He explains that when his father had a heart attack, he didn't shout about it. He just slumped to the floor, complaining quietly about shooting pains up his arm. It bothers Danny that you can't communicate someone slumped to the floor and quietly complaining, through a wall.

I don't say anything. I'm new here. I'm distracted because the brown-haired girl in the too-long lab coat hasn't come into the cafeteria yet, and even though I've never spoken to her, I like to know she's there. I'm embarrassed that I laughed and I'm looking anywhere else. They're aware of my silence, and shift a bit uncomfortably in their seats, and I know I'm still not playing the part right.

'So I guess I screwed up,' I say eventually, sipping my coffee. I try to say it casually. I force myself to stop glancing at the entrance for the girl, and glance at myself instead, upside down in the coffee-glazed spoon. It makes me look browner than I am, and I feel briefly reassured, that I have an identity, and a place in the world, a brown man in a white coat. Like my father before me. His father before him. As though there is a place for me to go, somewhere outside this prestigious Ivy League university, the medical convention in the big hotel, full of the coffee-coloured men in white coats, past and present and future.

I suck the spoon, to see myself more clearly, and wish I hadn't. Unlike my father, I'm not brown enough. I have my mother's milk-faced aspiration, although on me, it looks more like indecision. My sisters

5

aren't quite as light as me. They're nagged by our mother to bleach their faces and powder themselves pale, but Mae and Lana stubbornly keep their complexions the warm shade of burnt sugar and cream. My little brother, Jakie, is properly and proudly brown, and never needs to say a thing about where he's come from. I'm jealous of him. He's saved from the tedious explanations I have to give each new person I meet.

I pass off. People here don't know I'm foreign until I open my mouth. And even then they think I'm European.

My name badge says Sully, because that's what they call me here, and I'm not sure they realise how well the accidental nickname fits me. To sully. To screw things up. My real name didn't even fit on the name badge: Sulaman Osman Saddeq. Unless I got them to abbreviate it altogether. SOS. A cry for help. I was named after my grandfather, the first doctor in our family, and he was named after Solomon the Wise. The king who told two women squabbling over a baby to cut it in half, to see who would love it enough to let it go. The man who made terrible and tragic decisions, and lived by the consequences.

I can't live up to my ambitious namesakes. I can't make a decision, and I can't take the blame. So now I'm just Sully, a man impersonating another man doing a four-dollar job plus gas money, and I still did it wrong.

The other two nod. They're relieved I said it first. Like I was a girl they were trying to break up with after a third milkshake and a failed grope in the back of the local movie theatre, who has said sweetly, 'It's not working out, it's not you, it's me.' I've made it easy on them, and they appreciate this; they think that I'm probably a nice guy, even though I'm not very good at my job.

'You went kinda far,' says Jim. 'Once you'd got to 150 volts, and I'd run out of script, you could've stopped.'

'No one's going that far,' agrees Danny. 'We figured less than three per cent would go to 450 volts, with a man screaming behind a wall. Not just because a schmuck like Jim is asking them to do it. It's only meant to be a memory test.'

'He'd have to be one evil sonofabitch to get that far,' I say. 'But the difference is, I knew it wasn't real.' I'm making excuses, digging myself deeper. 'I thought it would be better to carry on, to get an extreme down. The pathological fringe, like the professor says.' I'm hiding behind my words, passing the buck again. It's so easy to do. It's like water flowing downhill. 'Just to let Danny record the screaming stuff about his heart. Get us through the new script.'

To my surprise, they look at each other, and seem to be taken in by this. 'Sure,' says Jim. 'But next time, don't just laugh. Argue or something. Get mad. Challenge it. Even the psychopaths who get to 450 volts will challenge it. Don't just do what you're told.'

'So you're telling me not to do what I'm told?' I say, as a sort of half-hearted joke.

I'm back in the room, and it's me and the machine. The smooth metal, the shining switches, the printed labels from 15 volts to 450 volts, from Mild Shock to XXX. It's big and impressive. It has a manufacturer's plate. It looks so real, it's hard to believe that it's just a hollow box. That the professor drilled the switch holes himself in the campus workshop.

'You ready?' says Jim-Just-Jim, coming in. He shrugs on the coat, buttons it up, and he's not Jim any more, true-blue eyes, cheap cut, good shoes. He's the white coat. I trust the whiteness of his coat more than I trust the whiteness of my thoughts. I trust him more than I trust myself.

'Sure,' I say, sitting down in the chair. It's not like I have a choice.

This story begins and ends in a place that no longer exists, and was even then disappearing. In Lahore, the Punjab, India. In the late thirties, the events were already in motion that would slice the Muslims off the west and east sides of India like dangling limbs, and rename our divided territory Pakistan. The year after I was born, my brother was born. A couple of years after that, my sisters were born, in quick succession, during the war. My father was a young medic; he worked for the Indian Air Force, and claimed much later in his after-dinner anecdotes that he had very little to do during this illustrious part of his career, as few people came back injured. They either came back whole, or didn't come back at all; their bodies burning to crisps in the air, or falling through the skies to feed the wild animals and the earth.

My mother was two people; comically girlish, or tragically severe. She watched all the movies that were imported, read magazines in private, and the Qur'an in public, and played with her babies. My sisters were born less than eighteen months apart, and the wet nurse that had been hired fed them both together, weaning her own objecting little brat, whom she left with her sister in her village. Our mother dressed the girls like dolls, put ribbons in their surprisingly thick fluff of hair, and praised their honey-cream complexions, although she still powdered them pale for public outings. For my brother and me, she changed her mask, frowned at us with silent disapproval, and then hit us with a ruler, a hairbrush, and even with a pair of scissors, if we did anything other than study. Or if we weren't studying hard enough.

Study. Study harder.

It was the mantra of our childhood, repeated more frequently than our prayers. She firmly believed that teaching and learning was best done by pain and punishment, and if she had been a volunteer in the New Haven test, she would have been surprised that they went to the trouble of using a shock machine and a separate room. She would have happily stood over the learner with a blunt instrument until he got the answers right.

I was jealous of my sisters, and teamed up with my little brother, Jamal Kamal, whom we called Jay-Kay for short, and eventually Jakie from convenience, as that was how he mispronounced his own name as a toddler. Our mother claimed it was easier to copy than correct him, but the truth was that she preferred Jakie, as it sounded more English, and she was the one who probably taught him to say it in the first place. My brother and I would seek out opportunities to torment the girls. We'd go up to them in the garden, where the servants couldn't see, and give them the hardest pieces of mango, to make them struggle and sputter, cough and cry as they tried to chew them down; when they saw us laughing, they'd run to Cook to tell on us. We would hide their stupid dolly-babies, the collection of hand-made rag dolls stitched by the ayah from bright sari offcuts, which they slept with at night. The ayah didn't find them until Jakie gave us away.

'They're definitely not on top of the wardrobe. No one could reach to hide them up there. Not unless they were the best thrower in the world,' he said too proudly. Jakie was the best thrower in the family; he told me that I threw like one of the girls. When the dolls were found, I took a set of our sisters' brightly coloured ribbons and fed them to the white worms that crawled up the latrine, watching them twist round like a hideous hairdo. Our sisters screamed when they saw them. Ribbons on worms, like a party dress on a pig, or dung decorated with gold dust.

I'm aware that I'm reporting this with something like pride. I think I'm still proud of our rebellion, even though we did mean things, because it was the last time I really did. Rebel, I mean. It was beaten out of me by the age of six. And how our mother would beat us. This was one thing, possibly the only thing, concerning our care that she didn't delegate to the servants. Amma beat us ferociously, as though it was exercise, and something that she needed to stretch and limber up for in advance. Like a local lawman in the villages, charged with administering a hundred lashes to a young rape victim for her adultery, whipping trees in the forest to keep in shape for his big day. She was a small and slender woman, and perhaps she felt it didn't hurt as much as it should, even with the tools she used, the slap and spit of the leather, the spikes of the brush; so she used the slap-spit-spike of her words to cut deeper into our skin.

'You dishonour me, and your father, when you disobey us,' she said before the beatings.

'I will make you into good boys. You will learn to be good,' she said after the beatings.

Like Jim's coat, almost twenty years later, there was no grey for my mother. The laundry she inspected for washing was separated carefully and came back gleaming and pressed, with no blurring or fading of shades. She was black and she was white. Boys were either bad boys or good boys. And the only good boys were invisible ones. Sons were a horrible inconvenience to her, I imagine. Made of slugs and snails and puppy dogs' tails, and nothing in our infant behaviour proved otherwise. She probably resented the fact that she needed to have us, Jakie and I, for her social standing, the spare and heir to be pounded firmly into their father, and so she crushed us like pungent chilli paste with a pestle, as though it were just another domestic duty.

Daughters were different altogether; girls were about indulgence and enjoyment; they were bred to be decorative and helpful, living dolls and housekeepers, and would one day be married off to men of means with movie star looks and letters after their names, and live their lives as light as birds in flight, indulging their own daughters. She nicknamed our sisters after the movie stars: Maryam, the elder, became Mae; little Leena, the younger, became Lana. She had no choice over our names, as Jakie and I had to be named for grandfathers, Sulaman and Jamal Kamal, in accordance with family tradition.

9

I wonder sometimes what she would have called me if she'd been allowed to choose. I wonder if she would have loved me a little more if she'd been indulged in this small matter. Perhaps she'd have been kinder to a son named Farid for Fred Astaire, or Daniyaal for Danny Kaye. I wouldn't have minded.

She could have called me Clark, Gene, Bing, Cary, Rock or Bob.

Any of these funny foreign names, short and shouting as brands in a boutique, unlikely nouns and verbs mislaid in neon on movie theatre canopies, would have been better than SOS, that plaintive cry for help. Or Sully, to smear and dishonour; to screw things up.

Our father felt sorry for us, and sometimes let us escape from home with him. He didn't tell our mother that was what he was doing. He would put it in the form of more study, of education through tough physical activity.

'The little boys must learn how to be big men,' he told our mother. 'Strong bodies make strong minds. Fresh air. Exercise.' The shorter his sentences got, the more persuasive he became. He was one of those good-looking, reedy-voiced men who was more impressive when he didn't open his mouth. Amma nodded, oiling and plaiting Lana's hair with silk ribbons, as she squirmed with discomfort, with the tight tugging of her braids, the stiffness of her frilled dress, which was too hot for even the early morning heat. Mae was lying on her belly at Amma's feet, within the cool of her shadow, wilting in her identical stiff dress like a flower flopping in a vase. Our fattest cat, Snow White, crept up to her with a needy mew, and she kicked it away with a sudden vicious energy.

'Air and exercise,' repeated Amma thoughtfully, throwing us a darkly glittering look, satisfied that it was what we deserved. She might as well have been saying 'Crime and punishment.' She turned Lana to face her, and became the other mother again, laughing gaily. 'Well aren't you a poppet, my darling? Aren't you the loveliest thing in the world?' Lana smiled with bashful confusion, unsure whether to be pleased at the attention, and gave us an apologetic shrug. Amma followed her gaze, and seemed surprised that we were still there.

'Well go on then,' she said impatiently, shooing us away with a flap of her hands. 'Go with your father for your air and exercise. Be good boys.'

Our father had been leaning over the veranda, pretending to look at something particular in the garden, some bustle of activity among the servants, or the chickens pecking over the ground for their scattered feed, but now he pulled himself back up and walked off, expecting us to follow him. He smiled and nodded at my mother, like a visiting dignitary rather than the head of the household, and she smiled and nodded back, like the Queen of England in a peach dress and tiara.

Jakie and I looked at each other. We realised that our father had been waiting for her to give him permission. And she had, and we were free. From books and rulers and hairbrushes and the sharp edge of the scissors. For just a little time. We scampered after him before she could change her mind. We didn't realise that our small bodies gave away what our faces didn't – that we were happy to go. That it wasn't a punishment. Then we heard an imperious voice behind us.

'Wait.'

We did, even though our father was already at the stairwell. We looked back, and it wasn't our mother who had spoken, but Mae, who had jumped out of Amma's shadow. She was blinking in the sunlight, her tight, ribboned braids shining.

'Where are they going?' she asked our mother. Amma shrugged with indifference, putting her ribbons back in the little box covered in deep velvet but embroidered with tough mirrors stitched on with stiff gold thread; she glanced at her many-mirrored faces reflected in the soft and scratchy lid as she closed it, leaving it on the low cane table beside her as she picked up a magazine instead. Snow White peered over the top of the box too, now that no one was using it, and pawed the textured lid experimentally, fur-trimmed pink pads on the velvet, and a sharp claw scraping the glass.

'For fresh air and exercise,' said Jakie impatiently, whispering under his breath to Mae, as she approached him, 'Didn't you hear, stupid?'

'You're stupid,' she hissed back, adding loudly, 'I want to go too. Mummy, can we go too?'

Amma raised her head from the magazine and looked at her daughter, surprised by the little rebellion. 'You want to go?' she asked Mae with interest. She glanced across at little Lana, 'And do you want to go too?'

she asked her for confirmation, and Lana was too shy and too good to say anything, but her hopeful face just said, 'Yes please oh please oh please.' I held my breath; I knew my sisters had spoiled it for us. That none of us would go. It felt like it was a long time before our mother spoke again.

'Don't be silly,' Amma said eventually. She said it indulgently, and her voice was warm. 'What silly little girls. Come, we'll get tea and sweets from Cook. Stay home and fun with Mummy. Let the boys do the hard work.' I breathed out with relief as she spoke, quietly so she wouldn't notice, and followed Abbu down the stairs, with Jakie behind me.

I glanced back with guilt at my sisters, knowing that we had won and they had lost. Knowing we'd lost something too, that we'd let them down, and failed to save them from our mother. We hadn't even tried. Mae ignored us, and followed Amma with flouncing resignation, kicking the fat white cat again, and when it didn't shift, she pushed it out of her way with the heel of her slippered foot. Little Lana threw us a stricken look as she was pulled away by her hand. Tea and sweets. Crime and punishment.

Our father dismissed the elderly driver, who had been cleaning the car and was dressed indecently with just an old cloth wrapped damply around the bony angles of his hips. Abbu told us he'd drive; none of us wanted to wait for Karim to dry himself off and tidy himself up, painfully pulling on the starched and braided uniform that seemed to hold him together. We got into the glistening car, still decorated with stray soap bubbles that left rainbow stains where they popped, and sat in the back as Abbu cautiously reversed out of our calm and dusty driveway and into the honking, stinking streets. Karim's peaked chauffeur's hat was hanging in the car, and our father put it on for fun. The edges of the hat were dark and stiff with Karim's hair oil, and the scent of slightly rancid coconut drifted from the front seat.

'I'm driver,' joked Abbu. 'Where shall we go today, sir?'

'The cinema?' said Jakie, joking back, looking at the movie posters outside the cinema as we passed it. Amma was always going to the cinema, and she sometimes took Mae and Lana with her. She never took us. Our father's back stiffened. Jakie couldn't see his face, but I was sitting on the other side of the car, and saw him struggling with the impertinent daring of the suggestion. It was one thing to take us out for an occasional game of tennis or cricket, but to take us to the cinema, while lying about what we were doing, was something altogether different. Too different. Too disobedient. I saw that he was tempted, as he never went to the cinema either, and I could suddenly see him as a boy like us, ignored or beaten by our beaming grandmother, and pounded into a career in medicine. I was worried that he'd change his mind about the outing too, or that he'd punish Jakie for suggesting we deceive our mother. I pulled off his hat to distract him.

'I'll be driver now, beep, beep!' I yelled a bit desperately, pretending I was driving with an imaginary wheel. I was too old for these antics, at nine and a quarter years, but Jakie wasn't. He yanked the hat away from me.

'No, MY turn to be driver, beep, beep!' he yelled back, with proper sincerity.

'Tennis club, driver, please,' I instructed Jakie, playing along and letting him keep the hat. I looked at Abbu as I said it, and caught his eye in the rear-view mirror, shrugging with a smile as I gave Jakie an indulgent pat on the flat part of the hat, which bounced on his thick curls as though amused by his excitement, while he went, 'Beep, beep! Vroom, vroom!' As though to say, 'What can we do with this little bother of a brother?'

'Tennis club, yes, sir, right away, sir,' replied my father, relieved that the terrible, tempting choice had been taken away from him. 'Tennis. The sport of kings. Fresh air. Exercise.'

We played on the dusty courts all morning, two against one, with Jakie and I on one side and Abbu on the other. When we did well, he ran across and hugged us, in the way he only could when sport was involved. Sometimes he picked us up and swung us around, which was uncomfortable because we weren't used to it. Sometimes he held us longer than we wanted, and I wondered about how little affection he got at home. I wasn't sure I had ever seen Amma hug him, or really hold him in her arms. Lana still hugged him sometimes, in her own way; she crawled on his lap after breakfast, and played with his tie while he was reading *The Times of India*, before he went to work.

Mae would look at Lana during those moments with a combination of scorn and envy. 'Daddy's girl, Daddy's girl,' she'd mock-mutter to her later. 'Daddy's little darling.' She was already six and didn't like to look so needy herself. She would have liked to sit with Abbu, but only if she was asked, and Abbu wasn't to know this. She wasn't soft and transparent like Lana; she was sharp-edged and unreadable, and so it never occurred to Abbu to pat his knees and call her over. If he ever did, she would have been so surprised by it, she would probably have tossed her head and stomped off anyway, like someone who can't take a compliment and assumes they are being teased.

Long before midday, the heat rising from the courts under our feet became unbearable, and so Abbu sat in the shade to smoke, on a bench under a flowering tree littered with slightly rotten blossom, which gave off a meaty, sweet stench, like a perfumed pink and white corpse. We watched Abbu light his cigarette, and wave it around to put off the flying insects that had gathered around him. We stayed on the court, but stopped scoring properly, and messed around with two other boys who had turned up, older boys who were in the big school. When we ran out of balls, we collected them on our racquets and gathered at the net, where the smaller boy, Ali, surreptitiously shared out some bright boiled sweets from his pocket like contraband.

'You're lucky your father brings you out to play,' said Farid, the bigger boy, who had the slightly stretched look of someone who had suddenly grown too fast for the rest of him to catch up. 'Our father just waits at home with a metal ruler, to beat us if we don't study, and then beats us when we do study, to remind us why we should.'

'Is he a doctor or a general?' asked Jakie as, in his limited experience, fathers were either one or the other. Medical or military.

'A lawyer,' said Ali, who still had the round cheeks of someone who had been lovingly overfed by their mother and indulgent ayahs; who despite a fearsome father still had sweets enough to share. 'He's upset because he's not a judge,' he added confidentially, looking around to check that no one had heard this flat treason. He didn't need to say any more. Their father had failed. They would have to do what he didn't, or bleed into their books trying.

Abbu was quiet as he drove us back through town, and when we swung past the cinema, he said, 'Another time, Jakie-jaan,' and sounded a little sad. As though worried that we'd revisit that dangerous moment, but wanting to revisit it in a small way himself.

Our mother wasn't like the other mothers we'd met. She didn't coddle and cuddle and overfeed us, and bewail the strictness of our education and the difficulty of our study and the fact that we didn't get to have fun. When other mothers said indulgently, 'Let them play, let them be little boys,' Amma would say, 'Let them study, let them be good boys. May Allah-the-All-Merciful make them obedient,' with a pointed piety that was difficult to argue with.

But our father was like other fathers. He wanted for us what he didn't have, what he never had as a child or as a man. When he took us out of our home, and out of our lives, to play for a few hours, every week or so, and when he held us longer than he needed to hold us, he wasn't just sorry for us. He was sorry for himself.

When we got home, we realised how dusty we were, how sweaty and sticky we felt in the cool of our shadowed hallway. Amma looked approving at first, as she swept in from the living room to inspect us. He had clearly made us work. And then she looked angry, a flickering transition that seemed as swift and inevitable as a wrinkled skin forming on the smooth surface of warm milk.

'Look how dirty you are,' she scolded. 'Look at all the mess you have brought into my clean house.' Jakie and I hung our heads, and looked obediently at our tennis shoes, caked with the clay of the court, and the dirt from the path that led to it, the faint traces crumbling on the scrubbed tile. There was a scrap of bruised petal, rapidly browning, thinner than skin, and tender as a stain. Jakie nudged me, and I saw the rest of the tear-shaped petal clinging to the underside of Abbu's sole. It gave the odd impression that there had been something indecently celebratory, something dissolute about our outing, because we had walked with flowers underfoot; as though we had visited a giggling henna party or a brothel.

Our house was gleaming, and much more sterile than the hospitals for which our mother raised funds as an excuse for her social events; our dark, hulking furniture was so highly polished it felt oily to the touch, and repelled our fingerprints. Amma made the domestic care of our home into a full-time management position, and frightened the servants into more efficiency than we'd seen in any of the neighbours' houses. Within the house, she even expected the servants to press their own clothes, or else dry them stretched out, smoothed and stiffened by the sun; even a wrinkled dhoti was unacceptable, which was why Karim had removed his before washing the car. The truth was that it wasn't really our dusty shoes that had made the house messier, but simply our presence.

We were the mess. Slugs and snails and puppy dogs' tails.

Jakie and I were the specks in her eye, offensive blotches that she saw everywhere she looked. Like smudges on her expensive sunglasses with tortoiseshell rims, ordered from an imported movie star magazine, but which she only wore at home, in the privacy of our garden, so that the neighbours wouldn't gossip and joke about her, saying she was dressing like a … hmm, leaving a swollen blank space as they hummed discreetly over the wicked word, showing what they themselves thought of the actresses and singers she admired too openly. She knew that they already laughed about the stuff she put on her face, the four types of coloured creams, powders, paints and pastes, for her cheeks, lids, lips and lashes; she dismissed them as plain provincials, villagers like their servants. Sometimes she made up Mae and Lana with her cosmetics, and they endured this suffocating attention, her fingertips on their skin, her own critical mouth close enough to kiss. They looked at themselves later, in the mirrors of each other's faces, at the painted, hard masks like their precious porcelain dolls from England, stiffly frilled and kept on the highest shelf. Their usual one-colour honeyed skin turned to many-coloured mournful brightness.

I glanced through the door of the living room, behind Amma, to see if she had done it to them today, but Mae was ignoring us, with her head in one of my comic books, and Lana was doing the same, pretending she could read, mimicking Mae exactly, right down to the way her legs were crossed. I knew that Mae had seen me look, though, as she turned her back more firmly away from us, with a 'hmph' and a little flounce. An abandoned tea party of rose-printed ceramic cups was beside them.

In the swallowed second between glancing at the girls and back at my feet, I realised that I'd made a mistake. Amma had told us to look at the mess we had made, and I had briefly disobeyed. Before I could mumble an apology, she stepped forward, into the darkness of the wide hall where we were standing, and gave us each a sharp slap, thwack-thwock, her hand moving in a graceful figure of eight, the distance between us precisely judged, so that I got the forehand, and Jakie the backhand, even while we instinctively ducked and swerved. Our mother would have been good at tennis, if she ever came to play with us. She knew how to hit small moving objects and make it look effortless. It cost her nothing.

'Next time, wash before you come into the house,' she said, pronouncing it like a judgement. She kept her eyes on us, not our father, who was hovering with uncertainty just ahead of us, standing to the side, as though not wanting to be associated with our punishment. She was probably just as angry with him – for his grubby shoes, for his sweaty presence, for walking us all straight back into the hall covered in city dust – but when she was angry with him, she got angry with us instead. She was like that. She communicated her dissatisfaction with her husband by punishing his sons; we were dirty, and we were disobedient. Not him. She knew that this was how wives were expected to behave. They had to keep their husbands in their higher place, or the world would end.

'Go. Go and wash now. Change those filthy clothes before lunch.' She was still talking to us, but my father led the way upstairs. Mae looked up and across at me as we carefully climbed the steps, making sure that we didn't accidentally touch the whitewashed wall or the polished rail; I looked back behind the bars of the banister, and saw her sitting in the prison of her stiff clothes. She'd been masked in rouge and kohl again. She looked older, and disturbingly lovely, just like our mother, with the same crease of dissatisfaction between her eyes.

Mae set her mouth with a smirk, as though it was exactly what we deserved. We'd abandoned them, but we hadn't got away with it after all. She made an elegant, swift gesture in our direction that looked like a queenly wave high in the air, until she repeated it and I saw the tiny figure of eight she was making with her hand. Thwack-thwock. Forehand-backhand.

Lana looked at us too, as though Mae's little mockery had given her permission to acknowledge us, but with sympathy. Our mother's morning of smothering had left traces of disquiet on her forehead, and concern around her eyes. Her expression was as transparent and clearly drawn as the kids in my comics, with brackets around dots-for-eyes, and wavy lines above them. It was as though Amma had marked them on with kohl and rouge.

Jakie stuck his tongue out at Mae, and made a clown face, turning out his lips and peeling back his lids, mocking her back for her make-up. I hustled him upstairs, pulling him along by his forearms, before our mother could notice.

By dinner, Jakie and I had been forgotten, if not forgiven. We had paid for our morning out of the house by being jailed in the windowless cell of the bathroom, trapped there with two buckets of tepid water, brought up too hurriedly by panicked servants to be heated properly. We had been punished with harsh scrubbing, soaping and scraping, and then humiliating oiling by the ayah, until we were as stripped and as polished as the furniture, with skins waxed enough to repel water. We had been dressed in stiff, starched shirts, and trousers that had been ironed to points on our knees.

'What little princes,' said Ayah, laying out our impressive clothes, and it was hard not to see an edge of criticism in her affectionate bustling, as she smoothed the skirts of her own worn sari, carefully mended at the hem, and printed with sun-faded flowers. Lunch had been sent up to us on tin plates, as we clearly still weren't considered fit for family company, and then we were beaten over the head by our tutor, a neighbour's relative whose family had fallen on hard times. A young man called Basharath, but whom we called Basher-the-Gnasher, as he hit us and ground his horsey teeth in humiliation at his lot, forced out to work to support his widowed mother and sisters. He'd rather have been beaten over the head by his own tutor, so he could be packed off to university with his school friends.

Everyone seemed to think that we were better off than them – our sisters, our father, our ayah, our tutor. It mystified me, this jealousy. As I leaned over my books myopically, equations blurring with the involuntary tears brought about by Basher's blows raining over the back of my head and shoulders, with the flat wooden ruler we used for geometry, I thought I'd rather be anyone else, anywhere else.

'The answer, Sulaman, the answer,' he commanded. I didn't have a clue. The blood was rising to my face, making me hotter, and I was starting to sweat in my collar and under my hairline. The triangle I had neatly drawn was in danger of being messed up by my sweat and tears. Dirty. Disobedient. I wanted to give an answer, and would have said almost anything just to make him stop. The triangle had three sides, a, b and c. The answer he wanted was the length of a, the longest side, but I couldn't measure it, because he had the ruler. The equation I had written out to solve the problem was neat and final: $a^2 = b^2 + c^2$, and b was 3 and c was 4. I had managed to work out that 3x3 was 9, and 4x4 was 16, but hadn't yet managed to add them together.

I saw Jakie to the side of me, working on a different problem, an easier one; he stretched out his closed fist towards me under the table, and opened out his fingers with a jazzy flash, spreading all five of them, wiggling them in a wave as though practising for piano, before closing and withdrawing his hand just as subtly.

'Five,' I said to Basher, with relief. 'The answer is five. That's the length of a.' It was obvious, but it wasn't easy, not for a nine-year-old. I looked with grateful humiliation at my little brother, and hoped that he'd just guessed it, and hadn't really worked out in his head that 9+16 = 25, and that the square root of 25 is 5. That he hadn't already surpassed me.

We were called for dinner, and the tutor was dismissed, treated like one of the other servants, although he was sent out by the front of the house, where the neighbours could see him, since having an educated boy of good family as a tutor was something of a coup. I watched Jakie as he took his place, fiddling with the mahogany napkin ring, and making popping fish faces at Lana so she'd laugh. Jakie the Joker. He had just guessed that the answer was 5, I decided. He could just as easily have guessed 6 or 7 or 8. But I still felt better, that he'd risked his own rain of ruler blows by helping me cheat. He didn't object when Amma didn't pass him the ceramic platter of samosas and pastries that was sitting on the table, probably the leftovers from some afternoon visit that must have taken place when we had been locked away, to be neither seen nor heard. Good boys because we were invisible. I didn't object when she walked by me too. I preferred that she didn't notice me. Forgotten, if not forgiven. And I didn't care for those little fried pastries, which were so often given to my sisters as treats. I noticed that Mae and Lana only took one each, and reluctantly.

Dinner was quiet and formal, in our home; it wasn't really a sociable occasion unless my parents were entertaining. We all ate with knives and forks, even little Lana. We wouldn't have dared eat with our hands, like the servants, or our neighbours, or our guests. Amma only ate with her hands when she herself was a guest in the house of someone who didn't offer cutlery, and when she did, it seemed to me that she ate with a certain girlish glee, offered the licence to mix her rice and dhal and koftas with her hands, and suck the fragrant and meaty juices off her fingers. It was clear that the food tasted better to her that way, and it seemed an odd privation that she wouldn't allow herself to do it in the privacy of her own home, when there was only us to watch her.

Our table was dark and polished, like everything else in the house, but covered with an oilcloth, and then a thick cotton tablecloth weighed with four metal acorns at the corners and two more centred at the long sides. It was partitioned by the acorns, as the girls sat on one side with Amma, and we sat on the other with Abbu. I liked the heavy comfort of the acorn in my hand, like smooth pebbles from the dirty river in town, and would set it swinging gently like the pendulum on a clock towards Mae, who sat opposite me, but too far away to touch. And like a message in the bottle, she would catch it, and sometimes swing it back to me. That evening, she caught the acorn first, and swung it towards me. Perhaps she had seen Jakie's fish faces with Lana, and decided it was too much effort to stay cross with us. I glanced at her as I sent it back, unsure of her intentions; she could just as easily have been setting me up to tell on me. She turned her face away, with a very correct smile, in Amma's direction, but then caught the acorn and swung it towards me once more. And I swung it back to her. Again, and again. Tick tock tick tock. A metronome without music. Pleased that I'd been forgiven.

Our table planning seemed foolish, despite its apparent symmetry – Amma on one side, with the girls either side of her, and Abbu on the other side, with us boys either side of him – as it required Amma to get up constantly, to wait and flutter about our father at the other side of the table. She did it so much, it was as though she was making a particular point, putting everything he might want out of his reach, the pickles, the salt, the jug of iced water, so she could jump up and pass it to him with gay subservience. A forced performance of happy spouse-willing servant. He never actually asked for any of the things she passed to him, never even glanced wistfully in their direction, but she would get up, scolding herself indulgently as though she were a dim but beautiful daughter who would be tolerated only for helpfulness around the house and the good marriage she might one day make, which would allow her to leave it soon enough. She only spoke English at the table, with the slight American accent of the nuns who had provided her convent education, and the British slyness of everyone else in Lahore.

'Oh, how silly of me, my dear. The pickles are so far from your plate. No, Sulaman, don't you dare pass them. You'll be careless and drip the oil on the tablecloth. Let me get them for you, dearest.' And she would flounce around, placing the pickles by his side, and then selecting a few of the choicest ones and putting them on his plate. As though he was the adored older son, to be fed and cosseted and publicly admired; in other families, that would have been me, I realised a bit grimly. It didn't upset me, though, as I certainly didn't want any more of Amma's attention than I already got. I saw the servants hovering, wanting to fill our tin water cups – crystal was for the grown-ups – but they were forced to wait until Amma sat down. A servant beside the table would expose her little charade: that there was no need for her to jump up and down and make such a fuss of our father, as there were other people to serve him.

Amma put Abbu up on a pedestal, but it seemed less for public admiration than for public ridicule, as though he were locked in the stocks for display. The ritual intended to establish him as head of the household made him seem as helpless as a high-chaired infant, and I think Amma, and Abbu, and all of us knew this. She used her servant's role to belittle him, to say, look how little you would be without me. Look how you would suffer and struggle.

At the end of the meal, when she peeled his fruit by his side, slicing off piths and pips, while the rest of us struggled with the tough skins, leaving Abbu just the jewelled juicy morsels of pomegranate, orange, pineapple, swimming in their sweet juice on his plate, she was the one who held the knife.

It was over coffee that evening, when we were finally let out of the cage of our stiff day clothes and permitted to wear pyjamas, that we first heard the word Partition. Jakie and I came out sleepily, followed by Mae and Lana from the opposite bedroom, and wound our way down the stairs. Our skin had been so used to the heat of the day, to our layers of impractical clothes, that we were now cold in the dark, sunless house. There was no electricity, and oil lamps lit the lengths of the corridors. In pious good taste, the only frames hung on the wall showed gold and silver passages from the Qur'an in lavish Arabic script, and when we reached the dining room, our milk already poured in our tin cups, scented slightly with cardamom and almonds, the final gilt frame hung in pride of place, large and boastful, a metre square of black holy cloth, protected behind glass. I knew that it was precious and prized, without ever truly understanding its purpose. Other families admired the cloth, and commented on how they only had a small piece themselves, kept folded with the family Qur'an.

I often wondered why we were brought down for milk, like puppets stripped after a play, when we could just as easily have drunk it in our rooms and gone straight to bed. Mae was obviously shivering in her thin cotton dress, bumps raised on the backs of her arms. Jakie and Lana were plumper than us, and seemed to give off a comforting heat instead, which made us squash on either side of them on the cloth-covered sofa, where we were allowed to drink our milk while our parents had their coffee. Again we were divided into boys on one side and girls on the other. I was next to Jakie, with Abbu on the winged leather armchair to the left of the sofa, and Mae was next to Lana, with Amma on the armchair to the right of the sofa. We never tried to switch from our allotted places; it was as though nothing would ever make sense again if we did.

'Partition,' said my father, leaning back in his armchair, looking down into his coffee, as though he could see himself reflected there. He drank his coffee pale and sweet with condensed milk; he'd look like a ghost in his cup, I thought, like the unhealthy white men who stubbornly continued to attend the cricket club at the weekends. 'Partition,' he repeated more loudly to Amma, who had either ignored him or not noticed that he'd spoken. He said it with such uncharacteristic emphasis I thought he'd just sneezed. Par-tish-shun. A-tish-u, a-tish-u, we all fall down.

'Bless you,' I said automatically, as I'd been taught again and again by Amma. I thought she'd tell me off if I didn't. It seemed unfair that she flashed me a hard, critical look instead, the silence softened only by

Jakie's giggle and Mae's snort; they both thought I was making a joke. Lana, looking between the two of them, tittered softly in sympathy, although she didn't know why, and carried on sipping her milk. Now Amma was annoyed with all of us, but she couldn't say anything, because her immediate business was to gaze with sweetly enquiring interest at our father. I looked up at the holy cloth, spread in its extravagant frame on the wall as a boast and a blessing, the polished glass that covered it so clean it was invisible. It looked like someone had carved a neat hole in our wall, and framed it in gold. A holy hole. I wished I could climb up the high dresser, and fall into it, like Alice, into another world. Down the rabbit hole. Through the looking glass. A heavenly place of mess and magic and kind and curious creatures.

'And what of it, dearest?' asked my mother, eventually, aware that Abbu wanted some encouragement. She might have been speaking about the weather. I was confused, because part of me still thought my father had either sneezed, or pretended to sneeze, although I didn't know why he would. Looking back, it seems affected that she always called him dearest, or my dear, rather than his name, or Daddy or Papa or Abbu, like the other mothers did in front of their children. At the time, we just accepted it as being true: he was the dearest thing in the house, as he was worth the most. At social gatherings, Amma made a point of looking at him with girlish adoration, as though she couldn't believe that such a man existed, as though she couldn't believe her luck: a doctor, a man with good looks and thick hair, a man with his own house, a man who had fathered sons. She was right that we were lucky to have him. Other unfortunate families, like Basher's, had been reduced to poverty on the untimely death of the husband and father; the sons forced to earn a humiliating living, the widows obliged to sell cakes and crafts and hand-stitched handkerchiefs to better-off acquaintances. It was probably the wives or daughters of such a family who had provided the dusty macaroons and pistachio biscuits on the coffee table, and the trimmed doilies the platters rested on. I imagined Basher's sisters straining their eyes by lamplight on the delicate work through the night, and Amma rolling up to buy them magnanimously for a few rupees. I imagined that Basher had to beg the rent collector for the small flat to which they had moved for just a little more time; that he made the same plea every first Monday of every month. No wonder he beat us over the head.

'Well, we have to make plans for it,' Abbu said. 'There'll be trouble.'

'What's Par-tish-shun?' asked Jakie, snorting the word out through his milk.

'It's separation,' said Abbu. 'Partition means separation. It means they're separating us.'

I glanced down the sofa and caught Mae's eye; she rolled her eyes at the foolishness of grown-ups, and I waggled my head in acknowledgement, neither agreeing nor disagreeing. It seemed to me that we were already separated, at the table, and on the sofa. I thought that might be all they were talking about.

'There won't be trouble here,' said Amma. 'This isn't Calcutta.' She said the word as though it were something degrading and disreputable, and strangely exciting. I'd heard of Calcutta before; it was our mother's home town, before she was sent to the Punjab for marriage, and it was suddenly a place I wanted to go.

'Dr Gupta and Dr Kapoor don't think so. They're moving over the border, to start a new practice with their relatives. I'm thinking of taking over their practice. Taking on a partner so I can specialise.' Amma smiled, and gave a delicate circular nod to show her consideration of this proposal, and her assent. At the next social gathering, she would describe her husband's promotion from military doctor to the owner of a successful medical practice in the neighbourhood, something that would normally take years of work and investment, but now gifted to him by the end of a war and the cracking open of a country.

Abbu toyed with his coffee for a while, looked into the depths once more, then put it aside; as though he didn't like what he saw there, as though he saw the ghost too. 'Still, there'll be trouble. I was thinking we should take the children out of the city for a while. Go for a holiday to the mountains. Take the tutor, to keep up their schooling.'

We had never had a family holiday in the mountains, although we knew of other children who went every year to escape the worst of the summer heat. The highest we ever got to go was to the top of our flat roof, where Jakie and I were occasionally allowed to sleep if the heat was unbearable. We would lie on our backs and stare at the stars, drawing pictures around the dotted constellations. We would catch the moon in the frame of our fingers. The girls were never permitted to do even this, as their room had a fan. Lana let out a milk bubble of excitement as she squeaked. She was the only one still drinking from her cup; the rest of us had finished, and were simply waiting to be dismissed.

But now we were all waiting for Amma to give that delicately circular nod again, or to ask us if we wanted to go. Our faces were already saying, yes please oh please oh please.

She didn't do either. She sipped her own coffee, which she drank black and bitter, and reached forward to the table, opening the decorative round tin that held the chocolates, which were damp with condensation from the ice box. She selected one, tipped with crystallised violets and angelica, and bit into it thoughtfully. 'This holiday, would it be with you, or without you?' she asked, with a slight edge.

Our father looked uncomfortable, as though he'd been caught out. He had said nothing to imply that he wouldn't be coming too, but I could see now that had been his intention, and he couldn't answer with a lie to a direct question. Perhaps he had thought we would make our plans, pack our bags, and he would have told us at the last minute.

'Without me,' he admitted. 'I need to maintain the practice. Protect the house. There may be riots. People died in Calcutta. Burned in their homes, like Britons in the Blitz . . .' He trailed off, and looked at us meaningfully as he said all this to her, as though there were more gory details to share, stories of maniacs with machetes, but he couldn't go on in front of us children. He seemed to think that he'd made a convincing argument; that they couldn't risk our innocent lives by keeping us at home.

'Even so, we will stay,' said Amma, her voice level, her eyes not leaving his face. 'If it's safe enough for you, it's safe enough for us.' Our father looked like he was going to argue, but Amma suddenly gave him that gaily melting smile she saved for company, for her public performances. It was like a flash of sunlight in that dark room. 'The children won't go without me,' she said. 'And I won't go without you. And you, my dearest, will not leave.' My father smiled at her, disarmed and won over by her show of bravery, of solidarity; she had used almost the same words that the Queen had used of the King, before bombs had fallen about Buckingham Palace, and she knew the effect these words would have. I looked at the rejected macaroons and nut-studded biscuits, and decided that my mother would rather we all died than be left a widow with four children, begging on others' charity. I don't know why I had such dark thoughts, as my mother wasn't yet thirty, and was still as beautiful as she was calculating. She would have probably just collected another husband, perhaps a widower with children of his own, and carried on with the same play she always put on for us. Her performance was relentless. Her show would go on.

Our father was right about the troubles. There were riots, and the practice narrowly escaped being burned to the ground; it was saved by the new Muslim name written on it, and the gold and silver frames of Qur'anic text that Abbu took from the house, to post prominently outside. Our mother took the holy hole of black cloth from its place on the dining room wall, and hung it above the entrance to the house, as a protection. She made us all wear small golden books around our necks, representing the Qur'an, with a prayer etched finely on the back. We provided sanctuary for Basher and his two sisters, as their apartment block was Hindu-owned; his mother had already gone to the safety of the mountains to provide care for an elderly relative, who was likely to leave them money. During the weeks of the curfew, our house became a more sociable place, as the grown-ups played cards and listened to music, and Basher's grateful sisters massaged my mother's feet and dressed her hair like a movie star. They made her more royal and radiant than ever, blossoming under their buzzing and constant attention, as suffocating as that which she imposed on her daughters, like a striped queen in a hive. And somewhere outside the genteel sanctuary of our home, further into the city, downtown, and over the borders, our Muslim brothers had their throats cut like halal meat for the feast days, and our Hindu friends were being hacked to bits, and children's heads were being crushed underfoot as they called for their mothers, as the riots spread like fire in a tinder-dry forest. But our holy cloth hung firm, and the angel of death never wandered down our street, and never stopped at our door.

'So this is independence,' said Basher at the card table, throwing down his bad hand, with the lack of formality that the day-and-night curfew had imposed. He was full of nervous, tense energy; he would normally put it into beating us, but he had less opportunity, as his sisters were always around berating him for our harsh treatment, and surreptitiously following our lessons for themselves. We had nothing else to do but study anyway, and were making fewer mistakes. My parents ignored him, and carried on playing, although Amma nodded in her queenly way at his older sister to join their game, and take his place. 'We're a nation of village idiots, slaughtering each other over our gods like dunces fighting for pennies in the gutter.'

'Tch,' said his older sister, Rania, disapprovingly. He looked at her scornfully, then his gaze moved unwillingly to our mother. He had never looked at her that way before the curfew, but the enforced intimacy had made him notice her as something more than the wife of his boss. He saw that she was despicable and lovely, treating his sisters like her indentured slaves to make herself more lovely still, like some witch-queen from a book of fairy tales. She saw him staring, and tossed her head with disdain and a withering look that seemed almost flirtatious; she now had a perfect balance in our household. One man to put up on a pedestal, and one to kick when he was down. Two girls to cosset, and two women to cosset her. Jakie and I didn't really matter to her; our presence was enough, the heir and spare, and we just had to do our assigned task of studying so we could leave the house as soon as possible, so she could boast about our achievements to her friends and acquaintances, and publicly mourn our absence.

'Tell Cook that it is time for the children's milk,' she said, without looking up. We all glanced around at each other, unsure who was being commanded. Jakie and Mae and I didn't think it could be any of us, as we were the children. Lana was already with Cook, watching him shred pistachios and toast almonds for the sweet milky puddings we liked. Rania saw the hesitation, and started to rise obediently with a smile, but Amma stopped her, with a cream softened palm placed firmly on Rania's card-holding hand, reminding her that she was still playing, and hadn't been dismissed.

'And Basharath,' continued Amma, placing her next card carefully on the pile scattered at the centre of the table, 'remind Cook that we are all waiting for coffee, too.' She didn't need to say this, of course, as Cook knew that coffee came with the milk. She wanted to remind Basher of his place. He looked at her with hate, confused with longing. He wanted to slap her, and he wanted to touch her too-soft hands. He really was her indentured slave, more than his sisters, who murmured his name warningly and looked at him impatiently while he stood there like the village idiots he was denouncing.

'Yes, milady,' he said, with an irony that was lost on us at the time. 'Coffee for your court, and milk for the two princes and your little princess.' Little Lana appeared in her nightdress, clutching a teddy and chewing a fistful of pistachios, and so he added, much more kindly, 'And for Baby, of course.' No one could resent Lana; it was a sort of gift she would always have; she was blameless in every situation. And with a flourish and a bow, Basher went out of the room.

'*Uff*, such a silly boy,' said Rania apologetically. 'He was always a good child, so obedient, he worked so hard. Always working, even now. Our father's death has been difficult for him.' Amma ignored her, and carried on playing.

'He's young,' said Abbu kindly, accepting the apology on her behalf, receiving a grateful look from Rania. 'He'll learn.'

Later that evening, Jakie was restless, and although he didn't wake up, he woke me with his tossing and scratching in the night. He had a light eczema rash, but refused to put on the rose-scented cream that Ayah left for him by his bed. I heard a door open in the corridor, and went to see who it was. I had the vague idea of begging for some more warm milk, if it was Ayah, but instead it was Mae, padding softly down the stairs in her bare feet. 'Where are you going?' I asked.

'For water. Go back to bed,' said Mae.

'I want water too,' I said, even though I wanted milk, and I still don't know why I couldn't just say this.

'Suit yourself,' she said. I followed her down, several paces behind as she didn't bother to wait for me, like a ghost floating through the shadows of the house in her cotton nightdress. The door to the dining room was slightly open, and as she walked past it, she stopped, and looked in the crack.

'What is it?' I asked, whispering. She shrugged, and carried on to the kitchen, and so I stopped and looked too. In the moonlight of the dining room, a man and woman were embracing on one of the large winged chairs. All colour was drained out of the room, to black, and grey, and the woman's pale sleeping sari was rucked up to her hips, her bare legs on either side of him, while she sat rocking on his lap. His legs were bare too, and his feet were pushing against the floor. Their arms were tight around each other, but it was strained, as though they were pushing and breathing with effort, as though their embrace was exercise. The woman's hair was covered with the loose end of her sari like a scarf, and I didn't see the man's face, as her head was blocking his. I stepped back and waited for Mae, who had brought out two glasses of water, then followed her up the stairs. I was so sleepy, I didn't question the presence of the embracing couple, and didn't even ask who they were until the next day.

'Just one of the servants, with a boyfriend,' was what Mae said in the morning, when I asked her. She didn't seem terribly interested in the couple; it was as though she wouldn't even have remembered them if I hadn't prompted her. I wondered if they were there often. I couldn't sleep the next night, thinking about them, and in the early hours of the morning I found myself imagining more terrible couplings, of Abbu with one of Basher's grateful young sisters, of Amma straddling Basher like a bicycle, squeezing him between her legs as some sort of complicated corporal punishment for his behaviour, of Abbu and Amma having a silent physical struggle in the night, because they knew that neither of them would argue or shout. I wasn't stupid; I knew that embracing in that way, between open legs, was how babies were made. I had seen dogs coupling in the bazaar. I think I was disappointed and relieved that it was just a servant, with a boyfriend. Although I didn't know how Mae could say this with such certainty.

When the curfew was over, Basher continued to come for our lessons, slightly more often than he needed to, to gaze with adoring repulsion at our mother, to feel her scorn. Abbu noticed this, and dismissed it. He knew that his wife was attractive to other men; it was why she had been chosen for him, and he had been chosen for her. They were both trophies to put on their shared mantelpiece, heads mounted on the hunter's wall. Basher's sister, Rania, went away to join her mother in the mountains, to help with the elderly relative. Then Basher was just left with his younger sister, but soon she went to the mountains too. I heard later that they had both got in trouble, as young, unprotected girls sometimes got in trouble in the city, in the villages, in the mountains. A hundred lashes given to rape victims, for adultery.

Years later, I thought of Basher's bitterness, and his unrequited lust. And his sisters who were so keen to keep him obedient, and to look after him. The white sari bobbing in the dark. And the skinny calves of the man, pressing on the floor. I had never seen Basher's calves.

In the university, I hear that they're modifying the experiment, again. It wasn't just me, it turns out. Almost every other student volunteer pulled the switches right until the end. It seems it's not getting us to obey that's the problem, it's getting us to disobey. Jim tells me about it while we're watching the news reels in the cafeteria; we see the unassuming figure of Adolf Eichmann, as he's being readied for trial in Jerusalem. He's going to be put on the stand in a bullet-proof glass box. Eichmann's the reason they started work on the obedience experiment, him and the Nazis like him; the ones who killed strangers without arguing about it, because someone in authority told them they had to.

'It's because it's too clean,' says Jim. 'It's a clean room, I stand there looking clean, the machine is clean, and the guy they're torturing is on the other side of the wall.'

'So the professor's thinking about making it dirty?' I ask, sipping my coffee, glancing a little anxiously around the cafeteria.

And then I see her walk in. The brown-haired girl in the too-long lab coat. She's late. I almost want to tell her she's late, and ask her why. She passes in front of us, and I can just see the cream edge of her cheek, the tip of her nose, as she stops and turns to watch the news too, and then takes a seat at a table a couple of rows down from us. There aren't many women here; no undergraduates, a few postgraduates, just one chair of medicine in the department. The younger students buy beer and drive out to Vassar to socialise. I guess I can't be the only one to look out for her. I turn to watch her sit, looking at the glossy back of her dark-brown head. I'm not as subtle as I think. She doesn't see me, but Jim does. He coughs, with the smugness of a married man, and smirks a little at me.

'Dirty? I guess so,' he says. Danny joins us, with a rattling tray, and it feels that the three of us have a dirty little secret already. We can look at the students and academics around us, and know what each of them would do if a guy in a colourless coat asked them to hurt a stranger in the name of science, for four bucks an hour plus gas. Even the brown-haired girl, who seems so clean and composed while she sits neatly and watches the news on the trial.

I'm in on the joke, but I've been finding it hard to look in the mirror. I don't see a monster there. It's not that. I'm not psychotic. I just see someone like Eichmann, a polite boy who has always done what he's been told. Who has never spoken up about injustice or atrocity. What Basher might have done to his sisters. What they might have done to him. The slaughter during the curfew, the card games that were played and milky puddings that were prepared. We fiddled while towns burned and children like us were squashed like ripe fruit, their juices running into the gutter.

'It was clean for Eichmann, too,' Jim says, and Danny nods. Encouraged, he carries on. 'A clean office. Papers to sign. He didn't see his victims. He didn't touch them. They were just statistics, numbers and names on the page.'

'No one ever talks about Partition,' I break in, and they look embarrassed, and I wonder if they even know what Partition is. I realise they do, but they like to pretend that I'm not Pakistani and that I never was Indian. That I'm just some slightly tan guy called Sully. I find I'm speaking louder than I need to, as though aware that I won't otherwise be heard. 'It made murderers of us. Hindus killing Muslims. Muslims killing Hindus. I was just a kid, and we didn't even talk about it. That wasn't clean. It was messy, and bloody. There were bodies on the streets.'

They don't say anything. They just want to talk about the experiment. About Nazis. Jim makes an excuse, and Danny follows him, taking his coffee cup from his tray. They're talking about setting up another version of the test, where you have to hold the hand of the learner on the pad. You have to force it down. I don't like touching people, not like that, not at all. It's why I switched from medicine to psychology. Otherwise, I could just as easily have specialised in surgery. I'm good with my hands. I can cut a loaf of bread as fine as paper with a sharp knife and a straight slab to lean on. I should really be excavating into the meat of our bodies, not the buzzing of our minds. If it wasn't for having to touch them: the cold, lifeless ones in the mortuary, the warm ones with a pulse pumping under the skin. I just couldn't do it any more.

I watch them go, knowing that I have to move off the project, as soon as I can. I need to get away from work, and out of my own head for a little while. I look through the newspaper that Danny has left, with the cinema listings. *Judgement at Nuremberg* is showing. Maximilian Schell got the Academy Award for his role as the Krauts' attorney. It annoys me that I know this bit of movie trivia, because the truth is I know far too much; the result of all those years of not being allowed to go to the cinema is that I now watch movies hungrily. The way I used to wait for water in the evenings on fast days, my tongue and throat parched, my lips dry. I've seen *West Side Story* three times this year. It won Best Movie. Best Directors. Best Music. I think Natalie Wood looks like she's Indian when she's crying over Tony, the way she covers her hair as his body is taken away. The edge of a sari covering a head, a dupatta worn like a scarf with the modesty of mourning. All those mothers taking away their dead children, their dead husbands from the dark streets, not so far from the street where I lived. I imagine I can hear the fighting, the percussion of pounding knuckles and flying feet, and the chanting: Hindus! Muslims! Our tragic allegiances; our gangs. I can still hear the fighting boys in the movie, singing and swinging their fists, dancing their challenges with nimble aggression, calling out fiercely: Jets! Sharks!

It takes me a moment to notice that the girl in the too-long lab coat has come up to my table. I guess she wants to take a spare chair, borrow the salt. I look up from the paper, and see that she's wearing a full pleated skirt under her coat, and that her eyes are as brown as her hair. She's sparrow-slight and small, and I guess they just don't make the coats in her size; it hangs below her knees. She looks back at me, and it isn't until she nods with a discreet sideways movement that I realise she's Indian too. I can't believe I never saw this before. Perhaps I knew, but I didn't know that I knew.

She's standing right beside me, in the genial bustle of a cafeteria full of clattering crockery and cutlery. It's like we're being pushed together by a swarming crowd at a national monument, the only natives in a sea of camera-flashing tourists. It's like we're suddenly alone in a room.

I imagine a shalwar kameez under the lab coat and the sensible skirt, which is full enough to hide one. Not one of the elaborate, jewel-coloured silks and satins that my mother would wear, but a discreet cotton print. The kind worn by the nurse who came to work at Abbu's practice, and by the local lady pharmacist who made up his prescriptions. A sensible outfit, loose-trousered, that could be easily washed, a badge of honour for the working women of Lahore, who took to their bicycles rather than be at the mercy of the rickshaw drivers. I haven't missed home since I got here, but suddenly I feel nostalgic for a town of practical women with careers and small everyday cares, that I never really lived in, and that I'm not sure really exists.

You're late, I want to tell her. Do you know how long I've been waiting for you? For the moment she is considering me, I feel a brief flurry of silent panic, as I realise that like her, I don't look Indian enough. I don't wear my nationality on my face, nor on my badge, where my real name is abbreviated to a mild insult. Sully. I am relieved when she addresses me in beautiful Hindi, a language I don't understand perfectly, and which sounds musical to me because of this.

'You're right,' she says to me. 'No one talks about Partition. Not here, anyway. Perhaps they thought it was a fair fight.'

She is wearing a charm at her throat, a little god. She takes a seat without asking, glancing briefly at the movie listings on the spread newspaper, which now divides us. She is on one side, and I am on the other. A Hindu, a Muslim. A fair fight. The girl I've been watching from a distance is now watching me. Close enough to touch. She's considering me, patiently, as though she is still making up her mind about something. She adds in English, as though it is of no great importance, just a couple of casual words to fill the blank space between us while she is waiting for me to speak, 'I'm Radhika.'

Chapter Two
Jakie

I'M JAKIE SADDEQ, AND I'M SITTING IN A DARK AND DINGY ROOM, but I'm staring at the stars.

When you don't have very much of something as a child, I think you either value it even more as an adult, or don't value it at all. Like money. Or chocolate. Or education. Or in our case, the movies. I'm not really interested in the movies; I don't even watch television. I'd rather talk to someone than watch fake people make fake conversation. Sulaman isn't a big talker, and so he loves the movies, where no one expects him to do anything but sit in rapt silence. We never went as kids, although our sisters went with our mother on an almost weekly basis. We didn't go until we were old enough to take our sisters as their chaperones, the year we left Lahore. Our favourite cinema was officially called the Balwant Rai Theatre, but we used to call it the Ratan Talkies, because it was a place full of chatter, on screen and in the foyers.

I didn't really listen to the odd, clipped conversations between the stiff-upper-lipped Brits, or the drawling Southern belle twangs of the Americans, or the Brits pretending to be Americans. I didn't listen to the wailing in Hindi or Urdu, 'But Ravi, I'm your wife now!' as another angry mustachioed villain mistreated his beautiful bride for an imagined offence, and had her dancing across broken glass, sobbing in song for his mercy.

I just went there to slide into another world, not the one on the screen, but the dark sanctuary of the cinema itself, the scents of toasted gram and sticky sodas the colours of cola, orange and lime, but which all tasted the same, of boiled sweets. I went there to sit beside my pretty sisters, who enjoyed the freedom of slouching and splaying their ankles rather than modestly crossing them. Lana would play with her braids, resting her head on my shoulder as though I was another bit of the cinema furniture, and stare puddle-eyed at the screen, hypnotised, her lips parting in wonder. Mae would hold her mouth firm, and toss her elaborately decorated hair contemptuously at the admiring boys in the row behind us. I honestly don't remember anything much about the films themselves, but Sulaman would come out humming the tunes. When he walked blinking into the bright light, like a soft creature of the night not used to the alarming nature of the day, he still had a smile on his face.

That's why I'm here at the pictures in London. Not because I'm nostalgic for home, or bloody-mindedly catching up on those lost childish years when the cinema was something we drove swiftly past. Back then, films were something kept for luckier, more frivolous boys. I'm here in this dark room, this grubby place smelling of sweat, hair pomade and melted ice cream, because I miss my brother.

I dragged a friend down here because Sulaman's been watching this movie. Three times now, although I'm surprised he'd admit this, even to me. He's told me about it in his aerograms. He always sends aerograms, Sulaman. Not postcards, they're too public. Not letters, they're too inefficient. Aerograms are private and efficient, like him. Sulaman tick tocks like a clock, with all his elegant and intricate mechanisms hidden behind his smooth face, his shining case, his soul unseen; and it feels that I'm the only one who really knows him, who really hears the ghost rattling in his machine.

When I watch the movie he's been watching, I can imagine that we're together, in this room where it's always night; so different from the operating theatres at the college hospital, where it's always day. The picture houses have names that promise luxury and tradition, the Empire, the Regal, the Prince of Wales. It turns out that they're usually dingy, depressing places, with worn carpet and stained wood, but I don't mind, because when I'm here, I can imagine that my brother is on the other side of the screen rather than the other side of the world. I can hear his calm breath, which sometimes turned to a deep snore at night and a puppyish snuffle in the morning. I remember the comfort I felt, hearing that sound from the bed beside me. My brother. My brother half of me.

35

We used to lie on the roof together when it was too hot to sleep indoors, and gaze at the stars. We'd join the dots, and frame the moon with our fingers. Sitting here, at least I know we're watching the same light show across the broad sky of the screen. It feels good, to know that the stars I'm staring at are the same ones he has seen.

We were always going to leave Lahore and go to college. That was never a choice. We were always going to be doctors. That was never a choice, either. We were always going to succeed, because otherwise it would be like admitting that our father and mother hadn't. I think my father's ambition was that we surpass him, so he would no longer regret what he had never done; that we would leave the brave new country he had defended and built, receive a foreign education, and come back glorious. My mother's ambition was simpler: she didn't want us back at all. Her job was done, once we had matriculated, and finished our final exams. She wanted us to remain absent and extraordinary, to put a sense of myth in our achievements for her gossip at the clubs, and with her society friends. Our physical presence was unnecessary, and disappointing; we were not the brilliant sons she described. We knew all this, we had known it for years; it wasn't a surprise.

The surprise was that they decided to separate us. We had never been separated before; we had even been put into the same school year out of domestic convenience, so Sulaman was always a bit too old, and I was always a bit too young. But then they decided to send us to different countries, in different continents. America and Britain. I never fully understood why. At the time, I assumed it was just the accident of college acceptance. Later, I suspected our mother of hedging her bets, between a large new-money nation and a small old-money one. The letters came not long after we had finished our exams. I remember that we felt strangely lost and emptied out. Sulaman and I had resented our education, resented the crime and punishment of it, the constant weight of expectation, but at least school offered escape. I don't mean in big terms; we weren't looking forward to leaping out of our little town into the wider world, a world where we would be self-supporting professionals. Where we would be doctors, or if we failed our exams, pharmacists, and if we failed those exams, medical administrators. Not that failure was ever discussed. It would have been like discussing the possibility of marrying us to homosexuals or Hindus or whores; failure was something decent families didn't even believe in. And those who did fail, in sending their children to college, or marrying their daughters well, were to be comforted in public with sly malice and sweets, and gloated over in private. In simple terms, school offered regular and almost daily escape from our polished home, and from our polished statue of a mother. From Basher's sexually frustrated beatings. Sulaman and I flew off to school in the mornings like caged birds set free, and we found excuses to stay, in extra study groups, in academic clubs, to cheat Basher of some of his income, and to avoid Amma's controlling switch over our study.

She let Mae and Lana come to school too. She didn't want to, as she didn't acknowledge the importance of school for girls, once they had learned to read, write and add well enough to manage their household accounts. But she was aware of the criticism of those who didn't let girls study – it was assumed it was due to poverty or villager-ignorance. She paid no attention to the girls' studies, beyond a cursory look at their end-of-term report cards. The day of the letters was the same day the girls came home with their reports. Lana's grades were acceptable and average, but Mae's were offensively good. Amma closed her face like the cupboard she locked the report cards in.

'What do you think, Mummy?' asked Mae, still in the long cotton dress of the convent, her hair in a regulation French plait and tied with plain white ribbons. Our mother had tried to persuade her to cut her hair into the movie star blunt bob that she herself wore, and which was no longer considered quite so show-off by the neighbours. She wanted to cut it even shorter, like Leslie Caron in *An American in Paris*, but Mae refused to be her living doll, and Lana didn't have the personality to carry it off. If Lana had arrived in school with short hair, they would have assumed it was a punishment, or else that she'd had nits.

Our mother didn't reply, and gave the impression of being busy and important while doing nothing at all, leafing through some paperwork on the polished sideboard, still standing by the cupboard the report cards had been buried in. The ticking of the carriage clock displayed on the dresser seemed far too loud, the space between the seconds swollen. Lana sprawled on the winged leather armchair, the one Amma usually sat in, and toyed with the end of her plait. When she was younger, she used to suck it unthinkingly, a bad habit for which Mae tormented her mercilessly. She looked as though she'd like to suck it now, the same way she used to suck her thumb when she was a baby – for comfort when the wet nurse or her bottle weren't available. Instead she splayed the loose hairs at the bottom of her plait carefully, and pretended to look for split ends. I don't know why that pretence made me feel so sad. Maybe because she had finally grown up too.

Sulaman never sat on those leather armchairs, he hadn't for years, and always inspected them suspiciously, as though they might be dirty. Whenever I asked him what he was looking for, he just told me, 'Spilt milk.' Which made no sense whatsoever. Given that we had always drunk our milk on the sofa, where Sulaman usually chose to sit instead. He was on the edge of the cushion, long legs bent underneath him, tensely twisting a lace doily that one of Basher's sisters had provided. It was a measure of how uncomfortable the moment was that Amma didn't even snap at him for this. I would have been relieved if she had, if she had swapped silence for snapping, and released the taut, elastic energy that was stretching, fraying in the room.

'Well, what do you think, Mummy?' repeated Mae impatiently, without any pretence of innocence, for all the clear sky-blueness of her cotton dress, the white ribbons in her hair. She said it with an edge, and hardened her own face in readiness, lifting her chin defiantly. For a moment she and our mother looked like the same person, caught in an unflattering light in the mirror.

Amma gave nothing away, and didn't waste a breath on Mae's challenge, not even a snort of impatience, although I noticed that her shoulders rose by an inch, almost to the swinging tips of her hair. Lana surreptitiously licked the end of her plait. She and I used to lick all of Mummy's violet-tipped chocolates, enjoying the sweetness of our duplicity, even though they weren't actually that sweet, as all we ever tasted was the icy condensation, the dew drops gathered on the dark polish of the couverture, on the crystallised flowers; we would then replace them, one by one, in the box, for Amma to eat later. And to offer to her friends. Lana's spit and then my spit, as she sensibly chose to lick them before me rather than afterwards. We started doing it as children, the first time out of genuine curiosity because the chocolates were never offered to us, and we never really stopped; it had become something of a tradition, whenever a new box arrived. After all, we weren't allowed to eat the chocolates, but no one had asked us not to lick them. Lana and I didn't argue, not like Mae, and we weren't sullen in our obedience like Sulaman, so we got away with more.

'The letters,' called my father from the hallway, banging the door behind him. I relaxed for a moment, knowing that the elastic wouldn't snap, and Amma's hand wouldn't rise and fly out in a slap. My own shoulders dropped the inch that Amma's had risen, and I sank back on the chair, not realising until then that I had shuffled my rear to the very edge, just like Sulaman, ready to fly out of the room on an imagined mission rather than witness the terrible thing that we all seemed to think would happen, with Amma's silence and the sealing away of the report card like a king in his tomb.

We all assumed our positions and put on our party faces. The little made-for-TV play that Amma expected us to put on for Abbu at the end of his working day. She smoothed her hair back, and smiled. Amma was a lovely woman, but to me, it seemed that this particular smile had something of the crocodile about it, and her jaws had the same vice-like bite. It was the way she smiled before she picked up the phone to call someone important, as though determined that they should feel her relentless blaze of charm through the copper wires, that it should worm into their ears. Like a wet tongue. I don't know if Abbu saw anything of this from the open doorway, where he found his family gathered in the cool of the living room. He seemed happy to see her, and us; he had brought Nasim with him, his junior colleague from the practice, proud to display his pious home, his smiling family sitting on his tasteful furniture. Lovely wife, heir and spare, and two daughters, one spirited, and one sweet. Ticks in every box.

'The letters have arrived,' he said, as he bounded into the living room. 'At last!' He beamed, keen to transmit his own energy and excitement to the rest of us; perhaps it seemed to him that we didn't understand the importance of what he was saying. 'Let's go to the garden, I've been inside all day.' He very rarely gave orders like this, as Amma disliked the heat of the garden, and preferred to remain indoors, but the presence of a guest gave him a right to establish himself as the head of the household, and Amma bowed her head with a geisha-like deference.

'A wonderful idea,' she said, clapping her hands girlishly, as though stunned by his intelligence, as though the rest of us were wilting listlessly in the living room simply because we were too dim to have thought of it ourselves. 'Mae, ask Cook to bring lemonade, and tea for Daddy and Nasim Uncle.'

'And sweets,' added Abbu. 'It is a special day. Fritters and sweets.'

We looked at Mae as though she'd dare to refuse, and Amma's smile was fixed to her face, but Mae smiled back without any sweetness, 'Of course,' she said acidly. Her obvious scorn was almost flirtatious, and Nasim took it that way.

'What a girl you have there,' he said in genuine admiration, as she left the room. 'What a love. You'll be fighting off the marriage proposals for that one.' Amma looked at him with a new interest, and took his arm to lead him into the garden.

The rest of us stayed in our seats, like players on an empty stage. It was like we didn't know what to do now the show was over, and the audience had moved on for drinks. It took our father's determinedly joyous exclamation over his shoulder, 'Boys! Come on, we have your letters!' to remind us that the show was still going on, and just the scenery was shifting. We were swapping oil-shined wood for dusty green leaves, heavy leather chairs for sun-bleached cane and a white metal swing. Tasteful artefacts for jasmine and bougainvillea.

Sulaman got up heavily, looking back with concern at Lana and me, to make sure we were coming too. Lana had started openly chewing the end of her pigtail, and I took her hand gently to stop her. She and Sulaman suddenly both had the concerned foreheads of cartoon characters, with wriggle-worms of worry etched across them. It took me a moment to catch up with them, and understand why. Mae was still at school, still in white-ribboned plaits, and although boys called out to her on the street, and my friends had started hustling into the cinema with us when they knew that we were escorting Mae and Lana there, this obvious eventuality hadn't yet occurred to me. That Mae and Lana had an end game to their education, as obviously as we did. The purpose of a boy's education was more education, college abroad, a foreign degree, and a glorious return to a big city practice. It was the price that our parents exacted from us. The purpose of our sisters' education was marriage. It was the price that our parents would exact from them, a debt that had been building since their birth, repaid on their wedding day. And then a new debt would begin in another household. Repaid by pregnancy and domestic duties. It now occurred to all of us that if Mae was already considered fit for marriage, then Amma would see no need to continue with her bothersome schooling, to risk her offensively good reports.

Marriage. It was the first time the word had been said in our presence, about our sisters. Love and marriage. Air and exercise. Crime and punishment.

Mae was already in the garden, swinging impertinently on the creaking seat, when we got there. She wasn't the sort to linger, and went to wherever she was going with a determined step. She had probably not even broken pace as she swept past the kitchen and called out, 'Tea, lemonade, sweets, fritters,' to Cook, who didn't mind this behaviour, and returned it in kind. He brought out the lemonade in a pitcher, filled to the brim and sloshing messily over the edge as he thumped it on the low table. Amma's eyelids flickered with instinctive disapproval, but she was busy charming Nasim Uncle, and pretended not to notice. Lana took the tumblers from Cook's tray, and handed it back to him almost apologetically. She would normally follow him back to the kitchen, to nibble on the pastries while he cooked, but it was clear that that wouldn't be possible, as Abbu was clearing his throat to get everyone's attention.

Our father waited for a moment, while Cook shuffled away. Abbu's chest was puffing with importance and a little jovial anxiety at being the centre of attention, as he laid two wilted white envelopes on the low table. He made a big show of producing a silver letter opener from his pocket, with which he slit them neatly across the top. Amma gasped as though rapt, as though she was the sort of silly woman who would join in the laughter at a joke without knowing why. Mae rolled her eyes at the two of them, causing Sulaman to frown, and Lana and I to share a surreptitious giggle, which we turned into coughs when Amma glanced at us. At the time, I think I believed the show, but now, I know that Abbu and Amma would never have risked the public nature of this letter opening if they hadn't already inspected the contents. I know that the letters had already been opened, inspected, and carefully resealed. There's probably a manila file stuffed full of rejections from various other colleges, the letterheaded paper as faded as flowers, somewhere in an attic or a cellar in our old town house. The excitement, though, was genuine. And so was Abbu's pride.

'Sulaman Osman Saddeq has been granted a place at Yale for studies in medicine,' he said, as though reading from the letter, although we could see that it was a great deal wordier than that, and contained caveats about achieving the necessary grades in final exams, and terms of payment. Abbu put the letter down, as though the effort of the paraphrasing, and his touching deceit in doing so, in making it sound more definitive than it actually was, had exhausted him. He took a long sip of lemonade, brushing the moisture from his upper lip with his cuff, causing Amma's eyelids to flicker once more with disapproval, even while she expectantly beamed widely enough to show her sharp white teeth. He then picked up the second letter.

'Jamal Kamal Saddeq has been granted a place at King's College for studies in medicine,' he said, emphasising the word 'King', as though that was where the King himself had gone. He sat down, and Cook arrived with the tea on the same lemonade-sloshed tray, with a batch of freshly fried fritters, and cold rose and pistachio sweets cut into cubes, already shining with condensation.

Nasim was impressed. 'Congratulations, bhai, congratulations, bhabi,' he said, overfamiliarly; he had been included in a family moment, and seemed aware of the honour. He and Abbu, both men with local degrees, glanced at each other with quick complicit sadness, as sudden as it was apparent. That these two squibs of boys had already surpassed them. The same look Sulaman gave me the day I solved Pythagoras' theorem for him when he was struggling with it, when I silently told him the length of the hypotenuse of a right-angled triangle with my fingers.

Abbu didn't even look at Sulaman and me; it was obvious that this was his moment, not ours. No one paid any attention to us at all, until Mae jumped off the swing and took the hallowed letters from the table while Cook was setting out the tea, muttering about having to serve it the funny foreign way, with tea, milk and sugar in separate containers, when any other family would be happy to trust their cook to mix it together in the kitchen first and bring it out ready for drinking, stewed and properly spiced and sweetened. He felt that serving tea in this way was infringing on his territory; he felt the same about the way that Amma insisted on cutting Abbu's fruit herself, after a meal. Cook repaid the slight by consistently failing to pour tea from the left, however many times Amma told him to do this. He got away with it by pretending that he didn't know his left from right, shuffling on his slippered feet from side to side, as though this would somehow prove his ignorance.

'They're in different countries, Daddy,' said Mae. No one was listening to her, in the flurry of misdirected tea-pouring from stubborn-slippered Cook and small talk between Amma and her guest about how much, how sweet, how milky, and so Mae thrust the letters under Abbu's nose. 'Daddy, they're in different countries. Yale and King's College. America and England.'

'Smart girl,' said Nasim approvingly. 'They're good colleges, too. The best.'

None of us corrected him, although we all guessed that they probably weren't the best, from the boasting of other families about applications made to Harvard, Oxford and Cambridge. 'But you can't send them to different countries,' said Lana, understanding the importance of this. 'Mummy, who'll look after them?'

Amma gave her a wide, impetuous hug, as though Lana was suddenly her adorable little girl again, her daughter-doll in a frilled dress. 'They're big boys now, Lana. Your brothers can look after themselves.'

Amma left the table briefly, and then bustled back with her round box of special confectionery. 'It's a celebration,' she said, generously offering her guest the shiny dark chocolates, tipped with violets and angelica and girl-and-boy spit.

'Thank you, most delicious,' said Nasim, taking one.

Mae took advantage of the moment. 'Could the boys take us to the cinema, as it's a celebration, Mummy?' she asked sweetly. She looked at Abbu too. 'And I did so well in my end-of-term report, Daddy. Mummy will tell you.'

Amma's face froze briefly, but then softened as she inclined her head gracefully. 'Why not?' she said, looking entreatingly at Abbu, as though petitioning on our behalf. 'We have so much to discuss.'

'Go, go,' said Abbu generously. 'Have fun. You've been good. You have worked hard.' Amma's eyes narrowed with calculation as she watched Nasim watch Mae walk away.

'I'll get changed, I can't go out in this old thing,' called Mae from the garden door, waving dismissively. 'Goodbye, Nasim Uncle, have a pleasant evening.'

Nasim kept looking at the space she had left, as he shook Sulaman's hand, then shook mine, and finally dropped a chaste kiss on the top of Lana's head. 'Girls are such a delight,' he said to Amma.

We sat in the cinema, the delightful daughters giggling within earshot of the schoolboys who were just a row behind, close enough to hear them whisper. Sulaman and I didn't say a word, and just stared at the screen. We had shared a room for the last seventeen years. We had shared beatings, and sometimes a bed, when we were cold, or afraid. The news that we were to be separated had not yet sunk in. Abbu had announced Yale and King's with a ringing of bells, but the words had fallen like a leaden echo in the air.

We didn't really believe it, or if we did, we believed it in the way we believed stories in books, or the film that was unfolding with energetic Hindi singing and dancing in the mountains. We were already plotting, like the shiny-haired hero trying to get his bride back from the clutches of a villainous bearded uncle, singing to the stars and snow that he would find her, and they would stay together for ever.

'I'll get you into Yale,' Sulaman suddenly whispered. 'Or I'll transfer to King's. We'll stay together.'

'*Yaar*, of course we will,' I whispered back, mimicking the hero's manly accent. The fact that he even needed to say it seemed to indicate doubt. I would look after him, as I had always done, as I had been born to do, and he would look out for me. The idea of being separated was absurd. As absurd as the idea of Mae getting married to some stuffy old man of means like Nasim Uncle.

Lana was next to me, her head nestled on my shoulder, her arm against mine, occasionally shushing Mae for talking too loudly. Mae was telling off the boys who were flirting with her, complaining at the screen as the heroine shrieked and fainted. Mae was spirited, and Lana was sweet. They seemed to have tried on these roles a long time ago, and didn't want to change out of them; they were comfortable in them, like old nightdresses softened with wear. Lana still seemed a little concerned about me, and after she heard us whispering, she reached out and held my hand. I squeezed her fingers, to show that I was okay, replacing her hand gently on her lap. Our education, their marriage. Our crime, their punishment. I remember thinking, with the witless optimism of youth, what is Lana worried about? I remember thinking, none of this will happen.

My friend comes back up the aisle, a bobbing torch beam ahead of him, and he must have said something charming or funny to the usher, as she giggles and shushes him as he makes his way into our row. The way

Lana used to shush Mae. The shusher-usher, I think, stifling a laugh to myself. I think it's quite good, and want to tell my friend, but he has already forgotten about the girl in the shadows, and is complaining about the fat man five seats down who wouldn't stand up for him.

'God almighty, I practically had to crawl across his lap,' Frank mutters. 'It's like it's what the dirty bastard wanted.'

He passes me an ice cream, which I didn't ask for, and I don't complain about how sticky the damp cardboard is, because it's like everything else in the pictures. Sticky seats, sticky floors, sticky soda. It's like they put grease and syrup in a bottle and sprayed it around, so we'd get stuck here like flies on paper, and sit through a double matinee rather than attempt to struggle out of the place. Instead, I take the paper towels, already dissolving into yoghurt around the containers, and ineffectively wipe my hands.

'That's probably what Fat Man's doing,' comments Frank, in a stage whisper. 'He's probably done jerking off by now.'

'Shush up,' I say, remembering my joke about the usher. 'Pretty girl, the one with the torch,' I add, leading into it. I think about saying something about the pair of pretty girls I used to sit beside at the Ratan Talkies, but decide it would be too distracting to start talking about my sisters. This is London, not Lahore, and I've accepted that I'm a long way from home. Frank distracts me instead, as the titles roll noisily.

'Course she was, I only talk to people who are prettier than me,' he says, leaning towards me as though his intention is to whisper discreetly about her, and sticking his tongue discreetly in my ear instead, using his cupped hand to hide from the row behind that he is nibbling my ear lobe.

I feel a small explosion of happiness, sitting there in the dark with my lover, and watching the Technicolor choreographed fight scenes that my brother's been watching on the other side of the ocean. I hope he's not sitting there alone. Frank's tan overcoat is spread over his legs, and eventually I slide my hand underneath it, familiarly between the warmth of his thighs, gently rubbing his thickening crotch, enjoying the deepening of his breath. I wonder now how many men must have pulled their dicks out of their dhotis in the Talkies back home, tugging in time to the music, while the slender actresses stamped and spun for them. Frank comes just when Tony is singing 'Maria', his own breath a stifled mixture of prayer and swearing as he grunts out loud, 'Oh Christ, Jakie,' as though he timed it with the loudest part of the song on purpose.

'Father Byrne's going to have a field day with me at next month's confession,' he eventually says, squeezing my hand, and then letting go so he can clean himself up with the remains of wilted tissues from the empty ice cream tubs.

'He must love you,' I say. 'Every priest needs a project.'

Frank stifles a laugh, and hums along with the song, changing the lyrics, 'Oh Jakie, I'll never stop singing, oh Jakie . . .' and then I'm the one that's laughing out loud, and being shushed up from the row behind, and the furious fat man five seats down.

My brother and I are now half a world apart, and I sometimes wonder whether we always were. My brother half of me. We both did what we were told. But no one ever told me not to fall in love with men, and make them come in public places. Sulaman, I think, would never have licked the chocolates.

Chapter Three

Sully

I SIT BESIDE RADHIKA IN THE MOVIES, AND HER HAND IS CLOSE ENOUGH to touch, but I don't dare. Sometimes she stifles a laugh, and tilts her head towards me, offering stray comments that don't seem to require replies. I guess this because she shifts back comfortably in her seat almost as soon as she has spoken, not giving me a chance to think of anything to say anyway, her short hair crackling against the rough velour with an electrical static. I imagine that if I do touch her, I'll feel a shock, and that she will too, and will cry out with annoyance. I think of the made-up man behind the wall, shocked to painful cries, cardiac arrest, and then silent, stubborn death; I think of the empty chair that Danny has left, and the recording he has made that spools in his place. When they tried including women in the experiment, they went just as far. But more reluctantly. I understand that. I understand that reluctance is better than nothing, but it's still no excuse.

Sitting here at the movies, I must look like every other man at the screening, deciding whether or when he should hold his date's hand. But I don't think I'll ever touch another human being again. I certainly don't think I'll ever touch a woman again, unless she's a patient, a machine under my hands in need of repair. And even then I'll wear gloves. I don't think I'll ever understand another human being again. The decisions they make, reluctantly or not. Least of all a woman. Least of all a woman like Radhika. I have no idea why she comes out with me. I assume it's politeness, but it has been three weeks of politeness now. I sometimes wonder if she's considering matchmaking me with a friend; she might consider me a suitable boy. She seems to show no interest in me herself. Her indifference is terribly attractive; I think that if she scorned me, and tossed her head in disdain at me, and walked away, I'd probably fall in love with her.

I'm a little bit in love with her already.

She is nothing like my mother.

I walk out with Radhika from the black and red womb of the theatre, and into the tingling night air, sodium street lamps like moons stuck on sticks, standing to attention in a long line down the street. She makes a few comments about Sophia Loren in *Two Women*; the film was her choice, not mine, but I'd already admitted to seeing *Judgement at Nuremberg*, and I didn't want her to think I was obsessed with the Nazis, like everyone else I've been working with.

I know she's saying something else to me now, I'm watching her lips move. But I don't really hear the words, because when she turns her head to smile at me, all the sounds around us fall away, and I can't do anything but smile back at her. A muscular reflex, like she's tapped my knee with a hammer and made it jerk. Like she's pulled my switch. And now she's smiling less certainly, and nodding at me, as though to say, 'Go on, then,' and it's my turn to speak, but I haven't been listening to a thing she's just said, and am still there grinning at her like an idiot.

'Sorry,' I eventually say, although I don't know how she's meant to guess what I'm apologising for.

'That's okay,' she says, as though she is apologising herself. Perhaps she thinks that she's been boring me, with her choice of movie, with whatever she might have said about the pretty actress, who come to think of it did remind me of my mother. Perhaps that's why I was watching Radhika, skinny and full-skirted, more than the look-at-me star on the screen.

I can't look Radhika in the eye now, and I'm staring blankly at the movie poster, waiting for her carefully polite 'Good night, then, Sully. This was nice, we must do it again.' I don't mind that she calls me Sully; I did tell her my proper name, when we first met, at the cafeteria. The second time, she didn't remember my name, I could tell, but she was too polite to tell me she'd forgotten, and dropped her gaze briefly to my badge, and said my name with such confidence, as she shook my hand, a little mannishly, that I didn't have the heart to disappoint her.

Other people call me Sully here anyway. Everyone does. Perhaps it really is my name now, and Sulaman was buried back in Lahore. Good riddance to him. Silly little Sulaman. Sullen little Sulaman. Who sat in the cold, and did as he was told, the child in a cautionary tale. Welcome, brave new Sully, who is too afraid to take a girl's hand, but can fearlessly hurt others with the flick of a switch. Sully, who smiles blankly when he's smiled at, but can't speak when he's spoken to; a cheap foreign import, unconvincingly rebranded for the States, poorly wired, with nuts and bolts all loose.

Radhika doesn't say good night, or goodbye, and instead asks if I'd like to have a coffee with her, somewhere further down the lamp-lit street, touching my shoulder lightly as she does so. She is standing behind me, which means I must have turned my back on her, because I was so worried with the anticipation of her leaving, again. This is our third week, our third date; it was up to me to ask her out for coffee. I've only just understood this. And she was waiting, and finally asked herself, because she is braver than me. And she is standing just behind me, touching my shoulder, because she is unsure. I was wrong to think I'd fall in love with her if she walked away scornfully, tossing her hair like a movie star. I've fallen in love with her now, for her uncertainty, for the barely-there brush of her hand on my jacket. She does not know if I'll say yes, she knows that little about me, and yet she is still asking.

'Sure,' I say. 'I'd like that. Sorry, I guess I'm kind of distracted.'

'It's okay,' she says again, and I wonder if we'll spend our lives together, and she'll say that to me every morning, like a blessing, and every evening, like a prayer. It's okay. It's okay. I feel all the tension trickling out of my body, like a toddler happily peeing himself in the warm water of a bath. 'You know, I get it, she's very beautiful,' she says, and she's nodding towards the movie poster of Sophia Loren.

'No, you're beautiful,' I say. It's the first time I've ever contradicted her. I think it's the first time I've really contradicted anyone in a long time. I don't like saying no. I don't like disagreeing. I'm better at consenting. Sitting in the dark and cold, doing what I'm told. I didn't say it to flatter her. I'm not sure I meant to say it at all. It's another knee jerk from that silver hammer she seems to have, just like the smile on her face, which pulled one out of me like a rabbit from a hat, and slapped it on so rigidly I couldn't speak or hear. But the words are out there, and I can't take them back. I have contradicted her. I have told her that she's beautiful. I'm such a fool.

'No, she's beautiful,' says Radhika, and she laughs a little, as though she's made a joke, or I have. I finally get that she's flirting with me.

'No, you are,' I say, and she pushes at me a little with her shoulder. I don't take her hand; I'm not wearing gloves and I still don't have the guts. But her shoulder is just there, and it's a cool night. I feel it's fine to put my arm lightly around her narrow shoulders, just to keep her warm, as we start walking down the street together.

'Where did you want to get coffee?' I ask. I keep my paces short so that I don't walk ahead of her, and make sure I'm just fast enough to keep up with her, so that she doesn't fly ahead of me like a swallow, with her swift and precise steps. I'm concentrating on my shoes. I'm not a big man here in America, but back home I'm the tallest in my family, and my feet look huge and ungainly clomping next to hers. Clown feet. I'm not confident enough to make a joke about it, like Jakie would; walking has never felt so difficult, such a complicated and graceless action. Her feet look almost blue, darting out from under her skirt in the dark. She's just wearing slippers, and stockings. It worries me, how cold her feet must be; I wish she was wearing socks.

'There's Mario's?' I suggest, noticing that she hasn't answered, that like me she doesn't always speak when spoken to, and feeling that it's my turn to fill the silence.

'I like Mario's,' she says, and I feel like I've passed some sort of test, and want to set one of my own.

'Or there's Luigi's,' I add. 'It's a bit further along.'

'I like Luigi's too,' she says, and she stops briefly and looks at me, as though daring me to go on. To keep on naming places that she will say she likes, because she has decided to like what I like, and she wants me to know this. I want to tell her she's beautiful again, in the sodium street light, her skin amber and shadowed, her cheekbones hollow, a faint scar on the edge of her eyebrow.

Instead I put my arm more firmly around her shoulders, and we stop at Mario's, and take the booth by the window. Her skin is cream again, without a trace of pink, and she shrugs off her coat and light scarf, her movements as determined as the small birds pecking at the crumbs on the sidewalk. She is unmade-up and scrubbed clean; she smells faintly of roses. I feel ashamed that the last time we met, after she said goodbye, and shook my hand, I went to the public restroom and banged my head against the mirror. I feel ashamed that after our date, I went home to my faculty apartment, the same size as a prison cell, and masturbated furiously on the chair, imagining a host of faceless, nameless women sprawled on me. I didn't dare to imagine her among them.

'The coffee's good here,' she says, as the waitress brings over two cups. She closes her hands around the thick white ceramic to warm them up; she didn't say please when she asked for coffee, and she doesn't say thank you now it has come. My mother would be shocked by her lack of manners. 'Chilly out, isn't it?' she says to us both, to the waitress and me, in a friendly tone. She smiles. She smiles and I smile. I just can't help it. It's like she's started something that I have to finish.

She is two years older than me, she has two degrees, and I'm guessing that she washes her face with rose-scented soap, or wipes her skin with rose-scented water. Her dark hair is cut short; practical short, not stylishly short, and she might even have cut it herself. She lets it lie unfashionably flat rather than teasing or curling it, although I'm sure she brushes it before she goes out, because it is shining under the electric light. She shakes sugar into her coffee, and doesn't ask how I take mine. When the waitress comes back to tell us about the pies on offer, cherry or apple, Radhika says, 'Mmm, they both sound great,' and suggests we share a piece of each. 'You slice, I'll choose,' she says. She presents me with the knife on a clean napkin, as though I've specialised in surgery after all and she is assisting in my final test. She has given away the knife. She is nothing like my mother.

'Do you want to talk about the movie?' I ask, hesitating just briefly before cutting the slices of pie into perfect halves with two smooth movements of the knife, and laying it back down on the napkin, clean and crumb-less. I'm proud of the precision; I could stitch them back together again just as neatly, and no one would see the join. I don't want her to see me admiring my own work, and so I casually sip my coffee, after shaking in my own sugar and pouring in cream. I prefer it black, but I'm feeling light-headed; I think I could do with the calories. She's right, the coffee's good. I relax a little, aware that we're invisible in the café, just another dark-haired couple in respectable faculty clothes.

She shakes her head, and I'm relieved. 'Good, I wasn't really paying attention,' I say.

'You do that a lot, Sully,' she says. I feel hopeful that she's saying my fake name. I like it when she says it. It's that Hindi accent of hers. I feel hopeful that she might be flirting with me again, however unpromising I might appear. Perhaps she likes the challenge of people who are hard work, or socially inept. It's what Jakie says, that some people prefer a project.

'You mean, I don't do that a lot, Radhika,' I reply instinctively, before I can stop myself. I like saying her name too, and I like that she doesn't abbreviate it, like almost everyone else I know. Jakie and Mae and Lana, Jim and Danny and now even me, all going around with our names chopped to friendly pieces. Radhika keeps firm hold of the three syllables she was born with. I suppose that if she were a boy, they'd call her Rod, or Dickie, and she'd lose all the music of her name.

'Wow, an Indian man who corrects grammar, that's refreshing,' she says. She's laughing at me. She is wearing a thin gold chain; it sits like a thread across her collarbones, weighted at the tender dent between them by a tiny god the size of a bracelet charm; the same one I noticed the first time she sat across from me. I don't want to stare at it, it would look like I'm staring at her flat bosom, but I think it's a form of Ganesha. Radhika is a Hindu, but she doesn't talk about it. Not since we had that brief conversation about Partition. She doesn't talk about anything much apart from her work, her papers, her research, and she only talks about these when I ask her. She seems just as comfortable to sit in silence, or comment on whatever happens to be around us at the time: the poster, the coffee, the temperature of the air. It's the first time she's said the word Indian tonight, and it feels like it might be a cue that I should pick up on.

'You could tell me about your family,' I say. I cringe. It hasn't come out right, it was just meant to be a casual suggestion. I genuinely want to know more about her, but now I sound like a suitable boy taking down dowry details and property prospects from a suitable girl.

'I'll tell you about mine, if you tell me about yours,' she replies, in a measured way. You show me, I'll show you. Like kids dropping their pants in the garden. I really don't want to tell her about my family, any more than I'd want to show her my diary, if I had one. I don't want her to have to swallow the most disgusting and private parts of me, my ugly thoughts and squirming liquid insides; it would be like sticking my dick in her throat, stirring my spunk in her coffee. She'd choke and sputter and gag. She'd puke like she'd been poisoned.

'There's not a lot to tell,' I say, keeping my voice just as level as hers. 'Jakie's in London now, and my sisters are at home in Lahore, with my parents. Lana's engaged. Mae's already married.'

She nods, disappointed in me. It seems that she has understood. She won't ask, and I won't tell. My mother had the same rule with the guests of social acquaintances at the club, if she suspected them of being Hindus, homosexuals or whores. There was a charity event once where she accused the much younger and very lovely companion of an elderly wealthy industrialist, visiting from India, of being all three. *Hijra*, she spat to us, when we came home, saying it like a swear word, almost delighted by the disgusting nature of the disease, but then she clapped her hand over her mouth and refused to say any more. Jakie had to tell me what she meant, after consulting with the boys at school who had older brothers. She was talking about the pretty rent boys who were docked and gelded like puppies, bought from villages or slums over the border, brought up in the Bollywood brothels, and less expensive than the real girls. Whores on happy hour. Cheaper than prison for men who liked to fuck men. Cheaper than a doctor for men who were trying to cure themselves of homosexuality.

'Well,' Radhika says drily, pulling out a cigarette from her pack, and offering one to me. 'Is she happily married, your sister?' I'm surprised how accurately she has read my expression, and worked out the blank space I left at the end of the sentence. It seems that I'm not terribly mysterious after all; even silence gives me away.

'I hope so. At least married men and women can do what they please,' I reply, taking the cigarette. I remember my manners, pull out a match, and light the cigarette that she is holding, her hand cupped intimately around the flame with mine for a moment. Our fingers not quite touching. I don't light my own, as I don't like smoking at all; I don't like drinking either, and only participate occasionally as a social convention, when it would look odd if I didn't. I wonder as she drags on the cigarette, the vile smoke working its way into the delicate architecture of her lungs, whether my own secrets would really be any more disgusting. She inhales easily, and she doesn't choke or sputter or gag. She blows out streaming blue-grey curls of pretty poison towards our reflection in the window.

'That's a touchingly lukewarm sentiment,' she says eventually. She's not laughing at me any more. Her voice has an edge.

'I'm sorry,' I say again. I think that this is how it's going to be. I'll keep saying sorry until I'm heard, or forgiven. 'It's just . . . they sent me away, and I know I'm never going back.' I don't want to revisit home in conversation; I try to avoid visiting it in my dreams. She understands; she really does. Her face softens, her hard edges seem to blur, but perhaps it's just the trailing smoke. Perhaps it's the sugar high of the pie and the caffeine rush that makes me think this. She puts her hand on mine. Warm from the coffee cup. Her nails are trimmed clinically short for her work with cadavers, so that there isn't any white to them; there's no place under her nails for dirt or blood, even if she was digging a deep hole in the ground, or an organ out of a corpse with her bare hands. She touches me, after all, when I was afraid to touch her myself, and her hands are so clean. With her touch, I understand something about myself. I know that I'm lying, and that I will go back. If only to bury the dead.

'My family's from Delhi. I don't have sisters, but I have an older brother,' she says finally, acknowledging that we had a deal. 'He's not married. Or engaged.' She isn't going to tell me any more, unless I do first. Tit for tat. Show me yours, and I'll show you mine.

Mae and marriage. It was inevitable. The brilliance of her school results was too much for our mother to put up with. It started the same night we got the letters announcing that our expensive educations abroad had been secured. We were allowed out to the movies to celebrate, and when we got back, we were told by Cook that our parents and our father's junior colleague had gone out to celebrate themselves. Probably spreading the news at the club. I heard them return late in the night. I wasn't sure if they'd woken me up, or if I was already awake, and a little while later, I went downstairs for milk, like a child.

The door to the dining room was shut, and when I returned from the kitchen, I found myself standing by it. I had a strange feeling, a little like the one you have when you know you're being watched, but it was that I was watching something instead. I was staring at the door, at the solid brass handle, and although there was no noise from the dining room, I felt that something terrible was about to happen, that something was just behind it. As though a lion was crouched in readiness beyond the frame, waiting to leap. I felt foolish, and took a sip of milk for bravery, as I had sometimes seen Abbu do with his whisky before embarking on a difficult conversation. I wiped my mouth with the soft cuff of my pyjamas, and taking the handle, I pushed the door wide. And I saw them coupling on the chair, dressed in white nightclothes in the moonlight, like ghosts.

The man and the woman were straining at each other again, her legs sprawled around him, his bare heels drumming silently on the thick pile of the rug, and even with the door open, all I could hear was hissing breath, and the rasping movement of fabric, the cotton of the woman's night sari shifting. I had often wondered if I had made up what I had seen during those troubled nights of rioting, and I wondered whether I was making this couple up now. Whether the world was asleep, and dead to itself, and I was in my head, in a dream, watching a phantom man and woman fuck silently on a chair.

They didn't notice me, it was as though I was the ghost, and it wasn't until I heard a plaintive whimpering, like the sound of a cat, that might have come from them, or might have actually been one of the cats, that I left them there. I didn't shut the door, and I walked swiftly up the stairs, and once I was outside the bedroom that Jakie and I shared, I drank the rest of my milk, shaking. I saw that my dick was swollen and hard. I gripped myself, and wondered if I could risk letting my own milk pour down the drain of the dark, damp bathroom. Just a servant and a boyfriend, Mae had said, that first time. I masturbated furiously, tugging at myself over the crested sink, newly installed with knotted pipework, imagining the lovely young companion of the elderly Indian, the one with breasts and buttocks so pert that my mother was convinced she was a eunuch, who had worn a sleeveless sari blouse that showed off her skinny arms, and four inches of flat childless stomach, stretched tautly from lower ribs to the stiff sweep of fabric below. I had no idea how things worked down there for eunuchs. They seemed as fantastical as mermaids, and more complicated than the new sink in terms of plumbing. She probably wasn't a man after all. She was probably just one of those undernourished girls from the slums who seem to be all bones and boobs, who had been picked out for her prettiness to be a mistress. I imagined her mouth on me, my dick in her throat, and tried not to think how I'd react if I ever saw her again. I thought it was unlikely; after my mother's cattiness had spread around the fund-raiser fair, she wouldn't come to the club again.

I knew my brother was awake, when I came back into our bedroom, and I put my empty glass on the nightstand, as though that was all I had been doing. Drinking milk, and rinsing out the glass. 'Sulaman, are you all right?' asked Jakie. It was as though my absence had woken him, that he needed me to be in the bed beside him so that he could sleep himself.

'I'm all right,' I reassured him. 'I've got a cramp, that's all.' I wasn't even lying: I had a solid pain in my gut, like I'd swallowed metal rather than milk. I couldn't go back to bed, and I sat on a chair, woven cane like the ones on the veranda. I tried not to think about what I had seen, and what I had just done, but I couldn't help it. I felt the blood leave my face and dick until I was as limp as the fabric of my pyjamas.

We knew of boys at school who regularly boasted about the servant girls they had slept with, who told us graphically how they had bent the girls over their parents' furniture, propped their naked buttocks at the end of their dining tables and pushed between their legs, and shoved the girls' shining oiled heads down into their laps. I knew that they were only half lying, that servant girls were groped frequently, although probably more often by fathers and uncles and the more senior servants than by the randy little squits at school, who simply spied on coupling couples in the night, or stumbled across them as I had. We all knew what it meant when a servant girl was sent back to her family, or tearfully passed on to another, less well-off family, with a bonus.

Whenever this happened, Amma would gossip with her friends over cards, and add cruelly, 'She's lucky. In the old days, she'd have been tossed in the river like so many kittens. Or broken her neck falling down the stairs.' She would add, 'Tragic,' but never made it clear where the tragedy lay: in the murder of molested maids, or the fact that these days they lived for someone else to tell the tale. She felt no sympathy for them, as their fates would never be ours; we were luckier than others, we would never be molested or murdered, we would never be molesters or murderers, and her iron rule made sure of it. The servants did what they were told, just like we did when we were children. I couldn't imagine any of our servants, even the gutsy new girls from the villages, who hadn't yet been broken down by city squalor and big house servitude, sitting in that commanding pose, with backs as straight, breath as controlled. The ghost woman in the chair was no victim; she was a spider, with arms and legs around her prey, and a paralysing bite, bargaining with her body. She was a more terrible animal than any gelded and docked whore in the Bombay brothels, than the poor girls who were regularly stabbed with their employer's flesh on unlikely household furniture. She was the one who held the knife.

I knew all this before, but I never dwelled on it in this dark way, never wanted to admit it to myself. It seems that since the experiment, since seeing what damage I'm capable of doing to others, the little moral mountain I built for myself, which said that I was better than the rest of them, has crumbled away. And now I sit here looking at a girl with a scrubbed face, knowing that I have a dirty heart. That I grew up in a place that pretended piety, but the truth was that we were all tangled up in revolting ways.

Mae never seemed to doubt the ugliness in our family; she took it for granted and dismissed it, even, as unimportant. The next morning, although I hadn't seen her leave her room in the night, I guessed that she had, as she asked Amma and Abbu pointedly at breakfast, 'Are you having more children?'

I almost dropped my juice glass at her impertinence, and my jaw must have dropped too, as Lana giggled at me, and Jakie threw a piece of fruit at my face, as though aiming for my mouth. Our parents didn't respond, and Mae patiently repeated what she had said with more precision: 'I mean, are you *planning* to have more children?' She said it too slowly and clearly, as though they had difficulty hearing or had possibly not understood; the way that British expats spoke to their servants, as though bleating more slowly and loudly would somehow translate their plummy jumble from bah-bah-bah to fluent Punjabi.

Jakie and Lana didn't seem to find it so shocking that she was asking our parents if they still slept together. That she was telling them she knew what they did in the night when they thought we were sleeping. Milk stains on Abbu's armchair. Stray hairs, too coarse to be from the head, too twisted to have come from the cats. As she spoke, Mae rolled her eyes at me for my overdramatic reaction, and although I was sure Amma went slightly pink under her bleached skin, she seemed grateful for the chance to snap at me, so she could ignore Mae.

'Be careful, Sulaman,' she scolded, 'or you can go back to using tin cups like a baby. And close your mouth when you've finished drinking;

you look like an idiot from the villages.' I obediently put my glass on the thick wooden coaster, and shut my mouth. When Amma wanted to insult us, she accused us of having inherited the family's secret genetic shame – a slack jaw, which meant that when our older relatives spoke, long streams of spittle dripping like icicles in a cave hung from their paan- and nicotine-stained teeth. And when they ate, all the food could be seen as it was ground to mush, and spilled freely on to their chests and the tablecloth, as did their juice or soda when they drank. Amma said afterwards, inspecting the stains on the linen, that they should all wear bibs. She didn't say it as a joke. She said it furiously, all the more furious after having been so honey-sweet during the visits from her in-laws, in which she claimed insincerely that her house was unworthy of her visitors.

Mae's question still lingered over the table, as Abbu studied the newspaper with too much attention, and Amma spread English marmalade carefully over a paratha, before rolling it up into a cigar shape. She hesitated about picking it up, as though there was suddenly something lewd about eating a paratha the usual way, and cut it into pinwheels instead, which she placed in her mouth one by one. I had never seen my mother so uncomfortable, and I think Mae was enjoying it.

'Daddy?' she asked, when she caught his eye and he couldn't escape.

'What a question, Mae-moni,' he said eventually. 'Your mother and I are too old for any more children.' We all knew that this was a lie, as our parents were only in their mid thirties. Our neighbour, Mrs Hana Alim, was having her seventh child; she was probably older than both of them, as her eldest son was already working for a big business in Karachi. Even no-longer-so-little Lana was about to say something about this, so Amma stopped the debate before it began.

'Your daddy means that we don't *need* any more children. You are all quite grown up, as anyone can see. If anyone should be thinking about children, it will be you, Mae-moni, and quite soon.'

Amma seemed pleased with this retort, thinking it would shut Mae up, and looked at her with a hard expression. It certainly stopped Lana giggling with Jakie, as they looked at Mae in her plaits and pale ribbons, trying and failing to think of her as a mother, like the little girls out on the street, and the young girls of good families fallen on hard times, sold to be second wives to wealthy old men who hadn't yet sired sons.

Mae was aware of the threat, and her face stiffened, but she refused to shut up. Instead she said brightly, 'Good, then you don't need the nursery any more. I'll use it for my studies.'

This seemed to be the final straw for Amma. She got up sharply, her chair scraping as she pushed it back. The maidservant had to hurry forward to catch it before it fell.

'Oh yes, your studies,' she said with poisonous sweetness. 'And to think I almost forgot to show Daddy.'

She went to the locked drawer, took out the report card, and showed it to our father, who reluctantly emerged from behind his newspaper, like a tortoise forced out of his shell, blinking and exposed in the glare of the light. He had hoped to get through breakfast without drama or discomfort, and I felt sorry for him at that moment, more sorry than I did for Mae, who brought it on herself. He had no idea how he was meant to react to Mae's excellent report, as he scanned the glowing comments and superb grades; he didn't understand how her doing well seemed to be such a confusing, ambiguous thing. Amma clearly appeared to think that there was something offensive about it, but he couldn't find the offending passage. He looked at our mother a bit hopelessly, and sipped his coffee to buy himself time. He eventually nodded at the report card, pretending he had finally understood, just as he must have done when he was a small boy who didn't quite get why he was being shown something: a holy scrap of black cloth, a passage in Arabic script framed on the wall, tatters and doodles.

'*Haan ji,*' he said, falling into the language of his childhood, then, realising what he had done, correcting himself to the language of our dining table. 'Okay, yes,' he added carefully.

Amma nodded at him with encouragement, as though he had done well, while pushing him further, like the recruits to the next stage of the experiment. The professor tries to force their disobedience by forcing their hands, literally. Instead of being on the other side of the wall, they have to sit in the same room as the screaming, inoffensive volunteer, and push his hand down on the plate, to get the shock. Many of these upstanding citizens don't flinch when faced with their duty to science. 'Like this, boss?' they ask, pushing their weight against the victim. They look expectantly at the grey-coated supervisors of the experiment, like children who've mastered a new trick: 'Did I do good, Daddy? Tell me, I did good, didn't I?' It seems that they'd have slapped their own grandmothers against the plate to get that approval. That they'd have smacked their own children in the face. And this was what Amma knew. How hard it is to say no.

'Exactly, darling,' she said, beaming. Reassuring him that his non-reaction was the reaction she wanted. 'She's done so well, there's no need for her to continue. What else can they teach a girl who is already top of the class?' Abbu nodded in dumb agreement. Her hand was lightly on his shoulder, fingers splayed, and I thought of the spider again, a spider crawling up his skin. Was she promising him another night on the chair if he agreed? Bargaining with her body, letting Nasim Uncle drool over Mae, and then selling her to him like a slave in a market. It was too despicable to imagine.

'Daddy,' cried Mae in outrage. 'Daddy! I have two more years of school. Sulaman and Jakie have only just finished.' Abbu nodded dumbly, again, and it seemed briefly, as he looked between Mae and Amma, that he was unsure which was which.

'They are going to be doctors, darling,' said Amma. 'You are going to be a wife. The things you have to learn are at home now. What use is your ninety-five per cent in mathematics if you cannot make samosas or French pastry? If you cannot knit, crochet or sew, or know when food is fresh when you are shopping for your family in the market?'

Mae scoffed openly at this, as Amma did none of these things, and we had no proof that she could. We had servants, and poor hangers-on, whom she paid. Mae looked at me for support, and I failed her miserably and stared at my hands. 'I could be both, if I finish school. I could be a doctor, and a wife,' she said, adding defiantly, 'When Sulaman learns to knit, I'll learn to knit.'

Abbu roused himself and said, 'Girls have to learn these things, Mae-moni. You'll need to know how to manage a household.' He didn't mean to betray her, and neither did I. We were just protecting ourselves. We were separating ourselves from her, passing the blame another way. 'Mummy is right,' Abbu said finally. It was as though he really had smacked Mae in the face, and he looked to Amma for approval, as though to say, 'I did it. Tell me I did good.' I felt a little sick.

'So I will give you the nursery,' said Amma magnanimously, knowing that she could afford to be generous, as she had won. 'When Lana goes back to school, you can help her with her studies, and use the room for yourself as you learn how to run the house. Cooking, cleaning and choosing a menu. Knitting and dressmaking. Shopping. Household accounts. Important things. We'll have such fun.' She clapped her hands girlishly. For a moment it seemed that she really believed it, and that she was pleased she had her daughter back again.

'You mean me to do our housework until I'm married?' said Mae, no longer in outrage, but with a slow, burning comprehension. This was her punishment, for being too smart at school, and for speaking her mind too often.

'Yes, just until you are married, Mae-moni,' said our mother sweetly, 'and then you'll be free to do as you please. Married men and women can do as we please.' She glanced complicitly at my father as she said this. He sank back behind his paper, and I wondered if he was blushing, with embarrassment, or shame.

I remembered sitting at the breakfast table, and looking around at my family as though they were a picture to be painted. Abbu-Amma, he behind his newspaper, she behind his seat as though she were standing behind a throne, her spider hand on his shoulder, a claw that could sink through the flesh like butter and hold him in place. That could hold his palm on the electric plate until he jerked and fizzed like a criminal in his chair. Jakie, our joker, with the suddenly sad face of a clown, his hand in Lana's, their fingers linked on the table in a grip strong enough to swing by, as though he was ready to run away, dragging her by the hand to safety. Lana, our sweet one, with the anxious puddles for eyes, reflecting the rest of them too clearly, sucking the end of her braid. Her mouth had dropped open when Mae had said that she could be a doctor too, and the plait had filled the gap. She was chewing bits of half-masticated paratha into the ends of her hair like a conditioning treatment. And Mae, the spirited one, no longer sitting at the table, but standing up, and I noticed for the first time that she was now the same height as Amma. Something horrible had passed between them, with Amma's deceptively irreverent words, a kind of tacit understanding, a sort of capitulation. As though the lesson that Amma had taught Mae that morning, with her hooks in my father and her tangled web around us all, would not be unlearned, but would sit in her body like a parasite, a tapeworm coiled and growing, and would never be drawn out from her.

Mae pushed her own chair all the way back with a careful movement, so as not to imply anger or impatience, and left the room, and the connection was broken. It was over. Even little Lana saying quietly to Jakie, 'Why can't Mae be a doctor too?' was unremarked upon.

A last whimper from a corked play-gun on an empty battlefield.

Radhika doesn't play with her hair, and doesn't fidget. She sits calmly, smoking her cigarette, and seems to have forgotten that I am there, even with her hand still on mine, casually draped on my skin in the centre of the Formica-topped table. I am beginning to think that I could slide my hand out from under hers, push back my chair as carefully as Mae did in another country, far away, not so very long ago, and leave without her minding. Without there being a ripple in the smoky air around her.

She looks out of the café window, and through her own reflection to the street outside. I wonder if she sees what I see, or if she simply sees what she has presented to the world, a practical haircut, an unmade-up face, a plain blouse with a charm at her neck. All her surfaces are smooth, stripped and bare. My mother would say that she looks like a washerwoman from the northern villages, a tender of fruit trees and goats, and it is probably true that Radhika looks most impressive in her white lab coat. Blank and brilliant, her expensive education and her achievements worn like a medal. Her smooth surfaces polished to white light. It would be impossible to imagine a woman like her on her wedding day, made up into a ghoulish cartoon of rouge and kohl (oh, poor Mae, poor little Lana), her hair primped and curled and pinned like a prize animal at an auction, swathed in fussy robes of scarlet and scratchy gold thread, stepping slowly around the fire.

'Your brother, is he in America too? Is he a doctor like you?' I ask her, reminding her that she owes me a little more information. I had told her that my sisters were wives, or wives in waiting, I had told her where they lived. She shakes her head, glancing back at me. I'm not sure if she is answering me, or is simply surprised that I am still there. She taps her finger thoughtfully on the back of my hand, as though reconsidering our deal.

'So you're not going back for your other sister's wedding,' she says, a statement rather than a question, and so I don't answer, and just sit back in my chair a little. My coffee is cold, but I pretend to sip it anyway. I feel so sad, thinking about Lana's wedding, and I know that she can see it, and that my silence has given me away again. For a moment I don't care. I betrayed Mae, back then, and I'll keep on betraying her, because I can't be any other way. I'll betray Lana too. Both of my sisters will be trapped in their marriages, each with a particular unloved man of means, until his funeral or hers. The punishment hardly fits the crime. Radhika drags on her cigarette a final time, and stubs it out on the cheap tin tray on the table.

'This stuff will kill you,' she says, pushing the tray of ash towards me, as though offering me sweets on a platter. 'That's something we're investigating. I've got bodies in the university basement; you cut them open, and they were dead inside for months before they died. Once the other patients heard the results, their prognosis, they smoked even more.'

'I guess it can't kill you if you're already dead,' I say unthinkingly, picking at the ash and rubbing it between my thumb and forefinger, as though to smear it on a forehead for a feast day or blessing. The pads of my fingers are greasy from the butter crust of the pie, and the ash sticks to my skin, making my fingerprints stand out in relief. Ash is dirty, and grease is dirty, but when you boil them together, you get soap, which gets your hands clean. Two negatives make a positive. For some reason, what I said strikes her as funny; she starts laughing, either at me or with me, and I smile ruefully back. She gets up, and so I get up. I pay the bill at the counter, where the waitress is listening to the radio, and we leave the café.

I find myself walking Radhika home, although she doesn't ask me to, and I don't offer. I just don't have the energy to say goodbye and walk in the other direction; it's so much easier to follow her, like a swimmer in her slipstream. The cool air ripples through my hands like water, and makes me aware of my skin, of her skin, and her exposed face, hands and ankles. She is showing no more of herself than a zealot's wife in a burqa. I find myself looking at her small, slippered feet with concern, as she walks on the cold, hard pavement. Even the tiny scraps of skin she is showing seem too much. I feel suddenly protective of her, although she is now not walking close enough for me to have my arm over her shoulder. I wish I could drape my jacket round her like a cloak. I wish I could give her my warm woollen socks.

At her building, she turns towards me, and I wait for her to shake my hand, and wonder whether she'll thank me, like she normally does, and suggest we do it again. I think that going to the café this evening was going too far, and I'm aware that I've failed and she's succeeded, as she has seen me for what I really am, and now knows not to waste her time with me. She has worked out that I'm not really a suitably suited man, not even a suitable boy, but just a machine with holes drilled for my eyes, bland and cold as grey metal, with less spark than the shock box we've been pretending to torture people with at the university. That I'm something that needs an order to take action. A thing, which when asked to jump will ask how high.

She doesn't reach out her hand, but leans back against the railing that leads to her basement apartment, and looks at me, her head giving a subtle sideways movement while she's thinking. I see her make her mind up, and I smile, hopefully, thinking it can't do any harm to show how much I like her. I called her beautiful tonight, and she took it as a joke.

'My brother's dead,' she says. 'He died during Partition. In the riots. Our ayah was Muslim, and they thought he was Muslim because he was with her. We found them together; his body was just a little further down the street from hers. Perhaps he was tossed there. Perhaps he was running away.' I have no idea what to say to this. I'm a machine, not a man, and I don't know what a man, a friend or a lover, would say or do in this situation. I realise that the smile is still frozen on my face, and I relax the muscles with an effort, drawing in my cheeks as though I'm sucking on a sour lemon sweet. I'm relieved that she is no longer looking at me, and that she has stopped talking, but now she seems ready to go down her stairs, open her door and shut it in my foolish face. I'll say anything to keep her here for a moment longer. I'll talk about the poster, the coffee, the air. I'll even talk about family.

'Your family must be proud of you,' I say. 'Everything you've done.'

'Oh yes,' she says. 'My grand achievements,' and she sweeps an arm towards the tiny flat in college-subsidised accommodation. 'I became a doctor because my brother couldn't. If he'd survived, it would be him here, not me.'

There is nothing I can say to this. I want to say that I'm glad she's here, but it would be like saying that I'm glad he's dead. I don't have the answer, and I ask her the question instead. 'Aren't you happy that you're here?'

She looks at me directly, with her brown eyes turned black with the night, and says, 'Yes.' She says it again, as though it is a relief for her to admit this: 'Yes, I am.' She starts fiddling with her door keys, and while her firm 'Yes' is still ringing in my ears, I have the courage to follow her down the few steps, and ask, 'Can I see you next week?'

'Yes,' she says, unlocking her door, and she turns towards me as she says it. I step towards her, and kiss her clumsily, with a dry peck on her mouth, my hands briefly holding her by the top of her arms, for my support more than hers. Her lips are warm and her nose is cold. I don't give her time to respond, to kiss me back or slap me, and step away hurriedly, and tell her again, so she knows it wasn't a joke.

'You're beautiful,' I say, backing up the stairs, my hand on the cold metal of the railings. I feel it's important that I have the last word in the matter.

Radhika thinks differently. 'Good night, Sully,' she calls after me, before shutting her door.

She sounds pleased, or at the very least amused, and I start running, because I want to skip, or dance, and know I can't do this in public, but I can at least look like I'm in a hurry. I kissed her. I liked it. And I think she did too. I called her beautiful, and one of the things I found beautiful in her was that under her smooth, luminous surface, she was as grubbily guilty as me. We'd both got away. We'd both survived. Ash and grease. They both make your hands dirty, but mix them together and they'll make you clean again.

I can't wait to go back to the silence of my cell, so that I can relive every moment of the evening in my head, lying in my laundered bed; but this time, in the café, I'll pour out my dirty heart to her, and I'll keep saying sorry until I'm heard. Until I'm forgiven. 'It's okay,' she'll say. 'It's okay.'

If only I could marry Radhika. And set us both free. Married men and women are free to do as they please.

Chapter Four

Jakie

MY LOVER'S NAME IS FRANK MCADAM, BUT HE'LL CALL HIMSELF FRANKIE as a joke, and sings songs from Elvis movies with an exaggerated slur: 'Frankie and Jakie were lovers, oh lordy how they could love, swore to be true to each other, just as true as the stars above, oh Jakie, you're my man, so don't you do me wrong.'

He winks at me as he sings, as he is far less faithful than me, and is always out at parties or pubs or clubs, while I'm studying or working or cutting into cadavers for my training. I have the smallest student flat in cheap digs on the north side of the river, and Frank fills it when he visits, so there isn't room for the both of us. I don't mean that he's a big man; he's slight, and wiry, but he has a big mouth and he spreads himself about as much as he puts himself about. He's one of those people who take up a lot of space in the world.

When I met him, I thought he was Irish, and then I thought he couldn't be, because of his name. I thought Irish names started with an O apostrophe, like O'Hara, and Scottish names with Mac, like MacDonald, and that most Welsh people were called Jones. The British equivalents of Ali, Khan and Singh. I was proud that I had picked up these snippets of local information. In fact it turns out that he's not Irish, and not British; he's from Northern Ireland, which is apparently neither. He talks a lot about this; he talks a lot about everything. And being from neither here nor there is something we have in common.

'God, my mother will think it's great that I've got a doctor,' he says to me. 'I've done better than my sisters. They just married into the New

66

York Mafia.' I'm not actually sure that he's joking. He says 'God' and 'Great' a lot, more than the butchers in the Lahore markets, who mutter the words in a businesslike way every time they kill a chicken for the flustered wives and flapping domestics with string bags and baskets.

But Frank never puts these words together into God-is-Great the way a Muslim would. He's not in the business of piety, and unlike the butchers and his brothers-in-law and me, he doesn't spill blood for a living. He's a writer; he spills his guts instead. He claims to visit his priest for confession, but I suspect he really goes to boast or torment the poor man, because I've never seen him pray.

His sisters did go all the way to New York, and they did marry Italian-Americans, cousins from the same family who courted them at a dance. Courted is Frank's word not mine, and he says it with an ironic twist to his mouth. He has a brother who works in a bank in Belfast, and another who's a teacher in the same town, who wanted to be a priest but couldn't keep up with the studies. Whenever he talks about his brothers, he says, 'Those sorry bastards,' and he says it with complicated affection. Like he loves them, but he's happy he left them behind.

He doesn't believe me when I said I had to learn the Qur'an by heart by the age of ten, and that everyone else in school did too; that not keeping up with the studies wasn't an option, even for the slow and simple ones, like Haroun-the-Baboon, who had to have verse after verse beaten into him. Haroun had three broken ribs from his beatings, each one teaching him a lesson he'd never forget.

'Do you still remember it?' Frank asks, testing me. 'Enough to quote, chapter and verse?'

'I guess I do,' I say, indulging him. Frank's a bit older than me, but he's the youngest in his family, and I think he's always been a little spoilt.

'Bollocks you do. Prove it, so,' he says. He's shrugging on his jacket and putting on his hat. It's the first time we've done it indoors with all our clothes off. It's the first time he's stayed over. He's leaving the morning after the night before. He's standing at the door.

'Remember me,' I say, looking at him framed in the peeling white paint of the doorway. 'I'll remember you.' He looks surprised, and pleased, as though I've just paid him an unexpected compliment, and then I say, 'Chapter 2, verse 152.'

'Well, that's just bloody lovely,' he says. I'm not sure if he means it, or if he's annoyed, and he shuts the door behind him on the way out. I love the ambiguous way he speaks, and he'd be offended by this, but I think he's exotic. If I had to come up with a charming Irishman, I'd have come up with Frank, light on his feet, free with his hands, and quick with his patter. He says 'Lovely' more often than any man should, and the waitresses and bank tellers and shop assistants all giggle like the cheerful bubble-haired heroines in the post-war movies when he talks to them, like he's the best thing since nylon stockings and knee-length skirts.

I met Frank in a café. Outside a café, in fact. Sitting at the only table set up in the street. Well, people can meet in cafés, can't they? You can pick up strangers anywhere, like pennies off the pavement, although I suppose I've done it more frequently at night with a few drinks, rather than in the morning, clutching a coffee and clutching my head.

It was a little place in Temple, off the Strand, and I was going into work early on a Monday morning. I realised as I walked towards the bridge in the crisp, biting air that I was still hung-over from the night before. I went into the café for coffee and dry toast, but the smell of frying fat and cigarette smoke made me feel even sicker. And so I went outside, and saw that the only table, set for four people, was taken up by a slight man with startling red hair. I finally understood the phrase 'a shock of hair'. He was bent over the table, his face practically touching it, and seemed to be writing in a notebook, which he had set in the centre of an open broadsheet. The corners of his newspaper were flapping like a loose tablecloth in need of acorn weights. The other chairs were taken up by his jumble of possessions: a flat cap, an umbrella, an old-fashioned briefcase with the battered air of a school satchel. He occupied his territory with an imperial sprawl.

My first words to him were 'Excuse me, sir, could I share your table, please?'

His first words to me, muffled into the newsprint, were 'Fock off,' followed by a mumbled 'Fockin' animals.' As he stirred fitfully, I realised that he hadn't really heard me, that he'd actually been asleep or passed out on the newspaper, but the stub of pencil in his hand had somehow remained in place.

My next words to him were 'Are you all right, sir? I'm a doctor.'

He raised his head with some difficulty, looking just as hung-over as I felt. Perhaps he thought exactly the same thing of me, as he glanced up, because then he stopped to look at me properly, staring openly at my face as though I was a museum exhibit. A curiosity in a cabinet. Something strange and captivating. I was trying not to stare myself; he had green eyes, and the combination of red hair and green eyes was more colour than I'd ever seen on a white man. I was clasping my hot coffee in one hand, with the dry toast balanced precariously on the rim, and holding my throbbing head in the other, for all the good that would do it. I'm not sure that I thought him slightly attractive until he smiled, his eyes crinkling at the edges as though he meant it.

'Did you hit your head when you fell?' he asked. I liked his accent. I'd never heard anyone sound so unapologetically Irish. I realised that I was smiling back at him.

'Fell from where?' I replied. 'From space?' I thought he was making a joke. Maybe something about illegal aliens. And if he wasn't, I was thinking about making one instead.

'From heaven,' he said, and started laughing at the line. I laughed too, but then groaned as it hurt my head. My coffee sloshed, and I hastily rescued the toast.

'Could I share your table?' I asked again.

'Sure, take a seat, fella,' he said, as easily as though he'd been waiting for me. 'It looks like you and I are both a long way from home.'

That was a few months ago, and although Frank wasn't my first lover, not by a long shot, he's the first I asked home and the only one I've spent the night with. He doesn't stay all the time, and I'm not surprised when I wake and he's not there. The alarm clock by the single student bed rattles off like a miniature machine gun, its tin hammer knocking between the bells, and I go deeper under the covers, ignoring it, until I hear a groaning from the floor, and an anguished 'For the love of God, Jakie, turn the damn thing off!'

I get out of bed carefully, and in the gloom I can see that Frank is lying flat out just inside the door, where he must have passed out as he stumbled in, sometime in the night. 'At least you didn't throw up on the carpet,' I comment.

'Ah, you wouldn't want to be looking outside the door, then,' says Frank unapologetically. I shrug, half smiling, and push open the curtain instinctively. A bright beam of sunlight sears the room in two, and Frank's groans are pitiful, as he howls, 'Jakie, you bastard,' like a bereaved wolf on the hills.

'Sorry, sorry,' I mutter, pulling the curtains back as swiftly as I opened them.

I walk the two steps to the gas ring, light it with a match, and put the kettle on. I realise that the kettle isn't nearly full enough to make coffee for two, and walk another two steps to the corner sink, fill it, and put it back on the burner. I do all this carefully, as though aware that I'm being watched, but when I sit back on the end of the bed, I see that Frank hasn't shifted, and that he might have even gone back to sleep. Using the thin rag rug as the sheet for his makeshift bed, just as he used the sheets of newsprint in the café that first morning.

For some reason, the sight of him, drunk as a skunk, and lying there peacefully, his flat cap miraculously in place over his thick red hair, a musky, sour scent of old wine and fag ash rising from him, fills me with affection, and a sort of grubby nostalgia, for the life we haven't yet lived. I reach out for the matches, and light them, one after another, staring at each flame, and waiting for it to tickle the ends of my fingers before flicking it in the sink. I'm great at throwing stuff. I make it every time, and then reach for another packet as I fling the last match. As I open the folded matchbook, I see that there's a number scrawled on the inside. The matches are from a bar that Frank goes to, sometimes with me, more usually without me. Someone must have given him his number, or he might have asked for it. I tear off the match, and start my game again, lighting and flicking them faster and faster, determined to throw this packet away.

'God, you're just a big kid, Jakie,' says Frank from the floor, where he has started watching me after all. His face has turned, and he is lying in the pillow of his arms. He begins to heave himself up, as unsteady and graceless as a baby gazelle. 'But bless you for making the coffee.'

'I'm good at games,' I say, tearing out and lighting the last two matches together. I don't wait for them to burn to the end, and flick them daringly towards the sink; the double flames fly safely over the carpet before they land and die hissing on the damp ceramic. I toss the packet into the straw waste-paper basket next to the sink, full of apple cores and nut shells, and the other remnants of the makeshift meals I occasionally fix for myself. 'I could beat anyone at tiddlywinks.'

'I don't mean that,' says Frank, finally on his feet, and going to the bin, rather than to me. 'It's like you don't want anyone else playing with your toys. Even when you're not playing with them yourself.' He picks out the matchbook, looks at it dismissively, and then drops it back in. 'I don't even remember the bugger. Definitely got off with him, though. He bought me drinks. It seemed polite.'

'Whore,' I say, getting up to take the whistling kettle off the hob, reaching for the mugs.

'Bore,' he says, coming to stand behind me, putting his arms around me briefly, and dropping a kiss on the back of my neck. 'It's your fault for never coming out,' he says. 'I'm going for a slash,' and he leaves the room. I hear him greeting the neighbour, and how her initially sniffy response warms to laughter. I imagine him linking arms with her and skipping down the corridor, before leaving her with a gallant kiss on the hand as he goes to the communal bathroom ahead of her.

I'm making the coffee in the gloom, and suddenly resent the fact that I have to sit in the dark just because Frank's hung-over, when he isn't even in the room. It reminds me of the time he insisted that I listen to the game with him, some football match between two teams I'd never heard of, and then went off to get fags. He left me sitting in the flat listening to a match I didn't care about, with commentators saying combinations of simple words that I didn't even understand. Offside rule. Corner from a defender. That's the trouble with Frank: even when he's out, he's still in.

I go and pull open the curtains, decisively. The sunshine is too bright for me, let alone him. The flash of light makes something throb in my head, like the onset of a migraine, and for a moment I feel confused, about the day, the month, the season; it feels it shouldn't be so bright this early. Even as I think this, even as I open the window and let out the stale, comforting air that smells of Frank's clothes, and lean out on to the street, I have already remembered that it isn't early after all; it's late morning, because I worked a late shift, and the reason Frank was still asleep on the floor when I woke, instead of at work in the newsroom of the paper he writes for, is because he's a feckless slut.

When he comes back in, his cap is stuffed in his pocket, his face is scrubbed and his hair is damply slicked back. It's only his veined eyes that still give away his hangover. He looks at himself in the mirror above the sink.

'Windows to the soul,' he comments, taking his coffee cup and sitting at the little painted table. I have so much to say to him, about the puke he says he left outside the door, about the stranger he got off with last night, about his drinking, about him losing his job if he doesn't get going or at least call in sick with a plausible excuse, that I don't say anything at all. I'm not his mother. I'm not his wife. I sit opposite him, warily, waiting for him to comment about the open window. He sips his coffee appreciatively, and then looks directly at me.

'Shouldn't you be at work, Jakie?' he asks seriously. He's telling me off. The unfairness of this hits me with a rush of affection. After everything he's done, he's the one who's telling me off. He's concerned for me and he's not afraid to show it. He's not afraid to nag. I want to hug him, but instead I grin.

'Shouldn't you?'

'Fair point,' says Frank. 'But it doesn't really matter if I'm not there to scribble copy about cats up trees to make tomorrow's fish wrappers. No one cares. And even if they do, no one dies. Your job's different. You've got to get to work and save people.'

'Well that's what I'm saving them for, isn't it? To read the newspapers at breakfast. People need to be entertained. Maybe more than they need to be saved.'

Frank sputters with laughter. 'God, entertainment over breakfast? Is that my highest contribution to the arts?' He finishes his coffee, and gets up to pour himself another. 'It probably will be. My book's bloody awful. Got smashed out of my head last night just to forget about it.' He gestures down at himself dismissively. 'Look at me. I'm a focking cliché. Another drunk Irishman, another muck-raking journalist, another writer in a café. I'm so many clichés you could bundle me up in them like a rubber-band ball, and throw me outside for the dogs to chase.'

'That's a good line,' I say. 'You should write it down. Advice from another cliché. The Asian doctor. Brown man in a white coat.'

'Fock off,' says Frank good-naturedly. 'Seriously, fock off. Go on with you, you need to get to work.'

'I did the late shift,' I remind him. 'I've got another hour before I need to go in. Do you want to get breakfast?'

'God, no,' says Frank. 'I'll only puke again.' He nods towards the door. 'By the way, you don't have to worry about the mess outside. Your neighbour cleaned it up for you. I said it was one of your patients.' There are lots of things that I could say about this. The casual way he said 'for you', as though his mess was my mess. The fact that I'm training in a hospital, and don't have patients who'd come to my flat, like some back-street abortionist. Instead, I'm lost between admiration and annoyance. Tenderness and exasperation. I must have something of a crush on Frank. I get too upset that he plays around with other men, but I don't know what I can do to change that. I can't impetuously ask him to marry me. I can only ask him to wake up with me, occasionally, and read the papers.

'I guess I'll get something to eat, then,' I say. 'If you're not hungry. There's nothing but apples in the cupboard. And a jar of something that was here when I moved in.'

'Why don't you throw it out?' says Frank, linking his hands and stretching his arms above his head with an indulgent yawn. He reminds me of a dishevelled alley cat, with just as few concerns. No one tells him what to do – I'm not sure they ever have – and so he does exactly what he wants. He doesn't seem to care where he sleeps, what he eats or whether he works.

'I'm leaving it to poison the vagrants who break in while I'm sleeping,' I reply. 'The intoxicated Irish who pass out drunk on my rug.'

'Sounds like a plan,' says Frank. 'Sure, if you leave it long enough, it'll grow legs and walk out of the place itself.'

I stifle a laugh, but then I see that Frank is shrugging off his jacket, not buttoning it up, and really has no intention of coming out with me. I start to rinse out my coffee cup in the sink, and am aware that he's watching me with amusement from the table, as though doing the washing-up straight away says something about me, that I'm a prig, or a mummy's boy, or I don't know what. I drop the mug in the sink with a clatter, half washed. I want to turn around and point out that in my family, I'm the fun one. I'm Jakie the Joker, and I drink, and smoke, and buy fried food for breakfast, and eat with my hands, and have sex with strangers in strange towns for the fun of it. But he knows all this. When I do turn around, unsure of what I'm going to say, he's standing up, and has shrugged off his shirt too, and I suppose he's intending to sleep it off in the warm bed I've just vacated.

'I just said I might puke,' he says, still with the edge of laughter that seems to cling to him, even when he's sad. 'I never said that I wasn't hungry.'

He tosses his own unwashed cup in the sink, where it chimes and cracks with the snap of broken glass, and takes a step towards me, so I can feel the pale heat from his pale skin, freckled on the shoulders. He moves closer, his forearms on either side of me, palms leaning against the mirror, and I'm pushed back against the cold ceramic and steel of the sink, not uncomfortably, as he drops one kiss and then another on the side of my neck, and then brushes his stubbled face against mine, kissing me as hungrily as he said, as though to prove a point. My eyes widen as I kiss him back, just for a moment, before taking his face in my hands and holding him away, just a little bit.

'You brushed your teeth,' I say accusingly, as though he was planning to seduce me, as though it was some sort of trick. I try not to sound too pleased. I try to look annoyed rather than flattered, like the women outside being whistled at by the road workers.

'You talk too much, Jakie,' says Frank, and the unfairness of this accusation from the man who never shuts up does stun me briefly into silence. 'Besides, I thought this was my job, providing entertainment at breakfast,' he adds, and then I laugh, and let Frank help me pull off my own vest, and we stagger back and fall on to the edge of the bed.

The window is open, and it is broad daylight, and he's hung-over and I'm stone-cold sober, and I don't think we've ever made love like this. Awake, aware, alight. We always do it at night rather than during the day. We used to do it outside more than in; it took us a whole month to get indoors. The sun is spilling on his electric hair, his alley cat eyes, and his winter skin, and I think again, a little unfairly, how exotic he is. How different. As though difference is everything that defines him. But I do love to see the contrasting shades of his body pressed against mine, the muscles moving in his arms as he wrestles me down, as I try and tug him towards me instead, and he wins, and pins me back, taking my cock deep in his mouth. And I grip his hair in my fingers, and worry briefly about the neighbours, and I hope they just think we're having a physical fight, as I cry out with the explosive waves of white light, because that's what it feels like. When I'm biting the sunlit pillow while Frank bites at the back of my neck, I just want to smash every dirty cup in the flat and holler with victory like a brass-beating Greek hero from mythology, and have them hear me all the way up the river to Parliament.

'God, I love you, Jakie,' says Frank afterwards. I wait for the 'but'; with Frank, there's always a but after those three little words, and he uses them freely. 'God, I love my mammy, but she's a terrible bitch,' and

'God, I love Hemingway, but he's a terrible bore.' I don't have to wait long. '... but you don't ever come out with me.'

I don't argue with him, as I get up to look for cigarettes. I don't point out that I just asked him out for breakfast, and that I go out with him late at night. I know exactly what he means; that I'll only kiss him in the dark of an alley, or behind closed doors, where no one else can see. He's right: I don't come out with him. I haven't come out. I can't. His accusation, this time, is perfectly justified.

I pull out a couple of cigarettes from his jacket pocket, still on the floor where he left it, with another matchbook. Another man's number scribbled inside. Frank's more honest than me. He knows his position isn't so very different from the secret mistress of a respectable man. Just like the ladies scattered all over Westminster, kept in nice apartments and maids by their married lovers in the Houses of Lords and Commons; probably fucked in the mouth or arse, like him and like me, so they can't get pregnant. He knows that one day I'll marry. Like Mae has done, and Lana will soon. Some domestically competent girl arranged from home will get shipped out to make a new home for me here, with children and soft furnishings. I know it too. It was Frank who described himself as the toy, not me. But it suddenly makes me so sad. That I'm the fun one, and I'm just not done playing yet, as though fun is all this is.

I light a cigarette, and take the other one over to Frank, but he's either asleep, or pretending to sleep, and his forehead seems tense, with the question he didn't ask and I didn't answer. God, I love you, Jakie, he said. I love you, but. He didn't say, Do you love me? which expects a yes, as much as a marriage proposal does. He didn't say, Don't you love me? which expects a nothing, or a no. I lean out of the window, blowing out the smoke for a while, watching the street. I can hear a church bell ringing, in the distance, as persistent as the barking of a dog. It's too late for Mass, and it's not yet noon. It's probably the end of a wedding service. Love and marriage, like a horse and carriage. Old-fashioned ideas that just don't go together any more. I can't marry the man I love, and I won't love the girl I marry.

I finish the cigarette, tapping the ash on to the windowsill, watching the grey dust trickle away in the breeze. The room is getting cold now that the sun has gone behind the clouds, and I think that Frank might be shivering, naked under the thin sheets. I shut the window, and pull up the blanket that we'd kicked to the floor. I'm sure that he really is asleep, as his breathing is deep and even. I don't kiss him, as I don't want to wake him, but I put my face close to his hair, breathing in his sour, sweet scent.

'You know I do too,' I say to him, and feel such a coward. For saying it while he's sleeping. God, I do too, but. It's like I left him a fifty-pound note on the counter, before sneaking off. I dress quietly, and go to work.

I take the bus over the bridge, towards the hospital; I usually walk, but despite a good few hours' sleep, I'm tired, and the cold air makes me feel clammy and uncomfortable. Like a corpse cooling to the temperature of the frigid mortuary air. Corpses don't bruise, but I'm bruised, inside and out. Sex with Frank really is like a physical fight; he likes it that way. I do too, but only with him. He's not so picky. He'll stroll in, cheerfully announcing that he knows he must have had a good night, because he woke up black and blue, and I think, God, he's been with some bouncer or a boxer, up against the bins in an alley. He cheats on me all the time, but I'm the one who feels branded now, with the love bites on my neck, hidden under my cravat, and the bruises on my ribs like a scarlet letter. I'm the one who feels faithless.

An old lady, dressed bravely in a smart hat and a tweed suit, as though determined not to let her age overpower her, steps on to the bus, and I stand up for her to let her have my seat. She looks surprised; she probably tries not to notice that brown and black people exist, thinking that the politest thing to do is ignore us. It's probably more polite than staring, which is what the smaller children do. A little boy is staring at me now, as the old lady gives me a curt nod and takes my seat, and I can't help noticing that she has the thin legs and high heels of a much younger woman. The boy's mother sees me glancing, and cuffs her son on the head, turning away from me furiously, as though afraid I'll notice her legs too. The child whines, and asks in a stage whisper, 'But does it smell of chocolate or poo?' and I know he's talking about me. I want to laugh and hold my hand out for him to sniff, like he's a puppy.

Instead, I grip the rail more firmly, until my knuckles force themselves with pale determination through my skin, and I notice a hair on my cuff. It's not mine, and it's not Frank's. It's pale brown, with a slight wave, and it must have transferred from his clothes to mine, when they were lying in a puddle on the floor. It's the hair of whoever Frank got off with the night before, or maybe one of the nights before that. I stretch it out, and it catches the light. I wrap it tightly around my finger, and it's strong enough to make the tip turn blue.

It's still there when I get off the bus, like the ribbon wrapped around the old oak tree. I pull it off, but instead of throwing it away, I stuff it in my pocket, to get lost among the shrapnel of change and lint lining. I'm jealous of a pale brown hair that shines gold in the sun, and a number in a matchbook. It hurts more than the bruises when I breathe. Frank is right to beat me up when we have sex, and he's right to betray me. He's a lapsed Catholic, but he still believes in retribution. He's giving me up before I give him up. And I will, I'll give him up when I get married, just like I gave up on Mae, when I let her get married. Like I'll soon give up on Lana. Mae was the first, and I'll be the last.

Mae's marriage happened sooner than anyone thought it would; Mae was the closest thing to a rebel we had in our family, simply because she was clever enough to get her own way, and pretty enough to manipulate our family visitors into indulging her. When our mother and father saw how she was admired, they pretended that they approved, that the admiration she elicited somehow reflected well on them, and in public they let her have the harmless little things she asked for. Trips to the cinema, and sparkling slippers to wear out on visits; Western music and literary novels. Textbooks. The truth is, they didn't really approve, and it made them feel uncomfortable, the way she got her own way; they felt she was slipping through their fingers. Sulaman and I never thought for a moment that we were masters of our own fates, and would never have dared to say that we were planning to be lawyers rather than doctors – we wouldn't even cross that line between the glamour professions expected of us. Mae was different, and when our mother announced that she was pulling her out of school, to do housework instead, we thought Amma would have a fight on her hands. We thought she wanted one.

Mae surprised us all, and outmanoeuvred Amma effortlessly, by simply agreeing. Or by seeming to agree. Our mother had the idea that

Mae would be some sort of Cinderella; that she would force her into marriage by making her do all the household chores, dismissing servant after servant until she became our only domestic, cleaning from morning to night, stopping only to sleep, and then being woken at 5 a.m. to go to the market and shop for the family, until tiredness and hard labour ground down her proud spirit. And that then she would fall into marriage, careworn and broken, as glad of the escape as a terminal patient escaping their pain or their morphine nightmares with suicide.

Our mother was wrong, and got much more than she'd bargained for. Mae took over the household, just as she had been asked to, making the old nursery her centre of affairs, and the servants were drilled just as efficiently as they had always been. She went into the kitchen, and took over Lana's stool by the cook, learning how to make his most complicated dishes, with a lighter touch than his fat, hot hands could ever manage. Mae's hands were always cool, like our mother's – a hereditary circulation problem had been diagnosed for both of them. When she was younger, she used to frighten us in our beds by drawing her chilled finger up the bumps of our spines, like a shiver, blowing a phantom's breeze along the line she drew, and only Lana's giggle beside her gave the game away, before we screamed in our dreams. Mae's corpse-cold hands were perfect for handling pastry, and her samosas were a crispy delight. It seemed that our mother was the only one who didn't have to lie to guests, when claiming that the treats on display had been made by her daughter's fair hands.

Mae even took to inspecting the household accounts, including our mother's spending, on the pretext of minimising pilfering by the servants, and then went too far when she started sitting in the front seat with Karim, the elderly chauffeur, and asking him to teach her how to drive. Our mother was afraid that she was sprouting wheels for wings, and would soon escape altogether, and called her bluff by inviting prospective in-laws to the house, sure that this would make Mae withdraw.

Again Mae astounded her, by dressing modestly, putting flowers in her hair, and keeping her head low as she served the samosas, like a model daughter-in-law, so that the mothers and fathers and sons were soon begging to see her face. 'So pretty,' the mothers would say, lifting her chin with their painted fingertips, and the fathers would nod approval, and the sons would look at her with yearning while she ignored them and charmed the parents. Mae knew that sons were easy to manage – she'd managed them at the cinemas and outside the school gates for years, tossing her hair and rejecting them, and then giving them the sly sideways glances that seemed to promise them something after all, and give them new hope all over again. Parents were harder to manage altogether – especially the mothers-in-law, under whose reign she'd be living, if she agreed to a marriage. She was too smart to swap our mother for one that was just like her. However appealing the groom, if the mother was haughty, difficult, high-nosed, or oozing complicated sweetness, she withdrew. When a mother came with plump cheeks from overindulging in ice cream and sweets, laugh lines and untidy hair from tossing her head with giggles, and a smooth, unblemished forehead that didn't have the habit of frowning, Mae took an interest, and shuffled closer, as though warming her hands on a flame.

'What a flower you have, Mrs Saddeq,' one of these mothers said. Matronly Mrs Kannon beamed at Mae with open admiration unedged with criticism, and dampened her forefinger delicately on her lower lip, to touch Mae for a blessing. 'A mayflower,' she added, laughing at her own joke, and looking eagerly around for the room to laugh with her. Mae accepted the touch, the spittle blessing, in the uncomplicated way a child would accept a kiss on an ouchie, graze or scratch, and laughed obligingly, throwing a glance at her mother over her shoulder. Amma was forced to smile in response, a rictus etched on her brittle face like a scratch on stained glass. As though if she smiled any deeper, her mask would snap, or shatter into sparkling shards.

Our mother had thought to have some fun with Mae. Those were her words, 'We'll have such fun.' She thought she'd teach her a lesson she couldn't learn at school. She thought by pulling her out of her classes, she'd tame her, and keep her to herself. Mae learned the lesson too fast, and now Amma had no way out. She had sanctioned and encouraged the visitors, hoping to dismay her daughter, and instead had given Mae her own *Mayflower* to escape to a wilder, kinder land. She had threatened Mae with a husband, and Mae had played her like a card shark, taking the husband, and raising the stakes by a new mother. A milder, kinder mother, grateful for Mae's beauty and accomplishments, instead of jealous of them. Marriage was going to be Mae's America, her

New World, not her sentence; it seemed that the punishment fitted the crime after all.

Our mother watched helplessly from her winged armchair as Mae became the centre of the household, and looked at her reflection in the polished glass covering our stretched black cloth as though aware for the first time of her own mortality. The wicked queen who didn't dare to ask the mirror on the wall who was the fairest of them all, because she didn't want to be told the truth. As the mother of the bride, she was of almost no importance; the most she received from the sons and fathers of the invited families was a cursory glance, and not even to see how Mae might age; they looked at the jewellery she wore, that their own family might one day inherit.

'I'm getting married,' announced Mae casually, coming in during a rainstorm, shaking her umbrella. We were on the veranda, enjoying the cooler air while the water ran off the guttering and the rubbery leaves of the shrubs. She had walked through the garden gate, rather than through the house, and had approached us across the damp grass and vegetable plot like an actress coming on stage with a line to deliver. I suspected her of having come in the front door first, noticing with annoyance that we weren't in the living room, and then going back out to make a proper entrance. Mae had her own ideas about the way things should be done; how proposals should be made, and how they should be announced. I wondered if she had given her groom a script, a specific location, and had made him repeat it until he got his lines right.

Our mother's back stiffened, and she turned from barking orders to the maids about drying the damp laundry they hadn't got down from the garden quickly enough. She had lost weight, as though she'd been trying to compete with the adolescent slenderness of Mae's hips, and it didn't suit her. Her breasts seemed deflated in her sari blouse, and her face was hardened by the sharpness of her cheekbones. She looked like she wanted to scratch Mae's eyes out, for daring to surpass her. Instead she took out the silver knife, and began to cut fruit for our father.

'Splendid, Mae-moni,' said our father, with a fearful firmness. Even he couldn't fail to be aware of our mother's stormy mood, but this was what she herself had arranged. A marriage rather than an education. And it was the natural order of things; although Mae was still younger than our unmarried cousins, she had been precocious in so many other

80

ways, it was natural that this flower of the family would blossom first. 'Which lucky boy has caught your eye?'

It was clear that he didn't mind which. All of the grooms who had been invited to the house had been thoroughly vetted: families researched, qualifications checked, incomes confirmed. The horror stories that circulated around the club and in the papers had made him cautious – brides murdered for their dowries, brides taken far away to the other family's house, to have their possessions and jewellery stolen and be turned into servants for an earlier wife, brides forced to wear Western dress and entertain foreigners, or sent out to work to support lazy, good-for-nothing husbands. Having assured himself that all these pitfalls had been avoided, and that the hopeful husbands came from suitable backgrounds – local, wealthy and traditional – our father believed his job was done, and that beyond this, marriage was a matter for women.

'Mrs Kannon's son,' said Mae. I exchanged a brief glance with Lana; it was obvious how Mae intended to twist the knife, naming the mother before the son. Mae then knelt down, and took the silver blade from Amma, so she could finish cutting up Abbu's fruit; that was her job now, and she never hesitated in pointing it out. She did it quicker and more efficiently than Amma, as though proving a point. Amma had always made it look laborious and full of hard-won effort.

'The older or the younger?' asked Abbu, looking perplexed, aware that she was being mysterious and had some purpose behind it. Mrs Kannon was the mother of Abbu's junior partner at his practice, Nasim, a man who we were expected to call Uncle. Nasim had previously admired Amma openly, and even flirted a little by dancing with her at the club socials, but had since transferred his besotted attention to Mae. He had a much younger brother, a good-looking but less than brilliant boy, who was pursuing a career with the army. Amma had initially approved their family's visits: Young Salim was far too dim, and Old Nasim was far too plain, and she probably thought that Mae would be dismayed by their interest, and that nothing would ever come of it. Amma had even joked about them, the delusional Kannon brothers who thought they had a chance to win her daughter, calling them Kannon-fodder and Coffin-fodder respectively, like a military-medical circus act. Now her jealousy was so white and throbbing it was a separate being in the room, like a cat curling around her as intimately as a witch's familiar, turning its head to snarl at us on her behalf, baring sharp, pointed little teeth.

Mae didn't look intimidated in the slightest. She smiled, baring her own white and even teeth, as though she had a familiar of her own. 'Does it matter?' she said to Abbu in an amused voice, as though she was making a pleasant joke. I was sitting opposite Lana, a board game between us, although we'd stopped playing when Mae arrived; we usually played simple ones like Ludo and draughts, as I beat her too often at chess and Scrabble for it to be fun for either of us, and she knew when I was letting her win, which meant she got embarrassed and red-cheeked in both victory and defeat. Lana breathed in sharply as Mae smiled, and I knew she was going to say something. I reached out and held her hand over the board, and squeezed it urgently. I did it instinctively to stop her, but she took my gesture as support more than warning, and squeezed back, just as instinctively, as though she thought that I was the one in need of comfort.

'Mrs Kannon's lovely,' she said to Mae, and the group at large, as though she didn't understand the discomfort of the moment, while diagnosing it exactly.

Mrs Kannon was one of those apple-cheeked mothers we had always envied, and she was already a grandmother to three children from her two daughters. Her hair was grey and straggly, and pulled back from her face in a walnut-sized bun, or else the wisps were unevenly pinned up at the back of her head by tortoiseshell combs, which kept sliding off. Amma laughed and said it would be kinder to her hair to put it out of its misery and shoot it off her head altogether, but Mrs Kannon didn't seem to care about how she looked. She laughed herself when her combs slid out, and offered boys and girls boiled sweets from her handbag if they could find them for her. Her eyes sparkled behind her bottle-bottom glasses, her hips and bosom were wide and deep, swathed in unfussy cotton shalwar kameez, and her skin was smooth and untroubled, apart from the smile carved deep around her mouth. Mrs Kannon's daughters had completed school, and made happy marriages; they did artistic things like designing dresses, painting and playing the piano. She didn't just socialise and imperiously donate at charity events and fund-raisers, like Amma, but actually helped run the stalls, potting the pickles and chutneys and arranging the flowers. Her family was too well off for her to work, and so she volunteered at local schools and the children's ward of the hospital, once her own children had left home. She always had pockets of small gifts for her charges – little knitted things she'd made, or decorated stubs of pencils and rulers. She was the closest thing to Father Christmas that our pious little community had. Mrs Kannon wasn't lovely like our mother was lovely – she had no beauty, wit or elegance; she was lovely in every way that our mother was not.

I saw Amma about to turn that witch stare on Lana, as though she'd change her into something many-legged and scuttling. If I hadn't managed to stop Lana, the least I could do was support her; her hand was still in mine.

'She is,' I agreed. 'She's really nice. She brought rasgullas to school on the last day of term, for the whole class.' I nudged my brother, sitting beside me, who seemed to have found something fascinating in his nails since Mae had come in through the garden and made her announcement. 'You remember, Sulaman?' I said. Sulaman didn't even dare to look up, in case he caught anyone's eye. I nudged him again, harder.

'Mm-hmm' was his only grudging response. The slightest possible assent, snorted through his nose. He didn't move his lips, as though words would be taken down in evidence and used against him.

'Well,' said our father, ignoring his three idiot children on the cane chairs, and looking at the only one that mattered: the smart, pretty one who was now standing by his side, wiping the fruit juice off the silver knife with the flowered tea cloth, her face reflected in the narrow blade. The fairest of them all. 'Which one? Or did the mother propose to you, instead of the sons?'

'The older,' Mae admitted. 'I've accepted Nasim's proposal. The family will come and talk to you tonight.'

'No!' said Amma, spitting out the word with such force that Mae actually stepped back, and sat down. 'No!' our mother repeated, and again there was a tiny moment of pause, like the echo of a gunshot, before she started to rage, her words spilling as freely as blood from a wound. 'You will not marry him! He thinks he can flirt with me, and have my daughter to boot! Have his cake and eat it! Inherit Daddy's practice from us! No! You will not marry him. You will never marry him. You will stay at home, and learn to be GOOD.'

'But I am a good girl, Mummy,' said Mae, looking as though she was about to cry. 'I've always been a good girl.' She was looking at our father as she said this. And our father was looking at our mother, in something like wonder; she was trembling, and almost ugly with her white anger. He had never seen her so weak and unguarded, so defenceless and disarmed, and he suddenly became a man. He shot up, and took her in his arms, shooing away the servants so they wouldn't see her this way.

'Don't fret, my dearest,' he said to her. 'You're not the first woman to lose a daughter,' and murmuring to her kindly, as though she was a bereaved patient, he led her up the stairs, calling over his shoulder for Lana to send tea to her room, and then, seeing Mae's stricken face, nodding to her and saying, 'Congratulations, my Mae-moni. We're happy for you. You've chosen well. He's a good man.'

As our parents left, the feeling of the stage around us dissolved, and players and audience, we all stood up. Mae appeared to wipe the tears that had never actually fallen, and even took a sort of bow, as she bent over to pluck a red lily, and tuck it behind her ear.

'Nasim Uncle? He's almost as old as Daddy,' said Lana. Mae shrugged, and smiled.

'That doesn't matter, silly. I'll live with Mrs Kannon, and he'll be at work all day anyway.'

'Congratulations, Mae,' said Sulaman, who had finally found his voice, and it took me a moment to realise that he wasn't talking about the marriage. 'Congratulations,' he repeated in a level tone. 'You've won. You don't need to do it now. Amma doesn't want you to get married any more. You called her bluff. You can go back to school now.'

Mae didn't pretend to misunderstand. 'Well, she's had her fun, and I'm having mine. And maybe she's had a chance to think it over, but so have I. I'd rather live with Mrs Kannon, and if you were honest, you all would too. I wish she really was my mother.'

'There are lots of nice mothers out there,' I said. I didn't bother saying what we were all thinking, that most of the mothers we had met seemed nicer than ours, although we couldn't really know what happened behind closed doors; everyone at school had always envied us our pretty, girlish mother. 'You picked Mrs Kannon, because when Daddy retires, you'll be the wife of the head of the practice.'

Lana sucked in her breath again, and Sulaman looked at Mae with a mixture of disappointment and admiration. Amma had said the same thing, but it sounded different said without anger, stated as a simple matter of fact. Mae had trumped Amma in every way possible; she had shown her what happens to trophy wives, and replaced her.

'I don't care about the stupid practice,' said Mae, and I wasn't sure whether she was lying or not. She was such a convincing actress, perhaps she herself didn't know any more. 'Mrs Kannon and Nasim are happy for me to stay on at school. I'll get my certificate. I'll be free to do what I want. Married men and women can do what they please.'

'Someone else said that,' Sulaman said, with accusation.

'What about me?' asked Lana, like a child. Abandoned by Sulaman and me for our studies abroad, and now by our sister. She'd be the only one at home, to be mothered, and smothered, to be gaily groomed like a prize pet, the weight of our heavy household on her narrow shoulders.

As though replying to her, we heard Abbu's voice echoing down the stairwell. 'Tea, Lana, your mother has asked for tea! Tell Cook now!' And she jumped up obediently like a puppet jerked on a string. As she went to the kitchen, she gave us all an accusing look, turning her head firmly from us while she walked away, as though to say, go on then. Leave me. See if I care.

'I'm sorry,' I said to her back. Sulaman was looking at his nails again; his head was hanging and I couldn't see his face.

'Yes,' said Mae, as though my apology had been meant for her as well. As though it should have been. 'I'm sorry too.'

I have to do a longer shift; there was a factory accident in Southwark, a tram accident in the City, and the nurses are busy on the maternity ward, as there are more births than usual. 'It's the full moon,' says a young sister-in-training in passing, as though she really believes it. 'We always get more births with the full moon.' The thought of babies coming out like howling wolves makes me smile, and she smiles back and carries on. She looks at the other trainee nurses for tittering approval, as though she won some sort of bet, speaking to the brown doctor. Proving to herself and the others that I'm just like anyone else, and that she's better than them, because she was brave enough to try.

I'm annoyed with her, but I don't show it, and muck in doing some of the chores that would usually be up to the nurses, changing dressings and fetching bedpans. I wonder what my father would think if he could see me now, the expensive education he lavished on his boys resulting in his younger son emptying out a factory worker's shit. I briefly envy Sulaman for changing his specialism, for the relatively clean work of the mind, but then decide that his desk job would bore me to tears: listening to the ravings of the criminally inclined and insane, writing research papers and working on fashionable shock-box experiments. Scribbling out prescriptions is about as much paperwork as I can handle. I like flesh and blood, the pulsing warmth of our meat, and all the pus and shit that goes with it just proves that we're not machines. So I don't complain about the menial jobs. William Godfrey, the West Indian doctor whose father fought for Britain in the war and now runs a grocery shop in east London, complains enough for the two of us.

William Godfrey is the black of bitter chocolate, although his father is half-white, and apparently much paler than me. I'm never sure why he keeps making this point, whether he's saying it competitively, or with disapproval. We have little in common apart from not being white, but I don't mind that he seeks me out, and not just because he's the only one who does. I like him. I like the way his skin sometimes shines blue in the light, and the contrasting pinkness of his palms. When he changes dressings, I can see a line down the side of his index finger, like the sunrise over the sea, where the satin blue-black shifts to textured rose; the horizon line in one of Turner's paintings. I try not to stare, but I find William Godfrey even more exotic than Frank, and for the same shallow reasons: the difference of his skin, and the richness of his accent. The deliciously incomprehensible turns of phrase they sometimes employ, the way William Godfrey says *cha nah, man* and Frank says *it's great gas*. I just sound like the English when I speak English, except when I say Punjabi names; I sense a relief followed by indignation in my patients when I'm introduced to them, and they hear me talk. As though I've tricked them in some way, because my face doesn't match my voice. As though I could scrape off my protective husk of brown, like so much stage make-up, and reveal milky white flesh beneath; like a Shakespearean actor blacked up to play the Moor. I'm excessively polite to patients, especially when I need to touch them. I sense their reserve, and feel I have to be. William Godfrey is curt to the point of rudeness, and tries not to touch them at all – he feels he has to be, or he's not respected. He says that the coloured patients are the worst of all; the Asians treat him like one of their cleaners or drivers, and accuse him openly of being an impostor who has stolen a white coat. The West Indians treat him like their youngest grandchild, the prized little prince of their extended family, and either dismiss his diagnoses with indulgent chiding – 'You stop fuss-fussing' – or accuse him of thinking too much of himself. I love it when he tells stories like this, with funny foreign phrases. Just as I love how Frank gets more Irish the drunker he gets, and starts speaking a different language with words like *craic* and *banjaxed*. It is, I admit, a little patronising to find them quite so picturesque. I don't mean to be. The truth is that I'm jealous; my family is wealthy, and has always been wealthy, and we've had nothing to drive us apart from social protocols and obedience to the club. The rich have no race, and we all speak the same language.

It's after midnight when we walk out of the hospital together, and on the pavement, the professional hardness falls from William Godfrey's face, and he tilts his trilby hat to a jaunty angle.

'Man, that was one hell of a night,' he says, a grin splitting the black of his face in two with a dazzling toothpaste smile that reflects the street light. It's unfair to compare Frank's teeth to William Godfrey's, but in his bone-pale face, and with all the cigarettes and coffee, Frank's are nowhere near as good.

This imperfection suddenly makes me feel affectionate, and protective towards Frank, and as William Godfrey sucks his own teeth thoughtfully, I wonder who's kissing him now, and which stranger's tongue is running around his flawed teeth and soft palate. The brown-gold hair is still in my pocket, somewhere. I can tell that William Godfrey wants to talk about the night, he's not yet ready to let work go; he's more driven and political than I am. He wants to complain about how we got stuck on nurses' duties as well as our own; he wants to talk about our careers and our rights.

'I'm going for a curry, Jamal Kamal, you wan' come?' We always double-name each other, as a sort of private joke, because that's how we were first introduced, even though he knows now that other people call me Jakie, and I know that other people call him Will. His professional accent has dropped too, and he doesn't sound like a briskly distant doctor any more, holding his clipboard before him like a shield, but like one of the cheerful black lads who always seem to work alone, driving a bus or mopping a floor, but who socialise in noisy packs in Notting Hill, nattily dressed. I know he means the place near the School of Oriental and African Studies, where his girlfriend works; perhaps she's already there, waiting for him. William Godfrey has a wonderful body, broad-shouldered and impressive, and I wonder why being in love with Frank doesn't stop me noticing this. I wonder why being William Godfrey's friend doesn't stop me noticing this either.

'No thanks, William Godfrey, I'm going to stop at a jazz night in town. I told a friend I might see him there, when I got off.'

William Godfrey laughs. 'A black man going for a curry, and a brown man going to the jazz.' He biffs me on the shoulder in a friendly way, and hurries off; his bus is approaching on the other side of the street. I watch him walk away, as I light a cigarette. When he turns and sees me looking, I raise a hand to wave to him.

I carry on down the street a little, undecided whether to walk a bit first, or get the bus too. But then I'm yanked into the shadows of an alley near the service entrance, and pushed hard into a wall. The wind is crushed out of me before I can cry out, one arm wrenched up high behind my back, and I hear a rough, drunk voice slurring in my ear.

'So who's the coloured fella?'

'That would be me,' I say to Frank, shrugging easily out of his grip, and turning to look at him. He's drunk, again, but I'm still delighted that he's here rather than somewhere else, with someone else. 'Were you waiting for me?' I ask.

I should be furious with him for messing about like that, but can't stop myself grinning. He presses his body against me as a reply, and kisses me with biting passion, slamming me against the bricks as though he wouldn't mind doing it here, outside, fully clothed, like we used to. When I kiss him back, he puts his hand briefly on my cock, but then backs off when he and I both realise how suspiciously hard I already am.

'I meant the other fella. With the arse you couldn't take your eyes off,' he says, and although he's smiling, his face is cold. I can see that he's not really joking. He backs up altogether, into the street, as though my erection has somehow betrayed me. I follow him hurriedly, but walking outside in public, even at midnight, it's not the sort of thing I can explain or excuse out loud.

'Frank, come on, you're being a child,' I say, catching up with him, putting my hand on his shoulder.

'Well maybe I don't like other people playing with my toys either,' he says, shrugging me off. 'That was disgusting, back there. Like sitting on a toilet seat already warm from someone else's backside.'

'He's a colleague. He's got a girlfriend,' I say, to show how ridiculous his accusation is.

'So, you found out that much already,' replies Frank, walking so quickly that he stumbles, and I have to run forward to catch him. To anyone else, it must look like I'm the Paki lackey stuck with escorting the office drunk back to his house. In the brief moment that he is in my arms, while I lift him back to his feet, and he struggles against me, trying to throw me off, I speak close to his ear.

'You talk as though I just want to fuck you,' I say. 'But I don't. Not any more.'

He stops fighting me off, and stands there. Listening. It is a moment where we are standing still, and everything else is moving around us. Late-night traffic. An ambulance going in the direction I just came from. An old man walking a dog, and another one howling in the distance. I actually don't know what I'm going to say. I wonder if Frank thinks he can guess. That we both know what this is, and we can't do it any more. That we're over, because he's drinks too much, and is too much hard work. That I love him. God, I love him. But.

I don't say any of these things. He's drunk, and the streets are wet and cold, and if I got down on one knee, I'd have no question I could ask, and would ruin my good trousers. I hold him by the tops of his arms, and see the blood pulsing in his pale throat, lit by the street lamps and the moonlight slivers between the clouds. Frank stands there in the stripped shadows, and he is black and white and blue, like a damaged vampire starved of blood, like he's waiting for the stake through his heart. He's not so good-looking; in fact he's not attractive at all until he smiles or speaks, but suddenly, in his sky-coloured sadness, he's beautiful.

'You don't,' he says. It's not even a question. He can't let any silence go unfilled.

'I don't just want to fuck you,' I say. 'I want to everything with you. I want to watch you fall asleep, and watch you wake up, and read the papers with you in the mornings.'

I see his anger deflating, and he just looks at me. Unconvinced. I know what he's thinking. That this would mean a lot more if he wasn't my dirty little secret. 'Well, as my mammy always says, I want doesn't get,' he says, not quite calling me out for it, but not letting me off, either.

He carries on walking, up towards the bridge, and calls over his shoulder, 'Let's just go home, Jakie.'

I notice that he's in the same clothes he was wearing this morning. 'Did you even go into work today?' I ask.

He doesn't answer, so I light a cigarette, and offer one to him. I can't nag him. I'm not his mother. I'm not his wife. He shakes his head, and presses the cigarette back into my hand, his cold palm enclosing my fingers. For a brief moment it feels as though we are simply holding hands.

'That stuff'll kill you,' he says, taking a silver flask from his pocket instead, and swigging from it; as though aware that he is sobering up, and taking precautions to avoid it.

Chapter Five

Sully

IT'S CHRISTMAS, AND I'VE BEEN FOLLOWING THE PREPARATIONS FOR THE Eichmann trial. There are photos in the newspapers of him standing in a neat suit, in his box of bulletproof glass, and I can't help but think how clean it all looks. Such a tidy end, a taut thread cut with sharp and shiny scissors.

There have been other trials, smaller trials, blooming like mould across the newsprint, discussed in the academic journals. One of the Lithuanian collaborators, a local soldier, has bought his life with his testimony. His words are printed and circulated, how the men, women and children were rounded up and marched through the mud, and then set to work digging the hole they'd be killed in. How he and his comrades shot them efficiently, one by one, taking care not to waste their precious bullets. He chose to shoot the children first, so they wouldn't see their parents die before them, and so he wouldn't hear them scream. The other soldiers went about it differently: they started with the bigger targets, so the cries of 'Mama!' 'Papa!' resounded round the pit. Some of his comrades seemed to enjoy it, but he didn't. He says he was just doing his job.

'It was like an experiment,' he said. Those were his words. They're printed here, and the transcript is pinned on my wall; I'm not making them up. 'It was like an experiment. I'd pull the trigger, and in the pit, someone would drop down dead. It was like it wasn't even me that did it.' He added, 'It's a real tragedy.' He's saved his own skin, and will be out of prison in thirty years, but most of his comrades have been sentenced to death. He never says what the tragedy was – the deaths of innocent people in a pit, or the fact that they asked him to do it, and he has to give thirty years of his life to make amends. Less than a year for each father, mother and child that he obediently killed, with damp, black earth under their nails from digging their own grave. Such a dirty end.

I wonder what Jim and Danny think about this, but I don't see them around so much. We're on the campus and in the cafeteria at different times now, as I've been accepted on to a new postgraduate programme; it's still research-based, but more theoretical than applied. I don't have to touch people. I don't have to get my hands dirty. I don't even have to flick the switches on a fake machine. Jakie writes to me, on humorous postcards with the tourist sights of London, and jokes about my 'desk job'. I stick the postcards on my walls, picture side out, and between the Eichmann clippings, with all their Third Reich marching photos, and the London landmarks like Big Ben and Tower Bridge and Buckingham Palace, it looks like I'm a Nazi myself, planning a British invasion. I don't realise this until Radhika knocks on my door.

'Sully? It's me,' she calls out.

She's never come into my room before, just as I've never gone into hers. I hadn't worried about her seeing what I do here, as women aren't really allowed in the residences, except at weekends, or holidays, and even then the hours are restricted. I realise that it is a holiday; it's Christmas Eve. I look around my tiny cell, probably smaller than the one that the Lithuanian soldier must be bunked in, and see no way that I can hide the walls. If I'd ever had the wit to think about this, I'd have nailed up a couple of throws. Or covered them with movie posters. I scrabble for my coat.

'Coming,' I call. 'I thought we were meeting outside the cafeteria?'

'My meeting finished early,' she says. 'And it's cold outside.' She's sounding impatient, and I open the door as minutely as possible, to slide myself out, blocking the gap as I do, so she can't see past me. I'm quite a bit taller than her, so I manage it easily, if not particularly gracefully.

'Hi, honey, what a great surprise,' I say, kissing her on her icy cheek, trying to repair the damage. I'm hoping that if I ignore my unflattering shock at her appearance, she might too. It doesn't work, and she looks at me frankly, without responding to the kiss, and so I apologise instead. 'Sorry, my room's a mess. Let's go.'

But just as I shut the door behind me, the cheap lock catches, and it bounces open again. The door swings back wide, displaying a wall of Nazi clippings and postcards through the wooden doorway like a framed exhibit in a Holocaust museum. Radhika stares at it, and then looks up at me, and smiles.

'Is there something you want to tell me, Sully?' she asks, walking into my room to look more closely at the clippings, flapping and overlapping so that there's no space between them. She takes off her scarf, and a shower of snow falls to the grubby wooden floor. She looks around for somewhere to put it, but every surface is covered with papers, books or clutter; even the bedspread, right up to the pillow, and so she keeps it in her hands, pulling at the dark cloth with lovely agitation, as she moves from article to article like a hummingbird.

'It's just some work stuff,' I say, thinking that pornography would have been less embarrassing. 'For my next paper. On conflict. And torture.'

'Fun,' she says. 'It makes my work on cancer sound positively light-hearted.'

She stops in front of the printed testimony by the soldier, noticing the text that I've underlined in the transcript, about the experiment, the children he shot first, the big tragedy, running a finger along my annotations and coded cross-referencing.

'This seems a little bit obsessive. Even for a psych doctoral candidate. It's like you're the one who needs a spell on the couch.' And then she blushes, a warm point on her chilled cheekbones; it sounds too much like an invitation, and we're both embarrassed by her discomfort. I don't think she's a virgin. I hope she doesn't think I'm one, either.

'Shall we go for lunch, honey?' I say. I've started calling her honey a lot, like the other guys call the girls they're seeing. I tried it experimentally the first time we met after the kiss, and she didn't object, and so I've kept doing it, so that everyone thinks we're not just dating, but going steady. I hope she thinks it too, but I've never actually asked her, as I'm too afraid she'll say we're not. I kiss her at the end of every date, on the cheek in public, on the lips if we're alone and there's no one around, and she doesn't object to that either, and seems a little bit amused.

She pulls the pin out of the article she's been reading, and puts the clipping in her pocket. She doesn't ask for it with a please or take it with a thank you, but she doesn't even say please or thank you for coffee in a diner. Still, the fact that she doesn't ask permission to pull something from my wall fills me with hope; it implies an intimacy we don't yet have. As though letting her into my disordered, mangled room has let her into my disordered, mangled mind. As though what little I have to offer is hers to take.

'Sure,' she says. She wraps her scarf, damp and sparkling with the melted snow, back around her neck, and steps out of the room. 'Honey,' she adds, as an afterthought, and then leans towards me with deliberation, and kisses me on the lips. Her own are fine and dry, and the tip of her nose is still cold. I want to press my face against hers, until she warms up, but think she'll scatter like the snow if I do, and instead step back. I must be looking at her with blank incredulity, as she feels the need to explain herself. 'I don't know why I'm always so interested in troubled boys.'

She pushes her hand through her hair, tucking a lock behind her ear, and even though she's talking as much to herself, to the air around us, as to me, I feel like I've been paid an outrageous compliment, and compromised at the same time. I like the way she says troubled; it makes me feel that being screwed up is sexy, like Brando on the waterfront, and Jimmy Dean in a leather jacket on a bike. I don't like the way she says boys, as though there are a long line of us standing outside the door, and as though she's so much more mature, and smarter than me. She's barely two years my senior. She sighs, as though I'm something to sigh about. Trouble. A boy. She walks ahead of me down the corridor.

'Maybe for the same reason they're interested in you,' I say, following her slippered feet past the chorus of her imagined lovers, the troubled sad-eyed boys, with phantom skin as pale as the concrete walls they're leaning against. I can't believe she walked like that in the snow, even on the scraped and salted sidewalks from her basement room to campus. Her feet look cold, her stockings nude and inadequate. Why doesn't she ever wear socks? I realise that I'm staring at her ankles, the only flesh on display apart from her patch of frozen face.

'And what's that?' she asks, glancing over her shoulder at me.

'They all want to be the one who makes you smile.' I catch up with her, and put my arm around her shoulders. She doesn't look up at me, and doesn't smile, but presses her head briefly against me, as though she might.

The cafeteria is almost empty, because most people have gone home for the holidays, and we've arrived before the start of service. The skeleton staff permitted by their fractious union are pouring out trays of turkey and beef and overcooked potatoes and baby carrots, which were probably there from the day before, and setting out the sodas. Radhika orders her food, and I can't decide. The cafeteria worker looks at me impatiently, which makes it harder.

'I guess I'll have what she's having,' I say eventually. I'm relieved he doesn't ask what I want to drink, because I can't decide between coffee and a cold drink, and end up with neither. We carry our trays to the table; the radio is playing, and Bing Crosby comes on, singing 'White Christmas'.

'I almost forgot, it's the big day tomorrow,' I say, as it doesn't seem that she's about to say anything. She's always accusing me of not talking, but when I do, she doesn't pay that much attention, and looks around. 'So, what are you going to do?' I ask her; I don't think she'll ignore a direct question, even a stupid one. No one does anything much for Christmas here if they don't have their family around them. Even if they do, the holiday seems to be over between lunchtime and dinner, when they pack up their unwanted presents to take back to the store for credit. Radhika smiles at me slightly, and pulls out the clipping from my wall. Perhaps she looked around because she didn't want people to see her reading it; as though interest in Nazi trials is a dirty little secret. Perhaps she's right, and it should be.

'The same old same,' she says eventually. 'I'll call my mother and her husband. They kind of expect it.' She pushes her plate to the side, sips her cherry soda, and spreads out the article, reading it carefully.

I sigh, as though she's someone to sigh about, and start to eat the meaty mush on my plate. I felt that we'd crossed some sort of line as we left my room, but now it seems we're back where we started. Either that or at the end of all things, a long-married couple who no longer need to make conversation over lunch. I talk to Radhika all the time, and she doesn't even know it. Since she first came up to my table, my distant crush has developed into a close obsession, although I try hard not to show it. I think I've become even more taciturn than I was to begin with. So much so that it's absolutely possible that she thinks I say 'honey' ironically, as a sort of joke, and that our first connection is all we have, that we are acquaintances united by the bit of brown in our background, and by the weight of family expectations, and not much more. That we're a simple case of us against them.

Still, when I'm on my own, I imagine thrilling conversations with her, across the tables at wine-scented restaurants, on the bridges in parks, walking animatedly down frozen streets. I tell her about myself, my dreams and fears wrapped in a tidy package with a bow for her to untie and release to the world, a Pandora's box with hope hiding at the bottom. I revisit my daily victories for her imagined applause, and my petty disappointments for her sympathy. I imagine her stepping lightly into my arms, as we tumble into a softer, larger bed than either of us actually possesses, and watching her face as she wakes in the morning, although I can't for the life of me imagine what might happen in between these scenes. I've had to stop masturbating, as thinking of anyone else seems like a betrayal, and thinking of her is too complicated. The woman I speak to when I'm alone in a room isn't really Radhika. It feels like I've made her up in my head, and that her slight flesh isn't as substantial as the fantasy.

It feels like that especially today, on Christmas Eve, when she is sitting here, as my possibly steady girlfriend, and isn't really here at all. It's like she's a photograph unfurled on the other seat, a lovely view from a car window that's really just painted paper rolling past in a loop. I want her to talk to me, and then I don't, as I'm so afraid of disappointing her, and myself.

I see another couple in the cafeteria, a few tables away from us, and they are holding hands and laughing. Her hair is long and ponytailed, her all-American teeth are gleaming, and she is with a man-boy in an oversized sweater with an oversized letter, instead of the usual uniform of sports jacket and tie. I think I know everything there is to know about them by looking at their shiny surfaces, at their smooth and uncomplicated foreheads. They are like the anti-us, and it seems for a moment that I have made them up too, as objects of envy.

I wish you were here, I tell the Radhika I've made up in my head. I wish you were her, and I were him. I wish we were ordinary, uncomplicated. But what if we were? she argues back to me. Then you'd wonder why you wanted to be ordinary more than anything else. Besides, look at me, and look at you, she says. We *are* ordinary. We're academics in a cafeteria, talking to ourselves instead of each other, what could be more ordinary than that?

'It's rude to stare,' says Radhika, glancing up at me. She looks amused again, and asks with a silver thread of laughter in her voice, 'Would you like to ask them to join us?'

She's not afraid to tease me, and I'm suddenly grateful that she's real, and not just a figment of my imagination. I don't care that she's laughing at me rather than with me. There's something amazing about a solemn person who smiles, like the sudden luminous smile of an infant; it's special because it is unexpected. I notice myself in my spoon, upside down and comically distorted, surprised at how pleasant I look as I smile back at her. I wonder whether, when I'm out with Radhika, this is the me that other people see. The-me-that-she-sees.

'You have a pretty laugh,' I say. 'You should laugh more often.' I don't know why the conversations in my head are so much more fluent than the actual words I manage to say. I realise belatedly how I must sound, like I'm trying to compliment her and criticise her at the same time. Belittle her with flattery. Grunting at her like a caveman so I can drag her back to my cave of shadows and monsters.

'My mother says that,' replies Radhika, unoffended, but still reading the article, not even glancing up. 'She's afraid I'll grow up into my father, either glaring or grumbling.'

I wish I'd never pinned up that damn clipping. I want to grab it from her, and shred it into confetti. I want to throw it into the air, and over her hair like the snow outside; like flour at a protest, or rice at a wedding. It feels like that's what it would take for her to look me in the face.

'So, what do *you* want to be when you grow up, honey?' I ask. The honey isn't honeyed, it has a tart edge, and she looks at me after all.

'I'm sorry, I'm being rude,' she says, as though she really didn't realise I wanted to talk, that I wanted to be seen, and heard. And now I feel guilty for making her feel guilty, just because she couldn't read my mind. To be honest, that's the last thing I'd want her to be able to do. 'I don't know, Sully. I guess I have to be careful what I wish for. You're looking at the woman who got everything she ever wanted.'

She looks at me and sits back assessingly, and I wonder if I'm one of those things. Whether she'll collect me like something broken, fix me, and then lose interest in me when I'm whole and healed. Pass me on to someone else. I wonder if that's the inevitable cost of getting what you want; that once you do, you don't want it any more.

'Why, what do you want?' she says, as though she's asking the same question I asked of her, although it's not the same at all, and we both know it.

'Honestly? What do I want? Hmm,' I half scoff and half laugh, as though she's leaned in earnestly instead of calmly sitting back, as though she's looking deep into my eyes like a tiresome heroine in a novel, chin in hand, breathily asking me what I'm thinking. I'm buying time, because my mind is blank. I can answer complicated questions from things memorised in books, but when it comes to simple things, I'm stuck. Put on the spot, I couldn't tell you what my favourite song is. What my favourite colour is. What I do for fun. I can't even say what I'd like for lunch. A child of four could answer these questions better than me. So how could I ever begin to say what I want? I'm just a machine, pre-programmed. I almost want to ask her what she thinks I should want; that would make it so much easier on me. I'll want what she wants. I'll have what she's having.

She's waiting, and I look at her, and for a moment I'm talking to both Radhikas: the one I made up in my head, and the one sitting impatiently in her full skirt and neatly crossing her bare ankles.

'I just want to be alone in a room . . .' I say, and she nods, as though it is a perfectly understandable desire. But I carry on, unable to leave it there even though I probably should. It feels that there's a force like gravity pulling me down, forcing me to finish what I started, a toddler tumbling down a slide, who wants to stop halfway but just can't. 'With you. I just want to be alone in a room with you.'

She stares at me, and I stare at the floor, unable to believe that I've said it. The other couple get up from their table, still holding hands, and we see that we're going to be left on our own in the cafeteria, with just the few staff chattering and clattering pointlessly among the reheated leftovers. We're sitting there, embarrassed by the sea of empty tables around us.

'Well, we're alone at last,' she says. 'You see what I mean,' she adds, almost kindly. 'You have to be careful what you wish for.'

The words that rattle around inside me get blocked at my teeth, like boiled sweets sticking at the mouth of a jar. It sometimes feels that none will come out at all unless you give me a damn good shaking. I never got in the habit of speaking my mind at home; it was a skill I wasn't taught, and the only shaking I ever got was from Basher, who beat me into ever-decreasing circles of silence.

I don't think I'll ever forgive myself for not talking to Mae about her marriage; a good-on-paper match to a much older man whom she couldn't begin to love. She was just fifteen, and a little part of me thought that she'd never go through with it, and was only pretending to go along with the preparations to annoy our mother. Jakie talked about it, but Mae didn't take him seriously, as he was always joking about serious things, and being serious about stupid things. I think that if I'd found the right words, and shaken them out of me in the right order, she'd have collected them together, and considered them. I spoke so little, I think she might have listened when I did.

Mae's marriage was the last time we were all together. The engagement was short, as the ceremony was planned for before Jakie and I went away to college; that was Mae's excuse, but really she didn't want to risk missing the start of the school year. And her husband-to-be, Nasim, whom we were no longer obliged to call Nasim Uncle, and were now encouraged to call Nasim Bhai, was keen to seal the deal as soon as possible. He frankly couldn't believe his good luck, to have been plucked from the crowd of younger, better-looking suitors. Amma was right: he had been flirting with her, and he'd managed to replace his fantasy of an illicit embrace with our mother with a legal marriage to her beautiful, ridiculously young daughter. It seemed to me that he couldn't walk straight around Mae with the anticipation, and it made me a little sick.

Nasim and his mother were the only ones pleased by Mae's marriage. Our mother seemed physically sickened by it too. She lost weight; her arms and legs got skinny, her face became gaunt. She looked genuinely ill. The frailer she became, the more our father seemed to love her. We hadn't realised how much he had needed to be needed, all those years. We heard him softly murmuring to her in the night, and in the early hours of the morning, and the unmistakable grunts, deep breaths and subtle rocking of wood on tile of quiet marital passion. He looked glowing and solicitous in the morning, as he seated Amma in her chair, called for her tea, and instructed Lana or Mae to serve her.

She sat stiffly at the table, unpowdered and as plain and proud as the washerwomen she used to accuse the other mothers of resembling. She accepted our father's kiss on her hair, and the squeeze of her hand, without a grimace or sign of pleasure. She no longer intimidated him, although she still intimidated us, and while she had stopped eating, it seemed that she resented every mouthful we took, following our forks and spoons to our mouths. Our father appeared to get plumper by the day, eating the spare food that was left on the table, and he took on the jovial manner of a fat and prosperous man. He continued playing tennis with his soon-to-be son-in-law, and delegated more responsibility to Nasim, leaving himself free to return home sooner to his suddenly fragile wife and grown-up family. Life seemed agreeable to him, and whenever Mae mentioned something about the wedding, he just nodded, and said combinations of 'Yes, very good, good-good,' without discussion or concern.

'So we'll need to pick out the flowers, Mummy,' Mae said to our mother one morning.

'Yes, good-good,' said Abbu, patting our mother's hand. Amma ignored Mae, but she couldn't pretend not to have heard her, not with our father's vague response. She waited until the silence became too thick to bear, pushing Mae to the brink of asking again, and replied just as Mae breathed in to speak.

'Too hot.' She said it curtly, as though it wasn't necessarily a response to Mae, but simply a complaint about the weather. As though it wasn't always too hot in Lahore.

'Yes, too hot to choose the flowers today,' our father agreed adoringly. 'Your mummy's not well.' We didn't really believe this. Our mother was perfectly capable of starving herself to prove a point, and we'd noticed that even though she dressed plainly as a poor relative when at home, she was still capable of making an effort if we had callers, especially the wispy-haired mother of Mae's groom. Although it was true that when she spoke, her breath reeked; at least that was what was reported by Lana and Mae, who sat beside her. I wondered if she simply had a tooth infection.

Still, it seemed that in the few months between Mae's announcement and her wedding, our mother's looks didn't simply fade, but were robbed from her, like a house stripped to mud and stones by looters. Her cheek-bones slashed through her thin skin, her cheeks themselves hollowed, her hair became coarser, and her arms as thin as the urchins who played outside in the streets. She stopped wearing saris, and wore voluminous shalwar kameez, and covered her hair with her dupatta; she went from butterfly to nun.

Our father bounced up from the table after breakfast, and helped our mother back up the stairs, saying she needed her rest, and we knew that he would be staying with her, alone in their room, until it was time to go to work. Jakie escaped from the table as soon as they had gone.

'Disgusting,' said Mae.

'What's disgusting?' asked Lana, and I looked at Mae, and caught her eye. I was relieved that she did seem to know what happened between men and women who were married, even those who had been married as long as our own parents, and who had no more children to plan. I tried not to picture the arms and legs of our parents, their naked calves, gripping hands, making some obscene spidery beast on the sheets upstairs. I wondered if Mae was doing the same, trying not to think of what they were doing, and trying not to paint herself and her elderly intended into that same, disquieting picture.

I should have said something; it still wasn't too late. Invitations had been sent, a hotel had been chosen, but they hadn't even picked the flowers as yet. No contract had been signed, and no fluids exchanged. Mae still had the narrow hips of a child; I couldn't believe they'd let her carry on with school if she was carrying one herself. I couldn't imagine what a pregnancy would do to her delicate insides, a child with Nasim's face stapled on, thrashing its way out of her, ripping and tearing as it went.

'I feel ill too,' I said instead, and went to the garden. I sat on the swing, thinking what a coward I was. After a while, Lana came out, and asked me if I was all right. At thirteen years old, she seemed to have taken on the role of mother in the family, now that Amma had given up on it, folding herself into her resentment like the folds of the modest scarf she wore over her head. I was grateful and sad that Lana felt the need to look after me, to look after us all. I wanted to tell her crossly to leave me alone, that I was a grown-up now, and she didn't need to do this, but I couldn't say that either.

'I'm okay,' I lied. 'It's just the heat, like Mummy said.'

'Why is everyone talking about the heat, all of a sudden?' said Lana impatiently. 'It's not any hotter than it usually is.' She went to the kitchen, and came back with a tumbler of ice-cold water, damp with condensation on the outside, and she thumped it down in front of me, just like Cook would. She was more of a doctor's child than Jakie and I. She sought practical solutions to problems, and filled her own prescriptions.

'So drink something, if you're so hot,' she said, licking the cold drops from her fingers, her little pink tongue like a kitten's. She was still a girl, and clearer than the smudged glass she brought me. Light shone through her, and you could see shifts in her mood as plainly as the weather. Mae had always been clouded by comparison, as though someone had poured something into her, something unhealthy, and stirred it around. It seemed to me that she was trying so desperately not to become our mother, she'd lost something of herself, and was already becoming an ironic version of them both.

'So, do you think Daddy has been poisoning Mummy?' Lana asked conversationally, sitting by my side on the swing.

'What! No! Why would you say that?' I turned to face her, utterly shocked. 'You can't just say things like that!' I looked around the garden, to see if anyone had heard. But there was only Lana and me, and some desultory chickens, who had wandered from the hen house, picking at our feet, where the servants hadn't swept properly from the day before. A spider dropped on a thread from a dense green shrub, dotted with small orange flowers, and hovered indecisively before diving smoothly all the way to the ground, and then disappearing back under the same shrub, like a jogger completing a circuit of the park.

Lana shrugged; she didn't seem to think that she had said anything controversial. 'He seems to like her more when she's sick. Like she's a patient.' She paused and added, 'I thought I did, too. But now it's just annoying, how *nothing* she is all the time.' I supposed that Lana, like most teenagers, would rather be shouted at than ignored. She'd rather be tormented than tossed aside. It had never occurred to me that an unkind mother was still better than no mother at all.

'She's just not been eating,' I said. I didn't say why. I thought it was clear that she was trying to punish Mae, perhaps make her feel guilty enough to call off the wedding, although it was also obvious that it hadn't had much effect. She'd probably have done better with a plot to outshine Mae at her wedding instead, leaving her sulking back in her mother's shadow where she belonged.

'She doesn't eat, because when she does, she throws up,' said Lana. 'I told you, her breath stinks in the morning. She's always vomiting, and then she's always brushing her teeth. I've had to order extra tooth powder for her.' She got up, deciding that I wasn't being any fun if I didn't want to debate her diagnosis with her.

'I've just brought her up some coffee, and juice, before I was even asked, and Abbu shouted at me to leave it outside the door. He said she shouldn't be disturbed, and sounded really . . . cross.'

She huffed at this, as if she really couldn't tell the difference between crossness and interrupted adult passion. She handed me the tumbler, expecting me to drink before she left, like a nanny who didn't trust me to take my medicine on my own, and added, 'So it would be easy for him to add poison to the coffee, before he brings it to her. Poison makes people throw up. Like bad fish.'

I realised that my throat felt dry, and I really was feeling hot, and so I took a couple of deep swallows. It did make me feel better, and Lana could see this as I wiped my mouth with the back of my hand. She took the glass back from me, satisfied. 'You'll learn things like that when you go to college.'

As she walked back towards the house, through the stiffly green bushes, she spat in the glass and swirled it around with a delicate movement of her hand. Jakie shouted down to her from the veranda, triumphantly holding our tawny tomcat, Pickles, just under the neck, so the long body hung down, revealing pink private parts. He was gripping on to Jakie's shirtsleeves with his front paws as tightly as though hanging from a high branch. In his jaws was a fat rodent. I couldn't tell if the thing was still alive.

'Look, Lana,' called Jakie. 'The fat cat finally caught the fat rat! And I caught him. I'm the fat-cat-catcher-fat-rat-catcher!' Lana squealed with delight.

'Don't let go,' she called back. 'I'm coming,' and she tossed the contents of the glass out over the cracked path, and ran inside. I watched the water and saliva shine briefly silver on the dust, before sinking and darkening it. The edges receded swiftly in the heat, like milk misting away from the flat surface of a pan.

I wondered at the expertly performed spit and swirl that I had just witnessed. It looked like it was something Lana had done many times before, something that needed target practice. I wondered if she spat in our mother's coffee or tea, experimentally, and then swirled it to see if she could hide it. I thought it unlikely, as our mother took her coffee and tea black. If she had it with condensed milk, like the other mothers, you could hide all manner of things under the thick white scum of the surface. All the bodily fluids that doctors like our father dealt with, and kept in sterile little jars for testing: spit and piss, blood and phlegm, egg yolk ear wax and the egg white soup that sperm swam in. The only thing you could hide in our mother's thin coffee would be the subtle salt of tears.

Water began running down the pipe on the side of the house, and over the leaf-clogged drain, spilling into the dust as well. Our house was high and the rooms were private, but the rattling plumbing was as open as a village sewer, and gave everything away. Our parents had finished what they were doing, and our father was washing himself before he went to work. Our mother's coffee would now be tepid, and she would probably sip it with disgust, and then throw it down the drain too, where it would coat the mulched leaves on the drain grille with a briefly brown sheen.

I realised, as I sat there impatiently swinging like an invalid grandparent waiting to be rescued from his daily constitutional in the garden and replaced in his wheelchair or bed, that Lana might be right. That in a way, Abbu might have poisoned Amma. That he was the one who had made her sick. And that it wasn't an infection she had in her mouth, sickly-sweet pus buried under an abscessed tooth, but a parasite buried in her belly. One that sucked the flesh off her bones, in order to feed itself. Vomiting in the morning. Loose clothes that hid skinny arms, but would also hide a puffing bosom and stomach.

It seemed stupidly obvious now, but I wondered, if that was really the case, why she wouldn't simply tell us. There was no shame or indignity in it, and it happened to plenty of women older than her. Amma wasn't yet forty. Her plan had worked too well, and instead of threatening Mae into being a good girl who did what she was told, she had lost her altogether, and turned her into a good daughter-in-law for another family instead, from trophy child to trophy wife. Perhaps she had decided to replace Mae with a newer model, just as Mae had replaced her with a kinder one. An eye for an eye, a tooth for a tooth. A new trophy. A child.

Perhaps now that Amma had got what she wished for, she regretted it. Perhaps she wasn't telling us about it because she was hoping to terminate the pregnancy before anyone noticed. Unlike my mother, I'm careful what I wish for.

There is a brief silence in the cafeteria, which is made sharper by the intermittent interruptions. My spoon scraping the remains of apple cobbler from my plate. The cash register at the other side of the room clanging shut. Radhika's trimmed nail tapping the side of her soda bottle, which is still almost full, the straw bobbing in the bubbles. My face is warm with embarrassment, and my throat is dry. I think of Lana's advice – 'So drink something, if you're so hot' – and I reach out and take Radhika's cherry soda.

'Do you mind?' I ask.

'Be my guest,' she says, and as I sip it, she adds, 'Sharing a straw. It's like we're kissing.' I sputter, snorting out the bubbles, and she apologises. 'Sorry,' she says, but she doesn't sound sorry enough. She sounds as though she thinks it's funny to see me so uncomfortable. 'It's just a bit of spit, Sully. It's not poison.'

'My sister used to spit in people's drinks. Maybe she still does. Just to get a little of her own back.'

Radhika nods, approvingly. 'I understand that.' And as though she's decided to get a little of her own back on me, for asking her to lunch and calling her honey, for boring her with my silence and making uncomfortable declarations, she asks me, 'So what would you want to do, in this lonely room, with me?' She's pushing me, and she still seems amused.

This might be the moment to take her bravely in my arms, but there's a table between us, and I'm not that guy. I don't have a letter on my sweater. 'I'd want to talk to you,' I say, and she just looks at me, unimpressed. It's obvious to both of us that I can talk to her right now. So talk, I tell myself. Talk. 'I'd want to tell you that I'm careful what I wish for. And that I want to take you home.'

Now she's the one who looks embarrassed. I've called her bluff. Now's the time when she might say, well, Sully, it's been nice spending time with you, but let's admit we're just friends. Let's call each other by our names rather than sweet treats, and stop doing so many little outings together. Let's stop hesitantly bumping lips at greetings and goodbyes, and shake hands firmly instead. She looks straight at me, not just at my face, but at all of me, as though she can see through to my beating heart and the messy, open pipework, and I wish the table wasn't between us, and I wish I was that guy.

'Okay,' she says, and then she repeats it more firmly. 'Okay.' She reaches for my hand, and says, 'Don't look so worried. I'm not. I'm not scared at all.' I'm not reassured by this; by the fact that she thinks I'm the one who's scared, and that she's the one who ought to be. She dismisses my disquiet. She squeezes my hand.

We get ready to leave just as the cafeteria becomes a little busier, with some of the postgrads who can't get home for Christmas. One of them, a dark-haired girl in glasses, her hair pinned up into a bun, and held in a neat mesh, comes over to say hello. She looks slightly more Asian than me, but Radhika introduces her as Dr Gloria Rogers, and it takes me a moment to realise that she's Mexican, or part Mexican. She wears a silver crucifix, not just a cross, but with an actual figure of Jesus delicately carved in white bone. Gloria notices the newspaper clipping just as Radhika remembers it is still there and starts hurriedly putting it away, folding it up across the wrong creases.

'I didn't know you could read German,' Gloria says to her with interest. I look at the newspaper clipping before Radhika finishes closing it into an untidy rectangle. She takes it off the table, and stuffs it in her pocket. I hadn't noticed that she had been reading the original German transcript, not the translated report next to it.

'Well, you speak Spanish,' Radhika says pleasantly, as a counter-accusation.

'I've got an excuse. My mom's from Guadalajara,' Gloria replies. 'Any other languages you holding out on us?' She adds like she's joking, 'Russian? Japanese?'

'Darn it, my mom! I promised to call her before lunch,' says Radhika, getting up smoothly. 'Thanks for reminding me, Gloria. Happy holidays.'

'Happy holidays,' Gloria says back, surprised at being so abruptly dismissed.

'It was nice to meet you, Dr Rogers,' I say, getting up to follow Radhika, feeling I ought to say something. Just as I feel I ought to say thank you for Radhika's coffee, when she doesn't say it herself. It's like a disease, a sort of reverse Tourette's. I can't stop myself being polite.

'Likewise, I'm sure,' she says, looking me up and down. She can't say my name, as Radhika didn't tell her it, making the barest possible introduction, with a 'Honey, this is . . .' Now Radhika surprises me by putting her arm around my waist, to lead me away. I don't mind this at all, and put my arm over her shoulder, speaking quietly into her ear.

'You don't like her,' I say.

'I like her just fine,' she replies. She shrugs off my arm at the exit to the cafeteria, but only to pull out the crumpled clipping, smoothing it ineffectively, and then folding it up properly and handing it back to me. 'Sorry,' she says.

'So, German? Did you take a course at college?' I ask, glancing at it and putting it back in my pocket.

'My mother's German. My father met her while he was studying. She went back to Germany after the war, a few years after my brother died. His name was Friedrich, but everyone called him Ricky.' I put my arm back around her, aware that a few people are looking at us, and kiss the top of her head. Like my father before me, I suddenly feel like a man, because I feel that briefly, at this moment, she needs me, and needs to be seen with me, rather than walking alone. I don't ask again if I can take her home. I just carry on walking with her, out of campus, down the streets, and hope she won't think to stop me.

She doesn't stop until her door, when she turns, and presses her face briefly into my coat. I'm so surprised that I cling to her, and then realise what I'm doing, and let her go.

'Thank you, Sully,' she says. 'For not asking questions. For walking me home. I appreciate it.' She's looking up at me, and so I bend down to give her our usual goodbye kiss, mouths closed, a little hesitant. Cold noses and cheeks brushing. She opens her door, and I feel the warmth rushing out in slivers from the basement flat. 'I guess I saw your room,' she says. 'Would you like to see mine?'

'You're asking me in?' I say, with such stupid surprise that I feel like punching the wall. She sees my tense hand, and before it tightens to a fist, she takes me by it, her palm around my knuckles. I feel my hand soften until it opens like a flower against hers, and then she draws me in.

Radhika's room is a converted basement in a house, and much bigger than mine, which is just one of the made-to-measure student rooms lined up with others along a narrow corridor, where every door is the same, and the name stickers change every year. There is no window at the front of her place, and the door is solid wood, so I had never been able to look in before. Instead, there is a small window at the back, with a view on to a metal stairwell that leads up to the garden. I guess the stairwell must be where they put the trash. There's a bed in the corner, a desk against the wall, a small table with a single chair, a narrow wardrobe, and a shallow sink, with a basin underneath it, collecting drips. It's only slightly tidier than my room, as her paperwork is everywhere. She has no bookshelves, not even makeshift ones of bricks and planks, like mine, and so her books and fat paper files are piled high in teetering towers, lining the walls on either side of the desk, built as unevenly and ambitiously as though a toddler had been using her books for blocks. Where the books end, the flapping clippings of papers begin, tacked or taped to the wall, and go as high as she can reach in her slippers. There's no decoration, no bright prints or pictures, no little boxes of trinkets, or vases waiting for flowers, not even a pot plant shrivelling in the corner. The only indication that it might be a woman's room is that there is a stiff blue bedspread, an Indian shawl, from which a musty tea and tobacco smell rises. It is highly embroidered along the edges in a traditional style, with a dull, brassy thread, and clashing red and green.

'So, this is your room,' I say, unsure if I'm dismayed or delighted.

It's only slightly warmer than outside, and I don't take my coat off, as she hasn't yet taken off hers. It wasn't as though I had thought of her as living in a magical place, that the plain wooden door in the brick wall where I usually left her would lead to a room of marvels, full of feminine frippery and the stuff that makes a house a home. Or that it would be softly furnished and smell of fresh-baked rolls, like Calamity Jane's cabin in the woods. Her room is much like mine, although the research on her walls is less obsessive and more scientific; unhealthy in a literal sense, a series of clean-looking charts with grisly titles about progressive lung decay and tumour biopsies. I've always liked the fact that she is nothing like my mother; I'm not sure what to think of the fact that she is so much like me.

She moves through the room, lighting the gas heater, and the gas ring, the brown and grey of her clothes disappearing into the brown and grey of the wooden floor and walls. It seems that if she stopped moving for a moment with that quick, bird-like energy, she would be painted into the background, and there would be a mirror-sized picture of her on the wall. She still hasn't replied to my bland statement, although it wasn't a question, so I suppose it doesn't need an answer.

'Yes, what gave it away?' she finally says, and she's laughing, and I feel like an idiot all over again. I'm a qualified medical doctor, and a PhD candidate, and I'm saying things like 'You're asking me in' to someone who just has, and 'So, this is your room' to the person whose room I'm in. A specialism in stating the moronically obvious. She takes off her coat once the heater flares up, and nods at me as though inviting me to take off mine.

'Not a lot, to be honest,' I say. 'But I'm glad I amuse you.' I pull off my coat, and look for somewhere to sit, but there's only the bed, where she's dropped her coat, and I don't think I should take up the single chair. I'd feel foolish sitting on the floor, so I just shift uncomfortably where I am, from one foot to the other, as though I'm in danger of getting painted into the background too. My sweater is grey, and my trousers are tan, and I suspect that if there were a mirror in the apartment, Radhika would look more like my sister, standing by my side, than my actual sisters. I think of Mac and Lana briefly, as butterflies fluttering over a flower bed, mournfully bright and fragile. Radhika is more like a thrush picking through fallen leaves in winter debris, drab enough to hide herself from danger, tough enough to make it through the cold seasons. I wonder if that's why people stared in the cafeteria and the corridor, when I had my arm around her, and she had hers around me. Perhaps we looked too odd together. Perhaps we looked too right.

'Do you like it here?' I ask her. I honestly want to know. I wonder if she'd like it to be nicer, to have something pretty to look at in her room. I've never brought her flowers, afraid of looking foolish giving them to her on a date, and then having to carry them around all evening if she didn't really want them. I've never picked her up from her place, but always met her wherever we planned on meeting. As though there were invisible other friends from our faculties who might be joining us too, but who never did. I've never been sure how much our dates are really dates after all. I'm not sure if meeting for lunch today was a date, and whether it still is one; and if it wasn't, whether it's become one now.

'Sure,' she says. 'What's not to like?' and she gestures around the room a little ironically. 'You know, my mother would weep if she saw how I was living. And my dad's family, well, you must know what it's like in India. They've got servants who do everything for them. They think that here in *Amreeka* it's all jukeboxes and dancing. That it's all automats and laundromats, and that you just push buttons to get things done. I don't tell them the truth. About how I have to chop my own vegetables, darn my own stockings, dust my own furniture.' She shrugs. 'They care about that sort of stuff.'

'Well, I guess we do have jukeboxes. And automats, and laundromats,' I say carefully, thrilled that she is really talking to me about herself. 'Do you care about that sort of stuff?'

'About housework, you mean?' asks Radhika. 'I don't do enough to care about it. Back in Delhi, my mother didn't work, and she spent all her time at home. She'd take up a whole table making an apple strudel, rolling out the pastry until it was thinner than paper. She'd knit me little cardigans, and stitch me dirndls, even though it was never cool enough to wear them. She embroidered tablecloths and throws, and had every surface covered with pretty little figurines in porcelain. She'd make sure they were dusted every week, and replaced in exactly the same way.' She looks at me, to see what I think of this, to search for traces of approval or disquiet. Her own face is perfectly blank, and I try to look the same; it's as though she hasn't yet made up her mind about what she thinks of it herself.

She goes to the wardrobe, and pulls out a couple of cups, and a box of tea; it sounds like she is still deciding as she speaks. 'Sometimes I think it would nice if I could be the sort of person who cared about things. Domestic things, I mean. A nice meal. A nice house. A lemon-scented floor. Whiter-than-white laundry.'

She shakes tea into a steel pot, not bothering to measure it, and then realises that she doesn't have any hot water. She fills a little pan from the tap, and walks past me to put it on the ring. It is only then that she notices I am still holding my coat, not sure where to hang it. She takes it from me, and throws it over the bed, where she left her own, the damp of the snow sinking into the dark blue bedspread, the musty smell getting stronger as the room gets warmer.

'But then I think, I just haven't got the time for that rubbish. I've got work to do. People keep dying. And people need saving. And soft-fucking-furnishings can wait.' She says this last bit sweetly, looking at me, like it's a challenge. I don't rise to it, and look past her, into her open wardrobe, where her clothes hang to midway, and the boarded base is covered with her provisions, rather than her shoes. There is also a cylindrical steel box, like a large coffee pot or Thermos, propped up on an old-fashioned bible, with gold-embossed leather cover. I guess the bible must have come with the room.

'Do you keep all your food in the wardrobe?' I ask, noticing how little there is: just the tea, a brown paper bag with some fruit, a plum-coloured bottle of something and a couple of bars of chocolate.

'I have to,' she says briefly. 'Rats.'

'You should get a cat,' I say, thinking of Jakie, cat-catcher, rat-catcher.

'I'd rather die than get a cat,' she says. 'If I ever become an old lady with a cat, you have permission to shoot me.'

'I'm not much of a cat person either,' I reply, leaning against the window. I wish I still had my coat to hold on to, as I am suddenly unsure what to do with my hands. I cross them in front of me, and then put them behind me, holding on to the damply peeling sill. 'Or a dog person.' I have to shift over as she comes to stand beside me and starts to heave up the heavy frame. The frayed rope and pulleys squeak as it finally slides open. She only manages to lock it open on one side, as the catch on the other side is rusted and stiff.

It only occurs to me that I should have helped her, that I should have put my spare and indecisive hands to some use, when she replies, 'No, you're more of a people person.' She says it with such a straight face, it's hard to tell if she's joking, or annoyed with me. She pulls the milk off the windowsill, and as she shakes it experimentally, a flurry of flakes blow into the room. 'Sorry, the milk's frozen,' she says. 'I forgot I left it out here this morning. Are you okay with black tea?'

'I'm fine,' I say. 'I don't really want tea, unless you do.' My legs feel stiff, still leaning back, and I help her shut the window again, and sit down on the single chair, unthinkingly. She smiles a bit ruefully, at herself rather than me.

'I didn't even ask you, did I?' she says. 'You can tell I don't entertain too often.' She looks in the wardrobe. 'I've got sherry, if you prefer? I don't know if you drink.'

'I'm not a big drinker,' I say. 'But I'll have whatever you're having.'

'You say things like that a lot,' she says, and pulls out the plum-coloured bottle. She pours a little into each of the teacups on the table. 'Bottoms up,' she says, and clinks her cup with mine. I realise that there's nowhere for her to sit. I'm on the chair, and the bed is covered with wet coats.

'I'll sit on the floor,' I say quickly, but she shrugs, and sits primly on my lap instead, her narrow shoulders brushing against me as she sips her drink. It feels like a practical solution, rather than a romantic one, and I'm terrified of moving, as the warmth of her body seeps into mine. I sit stiffly upright in the hardback chair, and drink my sherry, which burns my throat a little as I'm not used to it. I try to will myself not to have an erection, or do anything foolish that might get me thrown out. I can smell the rose water on her skin, through the thicker, cough syrup scent of the sherry, and she's close enough to kiss.

'For someone who says that he wants to be alone in a room with me, and talk, you don't talk a lot,' she says eventually. She finishes her sherry, and puts the teacup on the table. 'I have a little experiment I want to propose,' she says. 'A clinical trial,' and she kisses me, just as softly as she kissed me at the door of my own apartment. 'You know how to do this, right?' she asks knowingly.

She reminds me of Bacall telling Bogie how to whistle. Lips. Together. Blow. I realise that I do know, and I start to kiss her back, pulling her into my arms. A few swollen seconds pass, and her lips soften, but then sitting on the chair terrifies me suddenly. I think of those white ghosts coupling in the dining room in the night, and I stop, a little breathless, with Radhika tight in my arms, and her brittle body against me.

'It's okay,' she says. 'I'm not scared.'

'Why do you keep saying that?' I ask, and pull back. I want to stand up, off the chair, but I don't want to let her go. 'Why would you be? Have people been saying stuff about me on campus?' I'm thinking of the looks that Jim and Danny shared, after I flicked the switches all the way to XXX. I'm thinking of the evidence of my disordered mind plastered across my walls. I realise that I'm blowing it with Radhika, within seconds of holding her in my arms, just as her mouth was about to open under mine. That I'm sounding like a case study in paranoia, another annotated clipping with a pin in it.

'I just mean that I'm not scared of this,' she says. 'Of where this is going. And I want to tell you that, in case you are.' She puts her hand up to my face, brushing my cheekbone with the back of her fingers, and says, 'It's weird that you don't know this, but you're the good-looking one. It's like you don't see yourself when you look in the mirror; you always seem so unimpressed. If people stare at us sometimes, it's because they can't believe you're with me. I mean, look at me.' She smiles unrepentantly. 'I'm flat as these walls, and about as highly decorated.'

'I'm scared,' I admit. 'I'm mostly scared of scaring you off. I think I'd marry you tomorrow, if you'd let me.'

'Oh, shut up,' she says. But she doesn't sound displeased, and she puts her arms around my neck. I stand up after all, and I'm holding her in my arms as I kiss her again. She's light and sharp as a bone on the shore, and somewhere between my awkwardness, and her expectation, while we're kissing, we fall on our damp coats on the bed. It's like we're rolling on wet grass, from one edge of the narrow mattress to the other.

Eventually we're lying there, my back against the cold external wall, her head on my shoulder, and we hear stamping upstairs, and music playing. 'Rock Around the Clock', by Bill Haley. I feel Radhika's body tense, as her neighbour jigs upstairs to the music, and then relax as the record switches to something Latin American, and a sweet low voice sings about a girl on a beach. Radhika doesn't mind this one, and she stretches out her graceful arms towards the ceiling, flexing her palms and her fingers as though about to dance, like an extra in a Hindi movie.

I prop myself up on my elbow and look at her, at the eyelashes fanned on her cheeks, fine and straight rather than thick and curled. She grew up in Delhi, she'd let that slip before, and her mannerisms and voice were sometimes Indian with me, but always American with Americans. When she spoke to Gloria, her mother became her mom. I don't know why she did that. She doesn't seem to care very much, otherwise, about fitting in. She'd told me today, reluctantly, that her mother was German. She was as embarrassed at being caught reading a German transcript as an illiterate adult caught holding a newspaper upside down on the bus. She had lost her brother during Partition, and his name was Ricky. She was Hindu, but I didn't really know what she believed. The charm at her throat, the little Ganesha, remover of obstacles, might just be a charm. There is a bible in her wardrobe, kept with her food, away from the rats. I count these facts off on my fingers, the old-fashioned way that my father did, moving my thumb up the crease lines of my index finger to the top, and then starting on the middle finger.

She opens her eyes. 'What are you doing?'

'Adding up what I know about you. What you've told me. Doing the math,' I say. Studying in America had got me in the habit of saying mathematics like Americans, and I'm sure Jakie would laugh at me if he heard this. He would pee himself if he heard me referring to our mother as Mom. Radhika's short hair is loose on the pillow, straying across her cheekbone, and I hesitate before pushing it back, gently. It seems a more intimate gesture than kissing her. I spread my hand, and show her where I've stopped; I haven't even reached my little finger. 'Tell me more. Please.'

'I will,' she says, as solemnly as though she's answering a much bigger question, in a flower-filled chapel, or in a city hall in her flat slippers. Feeding a fire with rice in a temple, or seated in a scarlet sari with a gold chain looped from ear to nose. I see the inky dot of an old piercing on her nostril, and I wonder what she wore there: a diamond, a ruby or a plain gold stud. I wonder when she took it out. 'If you will,' she adds. She looks at me, frankly. Show me yours, and I'll show you mine.

'Okay,' I say. It's always easier to say yes than refuse, whatever the consequences. I know what the consequences are, this time, but I've always known. If she asks me a question, I'll answer it. Silence is a wrong answer.

She falls asleep after telling me about her brother. A handsome boy pulped on the street, his head open to the pink and grey core. She had hated him. He had teased her and tormented her, and treated her like one of the servants. He had told her that she was ugly, and skinny, and stupid. Her father had said she was silly to get upset. Her mother had said, 'He's the boy,' as though that was the end of the matter.

'I hate him and I wish he was dead,' she had cried out, and got slapped briskly by her mother, and sent up to bed without dinner. When he did die, they were never sure if his death was so brutal because he had attempted to fight and defend their ayah, or because he had been caught running away. Abandoning the woman who had brought him up, to save his own spoiled skin.

Radhika had said quietly, 'You know I didn't mean it.' To his covered body, and to anyone who would listen. But she was only eleven, and part of her knew that she did. She got the future that had been put aside for him: his education, his college funding, and all her parents' hopes, poured into her and stoppered firmly like an old-fashioned medicine, a cure for dropsy. Her parents had insisted that she bring her brother's ashes with her to America, from college room to college room. It was, she said, like being handcuffed to a corpse.

I watch her sleeping, flickering like a candle, and am unsure whether to stay or go. The moonlight is filtering through the four glass panes of her window, painting long white stripes on her floorboards, and when she breathes in, I can see her ribs, and the hollow beneath them. We haven't eaten anything since lunch, and I'm starving now, but she clearly hadn't even thought about dinner. She doesn't take care of herself. I pull the covers over her.

I wonder where her brother is, because I realise that he is probably here now, in this room. Throbbing under the floorboards like a beating heart. Packed into the cavity wall like a murdered housewife. I look around, and everything in the room is thrown into dark relief by the silver light. I leave quietly.

It is early morning when I come back, clutching a paper bag, and the day is just beginning to drip through the darkness framed by the windows. She wakes as I open the creaking front door, replacing the jangling keys I have borrowed on the hook. She looks at me with curiosity, as I sit next to her on the bed, and it feels presumptuous. I have to remind myself that I have slept there, beside her, for hours.

'Merry Christmas,' I say. I don't have the confidence to kiss her again properly, and I don't want to give her our usual greeting peck, as that might show that last night was just last night, and now it's over.

'Merry Christmas,' she replies, glancing down at herself briefly, checking that her clothes are still decent, before she sits up, letting the covers fall from her shoulders. 'I'm confused, Sully. Did you stay, or did you go?'

'Both,' I say. 'I left to get something for you. But I came back with breakfast.'

She looks in the bag, 'Where did you get hot rolls on Christmas Day?'

'There's a Jewish bakery right down the street,' I say. 'You really never noticed it?'

She shrugs. 'I'm not hungry right now,' she says.

'That's okay,' I reply. I give her another brown paper bag, pulled out of my pocket, tied up with a shiny string. 'Merry Christmas,' I say again.

'Darn it, I didn't get you anything,' she says. She looks cross with me, like I've shown her up.

'It's nothing, just open it,' I say, putting the bread rolls in the wardrobe. I'd already eaten a couple on the way back; I was so ravenous I couldn't help myself.

She shrugs, and rips the bag open, and pulls out a thick pair of woollen socks. With snowflakes embroidered on them. She laughs. 'Warm bread in bed, and warm clothes in winter. You'll make someone a great little wife one day.'

'I'm glad I nailed the audition,' I say. 'I'd have brought you flowers, too, if I thought you had anywhere to put them.' I stand by the wardrobe, unsure what to do with myself, again. Unsure where to look, and what to do with my empty hands. She sees me hesitating. She doesn't ask me to stay, or tell me to go. Instead, she shifts over slightly, pulling back the covers, and I gratefully pull off my coat, drop it on the chair, and take off my shoes, putting them neatly beside her slippers, under the bed. I slide in beside her.

'You're freezing,' she says, but she rolls closer, her breath warm on my cheek.

'Honey,' I say eventually, stroking the length of her arm from shoulder to wrist, 'can I ask you something?'

'Sure,' she says. 'You can ask me anything you like. As long as you don't mind what I answer.'

I'm not encouraged. 'It doesn't matter, it's a stupid question.'

'That's clever of you,' says Radhika approvingly. 'After that promising little review, I'm interested. What is it?'

'Forget it,' I say.

'You're not going to say it? Classic reverse psychology. Now I really want to know.'

'No,' I say, thinking that like my father, the less I say, the more persuasive I'll sound.

'Yes,' she says firmly, and I realise that this works both ways, and her yes is like a switch, and just as before, the ringing sound of it gives me confidence.

'Are we dating now?' I finally ask the girl I'm in bed with. The girl I've spent the night with. The girl who I've just bought breakfast.

'Yes,' she repeats, just as firmly. 'Sure. I mean, I'd say that this is a date, wouldn't you?' and she turns towards me, her face framed by the pillow.

I smile, so widely that I'm practically grinning, and this time, she's the one who smiles back at me. I smile and she smiles.

'You have great teeth, Sully. You're good-looking when you don't smile, but you're nuclear when you do. You should try doing it more often.' She's teasing me, a compliment and a criticism. I'm relieved; it means she really didn't mind when I did the same to her.

'I'm not sure I can risk it, for the sake of the good citizens of New Haven,' I say. I kiss her hair, and put my arm around her; I realise that I'm still smiling, even while I'm staring up at the dark ceiling. It feels good, but then it feels a little bit uncomfortable. I don't know why smiling should suddenly make me feel so sad.

'You're right,' she replies, leaning against me comfortably, her head on my shoulder, looking up at the dark ceiling with me, at the blotches of pale mould blooming on the painted plaster like they're soft white clouds in the sky. 'It's risky. And God forbid if you laughed or cried, the city walls might come tumbling down.'

I almost do laugh. I feel safe in her room, painted into her scenery, while the world shakes outside like a snow globe, tossing out flakes that splatter on the windows. I squeeze her hand, and briefly fantasise about sliding a thick gold ring down her finger. Her hand is so light, it would weigh her down like a gaudy flower head bowing a fragile green stem. Another heavy metal manacle, to another body. I imagine her belly, which sinks concave below her ribs, hidden by the folds of her skirts, swelling under my palm with a new life we've made together. Locking her in true love with me, keeping her inside, and everyone else out. A bulletproof glass box. Snow White asleep in a clear coffin. Waiting for a prince. A kiss.

In the wardrobe, there's a silver-plated Thermos that doesn't hold coffee, or rat poison, but her brother's throbbing remains; like a cockroach in a matchbox, trapped and tapping. I didn't mean it, she said.

But I do. I mean everything I said. I'd marry her tomorrow.

She says she's not scared, but she should be. She should be afraid of me. I'm afraid of myself. Afraid of being happy. Conflicted when we kiss. Sad when I smile. I'm crazy about her. But knowing what I know, about love and marriage, honouring and obeying, she shouldn't be resting in my arms. She should run and run, and never look back.

Chapter Six

Jakie

'IT'S NOT FAIR THAT YOU'RE WORKING TODAY,' SAYS FRANK, miraculously sober on Christmas morning. He's sipping coffee, and scribbling notes at the square table in his lodgings, spreading his books and papers and pens around with his habitual imperial sprawl, so there's not even a free patch of table for me to put my own coffee cup down. I hold it awkwardly to my chest, while trying to prop up yesterday's paper between myself and the table.

'I'm not the only one,' I say accusingly. 'At least I'm not working over breakfast. You could do all that later, I'll be out of here in an hour.'

'God, that's a terrible rag,' says Frank, looking at me struggling to read the broadsheet, shuffling the flimsy pages. He rolls his eyes, as though I'm the one being irritating. 'Read it on the bed, I'm not making space for it.'

'You write for it,' I say. The truth is I only bought it out of loyalty to him; I'd rather have got *The Times*.

'Not any more. I quit,' he says calmly.

'What? When? So what did they say?' I ask, surprised.

'Oh, I didn't *tell* them I quit,' he says. 'That would have been foolish. They'd have most likely stopped paying me. I have a dear old landlady downstairs to support. And a dear old mammy in the old country to keep in nylon hosiery.' He looks at me, obviously impressed with himself. 'I think I'll use that,' he says, and repeats out loud as he writes it down, 'To keep in nylon hosiery.'

'It sounds a bit fifties,' I comment.

'It's set in the fifties, shit wit,' grins Frank. 'Everyone's a bloody critic.'

Frank's book is about the Notting Hill race riots, just a few years ago, in 1958; he has articles, clippings and papers chronicling the clashes between the Teddy boys and the newly arrived West Indian lads, street battles placed and dated, sheets of immigration statistics, disquieting propaganda from the British Union of Fascists. He spends more time on his book than he does at his job. He drinks himself into depression about it, and sometimes I think he should get a more rewarding hobby. Other times I envy his passion, the fact that he thinks he's going to make a difference, and make something right.

I stand up, balancing my coffee between my arm and my chest, and inch my way over to the bed, to lay out the newspaper.

'Oh, stop pouting, Jakie,' Frank says, and he sweeps all his papers to the floor with one swift movement of his arm, lifting up his own coffee cup with a precisely timed flip just before it catches too, and sipping from it with satisfaction. 'Happy now?'

'About the mess on the floor?' I comment. 'Ecstatic.'

'Nag,' says Frank, joining me on the bed, and pulling apart the paper to look at the sports section.

'Fag,' I reply, because I can't think of anything cleverer; he always wins whenever we play this game. 'So what are you going to do today? I'm out all day; I've got an eighteen-hour shift.'

'Call in sick,' he says, looking at me seriously. He really means it.

'I can't call in sick on Christmas Day. It's skeleton staff. Anyone who's not Christian has to be there. I'd have to be dying not to go in.'

'Say you're dying,' he says, just as seriously.

'Then they'll send an ambulance, and I'll be in the hospital anyway,' I say dismissively.

'What if I came down with a sudden paralysis of both my legs,' suggests Frank, 'and got sent to Casualty. Then we could spend Christmas together.'

'Even if you *lost* both your legs, I couldn't spend Christmas with you,' I say. 'I'd just have to make sure that you were bandaged and anaesthetised.' I briefly wonder if I'd still love Frank if he lost his legs. I suspect that he wouldn't love me; he thinks I don't go out enough as it is.

'Spending Christmas legless, it doesn't sound like the worst idea,' muses Frank. 'Well, if you're so set on going to your office, I suppose I'll go to mine.'

'The Lamb and Flag?' I guess.

'The King's Head,' he says. 'I'm nothing if not patriotic.'

He surprises me by getting dressed, and walking me in through town, even though the pubs won't be open for hours. It's only slightly colder outside his rooms than it was inside, but even so, Frank's choice of coat is utterly impractical. He's wearing one of those ubiquitous bumfreezer jackets. I wonder if it's due to William Godfrey's influence; he cares about his clothes so much that he has names for his outfits, like they were his children. I'd introduced the two of them after work one evening; Frank had insisted on it, and they got on worryingly well. They discussed politics and sport, fashion and music, and I pretended I knew what they were talking about, nodding along to their strange language peppered with foreign words like Mosley and Man City, mods and Matt Monro. People stared at us outside Paramount Records in Piccadilly Circus, like we were another stylish black and white poster in the window. Our own jazzy trio in black, brown and white. Darkie, Paki, Paddy. 'Take a photo, it'll last longer,' Frank had said to a large man in a bowler hat. I think someone actually did.

'So, is Will working today?' Frank asks carelessly. So carelessly that I wonder if he's not so much jealous as interested in him himself.

'No, but he's asked us to his dad's place tomorrow,' I say. 'It's some Boxing Day party he's having. Just casual. Bring a bottle and a plate of something.'

'God, I don't want to have drag myself all the way out there,' complains Frank, but he seems pleased. 'I'll miss the races.' He pauses, and waits for me; he's walking ahead of me, as usual – he's quicker and he's got longer legs. Or maybe he's just waiting for me to comment on the jacket. 'So, am I coming as your date?' he asks.

'As my mate,' I say. 'Roommate, I mean,' I correct myself. Roommate. I'm aware of how distant and wholesome the word sounds, like I picked him from a public posting on the hospital noticeboard, or he was assigned to me by the college lottery. I try to stop myself apologising, but I say it apologetically anyway. 'He's a colleague.'

'Well, God forbid that your daily diet of meat and two veg gets in the way of your brilliant career, Dr Dick,' says Frank. 'You don't think all your esteemed senior colleagues weren't buggered senseless when they were fagging at Eton?' He points out a couple of old men, in long overcoats, dressed for lunch in shining shoes, as they turn into the Savoy. 'This is England. It's famous for its stately homos.'

'It's different for you,' I mutter, not wanting to have this talk now. Not wanting to have this talk ever. I wish we were back at his flat, so I could leave. If we were in my flat, I could make an excuse and go to the communal bathroom. In someone else's house, I could go to another room. But here on the street, out in the open, there's no swift exit I can make. I'm trapped, as we're both walking in the same direction, and I can't walk the other way, as that would take me further from where I need to go. And Frank's in no rush, and could follow me back down the street anyway. Reluctantly, I reply, 'And it's different for me. It's politics.'

'Sure, I'm a Catholic man from Belfast. What would I know about politics?' snaps Frank. 'It's not as though I'm ashamed of you.'

I'm starting to get annoyed. 'So now I'm meant to be grateful that you're not a bigot? That you don't mind being seen with the brown man in the street?'

'Yes!' explodes Frank, turning to face me, making a scene. 'You should be grateful for me. I'm grateful for you. And you're not just ashamed of me. It's worse than that, you're ashamed of yourself.' He's looking at me like I'm such a coward. I can't stand it.

'Oh, fuck you,' I say. 'I'm going to work.' And I step forward, and kiss him goodbye in the middle of the Strand, outside the bustling entrance to the Savoy, so that anyone who wasn't already staring at us stops and gapes, and the ones who were already staring at us avert their eyes and hurry away.

'Well, fock me,' agrees Frank quietly, as he steps back. 'Like we say back home, it's not Christmas Day until there's been a fight.' He grins at me, and I step back too, pulling my hat down against the cold.

'Christ, you always have to have the last word, don't you?' I say, walking off, stunned by own stupid bravery. I want to go away from him for a little while, and pull on a white coat at work, and think about what we said, and what I did. On Christmas Day, in broad daylight, in public. I want to sit somewhere quietly, and think about what it means.

I have no one to talk to about this, apart from the man I've been yelling at and kissing in the street. If there had been a policeman on the beat, swinging his baton cheerily as he turned the corner, he could have arrested us both. I think it's possible that I could have been fired, evicted and even deported. I think it's possible that I would have had to declare myself mentally ill – because that's what homosexuality is still officially filed under, a disease of the mind – and been unable to practise again. The land of stately homos. Wilde did time in Reading Gaol, and wrote a ballad. Turing helped win the war, but was prosecuted as a criminal, and had to have humiliating chemical castration treatments until he died of the shame.

'I know, it's a terrible habit,' calls back Frank, bloody-mindedly proving me right about the last word. 'It's like a disease. That's right, I'm diseased,' he shouts out, just to shock anyone still watching, so they scuttle away like fearful insects. I can't stop myself smiling, but feel a deep disquiet in my guts. Frank's walked around with a target painted on his back his whole life, a Catholic man in Belfast, an Irishman in London, an indiscreet homosexual, but I'm not as brave as him. I realise we're in trouble; I predict terrible trouble ahead. I love him too much. We've let this thing go on too long, and we've gone too far to turn back. We've crossed the line. Whatever happens to us now is going to hurt.

In the hospital, they've tried to make things a bit more jolly than usual, for the patients stuck with us. There's been a collection for the elderly who don't have family to bring them anything, and the local chapter of the Women's Institute has been distributing hot mince pies. They're for the patients rather than the doctors, and for some reason this makes them look irresistible; the pastry steaming on chipped ceramic plates in the chilled, clinical air. I don't dare take one.

A senior consultant, Dr Reginald Fletcher, has drawn the short straw and been called in today to supervise the rest of us. He comes out of his office to mark something on a clipboard, looking busy and important, and tells one of the nurses to fetch him a cup of tea, Mr Dearth's chart, and two mince pies. He doesn't look at her while he says it, and the way he buries the illegal request in a list reminds me of the first time I bought rubbers in England. I asked for tooth powder, shoe polish, cod liver oil, hair cream and matches, and everything else that I could see above the shopkeeper's shoulder on the shelf behind him, before I asked for what I really wanted. And he knew what I was doing, and he was one of those middle-aged men who'd fought a war, and hadn't fought it to have wogs invading his homeland, and he decided to have a bit of fun with me, forcing me to repeat the last item, loudly. He made me say it twice until the whole shop was staring at me, and it felt like I was in a special sort of south London hell peopled with middle-aged ladies in floral dresses and dowdy housecoats. He pretended he couldn't understand my accent, as though received pronunciation was a foreign language in Denmark Hill. I eventually said, 'I'm a doctor, sir,' as crisply and briskly as I could, somehow implying that I needed all the items for a patient, and he finally gave them to me, grudging me the business. After that, I discovered I could just buy them from my hairdresser, and I didn't even have to ask for them outright, but simply nod when he delicately suggested 'something for the weekend'.

The nurse is a south London girl too, a sparkier one than most, although Dr Fletcher wouldn't have known that, as they all look alike to him in uniform. Just like we brown doctors in white coats all look alike to him, distinguished by nothing more than height and haircut. Nurse Caitlin is of medium height, and most of her red hair, almost as bright as Frank's, is tucked away under her cap. I wait to see if she'll say that the mince pies are just for patients. I wait to see if she'll say no. But she doesn't even hesitate, and when she gets them for him, she moves with such vicarious authority that the beady-eyed WI woman doesn't even ask who they're for. I shrug, and turn away. I don't know why I'm surprised. It's a hospital, and the nurses here are used to doing what they're told by doctors. They're like soldiers in a war.

'Excellent, most efficient, dear,' says Dr Fletcher, pretending to look at the chart, but really sinking his teeth into the hot, steaming crust of the pie. I don't even like mince pies, but I want to steal it out of his mouth. I wish Lana had been serving it, as she might have spat on it discreetly first. He quotes Dickinson to Nurse Caitlin, who hasn't yet been dismissed: 'Because I could not stop for Death, He kindly stopped for me.'

'It's Mr Dearth, sir,' says Nurse Caitlin, who's not allowed to speak to the senior doctors or consultants, unless they speak to her first. Who gets locked into her residence with the other nurses at ten thirty every evening, unless she's on a night shift. 'Like hearth, as in hearth and home, he told me. It's quite all right. He's not stopping for you. He's finishing the crossword.'

In the corridor, two of the younger nurses are also having a discussion on pronouncing a patient's name. It's not a foreign patient's name, either. 'Mr Cockburn likes to be called Mr Co-burn. The cee and kay are silent. You can guess why,' she giggles, and the other nurse joins in.

'And so when Mrs Dipcock was admitted, I was mindful saying her name, and I said, "I'll just take your temperature for you, Mrs Dipco," and she said, "Whatever are you talking about, love? Who's Mrs Dipco when she's at home? I'm Mrs Dipcock, D-I-P-C-O-C-K, Mrs Dip-cock," and she said "cock" so loudly the whole ward looked.'

The nurses stifle their laughter as they see me passing. They look embarrassed, and I'm not sure why, as I'm just a junior doctor, and brown to boot, so they can say what they want around me. It's not until they greet me politely, 'Good morning, Dr Sad-dick,' separating the syllables of my name with careful precision, that I realise the joke is on me. They don't know how to pronounce Saddeq; they think I'm another unfortunate saddled with an embarrassing name, and I've only just got the joke that Frank made after breakfast, when he called me Dr Dick. I laugh out loud, thinking about how clever he is, and they look relieved, and laugh with me, although I'm not sure they even know why they're laughing. Perhaps they think I expect it of them; perhaps it's just another instance of nurses doing what a doctor wants them to do.

'Dr Saddeq,' says Dr Fletcher, calling me back with authority. He is no longer bothering to look at Mr Dearth's chart, and is burrowing into the second mince pie. His mouth is full of shortcrust pastry crumbs that cling to his moustache, and the open-mawed, slack-jawed chewing while he talks is both revolting and fascinating. I feel a disgusting urge to lick the crumbs off the self-important, flabby little man, like a dog, just to see what he'd do. I realise that I've been watching his mouth move, but haven't been paying attention to anything he's said.

'... so it's one of your lot, and I can't made head or tail of what it's all about, so you'd better go in, because the other one on the ward's in the middle of a surgical procedure.'

'What other one?' I ask automatically, instead of asking what he's talking about. I'm hoping that Nurse Caitlin will fill me in, as she's been standing helpfully to the side. She's the one who probably told him my name in the first place, so he could call me over. There are other doctors around with more experience than me, and I've not often been singled out and given particular responsibility for something that a senior doctor was too busy to diagnose.

'The other Paki chappie, of course,' he says impatiently. He's not saying it in an offensive way; for him, it's just a matter of fact. I suspect that if someone told him the joke about the Englishman, the Welshman and the Irishman in the pub, or the darkie, the Paki and the Paddy outside Paramount Records on Piccadilly Circus, he wouldn't even realise it was a joke until the punchline. I guess he must be talking about Dr Sharma, who's not a Paki at all; he's from Bombay, upper caste and upper class, and avoids talking to me, a polluted and impious Muslim. I sometimes wonder how he's resolved the conflict with his medical calling; all the Untouchables he has to touch with his scrubbed-and-gloved Brahmin hands.

Dr Fletcher nods to the nurse, who hands me the chart, and he walks away, his manner still so busy and important that it seems almost comic. No one is following his rapid, determined step down the corridor, no one is nodding to him or asking for his advice, and he seems a lonely figure, wrapped up in his sense of position, a ceremonial coat too clean to have seen any work. I suspect he is just going to the next plate of mince pies, and that he'll continue to graze around the whole hospital until his Christmas shift is over.

'Dr Saddeq,' says Nurse Caitlin, looking at me with a combination of sympathy and impatience. She's one of the few who gets my name right, which explains how Dr Fletcher said it with such crisp correctness. I realise that she's waiting for me, and that unlike our esteemed senior colleague, nosing around for nibbles like a truffle-hunting pig, she really does have other things to do. 'Would you follow me, please?'

She's quite pretty, and the red of her hidden hair is luminously lovely; a cleaner shade than the dingy henna-dyed hair you sometimes see in Pakistan, or even here, among the loud-mouthed prostitutes of both sexes in Soho. I wonder whether, before us immigrants came along – the darkies, Pakis and Paddys – she was the one who was picked on for being different, mocked or teased for her ginger hair. I wonder if she became a nurse so she could tuck most of it neatly beneath her cap.

'Is the patient Pakistani, then?' I ask her, as I walk beside her, rather than following her. She's holding herself very straight, as though determined to show that she doesn't mind walking with me. 'You know, just because he's Pakistani, it doesn't mean that I'll speak his language. There are lots of languages in Pakistan. I only speak a couple of them. I might not understand him.'

'I daresay, sir,' she says to me pleasantly, but firmly, as this isn't really her problem. Her job is to take me to the room or the bed of some poorly stranger, and leave me there; her duty will be discharged at the door. To show there are no hard feelings about this, she adds in a friendly manner, 'I've got cousins in Liverpool and I can't make them out for the life of me.'

'I don't mean accents,' I persist. 'I mean whole different languages. Like they don't just speak French in France, but Breton in Brittany and Basque in the Basque country. Or the Spanish speak Catalan in Catalonia and Galician in Galicia. Like the Welsh used to speak Welsh. And in Pakistan, we speak Punjabi where I'm from, but a different language in the hills, and in the south, and so on. There's no such language as Pakistani.'

She is nodding when I talk about France and Spain and Wales, as though impressed by my knowledge, but then laughs at the end, as though I'm teasing her. 'No such language as Pakistani,' she repeats, shaking her head. 'Well I don't know, sir, it's all Greek to me,' and she allows herself to laugh again.

She stops at a large room off the ward, with neat beds in rows, four on each side, and the curtains are drawn open on all of them, except a corner one, which is conspicuously hidden. She nods towards it expectantly, and when I don't move, she sighs, and walks forward. She pulls the curtain a little to let herself in, and waits for me to follow.

'Hello, miss,' she says loudly and clearly, in the ringing tones that people use with foreigners, and teachers use with young children, swollen with a false heartiness. 'The doctor's here now.'

Lying on the bed is a very young girl. I'm guessing from the glowing brown of her skin that she is Bengali, or maybe Tamil, and she is wearing a loose shalwar kameez, probably handed down from someone older and bigger than her. She is lying on the bed, rather than in it, staring quietly up at the ceiling like a stoical child. Her body is shuddering, and her jaw is clenched.

'She's clearly in pain but she won't let anyone touch her,' explains Nurse Caitlin. 'She turned up without anyone, and she hasn't said a word. We can't admit her or send her home without examining her.' Nurse Caitlin looks at me, looking at the girl. She's not just like a child; she is one. 'Are you all right, Doctor? You look like you've seen a ghost.'

Standing in the small space, partitioned by flimsy curtains, with a girl breathing rapidly on the bed, and a red-headed nurse's sugar-scented flesh by my side, I realise something that neither of them has yet worked out. I realise that the girl child on the bed is heavily pregnant, and that she doesn't even know it. That she is going to have a baby on Christmas Day.

'I'll come back,' I tell Nurse Caitlin hurriedly, repeating this to the girl in Punjabi, Hindi and Urdu. I'm not sure she understands, but she no longer looks so terrified. It's like she's seen my discomfort, and is worried for me instead. She nods, a slow, circular nod, and with this assent, her permission for me to go, it's like a release valve has whooshed open, and once I've nodded back and left her bed, I all but run from the ward, like something is chasing me.

Outside the heavy doors, I realise that people are looking at me, and I shorten my steps to a quick, determined-looking walk, as though I am Dr Reginald Fletcher, busy and important and faintly comical in my pitiful assertion of these facts. The bathroom is busy, it's always busy, and so I step into a supplies cupboard with confidence, as though it is an office, and shut the door behind me. I collapse on the floor, like a toy in a box, in a heap of my own bent bones and wet organs, among the labelled cartons of bandages and dressings, glass vials and syringes. I hold my head in my hands, and I cry.

I have sisters, too, and I miss them. Just as I miss my brother. They were everything to me, back home, I realise it more with each year of separation. I know I can't replace them and so I don't try. I don't seek out other anonymous Asians in the street in the way that William Godfrey greets every black man he comes across like a long-lost brother. He introduces me to them, and puts his arm around their shoulders, and flatters their nicely dressed lady friends, like they all arrived on the same boat and he's genuinely delighted to have bumped into them again, after such a long absence.

'You know a lot of people,' I remember saying to him outside the hospital one day. I was trying to make it sound like it wasn't a criticism, that I wasn't accusing or admiring him for his colourful behaviour. It seemed as exotic as the black-blue of his skin, the flame-red hair of the nurse in the corridor and the grass-green eyes of the nothing-if-not patriotic Northern Irishman in my bed.

'*Cha*, so they're strangers, man,' he replied, hearing the accusation anyway, and dismissing it, so I felt a little embarrassed for being so transparent. 'You never heard the saying? A stranger's just a friend you haven't met.'

'It must be nice to have so many friends,' I said.

William Godfrey snorted, as though he was about to tell me to fuck off, but instead he just laughed, and clapped me so hard on the back with his powerful hand that I fell forward a step. 'It is, Jamal Kamal. It is.'

I don't believe him. I nod to another Asian man if he nods to me, and if he speaks to me I'm polite, and nothing more. If he calls me brother, I'll call him Mr if I know his surname, or sir if I don't. If he addresses me in Punjabi, or Hindi, or Urdu, I'll reply in English. Besides, the Pakistanis in London are a proud, prejudiced and pretentious lot; they meet in social clubs, in other people's houses, not on the street. I've never joined the clubs; it would be like leaving Lahore to brick myself into exactly the same box I left, with a swarm of dark-suited and collar-studded spies reporting back home on what I was up to, and my funding would be cut off and I'd be sent back to Pakistan in shame. I'd finish my training on the cheap, and end up as the junior colleague to my brother-in-law, Nasim, who'd order me around like his flunky, before flouncing home, his withered ass in the car that was a wedding present from my father, and fucking my sister on the furniture.

And how I miss my sisters. My poor sisters, abandoned to my mother and to marriage. Mae has been married for a few years now, with a daughter I haven't yet met, and Lana is about to be married, in a few short days. Winter weddings are popular in the Punjab. I haven't really met another Asian woman here in London; they're wives and mothers, they stay at home, they move in cars to the houses and flats of other wives and mothers. They occasionally shop in Harrods, buying leather goods and soaps and scents, or take tea in Claridges. They have daughters who are sought after by the young men from home, for their British accents and British passports.

But this young girl isn't a Mae, or a Lana, and she isn't one of the wealthy daughters of an industrialist or landowner. She's not even one of the others that my mother wouldn't acknowledge back in Lahore: poor relatives sponsored by wealthier patrons with new, merchant money, sent off to London to run corner shops and chip shops and work in restaurants and live above the shop if they're lucky, and sleep in the basement with a crowd if they're not, like immigrants in the bowels of a sweaty boat. Over here, she's not someone's daughter or sister, but someone's servant or slave. One of the nameless ones, the child-maids sold in the cities who are abused in a household, and then passed on when evidence of the abuse grows in their bellies, tossed out like the rubbish, or tossed down the stairs.

The girl doesn't even speak the language of the strange, cold country she's been landed in. Her helpless baby concealed under adolescent muscle in her skinny body, her poor invaded territory. She is nothing like Mae and Lana, but she is my sister too. This is what happens to girls with no one to protect them; it happens there, and it happens here. It will keep happening, until it is made right. It's like Mae and Lana sent her over to me, as a message. Remember me, I will remember you. A girl's body in a bed.

I haven't seen my sisters in all the years since I left for college. They expect me back for Lana's wedding, but I haven't yet told them that I'm not going. I'm too much of a coward. I'm afraid of what they'll ask me, and what I might say; I'm afraid that when I go there, back to the place I once belonged, I'll weep in their arms and never return. I'll fail the test on the first attempt. I didn't need to go back for Mae's wedding; it was hurriedly organised to take place before Sulaman and I went overseas.

Our mother's curious sickness, which began shortly after the announcement of the marriage, evaporated as suddenly as it came upon her, like a vampire in the sunlight. She had spent months indoors, hiding her pinched morning face and stinking breath, with her skinny shoulders and bony arms swathed in fabric to conceal them. But just before the wedding, she shrugged off the shalwars and the shawls, a damp butterfly crawling out of a chrysalis, and shook out her glittering wings. She showed a new pleasing roundness to her bosom, and the apples of her cheeks. Her skin glowed, her uncovered hair shone and swung, and she painted a careful mask with her pots, powders and paints, with bleach, rouge and kohl, which seemed even more unbreakable and intimidating than before. She held herself proudly, as though she were wearing a medal, or guarding a secret, and looked at all of us with pity for having neither. Our father, who had been besottedly solicitous during her illness, faded again, and seemed afraid to touch her.

Our mother made up for lost time, and began interfering with Mae's wedding planning. From showing no interest at all in the preparations, for a full three days beforehand she supervised a frantic preparation of sweets and fried and baked goods, in our own kitchen rather than risk the purchase from shops and restaurants with unclean kitchens and God-knows-what contaminated cooks. Mae was forced to go around town to cancel the orders she had made, and Lana and I went with her. We took a rickshaw, as our father was teaching Sulaman to drive before he went to America.

'I knew she was faking it,' said Mae, fuming in the heat. 'Did you see how smug she was last night, with Nasim's family? That idiot uncle of his. "But which is the mother, which is the daughter? Either one of you could be the bride!" I wonder how many times we'll be hearing that one during the wedding.'

'You're the one who keeps repeating it,' said Lana, yawning a little. Her hair was still in schoolgirl plaits, as though she was deliberately trying to look younger, because Mae was trying to look older.

'Provincial idiots,' muttered Mae.

'Charming,' I said, flattening out Lana's skirt, which was flying up over her ankles in the rush of the traffic. She was wearing high white socks, which kept sliding down her skinny calves. She was leaning against me, with her chin and elbow digging into me a bit thoughtlessly. I didn't mind.

'I meant Nasim's family. They're the provincial idiots,' said Mae. 'They're just lucky they come from old money.' She tossed her head, and a flash of light came off her glossy hair; the rickshaw screeched to a halt behind an open truck with hens in cages, and the drivers in the stalled traffic all stared at her like she was singing on a stage. I realised that she'd never be as lovely as she was at this moment, that after this it would all be wasted.

'They're your provincial idiots now,' I said. 'They're your family, whether you like it or not.' I tried to say it like a joke, with humour, but I just felt a terrible sadness.

'I like them,' said Lana.

'Oh, it speaks,' said Mae. 'Why did you come out, Baby? You could suck your split ends at home just as easily. Don't you dare do that during the wedding. Not your hair, not your thumb. Don't you dare show me up.'

'I like them,' repeated Lana, simply ignoring Mae, so serenely it seemed that Mae was the one showing herself up. 'When you have babies, can I come and live with you, to take care of them?'

There was so much to say to this. Mae and babies. Lana leaving home. The hanging question of their unfinished schooling. We all knew that Mae wouldn't need Lana to look after her babies; she'd have servants, our old ayah, her kindly mother-in-law. Lana looked at Mae directly, across me, with puddle-wide eyes, hiding nothing. It was the candid request of a child. It was a plea from a frightened girl.

'Yes,' snapped Mae, hiding her affection behind her hair, as she swung it round like a curtain, and looked the other way, into the admiring crowd. 'Yes, of course you can.' She didn't call Lana Baby again, but it seemed as though she might; she was so afraid of showing any softness, or weakness. It seemed the more scornful she became, the more attractive she got. Even the rickshaw driver, his tough legs bearing down with the hard work of getting his fragile tin contraption moving again, his colourful canopy fluttering above our heads, turned to see what everyone was staring at.

'Uncle, look at the road,' Mae said sharply, making it clear to everyone who was in charge, even though I was older, and I was the boy.

'Yes, daughter,' said the man humbly, his forearms blackened to charcoal by the sun, cracked and hairless. Mae had something of our mother's power to command respect. It was to do with her refusal to use a balanced tone; she was either curt, or charming. People didn't like her, as they liked Lana, but they wanted to win her over, or were already won over themselves. It wasn't something I could ever do. I was uniformly friendly, with remarkably little effect; whenever I used a pleasant manner with a rickshaw driver, he would reply in an unpleasant manner. If I made a suggestion to a driver, with a smile, he'd tell me to mind my own business, without a smile.

Lana didn't say anything for a while, but grinned, looking at the other side of the road, before she suddenly squealed and threw herself across me to hug Mae, with the rickshaw dangerously swinging on a bend. She looked like she might fall out of the other side, but Mae caught her and held on to her like she was her own child, and I don't think I'd ever seen such extravagant, public affection between them. It was only just dawning on me that, like Sulaman and I, they'd shared a room as long as they could remember, and they were about to be split up too, into strange and separate lives.

'*Uff*,' I joked to Lana like an elderly in-law, embarrassed by how I was caught between them. 'You'll do yourself an injury throwing yourself around like that.'

They ignored me, and as the rickshaw turned another corner, Lana fell back across my lap and into her seat beside me, landing on her rump as neatly as a Soviet gymnast landing on the ground. Her elbow was digging into me again, more than before, and I realised that she and Mae were still holding hands across me. In a locked grip tight enough to stop someone falling from a building edge. Mae looked at me briefly, as though daring me to say something, and then stared fixedly ahead, barking another direction to the driver, whose dusty heels were pounding rhythmically up the street.

I did the only thing I could, and put my own palm over their two hands. Mae's was typically cool, even in the heat, which seemed wrong somehow, like she was ill. And Lana's was damp and slightly sticky, as though she'd been shuffling sweets in her pockets. My sisters. Spirited and sweet. Clever and kind. They didn't object, and it felt that we were taken back to a childish complicity that we had never really possessed; as though we had once built forts in the garden, solved local mysteries, and met in a secret clubhouse in the spread branches of the trees. It was as though all this had happened, and I remembered it clearly now, but had briefly forgotten.

I wished Sulaman was with us to share this moment, but Abbu had him busy with his driving lessons. He had suddenly got the idea from our new in-laws that a driving licence was needed to go to college in America. He didn't seem to think it would be a problem for me; he said London was like Lahore, and you could walk or get taxis anywhere. Truthfully, I think he just didn't trust me with the car. I was Jakie the Joker, and wasn't considered anywhere near as responsible as my brother, Serious Sulaman, Sulaman the Wise. I wondered if Sulaman sitting with us would make it feel more real, the brief feeling that we were all in this together, our hands joined and wrapped over each other.

Although, to be brutally practical, if Sulaman had come, we'd have had to take two rickshaws, and the girls would have been in one in bonnets, and the boys in the other in black hats, like a wagon trail in a Western. Separated again, like we were in our rooms, at our table, on the sofa. Another pragmatic partition.

The rickshaw pulled up outside Kwalitee's Sweets and Treats, and Mae remembered what she had been complaining about, and looked at us both as though we had deliberately been distracting her.

'I knew she was faking it,' she repeated, saying it with accusation. 'She's been flopping around the house wrapped up in shawls like a wet bit of linen, or lying flat on her back upstairs too weak to call for tea, with Daddy scurrying around her like she's some dying queen, servicing her every need,' she said, and stopped as I suppressed a snort of laughter. 'What?' she snapped.

'Nothing,' I said, realising that she hadn't been making a joke about their marital relations after all. On reflection, it seemed unlikely that she would.

'And then it's the week of the wedding, and suddenly she turns up for the relatives looking like a movie star!' Mae fumed, swatting the air in front of her with a swift and passionate gesture, snapping her palm shut as though she'd caught and crushed an imaginary insect. I could hear the slice of the air, and the smack of skin, even in the bustle of the honking, screeching street, as though she had briefly stopped time with her fury.

She stormed ahead of us towards the store, the assistant at Kwalitee's running out to open the door for her. Lana shrugged her shoulders, and trailed after her, looking back at me apologetically.

I realised the rickshaw driver was waiting for me to pay him, impatiently mopping his brow with the trailing end of his headcloth, wrapped to keep the sweat out of his eyes. He relaxed so obviously when Mae was out of sight that it was almost comic. He breathed out, pulling a rolled paper cigarette from behind his ear, tucked safely into the cloth, and playing with it. He didn't ask for a light, and he put it close to his lips but didn't suck on it. Perhaps it was his only one, and he liked to look cosmopolitan. Perhaps he had the dregs of a bottle of Johnnie Walker at home, which he poured into a dirty tumbler every evening, swirling it around, sitting and looking at it, breathing the fumes, before pouring it back into his bottle. I gave him a note, and waved away his fumbling for change, offering him one of my cigarettes. Our parents disapproved of me smoking, and only tolerated me doing it because everyone else used cigarettes as a manly sort of social currency. The way that ladies carried clean handkerchiefs to offer when needed. He took the cigarette, and placed it carefully behind his ear, keeping his old one in his hand.

'Your wife, sir?' he asked, as though aware that accepting the gift required something more from him. His face was closed as he said it.

'My sister,' I replied, and then, because it seemed unfair to leave out Lana, outshone so obviously by Mae, like a daylight moon, I added, 'My sisters.'

'*Haw, hai,*' said the rickshaw driver, considering this, and seeming less offended. Perhaps he had found it unthinkable that someone like Mae would be married to someone like me. He nodded, and with a regretful look at his old cigarette, replaced it in his headcloth with my new one, and put his dusty feet back on the pedals, his exposed heels cracked as the leather of his sandals. He gave a final glance towards the shop, where Mae could now be seen arguing in an animated way with the assistant, and I wondered if all pretty, scornful girls were considered quite so dreadfully attractive. His face softened as he watched her, and I realised that he wasn't so very much older than us. I wondered if he'd dream of her tonight, while he toyed with his cigarette, with his empty whisky-scented glass, in his hammock bed.

'Are you going home?' I asked suddenly. I don't know why.

'Home!' he barked, so offended as to be amused. 'I am already home,' and he jerked his head back towards the rickshaw, before pushing off, with a slow pumping of his heels, which quickly became more rhythmic and fluid. Without our dead weight in the back, he was flying down the street, avoiding errant children and animals and buses, like a sparrow flitting through trees. I realised how arrogant my assumptions had been. That he had a hammock, a glass, a bottle, a home. That he had possessions, and a place on the planet to call his own. He slept in his rickshaw. And if it rained, he slept beneath it, on the street. I realised with a slight start that I was looking at him with envy rather than pity.

'Jakie,' called Lana, and I turned back to see her framed in the shop doorway, slightly smiling at me, as though she had been watching me, watching him, and understood.

Lana tipped her head back towards the shop, where Mae appeared to have finished her negotiations. The shop manager had been called out of his lunchtime break, still wearing his sleeping dhoti, although he had put on a shirt for propriety's sake, hastily buttoned, and askew across the shoulders. The assistant was flopped back in her chair like a pile of laundry, exhausted and forgotten; her arms were matchstick thin, and her face was pinched, as though she hadn't been well fed, which was strange for someone who worked in a sweetshop. The trays of sweets, rose, pistachio and almond, glittered with dewy condensation, and Lana had either been given or purchased a jalebi, sticky and luminous orange, and was sucking the syrup from a stiff swirl of pastry like a straw. She had the same heavenly look on her face she had when she was scratching a persistent itch, or an insect bite; as though she was doing something naughty that felt nice.

I went to go into the shop, and she stepped back obligingly to let me through, but then we were both pushed out of the way by Mae, who scattered us into the street like skittles. '*Khuda hafiz*,' she called back over her shoulder. She said goodbye cheerfully, clearly feeling she could be generous, as she had won, while the owner shut the door firmly, as firmly as though he were shutting the shop altogether. His face was heavily pockmarked, and reproachful, as we saw him tenderly help the young woman up from the chair and lead her out, his shoulders hunched with tension, emphasised by the wrinkled fabric of his shirt.

Lana and I glanced at each other; we had both seen the same thing. It was exactly what our father had done with our mother during her illness. After every mealtime, after every stressful reproval of a servant.

Mae seemed pleased with herself. 'My God, if I have to hear some-one's sorry life story about how we've ruined them by cancelling the order, we'll be doing this until dinner,' she said, not really complaining, but reliving her triumph. 'He told me that they're having another baby, as though that's got anything to do with anything. Like it was an excuse.'

'You only need an excuse if you've done something wrong,' I said impatiently. 'It's not their fault. You're the one cancelling the order.'

'Only because Mummy's crawled out of her cave and is making me,' retorted Mae.

'Oh,' said Lana, with sudden understanding, looking back into the shop, at the space the shopkeeper and his young wife had left behind the counter. 'She's having a baby.' She looked at us and explained, 'I just thought he'd been making her sick. Because he liked looking after her.'

'She's probably made herself sick. Stuffing her face with leftover burfi and rasgullas all day behind the counter,' commented Mae.

'Not her,' said Lana, with a little frustration; it wasn't like Mae to be so dense. 'I meant Her.' The emphasis was unmistakable; Her with a capital H. She Who Must Be Obeyed. We'd all read the book, and had passed it around at home as secretly as though it was a political pamphlet or a pornographic drawing.

'Oh,' said Mae, looking as foolish as I felt. It wasn't her usual look, and she suddenly seemed nine years younger. That manipulated little girl in the stiff frilled dress all over again, sitting in her mother's shadow.

'Oh,' I said, and I knew that Lana was right. I couldn't believe we'd been that stupid. Morning sickness, for almost exactly three months. And then a sudden bloom, and plump cheeks and inflating bosom. It would be the size of a prawn. Or perhaps a large bee, buzzing in Amma's belly like a bug in a trap. Lana felt sorry for us, and snapped her remaining jalebi in two, handing the sticky pieces to us. I put the pastry straight in my mouth like medicine, and it was only as I bit down on it that I realised my mouth had still been hanging open with the 'O' of surprise.

'Why wouldn't she tell us?' I eventually said, after I'd chewed and swallowed. Mae had eaten hers too, and was wiping the syrup from her hands. The sugar did make me feel better; I felt my stomach settling. I gave Lana an appreciative look; she always took care of us, in the most practical ways.

'Other girls' mummies don't announce anything until after the first few months,' replied Lana. 'So that they're sure. In case it dies early, or doesn't grow.'

'She's waiting for the wedding to announce it,' realised Mae, with righteous fury replacing her shocked surprise. And as she said it, we all knew with certainty that it was true. That Mae would be upstaged and outmanoeuvred at her own wedding. And she would be able to do nothing but smile sweetly, with her eyes fluttering to the floor, while Amma worked the room and accepted congratulations on her own behalf: a new baby, a blessing.

'Oh, the bitch!' shrieked Mae, followed by a stream of Punjabi swearing that she must have heard from the servants. She stamped her foot in impotent rage, but her sparkling slippers made little impression in the dust outside the shop. She turned her fury on me. 'When's the rickshaw driver coming back? How long does it take for someone to find a place to pee?'

'He's not coming back,' I said eventually, after an embarrassed pause. 'I just paid him and let him go.'

'You idiot,' said Mae, and she looked like she wanted to slap me. She looked like she wanted to cry. 'You stupid *boy*.'

'You idiot-stupid-boy,' repeated Lana, but with affection rather than exasperation. And she went to the roadside edge to wait to see if another might be passing. She shook her head at us, and then went up towards the main road, with Mae and me following behind. The beating sun in Lahore had the same effect on rickshaws that rain in London has on taxis; they were all taken.

We were forced to wait for another, and stood in the slim shadow of the street light. The shade was no wider than a single body, so the three of us had to line up neatly, one behind another, like a row of tulips in a formal garden. First Lana, then Mae, then the idiot boy. Sweet and spirited and spineless. Clear and cloudy and craven. My sisters and me. I was such a coward; I was abandoning them, to my mother, and to marriage, while I ran away. I wasn't brave enough to stay. While we watched out for another rickshaw, I realised how I loved them, and how I had already let them go.

I wipe my face, and go back to the ward, and to the curtained bed. The girl is sitting up, in her baggy clothes. Her feet are bare, and boot-polish brown against the white of the sheets. I don't know how to explain her predicament to her; she clearly isn't much more than a child. She must be someone's daughter, someone's responsibility, but we can't afford to wait for her people to turn up and claim her. She doesn't have that much time. I sit beside her, at her level, so she doesn't have to look up to me, and take her blank chart, asking her questions with a combination of the languages I know and dumb play-acting. When I ask for her name, she looks blank, and so I point to myself.

'My name is Jamal Kamal Saddeq.' I try adding in Bangla, '*Amar naam* Jamal Kamal Saddeq.' And then I point to her, feeling foolish as the nurse returns. I think Nurse Caitlin will laugh at me, for my Me-Tarzan-You-Jane gesturing, and shake her head ruefully with another

'It's all Greek to me.' I wonder if she'll call over a small audience to watch the show, like feeding time at the zoo.

But then the girl places her hand on her chest and replies, 'Asha.' Her name is Asha. I breathe with relief at this small connection that we've made.

Nurse Caitlin beams at us both, and nods with encouragement. I carry on, play-acting my age, and Asha, breathing in and out with difficulty, shows me her age with her hands. She holds up a single palm, and counts up with her thumb along the creases inside each of her fingers. She stops on her little finger, at thirteen.

'You have the patience of a saint, Doctor,' says Nurse Caitlin, and then looks embarrassed, as she is perhaps unsure whether people like us have saints, and whether she's offended me. I ask her to see if she can find a translator for the girl, as I have finally worked out that Asha is speaking Malayalam, and that she understands some English even though she doesn't seem happy about speaking it.

I tell Asha that she isn't ill, but that she's having a baby, and although it is a shock to her, she understands that perfectly. She is older than she looks, but far too young to have consented to what has happened to her. She doesn't cry. She nods and closes her eyes, biting hard on her lip. I want to tell her not to worry. I think if I say, 'You'll be fine,' she'll believe me, because I'm a man in a white coat. I think if I say, 'Don't worry,' she might not worry, because she's used to doing what she's told.

I sit there, not because I have to, but because I'm unable to move. Another sister. Someone's daughter. I failed Mae and Lana, and I can't make that right. But they are there, and this girl is here. They are in their world, but Asha is in mine. She is breathing heavily, moaning with the waves of shuddering pain, embarrassed by the noise she is making, by the lack of control she has over her body, which is no longer hers, and has been taken over by someone else. Her abuser's child. Her child, too.

I realise that there is a chance for me, Jakie the Joker, Jamal Kamal, drinker and fornicator, doctor and faggot, coward and abandoner, to make amends. There is a chance for me, here in this clean white room, to make something right.

Chapter Seven

Sully

I'VE NEVER GONE TO THE DANCES AND MIXERS IN TOWN OR ON CAMPUS, although I've seen groups of Vassar girls in wraps, and boys in white jeans piled up six to a car, driving noisily to and from them, hooting their horns in celebration. Laughing and grinning like idiots. I watched from the outside, walking by on the street, looking on, looking in. Feeling dignified, and older. I am older, after all.

But then, after having never spoken about it before, Radhika looks at me across a table and says, 'We can finally go to the dance together.' As though it is something we'd have done all along, if we weren't so terribly busy. Like long-married people who don't have sex because of their schedules. I wonder briefly if she is talking in some understood code; if going to a dance, after months of dating, means we can sleep together. I walk her home all the time now, and often end up staying, but always fully dressed, just like the first time. And I don't put my hands anywhere that might not be expected while we kiss, and do my best to hide my erection. She falls asleep in my arms, and I watch her for a little while, before falling asleep myself. I memorise her face, looking for imperfections that make her more real, and attainable: a pore in the dip of the chin, pinprick-sized, the double fold in her left eyelid, the seasonal dryness of her lips. She's light enough to pluck from the bed like a flower, to swing like a doll, and carry home. My footsteps would sink just slightly deeper into the snow with her than they would without her.

I'm glad that there is no one to witness how I study her in her sleep, as obsessively as a collector, pinning a specimen to a board. I feel a yearning, for what I already have. For the woman I have already held, kissed, whose breath I have drawn deeply into my own body; she seems so far away. She never actually asks me to stay, before she falls asleep. I'm not sure whose feelings she is trying to save. I'm not sure if it's more polite to stay, or to go; practically, when it's a weekday, I have to go, as I have to get washed and changed. I don't know what she thinks when she wakes up without me, in her own world. I hope my absence carries the same weight as my presence, that it makes her think about us. She knows that I've made up my mind about her, but I know she hasn't yet made up her mind about me.

It is Gloria in the canteen who starts the talk about the dance. I've noticed that since we started going steady, the holding hands in public, carrying her heavy folders, paying for our trays together type of dating, people look at us differently. As though we were on the fringes before, just on the edges of people's thoughts, but are now suddenly accepted and acceptable. Before, we were both fairly aloof, involved in our work, and the effect this had on Radhika's colleagues was that they were fascinated by her, and constantly trying to draw her out. With me, it meant that they thought I was just introverted and strange, and left me alone. I mean, they knew that I was introverted and strange. I was. I am. But now, people smile and nod to me, and to us, and if I pass former colleagues, the Jims and the Dannys, they greet me like I'm some long-lost army buddy, promising that we'll have to get together for a beer. Something we never did the whole time we worked together.

'People like me better because I'm with you,' I comment to her, pushing her tray along with mine. She selects an apple, a plain roll and some thin, splashy-looking stew; I think there are hobos lining up outside church soup kitchens who eat better than she does.

'They feel more comfortable. There's something disconcerting about a good-looking guy sitting alone all the time,' she says. She squeezes my hand like she's made a joke. 'People like me better, too,' she adds. 'The girls are always asking me about my *boyfriend*, way too coyly, like you haven't got a name.'

'Well, it's a complicated name,' I say, paying for our meals.

'They say it with a French accent,' she adds, pulling out some cash, and dropping it on my tray as casually as a tip. She never fiddles with change, and looks annoyed with me when I do. I've stopped having the argument with her about me paying for stuff. Whenever I do manage to buy her something, it's as though she's done me a favour by letting me, and that I'm the one in her debt. I don't mind, it still feels like a victory, albeit a small one. 'Monsieur Sully Saddeq, to rhyme with Toulouse-Lautrec. Or Quebec. I guess they think you're French. I said you were from Lahore, and they didn't know what to say. They acted like I was making an inappropriate joke, until they realised I was serious. They said, really, there's a town called Lahore? La Whore? Good golly. Honest to goodness. Heavens to Betsy.'

She chooses a table, and I follow. I can't get used to the smiling and the nodding. 'Do you think they're just thinking, what a relief, the brown people have found each other?'

'You're not brown,' she says, starting with her apple instead of the stew. The stew will be cold by the time she's finished the apple, and she probably won't even eat that.

'I wish I was,' I say.

'I know,' she replies simply. 'It would be easier, wouldn't it? Instead of having to explain it all the time. I wish there was a badge that says Made in India. I guess it's why Christians wear crosses.'

Gloria waves to Radhika from across the canteen, her silver and bone crucifix glinting on her buttoned-up cardigan. She comes over with another girl, a tall blonde who isn't the same one who was there on Christmas Eve with the letter-sweater boy, but who might as well be. She has the same blonde ponytail drawn back from the same smooth forehead. She is slim, but she looks much more capable than Radhika; like she could ride a horse, change a tyre, and shoot a gun. Her name's Kitty, and I guess she must have been skiing, as she has a tan that makes her almost as bronzed as Gloria. There are lots of other tables free, but Gloria's obviously decided to sit with us. 'Mind if we join you?' says Kitty, as Gloria doesn't even bother to ask, but then neither of them wait for a reply, and carry on the animated conversation they've been having.

'There'll be a good crowd tonight,' says Gloria, toying with honey-dipped chicken, which leaves her fingers oily. She sees me looking, and dabs at her hand and mouth with a napkin, unembarrassed, then carries on. 'Most of us have finished marking the undergrad work. And you've already got that submission in, haven't you, Radhika?' she adds. 'The one for your research funding.'

'Mm-hmm,' says Radhika non-committally, eating her apple neatly around the core, tapping it briskly to shake out the pips.

'Well, you've got no excuse then,' says Gloria. 'You've been working on that for ever.' She seems to have a better knowledge of Radhika's work than I do. Radhika doesn't really talk shop; I suppose work on cadavers with cancer doesn't lend itself to dinner table discussions. I don't talk too much about my work either, and I have no idea what I would say if she asked me about it. Would I bore her with my research, or scare her away with my theories? 'That's settled. You're coming with us.'

'I can't,' says Radhika sweetly. 'I'm already going.'

'Well, who with?' asks Gloria, looking a bit offended.

'With Sully, of course.'

'Is that right?' says Kitty, delighted. 'I didn't know you danced.' It takes me a moment to realise that she's talking to me.

'I guess I could learn,' I say, and Gloria and Kitty exchange a significant look with each other.

'You're welcome,' Gloria says to Radhika, when they leave, as though they have done her a favour. Manipulated me into being a better boyfriend.

'Well, that's great, isn't it? We can finally go to the dance together,' she says, loudly enough for them to hear her, and then she laughs.

'Do you really want to go?' I ask her. This is when I'm thinking that it might be a code. That going to a dance means going to bed. I'm hopeful, but it doesn't last for long.

'No, of course not,' she says. 'I just didn't want to go with Gloria and Kitty, and be stuck making small talk next to a punch bowl, and have to fend them off in the ladies' while they badger me to fix up my hair.'

'I want to go,' I say. I'm not sure if I'm saying it just because she doesn't, like a child who's been refused a specific toy, or because I want to test her, to see if she'll do something for me that she wouldn't do for herself.

'But you don't dance,' she says, amused rather than annoyed.

'I could learn,' I repeat.

'Fine,' she says. 'Pick me up at eight thirty.' She leans over and kisses me goodbye, and collects her tray.

'Leave it,' I say. 'I'll stack it with mine.' She smiles, and I watch her walk away, reinventing her again and again in my head. I think I like to watch her walk away as much as I like to see her walk towards me. I like to think about her after I've been with her, as much as the moments when she's there. Her absence really is as big as her presence.

I see that people are still watching us, and I'm not sure why our little romance has suddenly become the object of such interest. I ignore them, and look at her tray. Her stew is barely touched, and half her roll is left. I pick it up, and dip it in the stew, eating it slowly, methodically, and imagine kissing her with reckless passion, instead of tender serious-ness of intent. I want to marry her, and she knows I want to marry her, and that does frighten her a little, for all she denies it. If I behaved as though I just wanted to screw her, have her for a night or a week or two rather than a lifetime, I suspect she'd let me in. She has at least eaten the apple, and she hasn't wasted a bit. She started at the remains of the flower, and has eaten her way up the core, leaving just the stalk, and the pips.

The pips are scattered on a white paper plate like frozen teardrops. For some reason they serve fruit on paper, not ceramic. Perhaps to take away afterwards, like the chips served in newspaper in London, which Jakie has written to me about. Fried food seems to be all he lives on. He writes less now, and I wonder whether he's found someone, like I have. Which means that there's much more to write about, but much less he wants to share. The dark pips on the white paper disc look clinical, mystical – like they're meant to mean something. Tea leaves swirled in a cup. There are exactly seven of them, shining brown, with sharp ends. I pick up the thin stalk of Radhika's apple, and hold it in my lips, like a toothpick, or a cigarette. A carpenter with a coffin nail, a seamstress with a pin. From her lips to my lips. I pick up one of the pips too, and crunch down on it, feeling the sharp cyanide sting, like bittersweet almond. Enough of these things could kill you. Pretty poison pips, on a paper plate. I could eat them all. I wonder if this is how I look at Radhika as she walks away, like she is beautiful, and bitter. With hunger, like she's dinner.

I'm far too early as I pull up outside Radhika's building. I see her there, letting herself in, rather than coming out to meet me, a paper bag of groceries in her arms. She doesn't see me, and it's only when I call her name and jump out of the car that she turns, and realises I'm there. I'm feeling a bit foolish, like a boy in a movie calling for a girl to go to a dance, expecting her to giggle and hop lightly into the front seat, laughing as the breeze ruffles her shining hair.

Radhika looks at me, up and down, as though amused, even though I'm not dressed very differently than usual. I'm wearing a jacket, though. The same one I wear to official events on campus. It's warm, rather than stylish. I hope that it looks like the jacket of someone who doesn't care about fashion. I've brought her flowers, not on a romantic impulse, but because I think that's what I'm meant to do. They're not particularly lovely, or expensive, but they were the most normal-looking flowers I could find. Flowers that might have been gathered lightly from the woods, instead of primped and fussed with curling bits of stuff and silly hothoused faces to them. It occurs to me that she might think I simply did gather them from the woods, but can't decide if this is a good or a bad thing. I walk down her steps and hand them to her, pecking her on the lips. She holds herself stiffly, still smiling in a slightly superior way, unwilling to give up her mask of amusement, as though it offers her some protection.

'I didn't know you drove,' she says, as she opens her front door and walks in, holding it open for me with her shoulder. She nods back towards the mud-coloured Cadillac I've parked in the street, and adds, 'I didn't know you had a car.'

'It's not mine,' I say. 'I borrowed it.' She seems impressed with this unexpected initiative, but I feel I have to manage her expectations. I add quickly, 'I'm not a very good driver. I learnt in Pakistan. You get a licence just for turning up and paying the fee.'

She smiles with approval. 'That's honest. Most guys like to say they're great drivers. Like most girls like to say they're great cooks.'

She dumps the groceries awkwardly, and some of her fruit rolls out of the top. I realise that I should have waited for her to put her bag down before giving her the flowers, which she is still holding, and which are now making it difficult for her to get her coat off. I think about taking them back from her, but she efficiently rips off the bottom three inches of paper around them, crushes the ends of the stems, and puts them in a tooth glass by the sink. Ripped, crushed, stored away, in much less than a minute. I can imagine her grace as she moves around her lab, test tubes in her hand, sliding specimens under the microscope, the economy of her movements, nothing extra or out of place.

'Thanks,' she says, as she takes off her coat. 'They're pretty.'

'Oh, they're nothing special,' I say, and I guess I'm trying to imply that she's the one who's special, but I'm not sure it comes across. It still feels like we're playing a scene: a boy and girl going to a first dance together. I don't know how I'm going to stand there with a smile and do this all evening, when all I want to do tonight is bring her back to this room, and put my arms around her and kiss her until we fall asleep in our clothes. And I'm annoyed about the flowers, because they are pretty but nothing special, and she has already dealt with them like a household chore and left them on the side. Done and dismissed. A little bit of me would have liked her to play her part better, to bury her nose in them, exclaim about their loveliness, and make a fuss of them.

'You okay?' she asks, and she's pulling clothes out from her wardrobe, so I realise that she's not already dressed for the dance. Of course she's not. She's just got back from picking up groceries, and I'm ridiculously early. Thoughtlessly early, in fact, although nothing she has said or done has implied this.

'I'm nervous,' I admit. 'You know I don't dance.'

'I do,' she says, and she looks at me steadily, a dress and nylon stockings on her arm, heels with straps hanging by a finger. She's waiting for me to say I don't want to go, and I can tell that she doesn't mind either way, but it feels like a dare that I don't want to lose. So I don't say anything, and just smile and shrug.

'It's okay. We'll be fine,' she says, when she realises that I'm not going to back out. She opens the wardrobe door, like a screen, and starts to get dressed behind it. I don't realise what she's doing until I see her toss her cardigan on the bed.

'Shall I wait in the car?' I say in a slight panic.

'It's cold out,' she says practically. 'There's no need.' Her skirt rustles down, and I realise that she is just in a slip, and it's not as though she's naked, but I can't bear that she's undressing in the same room as me, and isn't expecting me to do anything about it but sit there.

'I'm going to the bathroom,' I say, getting up and walking swiftly to the door.

'Okay,' she says, and she is sitting on the bed, pulling on stockings as I shut it behind me. I really do go to the bathroom, and hold my dick like an idiot. I should have crossed the room, and held her, and kissed her, and told her we weren't going to the dance. I should have told her that it was cold out, and that there was no need.

She's ready by the time I go back downstairs to her basement room. I knock on the door, and push it open to see her considering herself in front of the mirror that hangs inside her wardrobe door. She looks lovely, and I'm appalled. She's wearing a dress that falls to the knee, and pale shoes with a heel, and her hair is twisted up with pins. She's showing her arms, and her calves, and her neck, and it's turned her silhouette strange and desirable. I can imagine strangers whistling at this girl, and that makes me feel deeply uncomfortable.

I thought I was special, because only I could see how heavenly Radhika really was, under her plain clothes and her lab coat. Now I realise that I'm not special at all, and that everyone else knew it, herself included. I'm so shocked that it takes me a while to notice the details: that the dress is blue silk, with a flowered pattern around the hem, that the shoes are silver grey, that her calves have the slight gleam of nude nylon stockings, and her face has been dusted with powder, and made up with pale lipstick. I look at Radhika looking at herself, and she has that same amused, slightly critical look that she had when I jumped out of the car, as though she didn't like what she saw, but was too polite to say so. She seems to think that the girl in the mirror is showing off, or thinks too much of herself.

'That was quick,' I say, because it was. My mother took whole afternoons getting ready for events, but Radhika has done it in the time it took me to pee, wash my hands, and briefly press my forehead against the cold mirror, resisting the urge to bang some bravery into it. If only I had stayed in the room while she pushed her feet into her shoes, slipped the dress over her head, and put her hair up into that chic style, dusting her face with a brush as neatly as she would a specimen for inspection. I look at the flowers in the sink, the floppy stems already stiffening back into place, as though she'd cured them briefly with her swift treatment, and wish I hadn't given her something that was both pretty and dead.

'You look nice,' I say, having finally located the appropriate formula, the right line for the occasion.

'Thank you, Sully, but I look like a bloody clown,' she says.

She turns and shrugs, and the silk material shifts over her breasts. She is so shining I don't know where to look: at the hand smoothing the fabric over her hips, at the exposed skin between her ear and neck, at the pale painted lips. I certainly can't meet her eyes, and I find myself looking somewhere above, at the clear space between her eyebrows.

'I know it's just uniform,' she says. 'Like wearing a white coat in a lab.' She picks up a wrap, a silver-grey shawl that matches the shoes, and adds, 'But if I didn't wear it, everyone would be looking at me and wondering why. Like a bag lady at a ball. Last time I went to one of these things, I didn't bother, and all the girls hustled me into the bathroom, and did my hair and make-up, gave me their accessories like some street-side Cinderella.' She looks at me frankly. 'I just don't want to stand out.'

'If you didn't want to stand out, you shouldn't have worn that dress,' I say gallantly.

'You hate it,' she says shrewdly.

'I hate it,' I agree. 'I don't like anyone else seeing how magical you are.'

She laughs, like I've made a joke. 'So let's go, Sully. Let's have a magical evening.'

In the car, Radhika doesn't comment on my lousy driving. I get caught behind a bus, and don't know if I can overtake it, until a honking Chevy stuffed with noisy young undergraduates roars up behind me and does it first.

'I like cars,' says Radhika. 'I like the fact that you're not outside, or inside. I could live in a car, I think, and just drive from state to state.'

'How would you live?' I ask, although it seems to me that she is just speaking to herself, and isn't expecting me to reply. 'Dance for money at fairs like a gypsy? You said you could dance.' I'm joking, but she suddenly relaxes her body like liquid against the seat and turns to me, a movement so graceful that I believe she can dance after all.

'I'd rob banks and gas stations,' she says. Her tone is so matter-of-fact that I believe this too. 'I'd need a getaway driver, though, to keep the engine running.' As if on cue, the engine comically stalls, and the gears lock and then grind while I try to get the damn thing moving again, and she laughs. After a moment, I laugh too. It doesn't hurt. The city walls don't come tumbling down after all.

We get to the dance after dinner, and it's busy enough that we can slip in unnoticed. Radhika is right, and I was wrong; in her dress, she's just another clown at the circus, and another brightly coloured bird in the flock. Gloria and Kitty nod to her, and seem satisfied that she's made an effort. I get punch, and can't really hear her over the noise, and eventually realise that she's going to teach me how to dance.

'Not here,' she says. 'The best place to hide is in a crowd,' and she pulls me into the centre of the dance floor. It's a quick dance, and I realise that no one else can dance much better than me, and that no one is paying us any attention as we swing around to the music like kids in a playground. When a slow song comes on, everyone just moves closer, and sways. That's when I realise what a good dancer Radhika really is, the lightness on her feet as though she doesn't quite touch the ground.

'Are you having fun?' she asks, as though it's a serious question and there's a right and wrong answer.

'Mm-hmm,' I breathe into her hair, the non-committal way I learned from her. I almost step on her feet, as she is so much closer to me now, and she laughs, and steps on both of mine instead. She stays there, her toes tipped on mine, keeping balance perfectly as I move. Her hands are around my neck, her face tilted up towards me. It feels that we're invisible, alone in the room, a spotlight on us, and that everyone else has faded to shadow and dissolved to shimmering motes of dust in the air. I want to kiss her, but feel that if I do, it will break the spell.

'Shall we get some air?' she says, pressing herself closer. She wants me to kiss her too. For a wonderful moment, I know that she wants what I want. I dance her to the door, with her still on my feet, and feel as mannered and debonair as Fred Astaire.

'Is here okay?' I ask, when we are just outside, other couples milling around us.

'There's better,' she says, her arms still around my neck, nodding towards the borrowed car, parked across the street. I pick her up, and carry her across the road to the car. It's as easy as I imagined, all those nights I've watched her in my arms; she doesn't object at all. We've hardly spoken to anyone during the whole dance, and now we are leaving.

'So, what shall we do now?' she asks, as I start the sputtering engine, and put the car into gear. And that's how I know that she doesn't want me to take her home. That our magical evening isn't over yet.

'Let's rob a bank,' I say, and drive through town, the lights sparkling around us.

I drove to Mae's wedding, back in Lahore. Not the bridal car, which was a cream Rolls-Royce, hired for the occasion, with a cream and gold livery for the driver that came with it. The ladies went in that car, with Mrs Kannon fussing about Mae and Lana's clothes, and Amma taking the front seat to herself, with imperious command, to avoid her golden sari in Banarasi silk from getting crushed. It had been her own wedding sari, and she shone like she was on fire. Mae's traditional scarlet silk, edged with intricate embroidery, looked almost dreary by comparison, like blood pulled from a vein. The sober sunset after our mother's high noon blaze. Amma's choice of outfit was as inappropriate as a Western mother-in-law wearing her own white wedding gown to a ceremony, but no one dared say anything. Our father had shrunk back into his old role, propped up on the pedestal Amma placed him on, like a puppet king, and no longer dared to speak for her.

I drove our usual car, with Abbu, Jakie, Nasim, our soon-to-be brother-in-law, and his younger brother, Salim, who seemed glum at the prospect of having missed out on Mae, and resigned to the fact that he would be matched up with Lana. If not our Lana, then someone like her – a suitable girl, nice enough but in no way extraordinary, in her looks, studies, or her way of tossing her hair or stamping her foot. Nasim was so excited that he was dripping with sweat, and he had been drinking to steady his nerves. There was a small bottle secured to the underside of his sleeve with a neat bandage, which made him sweat even more. It made me a little bit sick to think of him with Mae that night, when the festivities were over. I imagined him lacking in any gentle finesse, and grunting like a boar in a fight, like he did when he played tennis with Abbu. I hoped he'd just keep drinking until he passed out altogether, so that Mae could slip out of the flower-garlanded four-poster bed she'd be made to wait in, and go and sleep with her mother-in-law in safety.

Jakie had been thinking something similar, although with less apparent alarm. 'If he keeps sweating like that, he'll slide right off the sheets like a greased pig, and Mae'll fix a ring through his nose to lead him by,' he whispered to me. He seemed to think that Mae had the measure of Nasim, and was more than his match. Perhaps he felt he had to think that to reassure himself, and me; concealing his concern with comedy. Our father didn't seem perturbed at all for Mae; if anything, he was looking at Nasim with a sort of pity, as though about to give him a kindly warning. As though he had accidentally exposed himself at a meeting, with his shirt caught in his fly. Perhaps he had; his lust for his bride was barely concealed, and he risked making a public spectacle of himself.

After the ceremony, Mae sat with Nasim, more made up than a mannequin and weighed down with family jewellery. A particularly elaborate piece, a heavy gold chain with rubies, which hung from ear to nose, seemed to be giving her discomfort. I saw her watching the crowd, and her face turned to stone as our mother spun like gold thread around the guests.

The band from the hotel were playing sedate dinner jazz in the reception area, and children were running around and dancing there, holding hands and twirling in tight circles. Jakie and I had been sitting together watching them, while Lana was running the gauntlet of elderly aunties, who kept comparing her unfavourably to Mae, and asking her if she was ill, because she'd refused to wear make-up. Her one-colour face was clearly causing them distress, although at thirteen her refusal seemed justified. Everyone had always thought of Mae and Lana as being the same age, just as they thought of Jakie and myself. But Mae's extra year and a half suddenly crossed the bridge from being a child to a woman. I wondered if Lana had actually bound her fairly flat chest, to make it seem flat altogether. It seemed exactly the sort of thing she would quietly do, claiming it made her shalwar kameez hang more smoothly, if the ayah or anyone else noticed. She didn't want to be seen as the next ripe fruit from the tree waiting to be plucked. Still, the aunties did pluck at her, and pinch her cheeks from apparent affection, but really in order to get some painful colour to them, like country heroines in a Victorian novel waiting to see their admirer. Kind Mrs Kannon came over to us, and sent us to rescue her, saying that we should all help look after the younger children, who were running riot.

Lana didn't mind being put with the children, and took her nanny role seriously; she took care of the ones who were shy or left out. She even danced with a little cousin on her feet, spinning him round. She could actually dance, having had lessons after school with Mae; it was what the girls did, rather than get beaten by Basher to do their homework. Basher and his sisters hadn't been invited; since the elder girl had got into trouble, they were no longer considered fit for society. After a while, Jakie shrugged and joined in too; a little girl jumped on his feet, and he didn't seem to mind making a fool of himself.

There was a rustling of silk behind me, and it took me a moment to realise that my mother was standing there. She put her hand on my shoulder. A spidery claw, with nails filed and polished to drips of bright blood; her palm was so cold, it felt that it might sink through my flesh, like a knife through warm butter.

I sensed that people were watching her as she stood with her oldest child and watched her others dancing, and that was her intention: for them to see her as the loving mother of happy children. For everyone in the room to be aware of how good a mother she was, by the measure of our apparent happiness, by the measurable inch-width of our smiles. She seemed pleased that she had won everyone over, and asked me, with flirtatious and girlish charm that she had poured over the guests like syrup from a pot, if I was going to dance. She asked it in Punjabi, with calculation, as though aware that not everyone in the room would speak English as fluently as we did.

'Nah, Amma,' I said, replying in Punjabi automatically, before realising what I was doing. I switched back to English; speaking in Punjabi at the table used to get our knuckles rapped, or the back of our heads smacked, unless we were speaking to a servant. 'No, Mummy, I don't dance.'

'Go on,' she said girlishly, adding with a steel tone, 'Dance with your little friends.' I looked at her with confusion; apart from Lana and Jakie, none of the children were older than eleven or twelve. She couldn't possibly think that I was one of them. I was older than Mae, the daughter who had just been passed off to a doctor in marriage. 'Go play,' she said, smiling with her mouth, but not allowing it to touch her eyes, so they wouldn't wrinkle. Wire was twisted into her words, and I wondered what I could have possibly done to upset her. She smiled wider, as though showing me how, and with the whiteness of her teeth, I realised what it was. I hadn't been smiling, and she felt shown up by this; that I had been sour and staring from the edges, instead of joining in. I smiled back, awkwardly, like a cartoon, and when I reached the acceptable inch-width, she breathed out and relaxed.

'That's better,' she said. 'Now you look like the big brother of the bride.'

And then, as though to mitigate the damage that my sour staring had caused to the pretty tableau of the golden woman looking over her golden family, playing with her children as easily as children play with kittens and puppies, she pulled me over to the crowd to dance with her. She was aware of how attractive she looked, making her sullen teenager smile and dance, as though I, like everyone else, was a little bit in love with her, and no other girl would ever be good enough for me because of her. Mae's in-laws were right: she looked like the bride, and I wanted to die right there with the shame, at what people were thinking of me. I wanted to walk off the stage, and slam the door behind me. I could even see my father looking at me with a little envy, and I wondered if his wife had spent any time at all by his side.

'So handsome, Sulaman, like a prince,' called over Mrs Kannon, and I grinned weakly back. Other guests, the ladies-in-law, the elderly aunts, echoed her 'So handsome' back into the crowd, repeating it amongst themselves until it seemed that they were mimicking her, and mocking me.

I glanced across at my mother, who in her high heels was able to look me almost in the eye. I hadn't yet had my final growth spurt, which would see me gain five inches in the States in the next couple of years, and leave me taller than everyone in the family apart from Uncle Grewal, who we called Uncle Ghoul behind his back; his looming, silent presence made it easy for us to make fun of him. He was simple in the head, but his mother, wife and children cheerfully ignored this inconvenient fact. They managed the factory he had inherited, and wheeled him out for public occasions, letting him wander about, sit briefly with other groups, nod blankly to their polite greetings, and then move on. I could see him in the crowd now, half a head taller than the people around him. He was actually an attractive man, his hair thick and curling, his moustache neatly trimmed and oiled, and I suppose this was how he was able to make a good marriage. His in-laws had passed him on his photo and income alone, and hadn't taken the trouble to meet him.

My mother followed my gaze. 'Poor Grewal,' she said, and looked at me with cynical interest, as though wondering whether I thought that would be my fate. She fluttered a hand at my father, looking at him with melting adoration, as though she would love only to be with him, but her children demanded her attention. I thought of the child that we had all guessed was in her belly; her sari was draped more modestly than usual, revealing just her right arm, and the deep vee of her sari blouse at her back, the gold silk wrapped around her like liquid armour. I wondered how she was going to tell the guests, whether she was planning to make an announcement, or inform them one by one and let the news spread like flaming gossip around the room, until it was all anyone was talking about, and the guests all tingled and shivered like dew caught on her web.

Perhaps Amma was thinking the same thing, as she cupped her icy palm on the side of my face, taking her regretful leave of me to join our father. She would tell them now, I decided, with Abbu shining with sweaty pride at her side: one child married off, another on the way. His prowess established; the fact that he still fucked a fertile wife, and fathered children with her. I wondered who would protect the poor prawn in her belly, and whether Lana had already resigned herself to being a proxy mother long before Mae became one. It seemed obvious that Lana would be the one looking after the child while our mother fluttered off to social events and card games and brunches.

I stared at our mother, like everyone else, like the children, for whom she held the fascination of all pretty, shiny things, even in a roomful of glittering women, as she moved into a crowd of admirers. But then I saw her cry out and stumble before she reached our father, as though she had been knocked off her high heels by a clumsy guest greeting her too effusively. She laughed, and everyone smiled, relieved at her good humour, but then she cried out again, and we all saw why. Her sari was ruined, covered in a deep red stain, blooming through the gold as though someone had decided it should be dyed bridal scarlet after all, and had tipped a bowl of pomegranate punch into her lap.

Our mother clutched her stomach, clawing at the stain as though it was acid burning her, the cause rather than the result of her injury, and tumbled to the floor, crying out with pain. Our father ran to her, surprisingly quickly for a man who now gave the impression of being prosperously paunchy, as though all his tennis matches had been preparation for just this moment, racing urgently to his wife's side through a crowded room.

Lana and Jakie pushed past me, and ran towards Amma and Abbu, and I saw Mae yanking out the heavy ear-to-nose jewellery, leaving a bright spot of blood on her nostril and ear lobe, and going to join them too.

I realised that I was the only one who wasn't playing my part, and when Amma looked up at them, I ran as well, snapping like an elastic that had been pulled taut and then released. I realised that she'd never forgive me for that moment of hesitation, although everyone else would think it was shock. The ticking seconds I had spent staring from the edges, watching other people go to help her. And when I reached her, the smell of iron in the air was overpowering. My father had swept her up in his arms. He was suddenly a man again, tender and strong.

'She's pregnant, and might be miscarrying,' he said to Nasim, authoritative and professional, the doctor with the patient. 'We'll take her to the hospital.'

I thought he meant that Nasim would drive, even though he had been drinking so much he couldn't stand straight. Nasim thought this too, and blustered, 'Yes, bhai, of course.'

'Not you,' my father snapped at him. Like they were back at the office, and he was berating Nasim for his stupidity. Perhaps Abbu realised how he sounded, even at this moment, and softened his voice. 'You are the bridegroom. Your place is with my daughter.' He nodded to me. 'Sulaman, get the driver.'

'He left,' said Lana, openly chewing the ends of her hair, which had been pulled high in a ponytail, and then braided and decorated with flowers. 'He had to take Zaida Nanu home.'

'Sulaman,' said my father again, and I nodded, and went with him. Lana followed us without being asked, collecting a clean tablecloth, dipping napkins in jugs of iced water, and taking a full one with her. I had no idea how she knew to do all of this.

'Lana, don't you ...' said Mae plaintively, finally finding her voice, as though she really wanted to say, 'Don't you dare show me up,' because it was what she had been hoping to say all night, and hadn't yet had a chance. As though she wanted to go back to the time when the worst thing that could happen at her wedding was her sister sucking her braid. We had all shown her up. Amma by bleeding, Abbu by picking her up

154

and leaving, Lana for knowing how to help, and me for driving them away. Jakie, who danced with children on his toes, had done nothing wrong. He put his arms around Mae as she started crying.

'Don't you . . .' repeated Mae, sobbing as she watched our bleeding mother carried out of her wedding, wrapped in cloth of gold; unable to say anything more.

'It'll be all right,' said Lana, not ignoring her this time, and we all tried to believe it. She spoke with such calm serenity, it seemed she couldn't possibly be lying.

I turned back and saw Mae clinging to Jakie as she cried, and her new husband standing apart from them awkwardly, the intruder in our family, swaying at the side.

When we got to where the cars had been parked, there was only the rented Rolls-Royce, which I had no idea how to drive. The driver had obviously taken our great-aunt home in our usual car, leaving the cream bridal car for the wedding party. The gearstick was different, and I didn't even know how to switch on the lights. Lana spread the thick tablecloth on the back seat for Amma, and put a cool napkin on her forehead. After watching me fiddle for a moment, she reached forward and switched the headlights on for me. She had travelled to the wedding in this car, and had watched our elderly driver struggle in the same way.

I set off cautiously, the car jerking until I reached third gear, and street children chased after us, surprised that there was no one else following a wedding car, no tooting and laughing, no gifts or coins thrown from the windows to celebrate. I pushed the beast of the car through the town, swearing and occasionally stalling, the engine complaining with my mistreatment, my foot pushing on the gas until it felt that I was kicking it uphill. Our mother was still conscious, but unable to speak; she just cried out with an occasional spasming pain, and she seemed to be losing a lot of blood. When we arrived at the hospital, our father carried her out, with Lana following. I stood there, unsure if I was meant to wait with the car as our driver would have done, or go with them.

Abbu saw my hesitation, and called over his shoulder as he hurried through the entrance, 'Go back, Sulaman. Tell them to carry on. Represent the family. Pray for your mother.'

When they were out of sight, I sat on the bonnet of the expensive car, as the inside stank of blood. My father would later be forced to purchase this car, having ruined it for rentals, and after it had been cleaned, he would give it as a wedding gift to Nasim and Mae, not wanting to keep it in our own driveway. I knew that I would do all of the simple things that my father had requested. Four orders, neatly delivered. I knew that I would snap my heels together, and put my hand to my forehead, as obedient and mechanical as a soldier on parade, with weapons spinning all around me in formation, and one pointed at my back, a bayonet screwed in place. Left, right, forward, turn.

Go back. Carry on. Represent. Pray.

'I'm sorry,' I said to the damaged squib that was pushing its way out of my mother's womb. That couldn't wait to be expelled from the cage of her bloody body and into a clean white cloth, in a clean white room. An almost-creature with a heart that pumped, ears that had just begun to hear, and hands that had just begun to reach for the cord that held it floating in that black and red space. My brother, or my sister. Tumbling out into the world, to be disposed of with hospital waste.

'I'm sorry,' I said again, out loud. 'I didn't mean it.'

I had thought, when I was dancing with my mother, that her baby would be better off dead.

Radhika has her hand on my thigh as I drive, as though she does it all the time. I try to drive one-handed, so I can cover her hand with mine. Just in case, for protection as much as affection. I'm not sure whether she means to put her hand higher, and I'm afraid that if she does, even by accident, I'll pop like a balloon, and crash the car. And be found by the emergency services with a damp patch in my trousers. I hold her hand in place, and it's like we've shaken hands on a deal, and that this is finally happening. Whatever this is.

She begins to direct me out of town, and I wonder if she really does mean to get on the freeway and drive until morning, until we're out of gas and we wake up as strangers on the run in a strange town, getting coffee in our fancy outfits and shiny shoes, like refugees from a prom. But then I find that we're on a country road, on a low hill with a view over town, where the street lamps are twinkling like dew on grass. There's a line of cars parked up, some with couples necking in the front, some where the couples have disappeared altogether, with just a fluttering of fabric from the back giving them away.

'You're kidding,' I say flatly, pulling up but leaving the engine running, for a quick getaway. I think on balance I'd rather rob a bank than break into her here, like this. I look at her, and she seems amused. 'Thank God, you are kidding,' I say with relief.

She leans over and switches off the ignition, as though it's her car, not mine, and she knows it better. She switches off the lights, and I try not to think of Lana switching them on for me, that other night in the other borrowed car. This is a brown Cadillac, not a cream Rolls-Royce, I tell myself, and everything is different. Radhika and her dress shine like moonlight, silver and grey, dappled with the shadows from the trees.

'What's wrong?' she says. 'It's an important rite of passage, isn't it? And it's meant to be fun. Losing your virginity in a parked car.'

She leans across and kisses me, while I try and decide what she means, whether she's thinks I'm a virgin, or is declaring that she is one herself. It never occurred to me that she would be; she's older than me, and always one step ahead. Even when we were dancing. Her dress rustles, and I wish it wasn't silk, and didn't have that deep vee in the back.

'What's wrong?' she asks again, but she doesn't wait for a reply, and kisses me more insistently. I begin to kiss her back, forgetting myself in her entirely, in the sweetness of her fruit-punch-scented breath. I pull her into my arms, until she is sitting on my lap, and then I just feel terribly confused. I'm thinking of the woman who was fucking the man on the armchair in our sitting room, and of Amma bleeding in a sari in the back seat of a car, and Radhika's dress keeps rustling like it's made of Banarasi silk, and it may well be, as it has that thick, expensive sheen, and I push her breathlessly away.

'Sorry,' I say inadequately, unsure how to explain myself, breathing too heavily.

'For God's sake, Sully,' she says, annoyed now, rather than amused. I feel certain that I've failed again, failed to meet what is expected of me. I'm meant to be the besotted boy who can't believe his good luck, grateful that he's about to get into his girlfriend's pants after one dance together. I'm meant to be staring at her with wonder, or kissing her with contempt for being suddenly so easy. Not teenage-terrified and adolescent-awkward at what might be under her dress, as though she might really be covered in scales, or have snakes sprouting from her scalp. She's no monster or myth; she is slight and small, and there should be nothing to be afraid of. But it feels as though that little hand of hers could pull out a human heart with one firm tug. I know for a fact that she's done it before, on dead bodies who had lived longer than me.

'It's the dress,' I say, and realise I have to add something more, before she thinks that I'm just saying again how I don't like it. 'I wish you weren't wearing that dress,' I try to explain, only working out how forward I must sound a moment afterwards. I just mean that I wish she were wearing her normal clothes, that make her feel and sound like her.

She either misunderstands me altogether, or understands me completely, because she says, 'If it bothers you, I can take it off.'

With an elegant gesture, she sweeps her hand behind her back and tugs the zip down smoothly, before pulling the dress over her head so she is wearing just the slip underneath. She undresses as simply as she dressed behind her wardrobe door, pushing off her shoes, and letting down her twist of hair, dropping the pins neatly on the passenger seat, where they gleam like sharp little weapons. She pulls my handkerchief from my pocket, and looking straight at me, wipes off the remains of her lipstick, and the powder from her nose. She gives that half-smile, her expression somewhere between sympathy and determination, and I realise how much she now wants this to happen, although I have no idea why, and I lunge for her with a sort of desperation that I hope she interprets as passion, and kiss her with the same steely resolve. With hunger. As though I've been starved of her flesh all my life, and now can't get enough.

She tugs open my shirt too, sliding her hand over my heart, and I wish we could keep undressing, stripping off not just dresses and shirts and shoes, but skin and flesh and nerves, until we are just soft, pulsing organs in the cages of our bones, and we can't be separated.

I don't just want her for now. I want her for ever.

I don't just want to fuck her. I want to everything with her.

And she should be scared of me, because I'm scared of myself, but she doesn't know anything of this, while her tongue slides over my gums, and she sits neatly across my lap, with my erection growing hard under her thighs.

'Well, it seems you're a real boy after all,' she says softly, laughing a little at her own joke as my breathing becomes laboured, and I'm biting softly at her skin, with my hands spread across her small breasts. 'My friends had this joke that you were just some beautiful robot that Professor Milgram and his boys cooked up in the lab for his experiment.'

'So, that's a little offensive,' I say, and it's impossible to ignore how she's sliding across my lap, and the painful tightness of my trousers. 'Do you want to go in the back?'

It's like a dare. We've obviously gone far enough tonight; we're half dressed, and halfway around the pitch, somewhere between second and third. I'm waiting for her to say no, and I'll be relieved when she does. I'll let her dress in the car while I run behind a tree or a bush and wank explosively, so I can walk back without discomfort. Then I'll drive her home. Kiss her good night, and tell her how pretty she was. Keep calm. Carry on.

'I think we should,' she says seriously, as though it's another clinical experiment that's been proposed. And now I'm thinking that the last thing I want is to be in the back of a car with Radhika, because I can't get my mother bleeding in the back seat out of my head, and if Radhika's really a virgin, she might bleed too, and the scent of iron mixed with car leather would make me puke, and that would be the end of us.

And I'm also thinking that if I man up and have the guts to screw Radhika, here and now, then she'll have to stay with me. And if I get her pregnant, then she'll never be able to leave, and I'll have trapped her with me, and can slide a ring on her finger, manacle her to me. I groan while I push her hair back from her face, sucking the rose-water scent from her throat, pressing my face between her breasts, and imagine myself sliding into her, invading and infecting her. An injection that stops other men getting near her. A vaccination. And I pull her hard against me, down on me, and inhale heavily, embarrassed by the depth of my breath, my helplessness. She's clinging on to me, as though we're going to keep going, and do it right here and now, and not even pause for the moment it might take to clamber into the back. And then I stop altogether, still breathing heavily, and prove to her that I'm not a real boy after all.

'I think I should take you home, Radhika,' I say.

I park outside her house. She is dressed, but her hair is still down around her face, and she hands me back the jacket she has been wearing to keep warm. It feels too final, and I tell her to keep it. 'You'll need it to get to the door,' I say, as it is already obvious that she's not asking me in.

'Thank you,' she says, a bit too formally, and I turn my hands slightly on the steering wheel, as I can see that she's looking at them. My knuckles are bleeding, from when I got out and punched the tree while she dressed. I headbutted it too, but the bruise is under my hair, and not too obvious. I still don't know why I did that. I wanked first, and I smelt of spunk, and blood, and wood. And so I wiped my hands on the damp grass, and cleaned myself up with the handkerchief that smelt of Radhika's powder, and then I smelt of grass and talc.

Radhika kisses me abruptly on the cheek, through the window, as dutifully as though I were an elderly aunt, or a simple uncle, and then turns to go. She starts down her steps, but then turns back.

'Look, I'm sorry, Sully,' she says.

'God, what are you sorry about?' I blurt out. 'I'm the one who should be sorry.'

'No,' she says firmly. 'It was a stupid idea, going up there. I didn't know how to tell you, and I thought we should, before I did. But I should just have told you straight. And I will. I mean I am.'

'Tell me what?' I ask. In the moment between my asking, and her answer, everything spins through my mind. She's met someone else, she's married, she's pregnant, she's dying . . .

'I'm leaving,' she says.

'Okay,' I say carefully. She's leaving. I understand now. She's going away, and it was meant to have been a farewell fuck. A promise to keep us both faithful while she's away. A promise to be good. I guess it must happen a lot on campus, before the long vacations. Before symposiums and semesters out of town. 'So, for how long?'

'For good. My funding's coming through. From that tobacco company. I'm going to be working in New York, out of Barnard.' I don't say anything, as I realise that she took me to a dance, and tried to fuck me, because she's dumping me. She's going away, and leaving me behind. Maybe not tonight, or tomorrow. But soon.

'I'm sorry, Sully,' she says, again. Sorry, Sully. Sorry, Sully. When you say it enough times, it sounds like a joke. When I don't say anything else, she walks down her stairs, and as she opens her door, I drive off.

I drop the car off at the faculty of the colleague who let me borrow it. I walk back to my room, and unthinkingly knock on the door. Someone, a guy who lives further down the corridor, who wears glasses and has a beard and a necktie, looks at me a bit strangely.

'I guess I'm not in,' I say to him. He sees my knuckles too, and thinks I've got into a fight. And I guess he's surprised, because I look like the last guy to ever get into a fight. At least, the last guy after him.

'Are you okay, man?' he says to me. Not because he wants to, but because he feels he has to. He has a pile of books under his arm, and a pile of paperwork under the other. He has a small bag of groceries, which he is gripping awkwardly, holding the paper bag by the rolled-up end. He'll have to put all that stuff down to get his keys out, but he doesn't mind. He has his evening planned, and he doesn't want to have to deal with me.

'I'm great,' I say. I'm not smiling. If I smile, in measurable inches, I'll look like a lunatic. I'll look like a cartoon.

I turn away from him, walk back down the long corridor, and carry on outside into the street. It has started to rain. Of course it's started to rain. Nothing dramatic, just a light, persistent drizzle that seeps into my shirt, and makes it stick to my skin. I start walking fast, and then running, and I'm not sure where I'm going to, until I'm running down the empty street where Radhika lives, past the spot where I waited to watch her walk away, and spring down her steps, banging on the basement door. I don't call her name, I don't know why. Perhaps I don't want to get her in trouble with her landlady, or the other tenants. Perhaps I'm worried she won't open the door if she knows it's me. I bang louder, like I'm the police breaking down the door, and she opens it, looking mussed up and bleary-eyed, like she's just got into bed, or just got out of it.

'Sully?' she starts to say, but I just push inside the door, and shove it shut with my back while I take her in my arms.

I tumble to the floor with her, my mouth on her mouth, her eyes, her hairline, down her neck and towards her small breasts, and with my weight on her, I can't tell if she's holding on to me, or pushing me away. My damp shirt is soaking through her nightdress, making her colder, and warming me up, and I feel us both shivering, and her nipples and the tiny bumps on her arms stand to attention, and in the dim light of the room, I pull down her nightdress to kiss her breasts, and to lick her glistening arms, and she's not saying no.

I yank my trousers down, my underpants, and push my hands up her nightdress, feeling her soft buttocks against the rasping carpet and the hard floor beneath, and she's still not saying no. I guess she feels she owes me this.

'Say you do too,' I say to her. 'Say yes.'

I think I'm begging. Perhaps she thinks I'm worried that I'm raping her, and it's true that what we're doing has as little sense or tenderness as a plane crash, and it feels like we're both going to be victims, and are just screwing to feel alive before we die, but she says it anyway.

'I do too,' she says. 'Yes,' she says, and I sink into her, and bang her against the carpet and the floorboards, with her legs locked around me, until all the strange craziness leaches out of me, and the feeling that we are just smashed human remains dissolves, and we fit back together again, and become ourselves, her and me, with me just sliding into her until her breath shudders and catches too, and I care about whether I've hurt her, and whether she's been able to enjoy it at all.

I gather her up, and take her to the bed, rubbing her back and shoulders where I pinned her to the floor. I pull off my wet shirt, and trousers, and shoes, and socks, and get in under the covers with her, so I'm naked, but she's not, and I smooth down her nightdress, as she is still shivering.

She doesn't seem surprised, and for once she doesn't seem amused. It's as though she always knew that I was capable of this; of passion and violence. Of need. I asked her to reply, I do too, and I asked her to say yes without telling her what she was answering. I was too scared to tell her first. She assented out of kindness, and she's looking at me kindly now, as she presses herself against me, and gives me what she knows I need most. Warmth and consent. I think she knows what it cost me to come back here tonight; I don't think she's yet worked out the cost to herself.

I place my face on her heart, and hear it beating. Her hand pushes through my hair, and rests on my neck, her arm around me draws me back until I am lying on her once more, and I'm held in place in the breakable world by the cradle of her, and her ribbons of breath and threads of blood around me. My heavy burden supported by such a slight body. I'm saved. I want her to say it again, and I know that if she does I'll explode in her once more like a confetti-filled balloon, like a gun going off in my mouth and signalling the end of one life and the beginning of another with a joyous flash of white light. Say it again. Please. Say it again.

I do too. Yes.

The shape of Radhika's lips as she forms the words like smoke rings, the mist in the cold air of the room. The answers that I've begged from her, the questions I've been too afraid to ask. This isn't an experiment, and this isn't a clean white room. It's real, it's cluttered and dark. I'm not alone here. I'm naked in her arms, and her thin nightdress is like a damp second skin against me. I'm not scared any more. She's given me her answer. She says it again.

I do too. Yes.

'I love you,' I say. 'Marry me.'

Chapter Eight

Jakie

THE YOUNG GIRL, ASHA, IS IN THE MATERNITY WARD NOW; SHE'S contracting every three minutes, and spasming with the pain, but with a first birth, she'll have some hours to go yet. She only complains with the contractions, and not in between. She only cries once, when she doesn't make it to the toilet in time to void her bowels; a contraction seizes her while she is clinging to the sink, and trying to lower herself over the seat. It's the shame that causes her to weep, not so much the indignity, but the mess that she made. The midwife tells me she was trying to squat, rather than sit, which makes me think that she hasn't been in England very long.

Nurse Caitlin arrives with the translator, a dapper Bengali academic with a specialism in Tagore and subcontinental poetry; he advises that Malayalam is his fifth language, and the one in which he is least well versed. Even so, the girl is relieved to be heard, and rattles off a long and passionate account of I don't know what, in between the contractions. The translator looks on, and nods, and doesn't disguise his distaste for the bloody situation, for the sweat and ooze and breathy vapour escaping from her as she chatters and puffs. The girl has been left fairly alone during her labour, with the midwife checking in on her occasionally, as it seems that the baby tunnelling through her is small for dates, but quite healthy. I think of all the white-clad nurses who fluttered around my mother like angels after her dead baby was born on Mae's wedding day. I never saw him, my almost-brother, just three and a half months in the womb, before he swam out of it. Lana told me that he was perfectly formed, and would have been neat enough to keep in a pickle jar. I imagine him there, bobbing and disconnected, like a lily plucked from its stem; his foetus face full of fierce concentration, his oversized head full of silent, unwitnessed thoughts.

The translator has told us that he can't stay long, so I wait in the room during their interview. I know it's not my job to think about this sort of thing; I'm just meant to diagnose and repair the damaged goods, I don't provide the after-sales service or chase up the paperwork to return the merchandise. But while she is talking, I start thinking about it all the same, about the people who might be able to help her. I'm trying to be sensible rather than emotional, to find a practical solution, just as Lana would. Sweets to settle a queasy stomach, an iced compress for a fevered brow, a cotton cloth to mop up blood.

The young girl is probably in this situation because of abuse, or rape. Her family or employers will either take her back and help her raise the child, or take her back without the child, or send them both away. And if they take her back, someone will have to keep an eye on her at home, and check that she wasn't being abused there; and if they don't take her back, someone else will have to take her on. Probably the sort of place where the unwed mothers go with their babies. But she needs to go to school, too. If she can't or won't keep the baby with her, it will have to go to an orphanage, and be put up for adoption. It occurs to me that she might be in England illegally, smuggled in on a boat, and in that case, we might not find her people at all. They might refuse to claim her, to avoid being deported.

It all seems too knotted and confusing, and I wish Lana were here. Lana's gift is for making complicated things seem simple. I'm encouraged that despite the disgusted reaction of the translator, the girl doesn't seem scared. The translator is holding a lavender-scented handkerchief to his nose while the girl speaks, as though to avoid infection with her disease, just in case poverty and pregnancy were things you could catch. She finishes telling him her story with a rapid-fire delivery; she speaks with the stoicism of an old village woman, hunched over a clay pot and providing for her family. As though the painful situation isn't really anything to do with her, but just the way things are, and needs to be accepted. I wonder if the habit of accepting things, without tears or anger, has been taught to her since birth. I wonder if this is what has led her here.

'So what did she say?' I ask the translator, nodding and smiling at the girl, to show that she did well.

'Nothing,' he says firmly.

Nurse Caitlin and I look at each other, with a rare moment of complicity. We're wearing the staff uniforms, and despite the fact that she is white, and the translator is browner than me, it is us against him. Nurse Caitlin starts to speak, but stifles it back, remembering that I am the doctor, and it's my job to do the talking; that she's not meant to speak unless spoken to, and certainly not if the ward sister is within earshot.

'That was a lot of nothing,' I say, adding, 'sir' to soften it, as I don't want to be rude, and lose the only translator who would come out on Christmas Day. He already seems to be regretting it. I imagine him as a sort of priest for his five-tongued community, summoned by the non-English-speaking residents to soften the blows dealt between the entrances and the exits: a child is born, and the doctors need speaking to; a man dies, and the undertaker needs to be summoned. The specific niceties of culture communicated with sympathy; our funny little ways explained and understood.

'Indeed,' he says agreeably, as though it is the girl, rather than him, who is being obstinate. She is watching him closely, and she's understood our exchange, apart from the 'indeed'. But the way he nods and smiles, beneath his neat Hitler moustache, says enough. The moustache is as tidily trimmed and well groomed as a favoured pet, and I'm half waiting for it to crawl off his upper lip like a furred insect, or for some bird of prey to come screeching through the window and rip it off his face as a snack.

'In-bloody-deed!' explodes Nurse Caitlin, while I am still thinking of what to say, waiting for that screeching bird to save me. 'That little girl's going to have a baby! We need to get in touch with her parents. We need to know her medical history. We need to thrash the bloody sod who did this to her. In-bloody-deed!'

I'm proud of Nurse Caitlin, for saying what I was too cowardly to come out with, but she's aware of what she's done, and claps her hand over her mouth, looking around to see who might have heard.

I can't stop myself smiling at her, and realise that she's started smiling too, underneath her hand. I pull myself together, and address the translator, who has pulled out his lavender-scented handkerchief again, flapping the floral scent in front of his nose and looking like more of a queer than Frank or I ever will.

'Sir, a moment in private, please?' I say. 'If I may trouble you. If you would be so kind. I'd be terribly grateful.'

He seems to appreciate the overelaborate politeness. It's something I learned during my training, that a few snippets of local vocabulary helps to put people at ease. He's one of those Oxford-educated Indians who speak a pure, pretentious English that they don't even use on the BBC any more. He nods stiffly, and follows me, and doesn't acknowledge Asha or Nurse Caitlin as he leaves the bedside. I know that he's hoping he'll never see either of them ever again.

We go into an empty room in the maternity ward, with a single chair for a pregnant patient to sit while a midwife or nurse takes her blood pressure, before she weighs her on the oversized scales, stands her against the height chart on the door in her stockinged feet, and ticks the boxes on her notes. He looks at me suspiciously, as though I have deliberately chosen a room with a single chair as a trap, when in fact it was simply the first place we came across on the long corridor. 'Do sit down, sir,' I say. 'I don't mind standing. I'm used to it.'

Again he seems pleased, and as he sits, he looks more comfortable. He is a man who does his work sitting down, at a desk. I'm not tall, and standing gives me a brief sense of seniority. Leaning against the shallow counter lined with tidy trays of instruments and sterile dressings, I can look down on him, and see his shining bald patch underneath the neatly combed-over and pomaded hair. I resist the urge to polish it with my sleeve.

'Would you be able to give me the young lady's address?' I ask, having finally worked out the most critical blank on her chart. 'And then we won't need to trouble you any more. We can send someone round to get in touch with her people, and take it from there. It's the paperwork, you see. We can't avoid the paperwork.'

I'm pleased at how clever I am. I think I have worked him out, that he appreciates paperwork over people. That he is happiest alone in a musty library, translating flowing Bengali and Urdu script into flowery English, and that the scent of dry parchment is the closest to heaven he comes. More heavenly than the sweet scent of a beautiful woman, or the salted sunshine scent of a beautiful man. That he is dead inside, and if you rattle him, all that will fall out, like coins from a slot, are worn-out phrases like withered petals.

'I'm sorry, old chap,' says the translator. 'She didn't say.' He says it politely, but his face is bricked up like a wall.

I resist the urge to rail at him like Nurse Caitlin, and wait, hoping that the uncomfortable silence that follows will encourage him to fill it. That my inability to come up with anything persuasive will somehow be interpreted as authoritative menace. But he's comfortable with the silence, and briefly shuts his eyes, as though enjoying it. He steeples his hands before his chest, palms apart and bringing the tips together, from little fingers to thumbs, as though in time to a swinging metronome, do-re-mi-fa-sol. He does it again, do-re-mi-fa-sol.

'So,' he says eventually, opening his eyes as a wheelchair rolls past in the corridor, a nurse chatting casually to the patient being rolled back to her ward, 'I believe my work is done. Good day, Dr Saddeq.'

'But the paperwork,' I say helplessly as he stands up. I unintentionally block the narrow doorway as I step ahead of him. I think that's what makes him suddenly lose control.

'*Kuttar bacha, shorer bacha,*' he shouts at me, his voice echoing in the room with a deeply righteous anger that takes me utterly by surprise. 'The blazes with your paperwork! You just want to send that unfortunate child back to the beasts that did this to her.'

I am too stunned to respond, and realise that just as Nurse Caitlin told him off, he has told me off. That just as I thought I had the measure of him, he thinks he has the measure of me. He thinks that I'm one of those crisp coconut doctors, white to my thin, liquid core under my thin brown shell. That I'm the one who cares about paperwork rather than people, and that stamping and signing them out of this place is the closest I get to heaven.

I feel a desperate urge to confide in him, to tell him that I have sisters too, that I'm in love with a fellow called Frank, and that I'm a doctor because that's what my parents paid for me to become. I'm almost certain that he just called me a bastard son of a dog or possibly a pig. Maybe both. I'm just a son of a bitch to him. A beast.

'You can't call them beasts,' I try to argue, implying that he's the one being bigoted. 'They're people. What about her parents, and her family? They have a right to know what's happened to her. And if they're responsible, we could prosecute them.'

'You don't know these people,' the translator says. 'They're animals.

They don't belong in a civilised country.' His look is eloquent, as though I am one of them, not one of us. And then he sees how miserable I look, and how confused, and he softens slightly as he says, 'It's like you really didn't know.'

And then I realise that I'm not one of us, or them, or anyone. That I'm quite on my own. I have misdiagnosed him, as a bigot and a snob, and he has mistranslated me, as an officious outsider. Our respective professions have failed us, and we are just two brown men in a foreign country, both speaking a foreign language and unable to understand one another at all.

'Good day, Dr Saddeq,' he says again. He makes a point of enunciating my name with careful correctness. I shift over to the side, standing against the height chart like a criminal, so that he can pass.

I walk back to the ward, and see Nurse Caitlin in the corridor. She turns her back to the wall, as though politely waiting for me to pass too, but in fact she is waiting to speak to me. She's dressed as though she's already left the hospital, in a green coat with a pointed fur collar, and her luminous hair has been released from her cap and hastily teased back up. Her powdered skin up close has that faintly translucent look that some redheads have, which makes her seem slightly fragile, without her starched white armour and cape. She's put on eyeliner, too. She's clearly off duty now, and I wonder why she's still here.

'Did you have any luck with him, Doctor?' she asks.

'He didn't tell me a thing,' I admit. She looks surprised, and I suppose it is a surprising failure, that he'd refuse to help me. I find myself filling the brief silence that follows, as though seeking her approval, or at least her understanding. 'He seems to think that she'd be in danger at home. He didn't want us contacting her people.'

'Ah, well that's something to go on, at least,' she says. 'It's good of you to have tried. Most doctors here wouldn't have given a little girl like that the time of day.'

I wait for her to move on, and wonder if she's waiting for me to move on first, as a matter of hospital etiquette. A trolley rolls down the corridor, with a nurse and a doctor marching smartly beside it, and she backs up closer to the wall, and pulls me with her, as though I had been in their way and hadn't noticed.

'I'm off my shift now,' she says. I nod; that much is obvious. 'The midwives are keeping an eye on the girl,' she adds, and that much is obvious too.

'I'm on until the morning,' I say.

'That's too bad,' she says. 'Another time,' and in the briefly empty corridor, she smiles at me so brilliantly that I am utterly disarmed, and grin back at her.

I have only just realised that 'I'm off my shift' is code for an invitation. It's not quite as obvious as telling someone what hotel room you're in, or suggesting a drink, and so the subtlety was lost on me. I realise how close we are still standing, quite unnecessarily, and in the grey and white corridor, she looks just like Christmas Day should, with her green coat, and snowy skin, and red hair. Holly in the frost.

And I think to myself that she's a truly pretty girl, and would it matter so much if I kissed her, and lost myself briefly in another life, where I am a doctor married to a nurse, and we have a litter of lovely little children, with nut-brown hair, and cream-caramel skin? It feels that I just have to lean in, tip my head forward, and then I'd belong, and I'd no longer be with the beasts, or the bigots, or the faggots, and I wonder if she'd look up at me with this sort of admiration if she knew the slightest thing about me. She thinks I'm brave, and that I'm good, and it doesn't help me at all that she looks like Frank's little sister.

'Merry Christmas, Jakie,' she says to me eventually, slightly embarrassed by my inaction, and I step back, and let her go. I watch her walk up the corridor with a genuine regret, and when she turns, and sees me watching, she smiles. I think she feels relieved that she hasn't made a fool of herself; that I was a little bit interested, even if I didn't kiss her.

I go and tell the midwife who is looking after Asha that we can't contact her family, for the meantime. I think about Frank, with the regulars in the King's Head, and wonder if he's got bored or drunk enough to move on somewhere like The Huntsman, to pick up yet another bloke, and take him home. Unwrapping a stranger in his lodgings, like a Christmas present to himself. I haven't got him anything yet; I don't know what you're meant to give a lapsed Catholic at Christmas. I suppose it's possible he's with someone else right now, and it gives me a dull sort of pain. Nothing like the acute physical pains that Asha is feeling, but at least hers will be over in a few hours; at least her pains are counting down.

I feel an odd sort of nostalgia for the days when I didn't care about anyone, and used to do what Frank still does. I would show strangers the room number on my heavy key fob in hotels, or suggest a drink in the bar, and then we'd go somewhere else swiftly on the pretext of a slash or a smoke. Hotel rooms, the toilets, the back alleys. It was less seedy than it sounds. It was more like a sport, a wholesome physical activity. It was like fishing, and seeing who would bite; it was like hunting, either stalking a quarry or waiting to see if he would come to you. And finally the wrestling, and the race, him against you, to see who would win, and who'd get there first. There would be no hard feelings afterwards; there would be a slap on the back, a punch on the shoulder, and a have-a-nice-life. I never went home with anyone except Frank, and never brought anyone else home either. I wonder what he would think if I brought another girl home instead; a Caitlin, as a wife; an Asha, as a daughter.

At 8 a.m. the next day, Nurse Caitlin is waiting on the steps as I come out of the hospital. She is pulling out a cigarette, and I pat my pockets until I find a light for her.

'I'm not on until nine, Jakie,' she says. 'Would you like to get a cup of tea?' I know how difficult it must have been for her, to wait for me and ask this, to call me Jakie rather than Dr Saddeq, and so I agree. I look around guiltily, as though Frank might be watching, like he used to watch me with William Godfrey before they became friends, and then I remember that he flirts outrageously with women all the time. The only thing he'd find suspicious is my twitching behaviour. We go to the Lyons tea shop near the hospital, and I buy us a pot of Earl Grey, and get her a sticky bun.

'I shouldn't,' she giggles a bit guiltily.

'Well, you don't look like you need to watch your weight,' I say. I mean it. She has a curvy, luscious figure, and twin dimples when she smiles. She probably looks like Marilyn Monroe in a bathing suit.

'I know *that*,' she says, unoffended. 'I mean the expense. The extravagance. Buying something you can make at home for nothing. At our house, you'd think the war never ended. Dad complains that beer costs two shillings a pint, Mum complains that bread costs sixpence a loaf. And they all go to bed when it gets dark because they won't cough up for the electricity.'

'My dad says he used to study under the street lights, when the electricity went out,' I say, sipping my own tea. I don't know why I'm drinking tea. I prefer coffee, especially this early in the morning. But she's drinking tea, and she asked me for tea, and I want her to like me. Because I like to be liked. I can't decide if choosing tea is selfless, or just dishonest. She sees me making a slight face while I think about this, and smiles.

'I suppose you'd want something stronger, after pulling a shift like that,' she says. 'I suppose your dad was a doctor like you.'

'And my grandad. And my big brother,' I say.

'So your kids will be doctors too,' she says innocently, as though she's not propositioning me at all.

'I'd prefer if they were astronauts. But I think we'd have to move to America for that.'

She nibbles the sticky bun, and she looks rather cute while she does, like a dainty dormouse, even in her primly starched uniform. She's not wearing her cap yet, and her backcombed hair is smoothed into a small beehive, with teased pieces straying out over her forehead and ears with a sweet sort of deceit, as though she wants it to look like she hasn't spent too much time on herself. As though she hadn't really planned on intercepting me at the door.

'Oh, will we now?' she says, and she laughs when I look briefly uncomfortable, and I laugh too. For some reason this offends a middle-aged couple in the corner, who I hadn't even realised were looking at us, and they leave, glancing back at us with hardened faces, just in case we thought it was a coincidence. I think about what William Godfrey and his almost-white girlfriend must have to put up with every time they go out; unlike Frank and me, they're a public couple.

'Oh, never mind them,' says Caitlin. 'Does it bother you, that sort of thing?'

'Not really.' I shrug. 'I only go out after dark.'

'Well it doesn't bother me,' she says resolutely. 'I don't mind being seen with you.'

'Good for you,' I say, realising that I have a slight edge to my voice. She's more perceptive than I thought, as she laughs at this too.

'Really I don't. My dad's hairdresser is coloured, he's browner than you. Tim Kapoor. My dad calls him Tim Cooper, and that's the name of his shop, Cooper's, but he's really Tim Kapoor. I don't even think he's called Tim.' She pours me a little more tea from the pot, and then pours more for herself, and I imagine her as a slightly older woman, welcoming her family with tea at the end of a working day, and saying, Shall I be mother? as she takes over the teapot. It seems a lovely sort of life she has ahead of her, that of caring and being cared for. 'I've heard his wife call him Timhu,' and she pronounces it carefully, 'Tea-Moo', trying not to look at the pot or the jug of milk as she says it, as though aware that it might seem that she is making a mildly offensive joke. She looks at me, shrewdly, and says, 'It's easier, isn't it, Jakie?'

'I've always been called Jakie,' I say. 'My real name's Jamal Kamal, and so I was Jay-Kay, and then I was Jakie. But yes, I suppose it is easier.' I stir my tea, unnecessarily, and look at her. 'I guess it helps to have things easier, sometimes, when everything else is so hard.' She puts her hand on mine, and her skin is meltingly soft, like a newborn. As soft as the baby that Asha is now cooing to back at the hospital, dissolving back against her flesh as she nurses him on her tough little breasts.

Another couple, not quite middle-aged, wearing scarves and heavy coats, leave the tea shop, the woman standing with a feather bobbing on her hat at the door, looking anywhere but at us, while her husband painstakingly counts out pennies on the counter.

'We won't be stopping for breakfast,' he tells the waitress firmly. 'This used to be a respectable place.'

The waitress smiles faintly, and shrugs, neither agreeing nor disagreeing. She doesn't apologise to him for my presence, or to me for his insult; the money from either of us is as good as anyone's. I've been in this place on my own plenty of times before without too much comment; it's my being here with a pretty white girl that they object to. I can hear the man muttering outside to his wife, *they're taking our jobs, they're taking our women*, her hat feather bobbing even more vigorously as she nods her agreement. Caitlin looks back at them steadily through the painted signage on the window, her hand remaining where it is, and I appreciate her solidarity, and wait until they have gone before patting her hand and pulling mine back.

'You're a great girl, Caitlin,' I say. 'I saw you yesterday, and I thought to myself, that's a girl who'll make every day feel like Christmas.' I don't say But, and I don't need to. She's bright enough to say it for me.

'But, you've already got someone, haven't you?' she says.

'I have,' I say solemnly. 'And I've got them bad. I think I'm in love.'

'Good for you,' she says, without an edge, but with a brave disappointment. 'So who's the lucky girl?'

'I guess that would be me,' I say in a low voice, and I don't know why I'm telling her, except that I think it would make her feel better, and it makes me feel better to admit it. She could shriek out loud and get me arrested. But she just stares at me, her eyes as round as marbles, and then yelps with a short burst of laughter and claps her hand over her mouth again. She's adorable. I wish Sulaman were here so I could introduce them, and they could have those nut-haired, cream-caramel children for me.

'Oh my stars,' she says. 'I had no idea, no idea at all.'

'But if I weren't that way inclined,' I say to her quietly, as everyone is staring, and I think I might get arrested anyway, 'you'd be the first girl I'd take dancing.'

'Well if you won't take this fine lass dancing, I know a fella who will,' says Frank, looking in the door. He is wearing a clean white shirt, with a thin tie, and looks far more respectable than usual. The resemblance between him and Caitlin is startling, and everyone in the tea shop visibly relaxes, assuming that he must be her brother, and that I'm probably there as his friend or colleague, and not as her lover.

'I've heard he's already spoken for,' she says, blushing, and stands up. 'I'll see you later, Jakie,' she says, and pecks me on the cheek as quickly as a sparrow, before darting off. 'Thanks so much for the tea.'

'Lovely girl,' says Frank, taking her place and sipping from her cup. He starts to eat her leftover cake with his hands, breaking off a piece and passing it to me. 'I thought I'd find you here,' he says. He's grinning, and I'm not sure how much he heard. 'What was that thing you said, about not telling colleagues?'

I change the subject. 'I've got you a Christmas present,' I say. 'I was thinking, what could be the best present you could possibly give a lapsed Catholic at Christmas?'

'What is it?' says Frank, more interested in the cake. He looks at me, empty-handed, and at the flat pockets on my jacket. 'Where is it?'

'It's back at the hospital,' I say.

'You're focking having a laugh,' says Frank, looking through the doorway into the maternity ward at Asha and her bundle of baby. 'A focking virgin birth? That's your idea of a present? You want us to bring a baby home? A kid?'

'Two kids,' I say. 'She comes with him. She has to. Once her people find out, they'll kill her.'

'Well, no one's ever thrilled about a bastard baby, but people get on with it,' says Frank.

'No, I mean that they'll really kill her,' I say. 'Kill her dead. It's happened before. It's the opposite of honour and obey. Dishonour and disobey. An honour killing.'

'That makes no sense,' says Frank. 'She was probably raped by some perverted family friend. If they're so keen on lynching, they should get the culprit, not the victim.'

'I doubt I'll get a chance to make that case,' I say. 'Where she's from, where I'm from, a village woman would get a hundred lashes for adultery if she admitted to being raped. A woman in a city, in front of a judge, would get jailed and stoned for fornication.'

Frank is looking at me like he doesn't quite believe me, like I'm an unreliable witness he's interviewing for a piece, someone determined to use sensationalism to push their case. He's looking at me like he's only just worked out that I'm not just brown, but foreign, from a place where they do things differently.

I breathe deeply. 'Look, I don't think I've got a choice here. I've got sisters. This is what happens if you're not there to look out for them.'

'I've got sisters too, you know,' says Frank. 'Although I don't need to look out for Maggie and Niamh. They've got Italian surnames, and their fellas own firearms.'

He turns and watches Asha as she lifts her baby with all the excitement of a little girl with a new doll. She has already named him; she's called him Hari, after her dead father. Her mother gave her up when she was widowed. Asha clearly has no intention of giving Hari up, and it probably hasn't occurred to her that she might be obliged to do so. She is practically bouncing on the bed with the rubber ball resilience of youth, the pregnancy and birth already left far behind her. Her skin is shining, and her hair has been fixed into a neat single braid that falls over her shoulder. The other mothers look ancient and exhausted by comparison, even though most of them are in their mid twenties, not much older or younger than me. One of them reads a magazine with determination, even while her newborn baby is squalling, and eventually a nurse comes and firmly suggests that she check on him.

'Oh, I'm not touching him,' says the woman, not looking up from the magazine. 'I've got three more of those at home. Until I'm sent back there, that one's all yours.'

'Sensible woman. Now there's an attitude I can understand,' says Frank. He glances back at the brown girl in the bed, with her living toy, and says quietly, 'I know you want to do something good, Jakie. You're a good boy inside, where it counts. There's a kindness to you. A selflessness. It's what I . . .' He pauses, and grins at his own hesitation. 'What I really *like* about you.' But he is shaking his head. 'I just don't think I can do this.'

'I know I can't do this,' I say quickly. 'But I think *we* can. I think we'd make, I mean we do already, I think we make . . .' and this time I'm the one laughing with embarrassment at my own hesitation, at the missing words. Eventually I say, wryly, '. . . a great team.' I say it again, more firmly, loud and proud, because now it's out there, I've nothing to lose: 'We make a great team, Frank McAdam.'

Frank looks shocked. 'God almighty. Dr Jamal Kamal Saddeq, are you propositioning me?'

'I think I'm proposing to you,' I say. I'm not whispering. I'm not even speaking quietly.

Frank grins. 'Well do it properly, then.'

'I'll get down on my knees later.' I'm not sure I'm actually joking, and I hadn't even been thinking about sex, but we both realise how it sounds, and laugh loudly enough for Asha to notice us. She waves at me, and smiles, lifting baby Hari so I can see him better, and then carries on playing and fussing over him. 'I don't have a diamond,' I say.

'I don't like diamonds,' says Frank. 'How about a fast car, with a full tank of gas? I'm guessing we'll need one when her people track us down.'

He smiles, and I look at him, looking at me, and I know I'm not a coward, not any more. I'm a man. I'm finally a man. He's burning like a candle in the grey corridor, so bright I could warm my hands on him, and the air is vanishing between us, and I can see myself reflected in his green, green eyes, and I don't think I'll ever be happier than I am at this moment, when I know I am going to do something reckless and right. When the man I love has told me that I am good.

PART 2

GOOD SISTERS, GOOD BROTHERS, 1961–1997

Chapter Nine

Mae

'SO, ARE THEY COMING?' MAE'S MOTHER ASKS HER, WATCHING AS SHE hangs up the phone. Mae turns towards her; for a moment she doesn't recognise the woman in the armchair, a small pile of pale cloth, sitting stiffly, like a bedsheet wrapped white and tight around a mannequin. The mother in her head is more fearsome and beautiful than the slight body present in the room. Was she always this little? Mae nods at the bundle, and perhaps her expression is too soft, too pitying, as the dark eyes flash in the washed-out face, and her mother sounds like herself again as she adds curtly, 'And are you coming?'

The voice doesn't match the face. It matches her memories instead. It is as though there is a vengeful ghost in the room. It is as though Mae has conjured it up. Summoned it with a ouija board. Like those converted Christians in Karachi who practise their new faith with the intensity of superstition. The ones who believe in miracles, and magic. Witch doctors. Witches.

Mae turns to face her mother properly, drawing herself up, standing tall. She looks down on the seated figure in her armchair, a puppet queen on a cardboard throne. She wonders if this is what she looks like herself, seated in her office, behind her desk, receiving petitioning suppliers and throwing out commands to her assistants with that same curt voice. She dislikes seeing the resemblance between herself and her mother; she always has. But all the same, she finds herself rooting it out, like a woman who is no longer young seeking out her pores and flaws in a mirror, to cover with concealer; raking her fingers through her hair so she can locate and tug out offending greys. She is twenty years younger than her mother, but they could be sisters, if Mae covered her carefully dyed hair, stripped off her make-up, and wrapped herself in widow's weeds.

'What a question,' she says to her mother, and at the withering glance her mother gives her, she feels forced to elaborate, as though she's failed some test by refusing to answer. She's a grown-up, with a grown-up daughter. She is well dressed in an outfit of her own choosing; she is wearing sturdy leather heels, and standing tall, so why does she suddenly feel so small?

'I'm here already, aren't I, Mummy?'

'Always a gift for stating the obvious, Mae-moni,' says her mother. 'And your father thought you were the smart one,' she adds, as though she always knew better.

She gets up from the armchair, and walks past Mae, towards the door. 'Tell the maid to prepare the rooms for them,' she says, as though Mae is a maid herself. 'Your room is already prepared. Daddy ordered it before he died. He thought you'd get here faster.'

Mae isn't in her fifties; she's five going on six all over again, trapped in a tight frilled dress, lying in her mother's shadow. She can't remember the last time she was alone in a room with this woman. She misses her father, who has been dead for twenty-four hours and is already in the ground, in the family plot, next to his father and grandfather before him. She is angry with him for dying first, for not sitting in the armchair instead. He would have looked at her with kindness, held out his arms. He would have said as little as possible, to avoid saying the wrong thing. He knew how words could be weapons.

'He called for you, Mae,' says her mother, twisting the knife, twisting her mouth, as though she is amused by this, or else has swallowed something unripe and bitter. 'He said, where's my Mae-moni?'

'I came as fast as I could,' says Mae. She knows that she has no reason to defend herself. She knows that she shouldn't. Mae isn't in her fifties; she is a teenager with an umbrella, walking in from the rain, defiant and defensive. She is watching herself, shaking her head with frustration. A mother at a school play, witnessing a disappointing performance, mouthing the missing words to the stage. Mae needs a stage, an audience, so she can deliver the killer line and take her bow, but there is no one else here. 'I took the first plane from Karachi,' she adds weakly.

'You should never have gone there in the first place,' snaps her mother. 'You should never have left.'

Mae is surprised that her mother has finally said this, some twenty-five years after the fact. It implies a weakness that her mother is aware of too. Her anger at her absence gives away too much; it shows that she missed Mae after all. Her mother clambers back to higher ground, like a call to prayer from a minaret on a mountaintop. A spider clambering up a wooden cross hoisted on a hill.

'He called for you, and you weren't there,' she says. 'He died without a single child of his by his side.'

Mae wants to sit on the sofa and flop back, defeated, but refuses to let her body betray her. She wills her weak knees, her veined calves, to stay firm until her mother leaves the room. Why is Amma wearing white? It's not her funeral, but she looks like a murdered Hindu devi put to rest on a funeral pyre, waiting to be set alight by her children; the Indian prime minister, wrapped in her white sari, shot by the men paid to protect her in her own garden. Perhaps she has dressed to ward off treachery and terrorism. Perhaps she thinks it will make her particular tragedy stand out, amid the darkly dressed sadness that will surround her. Perhaps she simply thinks that white suits her better.

It seems that Mae's stricken face has betrayed her in any case, as her mother stops, and turns at the door, her cream-softened hand on the frame a shade darker than her face. The same door she once stepped through to slap Sulaman and Jakie with a firm figure of eight, taking two bodies with the same bullet. Like a soldier economising on his ammunition, testing shooting strategies on prisoners of war. The stories that Sulaman seems so keen on dragging up from the past for his research: Nazi collaborators who made their prisoners dig the pits they'd be shot in; West Pakistani soldiers who slaughtered the East Pakistanis on their own land and raped their wives. Big wars, little wars. Victims and survivors. Slapped boys, spoilt girls. Mae remembers at the time that she thought her brothers got what they deserved. She remembers that at the time she'd rather have been slapped and sent away than spoilt and forced to stay.

'Well, Mae,' says her mother. So here it comes again, the transition that she used to see several times daily between her two mothers, the harpy and the houri, the scowl and the smile, the bad and the glad. The shimmer from black to white; there is no grey for her mother, no comfortable middle space. Amma looks at her, and she doesn't exactly soften – there is nothing soft about her; she is as sharp as cut crystal – but her teeth shine white as she smiles.

Mae steels herself, and waits to accept the affectionate words, waits for the confusion she felt when her mother made her up with her cosmetics, her perfumed skin next to hers as she drew the lines around her eyes, close enough to kiss, and told her that she was such a poppet, the loveliest thing in the world. Wrapped in ribbons, decked in baubles, bangles and bows. A living doll. She does the same thing herself now; not with her own daughter, never with her own daughter, but with the mannequins in her boutique, apricot-skinned, auburn-haired and smooth-browed, to match the bleached and Botoxed ladies of means who keep her in business.

She waits for her mother to tell her that she is glad she has come. That she is a good girl for coming. That she is good.

'Thank you for calling the others for me,' Amma says eventually, with frigid formality. Always that pause before her words, to make people wait for her, to keep them guessing and hoping. This little woman in white, bleached and Botoxed like the rest of them. It seems to Mae that her mother's eyes flicker to the empty chair, the vacant sofa. She realises that her mother needs an audience too. That she misses Abbu, that she would miss him for this fact alone. His presence in a chair. She must be furious with him for dying first; she would never let Abbu so much as leave a wedding without her, even if there was a medical emergency. And now he has walked out on her altogether. Mae thinks that her mother is more mad than sad; that she would dig him up and slap him too, if she could, on both cheeks with a firm figure of eight, forehand and backhand. Look at what you've done! All the miserable mourners who came trailing to the house on the day of his death, who lingered after the burial that same evening, and who will return for the Qul, bringing sticky sweets and salty fried food, flowers from their gardens and the dirt they have grown in, a series of unpleasant social events she is now forced to host alone. Look at the mess you have brought into my clean house! The filthy feet of his friends, family and former colleagues. The stains of smeared petals crushed underfoot.

Mae nods. 'You're welcome,' she says, just as formally. She remembers how the less her father said, the more effective he was. It was the best lesson he ever taught her, especially with regard to dealing with her mother. She knows that her mother is at least being sincere, as she could never have called Sulaman and Jakie and Lana and asked them to come herself. She knows that her mother is being practical, that there is a purpose to her politeness, as she may need Mae to call them again, to organise transport and other arrangements for their visit. She may need her to fend off the visitors who choose to ignore her instruction that she be left in peace until the Qul, the gathering of mourners and prayers for the dead that will be said in the house. Mae knows this is the best she's going to get. She returns the crocodile smile with one of her own; her mother inclines her head with the slightest acknowledgement, and leaves.

White witch. Bleached bitch. Black widow.

Mae sits down, still cursing under her breath towards the empty doorway, and glancing up, sees her reflection in the polished frame over the taut black cloth. Witnessed by the sacred space on the wall. She feels compromised, caught out. A manipulated little girl, caged in her dress. A rain-soaked teenager with garden mud on her feet. A grown-up fresh off a plane from Karachi, who needs a shower. For God's sake, she's a mother and a mentor. She runs a successful business. She is respected and revered by her staff. People seek her advice, on fashion and finance. She is better than this, and she stops herself swearing at her bereaved mother in the empty room.

Mae stands up, and goes to the sideboard. There are polished frames of family events, including her own wedding, the family seated on cloth of gold that matched her mother's sari. She picks up the picture, looking closely at all their faces. Serious Sulaman, Jakie the Joker, sweet Lana, spirited Mae. Their prosperous, proud-looking father. Her mother is gleaming out of the frame, looking more bridal than Mae herself did. The day her mother lost her last child. Blood on the dance floor. Scarlet on the gold. Carried out aloft in her husband's arms, gilt-edged and flame-red, like a blazing torch, in front of the crowd.

A less charitable woman than Mae might say that her mother would do anything to get attention.

'Tea, madam?' asks the maid, scurrying nervously into view. Mae suspects she waited for her mother to leave before appearing. She's a new one, from the same village as the last one. Mae doesn't know what happened to the last maid; she can't even remember her name, something like Bibi or Bitsy. She probably got homesick, or pregnant, and went back home to her family. Letting another girl swap her stinking village for the glamour of a Gulberg house in the Garden City. It takes the new staff a few years to realise that the city stinks too, and that cleaning a stranger's dirt for a wage isn't so much better than cleaning your own for free. Just as it took Mae a few years to realise that swapping one husband for another was like switching deckchairs on the *Titanic*; that under the smooth looks and nice manners, the new one was just as much a jerk as the last one. Her daughter has learned from her mother's example at least: Sherry has never married, and goes through boyfriends like disposable wipes. Mae jokes to her daughter that she's the reason why they installed a revolving door in her building.

The maid looks fearfully at the frame that Mae has touched, and Mae recognises the fear: that there might be offending fingerprints left on the polished surface, a speck of transferred lint or dust that visitors might discover, if they wore white gloves and ran their hands over the surfaces. Burglars breaking in during the night would find nothing to fault in the house; they would take tea in the well-stocked kitchen while they emptied the safe, and leave a note complimenting the lady of the manor on her superb housekeeping. Her mother is always prepared, like the Queen or the first lady of Pakistan, to receive company with no notice at all. Mae sees the maid's hand twitching in her apron pocket for the duster, but she doesn't dare to clean the frame while Mae is still in the room, in case this is interpreted as criticism.

Mae wonders what they must say about her family, the people in the maid's home village, where they live in stone and wood cabins, plastered with puddled mud and cow dung. Where they sweep their own floors, grow their own vegetables, and wash their own clothes by a river. Where the few families who have electricity stick their ancient black and white televisions outside their homes, for everyone to admire and for everyone to watch. How they must laugh at us, thinks Mae, when the maid goes back for her annual two-week vacation, or to attend a birth or funeral. The children probably put on little plays mocking them, and the maids and their sisters, and sister-cousins and aunties and great-aunties, must laugh until they cry. Who needs television when the stupid rich people provide such rich entertainment?

'Yes, thank you,' says Mae. 'Put it on a tray, please. I'll have it in my room.'

'I don't know why you're so hard on her,' says Sherry, her voice echoing on the poor long-distance line from Singapore. Mae's daughter has a masala accent, part Lahori convent girl, part Karachi socialite, part breathy West Coast American from her masters education, part Singapore expat. Her international anywhere voice is well known in her adopted town; she has an arts show on the radio, where she flirts with local celebrities and is adored by her audience. 'I know that you guys have had your moments. But she's an old lady now, she's all alone in the world. Poor Nanu. Imagine what she must be feeling.'

'Yes, yes,' snaps Mae impatiently, feeling like herself again. 'Your grandmother's a sweet, helpless old lady and I'm a dreadful daughter.' She hears her own voice echoing down the line, and stops to let herself finish. 'A dreadful daughter,' she hears herself say. She doesn't sound as ironic as she intended.

'Oh honestly, Mummy,' says Sherry, amused and a little impatient. 'It's not a competition.'

'Do you know what she said when she saw my outfit? How she greeted me when I'd just got out of the car from the airport? She went and took out one lakh fifty from the safe, and told me to get something new for the funeral.'

'Well that's sweet. She knows you got there in a rush.'

'I run a clothing store, Sherry. A designer clothing store. It wasn't sweet. It was a thousand-dollar criticism.'

Sherry laughs. 'Oh Mummy. I'm putting that in my show. A thousand-dollar criticism.'

'Don't you dare,' bristles Mae. 'I'm your mother, young lady. Not material.' At the same time, she's impressed by her own wittiness. It seems that the ability to flatter and compromise at the same time has been passed down through the women in the family. She wonders if Lana's daughter, Minnie, can do it too.

'She said I looked like new money,' she adds. It sounds like a joke, but Sherry picks up on something almost plaintive in her mother's voice. This isn't to do with clothes. It's a judgement by her grandmother on who Mae is now. Old money to new money. Trophy wife to career woman. The paths she has chosen.

'Are you going to be all right, Mummy?' Sherry asks seriously. 'I don't want to think of the two of you fighting.' Mae doesn't answer, and Sherry asks more brightly, passing over the responsibility, 'So when are the cavalry coming? Uncle Sully, Uncle Jakie? Auntie Lana?'

'Not until the Qul,' says Mae. Sherry knows that this will take place three days after the burial. It had seemed unlikely that they would make it, but Lana confirmed on the phone that they'd all be there. Their father was thoughtful enough to pass away before the peak summer season, so there were still some seats on the planes. 'You know, Sherry-moni, they'd all love to see you. Your grandmother especially. Could you come too, sweetie?'

There is a pause. 'Could you come too, sweetie?' her voice echoes, sweetly pleading, rather than casually offhand. The pause is too long; tumbleweed is blown through the deserted space it leaves. It is as though Mae has asked a question that she promised she never would. She knows her daughter doesn't want to come for the Qul; she is sparkling and selfish and Mae rarely encouraged her to be anything else. She has never pressured Sherry to be dutiful. She knows that Sherry was fond of her grandfather but has no interest in praying over his body now that it is already in the ground.

'I'm sorry, Mummy, you know I'm not into all the old-world bullshit. I'd have come for the funeral, but you bury your people with such indecent haste.'

'You?' asks Mae. 'Your people?' She's cross, but she's relieved that Sherry has given her something to be cross about, a way to vent her disappointment. 'For God's sake, Scheherazade.'

'We,' says Sherry, in a conciliatory tone. 'I meant we. I meant our people.'

Mae has always told her daughter that she can make her own choices, be anything she wants. And Sherry has chosen to live as a career girl in another country, and become a champagne Buddhist, and has even less to do with her family than her mother does. But Mae knows that Sherry is feeling guilty about her, and would come if she pushed her. If she said, 'I need you, Sherry.' She wants to say it, but she doesn't. She won't manipulate her child, not even with the truth. She realises that it's what her mother meant, exposing herself by saying it, when she told Mae she should never have left. Because her mother needed her. I need you, Mae-moni. She would never say this out loud to her, even if Mae wanted

188

to hear it. And Mae can't say it to her daughter, because she knows Sherry doesn't want to hear it. She sighs.

'I love you, sweetie,' she says. 'I'll let you get back to work.' She's proud of herself for saying this. She feels like a good mother. She even feels a little sorry for that slight woman in white. For messing things up so badly with all her kids. The four that are living, and the unborn one that died. Sherry's wrong, it is a competition. And for the moment, Mae decides that she has won.

'Thanks, Mummy,' says Sherry gratefully. Not for the love, which she expects, but for not being pushed into coming. They both know this. 'You're the greatest,' she adds. 'Be nice to Nanu.' Delegating responsibility again, passing the buck. Sherry doesn't promise to call later. She won't make promises she might break.

Mae remembers the tea, and goes to the kitchen to find it. She sees the maid in tears, hunched over a steel pot in the corner. Mae doesn't know what her mother might have said to her, and can't see the problem with the pot. The girl is quite pretty, and very young, and Mae imagines her mother might have held this against her, and has ordered her to polish the pot until she can see her face in it. A wicked stepmother to the maid's Cinderella. Mae wants to tell the maid that she should stop playing this role before she is trapped in it; there is no prince coming to save her. She won't find one in this dark house, and she is unlikely to meet one on her afternoon off.

'Are you okay?' she asks kindly, just to let the maid know that she is there. The question itself is meaningless, and answers itself, as she obviously isn't.

'Yes, madam,' says the maid, hurriedly wiping her eyes with the back of her hand, like a child, even though she has an apron that would be far more effective. 'Your tea is ready.' She puts down the pot, and pours the tea that is bubbling and stewing on the stove into a steel teapot. She puts one of Mae's mother's precious rose-patterned cups on the tray, shipped from England and kept for company only, and then punctures a tin of condensed milk and puts that on the tray too. No spoon. No strainer. No saucer. The tray doesn't even match.

Mae knows exactly what her mother would do to this girl if she presented a tray of tea like this. Lift the precious patterned cup carefully, slap the maid with her ringed hand, and then fling the tray with the rest of its mismatched oddments across the room in a satisfying crash of tin on tile, cymbals clashing to the music of the poor girl's tearful howling. Mae is tempted to slap the child herself; how could she be so foolish? Like a crawling baby insistently headbutting the wall, wailing and failing to learn that it will hurt. Like an idiot wife going back obediently to a husband who beats her, with a please, sir, can I have some more. Look at what you make me do, he'd say, slamming her head against the floor. Mae has no sympathy for stupid women; she suspects she was one herself, once.

She notices that she has clenched her hand, and opens it out, hoping the girl hasn't seen this. Mae has learned from her mistakes. She is a good mother, a good employer, and she won't make the mistake of being kind or unkind. She will be firm. She will do what good mothers and good employers do, and create a sense that all is well with the world, and that they are in a safe place.

'What's your name?' she asks the maid, brisk and practical.

'Pussy,' says the girl, blinking with fear. Mae is reminded, unpleasantly, how much she must resemble her mother. She tries not to roll her eyes. She can imagine the cruel jokes that the poor girl must have suffered from her mother's friends, from the senior servants, even. Here, pussy, pussy. Stinking pussy from the stinking village. Damp pussy let out in the rain. Drowned pussy in a sack. Not that there aren't plenty of Pakistani princesses with moronic Bollywood-Lollywood movie star names like Pussy or Twinkle or Dimple, but they have the family background and diamonds dripping to their shoulders to carry it off.

'And what's your good name?' perseveres Mae.

'Pari,' says the girl.

'Pari,' says Mae, hiding her relief. Even though the girl mangles it with her village dialect, it still sounds better. It'll do. She was worried that Pussy was the girl's real name after all. She adds firmly, 'That's not how you make the tea. Let me show you. I'll show you once only, and after that you can do it by yourself.'

'Yes, madam,' says Pari. She's comforted by Mae's no-nonsense attitude. She's grateful. 'Thank you, madam.'

Mae puts away the precious rose-patterned cup, and gets her mother's usual willow pattern service in green and white. She pours the condensed milk into the matching jug. She decants the tea into the right teapot. She puts the saucer and tea strainer on the side, and shows Pari where the butter cookies are, and what plate to put them on.

'Now you can make another pot of tea for my mother, please,' she says. 'No milk. Put the tea leaves straight in the pot, and pour on the water a few minutes after it's boiled.' Pari obeys, and gets it right. Mae nods her approval, and the maid beams with her achievement.

'Follow me, please,' Mae says, nodding towards the tray, and Pari picks it up awkwardly. For a terrible moment Mae thinks that she is going to try to put it on her head, so she turns and steadies it in the maid's hands, showing her how to balance it. Pari probably carries three pots of water on her head with ease in her village, each stacked on the other, with a plaited rope circlet on her crown to hold the first round base in place. She probably wore a hijab, not from modesty, but because headscarves provided protection from the sun, and she looks uncomfortable and exposed without one, pulling her hair over her ears rather than tucking it neatly behind them.

When did Bibi or Bitsy leave? Mae is beginning to suspect that her mother fired her in a fit after Daddy's death, as it seems that no one has taught this girl anything at all, except to be afraid of fingerprints. She wonders if anyone has even told her how to use a Western toilet, or if the poor thing has been squatting with her feet on the seat, and wiping away the marks of her slippered soles afterwards. She'll ask the sweeper when she comes back from running her errands at the market.

'Okay,' Mae tells Pari rather than asks her, and Pari nods with the confidence Mae has shown in her. She follows Mae with steadier hands, and just the slightest rattling of the saucer on the tray. Mae goes up the steps to her mother's room.

'Mummy?' she calls. 'I've brought us some tea.'

'Leave it outside, thank you,' says her mother, curtly and correctly. Mae nods to Pari, who understands to put the tray on the stand outside the door, and leaves, her shoulders more relaxed than before.

'I've brought it for both of us,' says Mae. 'I thought it would be nice to catch up.' She resists the urge to take her own cup and pot and walk off. Be nice. That's what Sherry told her. She bites her lip; so easy to give advice you don't have to take yourself. Sherry's probably tapping away on her computer now, sipping her imported Chardonnay, and has already forgotten all about the bereaved and the dead. Happy and thoughtless. Mae's done her job a bit too well.

She goes to open the door, and finds her mother standing on the other side of it, as though she was listening for Mae to leave. She doesn't seem embarrassed to have been caught out.

'Thank you, Mae,' she says sweetly. 'I'll have it brought in a little later. I'm praying,' she adds piously, as though that's the end of every conversation. You can't argue with prayer. She goes to shut the door in Mae's face, and Mae finds herself pushing it back open, almost as an instinct.

'*Uff, Allah,*' she mutters less piously to herself, immediately aware of how ridiculous she must look, fighting for the door with her mother. She is almost sorry that there is no one to see her, and laugh. It would make poor Pari feel so much better, to have something to write home about. She reminds herself that her mother is a little woman with soft hands who has never hung out laundry or washed a plate, and that New Money Mae has done all this and more. Mae has humped sewing machines from one side of a shop to another, taken fittings, and flung out bales of cloth on long trestle tables for inspection. She knows that she could win this fight with her elderly mother; that she could throw open the door, and send the old lady tumbling to the floor, scattering like an overturned tea tray. Be nice, Mae.

'Sorry, Mummy,' says Mae, backing off. 'I thought my shalwar was stuck in the door,' she lies, unconvincingly. 'I'll take my tea in my room.' The door clicks heavily shut behind her, hard enough to sever a little finger.

Mae puts her cup upside down on the teapot lid, the jug of condensed milk on the saucer, and carries them down the hallway. She pushes open her bedroom door with her sandalled feet, a bit awkwardly, and Pari comes around the corner, rushing towards her to help. Perhaps she witnessed the scene at the door after all. Mae wonders if anyone would believe it if she told them. She is tempted to stride back to her mother's room, to push the door wide and see if a lion leaps from behind it. It seems more credible than the fact of her mother waiting at the door, ready to shut it in her face.

'Let me, madam,' says Pari. She glances behind her, nervously, as though she's being followed.

'My daddy's dead, and my mother shut the door in my face, and my daughter told me to be nice to her,' Mae says to Pari, conversationally, as the maid holds the door for her and then relieves her of the teapot and milk jug. Mae flops heavily on her old bed. Four-postered, with a mosquito net swagged over the poles. Her daddy. It should be about him, and instead it was about them. Mae had almost forgotten Daddy, like she had so often when he was alive. She notices his absence now, in a way that she rarely noticed his presence. The empty armchair. The space he has left. Poor Daddy.

'Sounds like someone needs a hug,' says Jakie, coming in the door, following Pari into the room as she sets down the tea on the dresser. He is wearing a travel-stained white kameez, and loose trousers, with faded chappals on his feet. He reminds her so much of their father, who in his later years dressed traditionally at home, that Mae thinks it is him, and that she has conjured him up, just as she did their mother. An angel, this time, rather than a ghost. But Jakie is grinning, a bit ruefully. He has a cane, and Mae isn't sure if it's an affectation or necessity, as it seems to suit him so well. The light from the corridor is shining behind him. She is so pleased to see him that she can't let herself show it.

'You look like bloody Gandhi with a staff and loincloth,' she snaps. 'What are you doing here?'

'Same reason you're here,' he says. 'My daddy's dead too,' and he holds out his arms to her. Jakie's always been quick to comfort, and generous with his affection. Mae remembers how he instinctively put his arms around her at her wedding, when she started to cry, while her husband stood stupidly to the side. She gets up and goes to him.

'I don't *need* a hug,' she says, stepping forward and burying her face in his shoulder.

'Maybe you don't. But I do. So humour me,' says Jakie. Perhaps it is her imagination, but just as her mother seems smaller, Jakie seems taller. Not as tall as Sulaman, but still. Perhaps it's something to do with the cane. Perhaps he's lost weight. It doesn't matter. He is here. He is holding her in his arms.

Their mother is still praying, so they escape from the house for tea. They are heading out to a place near the Main Market when Jakie asks the driver to stop and let them out. Mae gets out, complaining, 'What's this dump?'

'You don't remember it?' asks Jakie. The sign has changed, and the storefront is different, but it's still a sweetshop.

'Kwalitee's Sweets and Treats,' says Mae. 'Funny.'

'I always come here when I'm in Lahore,' says Jakie. 'I figure we owe them the business.'

'Same old selfless St Jakie,' says Mae. 'Paying other people's debts, raising other people's children. Forgiving other people's sins.'

'Same old Mae,' says Jakie. 'Like a chocolate, or a jalebi. Hard on the outside, and goo on the inside.' He opens the shop door for her, bowing before her like he's her butler. She's aware that that's what he looks like. Dressed the way he is. 'I'm not as selfless as you think. The sweets are good here. And much cheaper than the other places all you ladies who lunch go to these days.'

He orders tea, and Mae bossily orders the sweets, more than they could eat, as she wants to look generous, and will take some back for the servants. Jalebi and rasgulla and burfi. Gold and white and pistachio-coloured. 'PIA colours,' says Jakie. 'Very patriotic. See, this place isn't so bad.'

'It's okay,' admits Mae. 'I'd rather have gone to a hotel and had a drink, but I guess I can't go back to that house stinking of gin.'

'Minnie will bring some,' says Jakie. 'She's thoughtful like that. She went to Greece with her boyfriend, and brought back a litre of ouzo. Frank got so pissed on the stuff, he smashed half the crystal in the cupboard. Walked into it thinking it was the bathroom.'

'Nice. Congratulations on landing the clumsy alcoholic,' says Mae, laughing.

'He's a catch all right,' says Jakie, 'definitely drinks like a fish.' He grins and carries on, 'Smokes like a chimney, swears like a sailor, skips work, can't cook, and he doesn't come from money. That's my Frank.'

Mae looks straight at him, and seems less amused. 'I know what you're doing. You've learned something from Frank over the years. You're burying the bad news.'

'What bad news?' asks Jakie innocently.

'That Lana's daughter is coming all the way from London. And mine won't even come from Singapore.'

'I didn't know that Sherry wasn't coming,' protests Jakie.

'Oh, we all knew that Sherry wasn't coming,' says Mae. 'I don't know why I even bothered to ask her. I should have known better.'

The tea arrives, already mixed with condensed milk, scented with cardamom, and as thick and filling as soup. Mae drinks it hot, and almost downs it. Like she's swigging a gin and tonic after all. She is relieved that she doesn't have to sip it daintily, under the critical eye of her mother. 'You've not said why you're here already,' she points out. 'Lana didn't say you were in Lahore. She just said that you'd be here for the prayers with the rest of them.'

'Lana doesn't waste words. She didn't know I'd be back in Lahore so soon. I'm still meant to be up in the hills with the aid workers. We got evacuated yesterday. Drug gangs. Terrorists. Fundos fighting fundos. Same old same.'

Mae nods. Jakie spends two weeks of his precious annual holiday working for an aid agency in Pakistan, vaccinating smelly little orphans in the smelly little villages and sprinkling polio drops like fairy dust. Mae thinks that Frank's the real saint to put up with this, year after year. If Jakie was her husband, she'd put her foot down and insist on going away together for a fortnight, somewhere nice, with good shopping and restaurants. But Frank doesn't mind; she supposes he travels enough with his work as it is, and he lets Jakie get away with it. Jakie's been doing the charity work since their adopted children, Asha and Hari, grew up and left home. Mae supposes he needed another cause, another set of children to save. It seems everyone has their faults, their particular diseases: Mae has poor circulation, Lana has religion, Sulaman has suited-booted success, and Jakie has charity. Mae is a little perturbed by Jakie's commitment, and disguises it by making fun of him. St Jakie.

'You kept that quiet. I thought you normally do your stint in October,' she says. She is proud of herself for avoiding saying anything bitchy out loud about his work for charity, for resisting the urge to say the word itself with a mocking edge. Charity, sweetie. Charity Junkie Jakie. She privately thinks it's like he's overcompensating for something. An errant husband turning up with flowers for his wife after a night with his mistress.

'It was last minute. Someone dropped out, and they called me. I'll still come in October, though. I'll spend some time with Mummy. And then I'll come and see you.' Jakie says this with a wink, as though he knows that lumping her in with their aged mother will annoy her.

'For God's sake, Jakie, I'm not someone you have to look after. I'm not some withered old woman melting into a screeching puddle of cloth.'

'I know that,' says Jakie. 'You're the most impressive woman I know.'

Mae is taken aback. She suspects Jakie of something, although she's not sure what. What can he possibly hope to achieve by paying her an extraordinary compliment? She refuses to accept it. She suspects the rest of her family of laughing behind her back. New Money Mae with her designer boutiques and frivolous fashions. Mae, the only one who didn't get away.

'Really?' she says coldly.

'Of course,' says Jakie, surprised that she seems surprised. As though he expects her to be able to take a compliment, and she has disappointed him by showing she can't. 'Look at everything you've achieved, for yourself, for your daughter. Everything you've done.'

'More impressive than Lana?' asks Mae sarcastically. She doesn't say Little Lana, but it sounds as though she might.

'Oh Mae,' smiles Jakie, 'it's not a competition.' Mae wonders why everyone who knows her accuses her of this, as though she's always playing a game she intends to win. Jakie drinks his own tea thoughtfully, and says, 'I think you're the bravest of us all. It's easier to run away than to stay. You stayed. You were here.' His voice breaks a little, as he adds, 'I wish I had your guts.'

He's smiling, but his eyes aren't. Mae finds herself reaching across and putting her hand on his, squeezing gently. She thought Jakie had wanted to comfort her, but now she realises that she wants to comfort him. Their daddy's dead, but Jakie was already here. He'd run back to Pakistan, reorganised his work and life on a spur-of-the-moment call, and now she's wondering why.

'Don't be like that, Jakie,' she says. She finds it unbearable when Jakie isn't happy. Whenever she thinks of him, in all her memories and photos, she sees him grinning under his roguish tumble of untidy curls. A cheeky child, pulling faces at the table. A maverick teenager, licking chocolates with Lana. An irreverent adult, living openly with his lover. Jakie the Joker. She can't take him with the suddenly sad tears of a clown. 'I'll have that hug now, please.'

He grins, and kneels beside her, like a prospective groom about to propose, and puts his arms around her. The other people in the shop are staring, and giggling at them. Two middle-aged people, showing foolish affection in public.

'What?' she says sharply to the spectators. 'Go ahead, enjoy the show,' so they look abashed, and go back to their business. At least she's succeeded in cheering up Jakie; he stifles a laugh in her arms. She's the same old Mae. Hard on the outside, and goo on the inside. She isn't crying, and she doesn't know why she brushes at her eyes with the back of her hand, as though she might.

Mae left her husband, Nasim, a man she had once called Uncle, in 1971. The year of the war with East Pakistan. Nasim's brother, Salim Kannon, once nicknamed Kannon-fodder by her mother, was sent off to fight in the Bengal. Otherwise, it seemed that the cracking open of their country wouldn't really affect them. Mrs Kannon sent care packages to Salim, and Mae's mother, originally from Calcutta, in the Indian Bengal, refused to participate in partisan discussion that might reveal that once again she was from the wrong side of the political tracks: an Indian in Pakistan, a Bengali in the Punjab.

There were protests, disquieting news of what the military was allowing in the East Pakistan campaign: beheadings of civilians in the countryside, children murdered and mothers raped. Martyrs and heroines. Blood on the fertile fields. But it was happening far away, on the other side of India, and it flew over Mae's mother's head like the Pakistani Air Force on ceremonial display. The petty personal rift between Mae and Nasim bothered her mother more. Perhaps surprisingly, she was as against the divorce as she had been against the marriage.

'What will happen to Daddy's practice?' she shouted at Mae, who had come back to her parents' home with her daughter. 'He'll marry that cow-faced slut, and have the sons you refused to give him, and your Sherry will get nothing. Nothing!'

'What would I do with the practice?' said Mae calmly, fastening on emerald and diamond earrings, and tucking back her hair to make sure that they could be seen. 'I'm not a doctor. Get one of your doctor sons back here to run it, if you're that bothered about it. I'm sure Sulaman and Jakie would love to move back to Lahore. They must miss it terribly. Pakistan in wartime. Like Paris in springtime.'

'Disgrace, dishonour, disobedience,' her mother muttered, as heavily and incoherently as though she were reciting a verse of the Qur'an to herself. 'Nothing but disgrace, from all of you.'

Mae's mother rarely mentioned her sons, and didn't tolerate family members mentioning them either. Jakie had set up home with a Catholic homosexual a few years before, taking in a molested maid and her rape baby, raising them in his house, as his children. Paying for their expensive British educations with his own hard-earned money. Asha, the girl, was in law college, while Jakie and Frank looked after her son, Hari. Jakie's adopted children both called him Abbu. They couldn't call him Daddy, or Dad, because that was what they called Frank. Mae and her daughter had taken to using a code if they ever had to mention Jakie's partner; instead of Frank, they called him the Saint, so that Mae's mother would think they were talking about the television series. Even Daddy understood the code, although he didn't mention Jakie much either, and certainly not in front of Mummy.

And Sulaman, who had dutifully married and produced a son of his own, was considered little better. The suitable Indian girl with the medical degree he had described in his letters turned out to be a Hindu half-blood Hun with a career. He had managed not to mention this until the first time their mother and father had visited him in the States. Their mother had changed the tickets within a day of arriving, and left the city forty-eight hours later. Sulaman's letters had since dried up to birthday greetings, and he hadn't visited the familial home since he left.

'I'm not the disgrace,' said Mae, inspecting her more-than-acceptable reflection. 'Nasim's the one flaunting his mistress around the town.' Was Mae still the fairest of them all? She wouldn't see thirty again, but she probably was. She was occasionally surprised and disappointed at how good she looked, when she saw herself in passing, in a shop window, the black mirror of a switched-off television screen, upside down in a tea-stained spoon. It seemed that this was all that defined her. Her persistent beauty. That mouth, those eyes. Liquid hair that hung smooth, and flashed with a shampoo ad shine in the sun. People looked at her in the street. People occasionally assumed that she was her daughter's sister, rather than her mother. Until she opened her grown-up mouth and said what she thought. Which made the reason for the separation all the more unlikely. Nasim had taken a mistress, and had chosen a woman far less attractive than his wife.

It was to do with the war, Mae decided. Nasim was keen to have a son, and she didn't want any more children. He had no idea that she'd already had two abortions in secret. Despite her refusal, she had never thought that Nasim would have it in him to do anything as interesting as have an affair, much less a public one. She supposed that war was liberating; people did things differently, they realised they had less time, and less to lose.

'And you let him!' shrieked her mother. 'Disgrace, dishonour, disobedience! We gave that man a Rolls-Royce. We bought it with your dead brother's blood. With my blood.'

Mae said nothing. She remembered when the cream Rolls-Royce had arrived. The iron stink of it, even after all the hours of cleaning that went into it. She had hated the car. Nasim insisted on driving everywhere in it, with her positioned next to him, with the windows rolled down, for everyone to see. A trophy in a trophy. Mae pushed on her heavy gold bracelets, unfashionable and ancient. A gift from Nasim's mother; she knew that they were treasured family heirlooms, and so she had dutifully worn them every day. Manacles to her marriage. Poor Mrs Kannon was mortified over her son's behaviour.

'If it's the car you're worried about, I'll get it back for you,' said Mae. 'I'll even arrange for the guards to point the security lamps at it. We can put it up on a podium, and light it up like the Lahore Fort, so all the dinner guests can admire it in the drive.'

'Don't be facetious,' snapped her mother. 'You should go back to your house. The longer you stay here, the faster she'll get there. She'll take over your room, your keys, your safe.'

'He has a *mistress*,' said Mae, slowly and clearly, as though speaking to a child. Her mother thought she could still treat her like a teenager. Her own daughter was almost a teenager. She couldn't imagine doing to her daughter what had been done to her. Sherry took her expensive convent school education for granted, and wasted her time and generous allowance money on imported magazines and fashion accessories. She shifted herself around the house from cushion to cushion with the latest *Cosmopolitan* and a clutch of Archie comics, and watched domestic family dramas on television, shoulders slouched and long legs stuck out in front of her. She made asking the servant for a cup of tea into something that smacked of too much effort, but managed to leap into action if any of her giggling friends called round, and would dash downstairs and disappear into their chauffeur-driven cars, gossiping conspiratorially. Occasionally Mae resented how easy it was for her, and had to remind herself that this was what motherhood was meant to be, correcting the mistakes of her own childhood, rather than getting her own back.

'So?' said her mother. 'This is Lahore. Every man of means has a mistress. I expected this stupid naivety from your sister. But from you?'

'Sherry, sweetie,' called Mae. 'Mummy's ready. I'll wait for you in the car.' A whining groan came from upstairs, which Mae seemed to understand perfectly, as she replied briskly, 'Well never mind that. I'm not keeping the lawyer waiting. We'll see Dadi afterwards.'

This seemed to persuade Sherry, as there was no more whining, and the sound of shuffling activity on the floor above. 'Dadi?' sneered her mother. 'You're seeing Nasim's mother?'

'She's paying for my lawyer,' said Mae, and shook the gold bangles to prove the point. She was tempted to clang them together in the manner of a mourning widow, but decided that would be too dramatic, too cruel. Nasim wasn't dead to her; he was simply a man to whom she no longer wished to be married. 'At least, her jewellery is. You don't know how long I've wanted to melt these down. I didn't want to offend her.'

Her mother was about to say something about this, but they were distracted by Sherry flying into the hall, dressed like a brown Barbie, in a long flowered kameez, but with Western trousers underneath instead of a shalwar. White denim flares. Her long hair was untidily looped up into a double-knotted ponytail, and her fringe was hanging in her eyes, because she was wearing her white hairband around the top of her head in a circlet, rather than using it sensibly to push back her hair. She had gooped so much Vaseline on her lips, it looked like lip gloss.

'Hi, Nanu,' said Sherry, kissing her grandmother stickily and imprecisely on her cheek, too close to her ear. She didn't see her enough to know not to do this. She was used to her dadi, Mrs Kannon, who was generous with her kisses and expected them returned. 'Bye, Nanu,' she added, dashing towards Mae and the door.

Mae saw that her mother was somewhere between offended and amused, and torn between making a stinging comment about how Mae's daughter was dressed and returning the kiss with a delighted 'Aren't you a poppet? Aren't you the loveliest thing in the world?' Sherry was the only granddaughter close enough to touch; Lana's daughter, Minnie, was only seen in photographs, sent regularly with letters written in Lana's schoolgirl-neat script. Mae was a little embarrassed to be seen out with Sherry, and a little proud too. Her ridiculous outfits were like a child's homework: so full of fault that they were above suspicion; it was obvious that she got dressed all by herself, with no interference from her mother.

'Tch, I told you, don't call me Nanu, it makes me sound like an old lady,' tutted Mae's mother. 'Call me Buri Ammie.' Mae had to turn her head so that her mother couldn't see her snigger. Buri Ammie. Older mother. What was wrong with Nanu, Grandmother? This was a new affectation; perhaps her mother hoped that people would think that Sherry was her daughter rather than her granddaughter when they went out together

'So, Buri Ammie,' said Mae, with a straight face, 'shall I ask for the car back? I could get it in a heartbeat. You just have to say the word.'

Her mother said nothing for a moment. She waited for Sherry to carry on out of the door, to the car, and then turned to leave herself, going up the stairs. She was skilful with her pauses; she always knew how long to make people wait, the importance of the white and black space between the words she chose. She would have been a gifted actress, thought Mae; she was a gifted director already, a puppet master, pulling at all their strings, handing out their scripts. She wondered who had handed her mother her script, all those years ago, to make her what she was.

'I can't tell you how much you've disappointed me, Mae,' her mother said finally, just as Mae was ready to stop waiting for her reply, and walk out after Sherry.

'You say that as though I haven't already disappointed you,' snapped Mae. 'It's an old record, Mummy. Disappointing you is "Blue Suede Shoes". We're all members of the Disappointing Mummy Club, aren't we? It's easier to get into than Nasim's slut's knickers.'

Mae stopped her rant, suddenly sure that she had gone too far. But her mother surprised her by laughing, not a cackling witch laugh, but the tinkling silver laugh she used for company, sharp-edged when she wanted to be critical, sparkling when she wanted to be noticed and admired. Mae had to stop herself laughing with her; it was so unexpected, and oddly flattering.

'You see, Mae?' her mother said. 'I have three children as spineless as soup. Too scared to look me in the eye. And I have you.' She shook her head as she carried on upstairs. 'Running away because of a stupid slut, instead of standing your ground. And you wonder now why I'm disappointed.'

Mae walked firmly into the shining entrance of the Hilton, wearing her oversized sunglasses and her scarf over her head, like a woman about to have an illicit meeting over a drink, who wanted to be recognised as this and left alone. Her teenage daughter, trailing behind in her hotchpotch clothes, a magazine shouting with movie star names in one hand, and her favourite sequinned butterfly-shaped purse in the other, gave her away.

'Welcome, Mrs Kannon,' beamed the doorman, as though he was family.

'Mrs Kannon, Mrs Kannon,' trilled the hotel receptionists, as though they were old friends, and waved urgently to the maître d' of the café area, who scurried over, nodding with delight to show that Mae and Sherry had just made his day.

'Mrs Kannon, madam,' he said, beaming too, mopping his shining forehead with a clean napkin. It seemed that he was going to pop out of his collar stud with pleasure at their chance encounter, and Mae felt an urge to reach over and pull it out for him, before it pinged her in the eye. 'Dear madam, it's been too long. Your mother is waiting for you,' and he gestured towards the other Mrs Kannon, who was waving to them excitedly, seated prominently and visibly in the window of the café, knitting something long and colourful.

'Oh,' said Mae, realising that her dime-store disguise was an unnecessary precaution. She pulled down her scarf, and propped her sunglasses up on her hair, then turned, smiling and nodding her thanks to the maître d', only realising as she sat that she hadn't actually said thank you. She suspected uncomfortably that she had acquired something of her mother's regal formality after just a few days back in her old house, her father's cautious way without words, as though using them unnecessarily gave too much away.

'Dadi,' squealed Sherry, Teflon-coated and unaffected, and ran over, giving Mrs Kannon a bear hug, and a sticky Vaseline kiss. She waited expectantly, and Mrs Kannon didn't disappoint; she reached into her purse, pulling out a set of plastic butterfly clips, and a small packet of colourful mints.

Everyone adored Mrs Kannon at the hotel. They adored her at the school. At the hospital. They'd adore her walking down the street, even. Everywhere. Mae half expected the staff to burst into spontaneous song, and offer her flowers. She adored Mrs Kannon too, but she made her feel unworthy in exactly the opposite way to her mother; she got some of the warmth of the golden light spilling around Mrs Kannon, the reflected glow. The splashback. She supposed it was better than sitting in the shadow of her mother, however cool it had been, in the morning heat.

'Mae-moni, my mayflower,' said Mrs Kannon, getting up to give Mae a hug as wide and deep as her talc-scented bosom. 'Why are you all covered up? Is it too hot out there?' She patted the seat next to hers, where anyone passing in their car, going in or out of the hotel, could see them. 'Have some iced water. I've already asked for tea. Just the way you like it. I can't bear to think of you being forced to drink Earl Grey or God knows what at your mother's.'

'*Na*, Ammie,' said Mae. 'It's not too hot. I just thought we were being discreet,' and she laughed a little; the idea of Mrs Kannon requesting a private table, or a private room, a secret meeting with coded greetings and made-up names, now seemed ridiculous. She was clear and soft as rainwater. Mrs Kannon seemed so surprised by this comment that she looked almost hurt, and Mae hastily added, 'I meant, for your sake. It's not that I don't want to be seen with you, of course not. I just thought it might be embarrassing for you, if Nasim heard we'd met.'

'What nonsense,' sniffed Mrs Kannon. 'As though Nasim could stop me seeing my youngest daughter for tea.' She added, with characteristic bluntness, 'And if he is so concerned with being discreet, he shouldn't be displaying his strumpet at social events.' She turned to Sherry, who was flicking through her magazine, slouched against the banquette. 'I'm sorry, *beti*, I should not speak this way about your father in front of you, but he's an idiot. All men are idiots.' She carried on, 'And I shouldn't call that woman a strumpet. I know I shouldn't. It implies she's good-looking, or at least young. She's neither. Oh Mae, I can't tell you how ashamed I am of Nasim.'

'Ammie,' laughed Mae. It was like hearing a child swear, hearing her mother-in-law being critical of anyone at all, especially her son. 'It's so good to see you. I've missed you.'

'Then come home, Mae. Please. We all miss you and Sherry.'

'I can't. I can't go back to his house. Not after this.'

'It's still my house,' said Mrs Kannon. 'And if Nasim doesn't like it, he can leave and live somewhere else.'

Mae stopped laughing. 'You'd really do that, Ammie?'

'Of course,' said Mrs Kannon. 'Here in Lahore, I only have one daughter, one granddaughter. Nasim doesn't know how lucky he is. I should have married you to Salim. So much younger, so much better-looking. All those years he's spent away in the army, refusing to meet girls from nice families. And now he's stuck fighting a war. I think he's still in love with you.' Her voice rose with a hopeful lilt. It would have been faintly comical, more Mrs Bennet than Mrs Kannon, if she hadn't looked so wide-eyed and sincere.

The drinks arrived, giving Mae a chance to think about what her adopted mother was saying. Stewed spiced tea, syrup sweet, and lemon and lime sherbet for Sherry, served with an umbrella and a fancy straw. Little saucers of imported salted biscuits and sweet cookies in crinkled cases were brought by the maître d', with some sliced oranges, which he knew Mrs Kannon had a fondness for.

'You're too kind,' she beamed, asking him about his children, remembering their names and their ages. She sprinkled salt and chilli on the orange slices, and shared them around, as though she were in her own house, at her own table.

Sherry sipped her sherbet. Now that she was sitting upright at the table, snacking on the sweet cookies, sucking the salt and spice off the oranges, she seemed to have revived out of her adolescent stupor enough to join the conversation. 'So when are we going home, Mummy?' she asked Mae, adding to Mrs Kannon, '*Haw*, Dadi, I'm so bore-bore at Nanu and Nana's.'

'Sherry!' said Mae, and her daughter misunderstood the admonishment, and corrected the schoolgirl-socialite slang.

'I mean, gosh, I'm so very bored,' she enunciated carefully. 'It is so terr-ib-ly dull.' She turned to Mrs Kannon. 'You know, Dadi, all they do is eat and pray. Pray and eat. Eat and pray.' She chewed on a salted snack. 'And they don't even eat that much.'

Mae tried and failed to find something she could argue with in Sherry's succinct summary, but it was all true. It was the school holidays, so Sherry couldn't even escape to the convent for the day with her friends.

'I know it's not fun there, but it won't be for long,' she started to say, but Sherry squealed with excitement, and waved across the café to a pair of smartly dressed girls who were wearing their hairbands, brightly coloured and embroidered, rather more conventionally, showing off their smooth, peach-coloured foreheads.

'Pinky, Dinky,' she shrieked, and jumped up and ran over to them. She joined them at another table, where they began noisily admiring each other's outfits. Mae knew the girls from Sherry's school, although she couldn't for the life of her remember their real names. They'd been Pinky and Dinky as long as she'd known them, the Akbar twins. She supposed their mother was out shopping, or getting a massage or a manicure.

'*Yaar*, so bore-bore, *na*,' Sherry complained to them, casting a significant look towards her mother, lightening it with an irreverent grin when she saw Mae looking back, as though she was just making conversation and didn't really mean it.

Mrs Kannon smiled indulgently in Sherry's direction, and waved at the girls, who waved back politely. She seemed pleased to have the chance to talk to Mae more privately. 'But where will you go, Mae-moni, if you won't come home? I know you don't want to stay with your mother.' She added quietly, 'Salim will come home if you divorce Nasim. I know he will. I have a house I'm building in Defence for him, when he has his family. I know it's not Gulberg, but still . . .'

'Ammie, I'm sure Salim's not been pining for me,' Mae said pointedly. 'And I'm sure he's not been praying for Nasim's divorce or death while he's out on the front lines. And it's useless if he has been, because I don't care for him. I don't even think this is all Nasim's fault, because I didn't really care about him either. I never loved him and he knew it.'

She remembered what she had said to her daddy, the day she had announced the proposal, when he'd asked if she had chosen the older or younger brother. She had replied, with Sherry's insouciance, does it matter? He had astutely asked if she was marrying the mother or the son, and he was right. She hadn't gone into a marriage. She had adopted a new mother, just as surely as Jakie had adopted his son and daughter.

'Well of course he knew it,' said Mrs Kannon practically. 'No older man ever married a beautiful girl of good family and expected her to be *in love* with him. It was a match. A marriage. Do you know how many men dream of marrying their boss's daughter? You've been a good wife to him, Mae. He made a promise to you, and he broke it. He has no right to make you a divorced woman. He should be grateful for you.'

Mae shrugged; this much was true. 'Well, I've had sixteen years of his gratitude. I think now he wants someone to be grateful for him instead,' she said. 'He really should have married someone older and uglier. Someone like the strumpet,' she added wickedly, and would have laughed, but she caught sight of her reflection. She was too good-looking. She was joking animatedly about her divorce. She looked as giddy as the three girls in their hairbands on the other side of the café. She forced herself to compose her face, to look serious and more careworn. That's better, she thought, sucking in her cheeks and letting her mouth fall; now you look like a mother.

'I was thinking of moving to Karachi, Ammie,' she said. 'A clean break. I'll set up home with the divorce settlement.'

'Then *all* my daughters will be in Karachi,' sighed Mrs Kannon. 'I miss Shamila and Nazneen. Sons stay, and daughters leave. I don't know why I don't just move there myself.'

'Lahore would miss you,' said Mae. 'You're the most gracious lady here. Everyone knows that.'

Mrs Kannon giggled, and the apples of her cheeks flushed pink with the compliment. 'Oh Mae, you shouldn't tease your old ammie so.' She sipped her tea, and composed her face too. 'Still, what you will do out there?'

'We'll have Shamila and Nazneen,' said Mae. 'So Sherry will have her aunties and all her cousins.' She added, with uncharacteristic hesitation, 'You know, when Shamila heard about Nasim's . . .' she paused over the word, and finally decided on something mild, as Sherry was in earshot, 'behaviour,' she whispered finally, making a face, 'she suggested that we come and visit. You know that place she was designing outfits for has gone out of business, with the war.'

'Bengal Silks and Satins,' nodded Mrs Kannon. 'A lovely shop. So artistic, Shamila, always keeping busy. She painted the quotation from Tagore that's framed inside the shop.' Mrs Kannon shook her head. 'It was never going to stay profitable, with a name like that. Why didn't they just call it Silks and Satins, and board over the Bengal?'

'I was thinking of visiting the shop,' said Mae. 'And taking it over. I can do accounts. I can design and dress-make, even; Mummy forced me to learn the summer before I married Nasim.'

'Of course you can, Mae-moni,' said Mrs Kannon, a little sadly. Mae knew what she was thinking; she wasn't the first in the family to profit from someone else's misfortune in a conflict. Her daddy had taken over the Hindu practice during Partition. She was taking over the Bengali dress shop during a civil war. She refused to be embarrassed.

'Are you certain you want to do this?' said Mrs Kannon. 'I'd make sure you were comfortable. You'd never need to work.'

'Well, what else would I do?' said Mae. She nodded at Sherry, who had finished squealing, and was now talking intently with the two other girls, casting significant looks at the magazines. Probably talking about boys. In a few years, Sherry wouldn't need her at all, except for her allowance. She would do a fluttering artistic degree, just like her friends, while they waited for the boys of good backgrounds to send them proposals. They'd become corporate, co-operative wives, not so different to Mae herself, and if they were motivated, like Mrs Kannon, they might knit and volunteer in their spare time.

A year before, Mae had taken Sherry to see her family, after waiting in the sun for hours to get the visa. They had visited Jakie, Lana and Sulaman. They had met the adopted cousins, Asha and Hari, and the real cousins, Lana's daughter Minnie, and Sulaman's son Buzz. They lived in nice properties; Jakie and Lana both had places in Notting Hill, a colourful part of central London but still close enough to the good shops. Sulaman had a sprawling family house in Long Island. But all Sherry could do was whine about how small their houses were, how bad the food was, and she was more than appalled that they had to make their own breakfast, wash their own dishes, do their own laundry, and squeeze their own juice, if they bothered at all. That Sulaman's wife, Radhika, had put on a coat and left for work in the morning, along with Sulaman. Wage-slave wallahs.

Mae had been embarrassed, more than embarrassed, at Sherry's behaviour. Behaviour that was tolerated and even indulged in Lahore was shown in a sharper light abroad, in London and Long Island. Sherry was spoilt. Her family were too polite to call her a Pakistani princess to her face, but Mae knew that that was what they were all thinking. In the cheap Chinese restaurant, famous for its intolerant staff, she had been ruder than the waiter. 'Why is all this stuff steamed and boiled?' she'd hissed about the dim sum and the noodles. 'It's like an ashram. In the Ming Palace in Lahore, they know how to *fry* the food.' She spoke to people in the shops like servants. She'd had servants all her life. She had never seen a woman of her class work in Lahore, and she never expected to work herself, so Mae knew that all this wasn't really Sherry's fault. It was Mae's fault.

'Like you say, daughters leave home,' Mae said. 'And before Sherry does, I'd like to show her that women work too, and that their work matters.' She added appeasingly, 'I know you work, Ammie. More than anyone I know. But you work because you want to, and Sherry's just not like that.' She paused. 'She needs a break from all of this, from Lahore. And so do I.'

'I see why you're not more angry with Nasim,' said Mrs Kannon. 'He's set you free.' She said this sadly too.

'I don't want to be free from you, Ammie,' said Mae. 'Come with us to Karachi, to visit Nazneen and Shamila. Look at this shop with me, tell me what you think of it.'

'Of course, of course, Mae-moni,' said Mrs Kannon, and her eyes were leaking a little behind her thick glasses. She pushed her frazzled hair back distractedly, so that her heavy tortoiseshell comb fell from it, and into the jug of water. 'Oh dear,' she said mildly. 'Always so clumsy,' and she tutted at herself. Mae retrieved the comb, wiped it on her sleeve, and replaced it on her mother-in-law's hair, her sleeves falling back as she used one hand to push back the thin locks, and the other to fasten the comb in place as best she could.

'Lovely,' she said, and she was aware that Mrs Kannon was staring at her bare wrists, exposed briefly. She was aware of the absence of the jingling sound of the gold bracelets tumbling down towards her elbows.

'Mae?' asked Mrs Kannon.

'I've sold them, Ammie,' said Mae. 'I needed to be free of them too. I hope you understand that.'

Mrs Kannon looked stricken for a moment, but then she recovered, and smiled. 'Of course, Mae. They were a gift to you on your wedding day. They were yours, to do with as you wished.' She added, conspiratorially, 'They came to me from my husband's side of the family. I was touched that you wore them, when you had your pick of so many flashier, more modern pieces. That you took such good care of them. But I'm not sure they ever suited you. They were far too traditional and heavy for your light Lahori wrists. They must have felt like millstones all these years.'

Mae finally realised that her mother-in-law wasn't just talking about the jewellery. 'I'm sorry I never told you this before,' Mrs Kannon said. 'They were your choice, and I didn't want to offend you.'

Mae laughed so loud that the people in the café stared at her, and she could see her daughter looking embarrassed, as she mouthed a mortified 'Mummy!' in her direction. 'We'll go tomorrow, Ammie. Sherry can't stand more than another night with my mother, and I want to get to Karachi before someone else buys that shop.'

Mrs Kannon nodded. 'You'll need to think of another name for it. Something to show the West Pakistani ownership, so the customers will go back.'

Mae smiled. 'I've thought of one.' She lightly touched the comb in Mrs Kannon's hair, and moistened her forefinger on the inside of her lip before putting it to her mother-in-law's cheek, as a blessing. 'I'll name it after you. I'll call it Gracious Ladies of Lahore.' She finished her tea, and began gathering her things. 'Well, I suppose I'd better go back to the least gracious lady in Lahore, before the old witch blows on our baggage and turns all of Sherry's tennis shorts into shalwars . . .'

'Mae, I'd like you to be kinder to your mother,' said Mrs Kannon. She said it with the loving firmness of a parent who had left their child a certain amount of time to make the right choice, and had finally decided to step in and guide them in the right direction. 'It is a difficult time for her. You're Lahori through and through. You forget that she was born in Calcutta. You can't imagine what it must have been like to be shipped across the country at the age of ten, and taken away from everything you knew. Your daddy, you and Sherry are all she has.'

'I'm not sure what that's got to do with anything,' said Mae.

'Do you know why your mother almost always speaks English, even at home?' said Mrs Kannon. 'She doesn't want people to hear her Bangla accent when she speaks Punjabi. She still has one. Even after all these years.'

Mae thought about this. She had never imagined her mother as someone who lived her life in fear. Afraid that someone would hear her accent and make an unkind comment. Attacking others, as foreign or common, before anyone could attack her for it. She tried to imagine her mother as a girl the same age as Sherry, keeping her head low and serving tea to her prospective groom's people, only speaking English in case they heard her imperfect Punjabi and decided that her voice wasn't as suitable as her face.

'I'll be kinder to her,' she said to her other mummy. The one who was lovely in every way that her own mother was not. 'I'll try to be good, I promise.'

As Mae and Jakie leave the sweetshop, their waiting driver waves to them from the car. He's their old driver's grandson, and he wears tan slacks and a shirt rather than a uniform. 'You know what?' Mae says to Jakie. 'Let's get a rickshaw home. For old times' sake.' She hands the boxes of sweets to the driver to take back with him, giving careful instructions on how to carry them from the car to the house so they won't leak or crumble.

'Are you sure?' says Jakie. 'I'm already a mess. I wouldn't want you to ruin your outfit.'

'According to Mummy, I need to buy another one anyway. She disliked what I'm wearing so much, she gave me one lakh fifty from the safe.'

'Rubbish. You look wonderful. You always look wonderful. It's possibly your only fault,' says Jakie. He adds, as though it is a separate conversation altogether, 'Do you know how many children I could vaccinate with one lakh fifty?'

'It's yours, old man,' says Mae abruptly. 'Just save me the St Jakie speech. Cholera before clothes. Food before fashion.'

'A pleasure doing business with you,' says Jakie. She notices that he's limping a little, and actually using his cane rather than swinging it about like a natty dancer in an old movie.

'Are you all right, Jakie?' she asks. The truth is that she had forgotten about the cane when she dismissed the driver. She slows down her determined step and puts her arm around him, to support him.

'I'm fine,' he says. 'I'm always fine,' and he squeezes her hand, and lets it go. 'It's just a bit of arthritis. I keep thinking I'm too young for it, so I don't take it seriously. Gets worse when I'm out here because I don't keep up with my exercises.' He uses the cane a bit less, as though suddenly self-conscious about it. 'I'm not often on the receiving end of that question,' he comments. 'It feels odd to be asked.' He really does seem genuinely uncomfortable.

'Well, St Jakie,' says Mae, once they reach the main road, and are standing in the shade of a street light, just as they did before. One behind the other, like Britons waiting politely for a bus. 'How's the real saint? The one who puts up with you. St Francis of Assisi. Frank the Sissy.'

Jakie smiles at the old joke, and waves his cane for a rickshaw. The cane is surprisingly effective; one stops immediately. The sharp-boned rickshaw driver is solicitous with Jakie, and helps him up as though he's a more fragile man than he is, and seems impressed when Mae gives the Gulberg address.

'Look after your uncle's cane, daughter,' the driver admonishes Mae, as it rattles across the rickshaw.

'Well that's flattering,' mutters Jakie to Mae, picking it back up. 'She's only a couple of years younger than me,' he complains to the driver, who isn't listening, and is humming a song to himself, waving his head in time.

'How's Frank?' asks Mae more seriously, reminding Jakie that he hasn't answered her question.

'He's less fine,' admits Jakie eventually. 'His mother had it. His older brother has it. And now he's been diagnosed. I made him get checked out, because I could see it was affecting his work. He wouldn't have bothered otherwise. He's got early-onset Alzheimer's. Dementia.'

'I don't know what those words mean,' says Mae. She wonders whether it is a euphemism for AIDS, and is relieved when she realises it can't be, not if Frank's Catholic mother had it too.

'It means that he's forgetting things. Little things at first. And then big things. And then maybe everything.'

'How long?' asks Mae. 'How long before everything?'

'Can't really say,' says Jakie. 'Maybe years and years. But there's no cure.' He pauses, and says simply, 'Frank's the one who's too young for this. I've treated patients with dementia. Treated is too big a word; there's nothing you can do. Care analysis. Assisted living. They were elderly people, much older than Daddy, and they'd lived full lives. But their minds were shredded to confetti. They didn't remember their partners or their kids. They played with pets and therapy dolls to keep themselves busy.'

He turns to Mae, to look at her, as the rickshaw spins around the corner. A group of children on bikes scatter ahead of them, shouting abuse at the driver, who swears back at them. It is getting hotter, and Mae is more used to the heat than Jakie. He's shorn off his thick curls for the trip, but he's still sweating a little under his hairline, under the three-day stubble of his beard. 'When I try and talk about this stuff to Frank, he just tells me that I talk too much. Do you believe that people are made up of their memories? Their past? Is that all we are?'

'No,' says Mae, so firmly that the rickshaw driver turns to face her, thinking she is addressing him. 'Eyes on the road, Uncle, please,' she says briskly.

The driver nods with such appreciation, before he turns back, that other people on the street turn to look at her too. Perhaps sitting next to travel-worn Jakie makes her look even more impressive. She still has those eyes, that mouth. Her hair is fashionably coloured in shades of dark espresso now, but still shines with a white liquid light, like a shampoo ad.

'No,' she repeats, just as firmly. 'I think people are made up of what's to come, not what we've left behind. What we're trying for. Where we want to get.' She looks at him frankly, taking his hand. 'Our hopes. I think our best is still ahead of us. It is always ahead of us.'

'You're a good sister, Mae,' says Jakie. He leans back on the rickshaw, closes his eyes. 'I'm a doctor, and I can't help him. I don't help anyone, these days. I'm just not made for general practice. I'm really no different to Daddy now, treating his Gulberg-begums with anaemia and high blood pressure. Instead, I've got Notting Hill-wallahs with asthma and eczema. Coughs and sneezes and city diseases.' He's smiling, like he's made a joke, but the smile doesn't reach his eyes. 'It's a desk job. A decent pharmacist could help half of my patients, and the other half just go home and get better themselves.'

'I'm glad that expensive medical degree is working out for you,' says Mae. She is tempted to say more, to make him laugh, or tell him off for whining, but stops herself. She supposes that he needs to get this off his chest.

'I should have done some good in the world,' says Jakie. 'Two weeks a year helping out in the hills, it's not enough. It's never been enough.'

He turns to Mae. 'It suits you when you say no. You say it so loud, it's like you're on a stage with cymbals crashing. I should try saying it more often. It's a powerful little word.'

'Frank's right. You do talk too much,' says Mae impatiently. 'Try saying "You're a good sister" again, and this time just shut up.'

'No!' says Jakie. They both laugh. 'You see, I need to practise it. That just feels wrong.' He adds, 'You're a good sister, Mae.' He makes a big show of zipping his lip, and then leans back and grins. He recognises the refrain the rickshaw driver is singing, and carries it on.

Mae decides it's time to show that she can take a compliment. 'Thank you, Jakie.'

She sits back and lets the city dust settle into her clothes, and pulls her scarf over her hair against the sunshine, but loosely, so that her long earrings, made with the leftover gold from one of her melted-down wedding bangles, sparkle and shimmer with schoolgirl giggles. Silly, pretty New Money Mae.

She isn't surprised that they make it back before their driver, who must have got caught in the traffic around the market, but is more than surprised to see another, more familiar car blocking the drive. The cream Rolls-Royce.

'Bloody hell,' says Jakie, suddenly sounding very British. 'Does that thing still work?'

Mae is furious. That Nasim has the nerve to visit, and in that car. Their wedding present. 'Of course it does,' she tells Jakie bitterly. 'Nasim always took better care of it than most people take care of their children. He used to polish it himself. He's replaced so much of it, you could make a new car out of the bits of the old car, and Sherry says that those are still in the garage too. The Rolls and the Zombie Rolls. I don't know why he doesn't cuddle up with it at night. It won't talk back to him, and he can honk the horn all night long.'

'Be nice,' says Jakie. 'He's probably just here to be polite, because of Daddy.'

'Be nice, be nice,' Mae parrots back to him. 'Everyone is always telling me to be nice. When are people going to start being nice to me?' She leaves Jakie to pay the driver, with the casual rudeness reserved for siblings or spouses, and strides into the house, calling out, 'Mummy, we're home.'

There is no answer, and so she goes into the sitting room, where an elderly man is sitting stiffly, his hands spread on his knees, being served tea by Pari. She notices that Pari has replicated the tea that Mae showed her to make earlier in the day, a stewed pot of traditional tea, a second pot of English tea, and has done it perfectly. She learned quickly, and just needed someone to show her how. Mae is more interested in the tea, after the hot ride, than the old man, whom she doesn't recognise at all, and it takes her a moment to realise who he must be.

'Oh,' she says, and this is the only thing that gives away her surprise. Nasim is in his seventies now; he is almost the same age as her dead daddy. She hasn't seen him for a dozen years, not since kindly Mrs Kannon's funeral, and didn't really expect him to have changed, as she hasn't at all.

'Mae,' says Nasim, standing up, taking refuge in good manners. He is clearly astonished at how good she still looks, even dusty and crumpled after the rickshaw. Especially dusty and crumpled after the rickshaw. She sees herself in his eyes, reflected in his sober square glasses, and astonishes herself. 'You look wonderful,' he adds sincerely, as though to say anything else first would be a lie by omission. 'Just like our Sherry. Whenever I see her, I see you.'

'Do sit down, Nasim,' Mae says, realising that once again, she has won whatever battle it was she was fighting, and that now she can afford to be kind. She has to resist calling him Uncle, or sir. She doesn't ask why he's come, but waits for Pari to serve her tea, rewarding her with a sincere smile, which has Pari looking so delighted she practically skips back to the kitchen. 'You're looking well,' she says, and then regrets it, as it is too obvious a lie.

'I've come to pay my respects to your mother,' says Nasim, answering the question she hasn't asked. 'I wanted to tell her that my thoughts and prayers are with her, and with her children and grandchildren.' His voice breaks a little. 'I was so sorry to hear about your father. That man gave me everything I had. My professional success, my place in our community. Even my wife and my child. I owed it all to him.'

Mae smiles a bit stiffly. 'Is my mother coming down?'

Nasim shakes his head. 'The bearer said that she is praying and can't be disturbed. He asked me to wait, and take tea. If she's not ready to see me after this, I'll leave. I don't want to intrude.'

'If you didn't want to intrude, you shouldn't have come in a car that takes up the whole drive,' says Mae, sipping her tea.

'Sherry called me,' says Nasim. 'She said that perhaps your mother might want the car, that it might help her. She used one of those modern words. Closure.' Mae's eyelids flicker at this. Closure. Like shutting a door. A lid on a box. She nods politely, while Nasim carries on. 'It doesn't run any more. I had it brought here on a handcart. It's hers if she wants it.'

Mae laughs. 'The Rolls rolled here on a handcart? Like the President on the back of a bike. I'd have liked to have seen that.' She smiles, thinking of her daughter picking up the phone and making the call to her father. Her Sherry isn't quite as self-centred as Mae thought; sometimes, it seems, she listens to what Mae has to say, about her marriage, and her mother. Perhaps she was even listening while she glooped on Vaseline and read her magazines, as the spoilt teen she used to be. Her daughter has surprised her, and it is a pleasant feeling. Her working daughter, who made her own way in the world. Mae feels that she had done something right, after all.

'Thank you, Nasim. I think that Sherry's right. I think Mummy might want it, if you don't mind giving it back.'

'Well, it never felt like it was really mine,' shrugs Nasim. 'Still, that car was the best thing anyone ever gave me. The second best thing,' and he nods towards her, with a slightly sad gesture that reminds Mae of his mother, who passed away after a mercifully short battle with cancer.

It is only the memory of Mrs Kannon that stops Mae snapping at Nasim, as she says briskly, 'If you're talking about me, I was never a thing to be given. And I was never an "it" to be owned.'

'Of course, Mae,' says Nasim. 'I'm sorry. I don't have your and Sherry's way with words.' He adds, 'And I'm sorry that I wasn't a better husband to you, all those years ago. I'm sorry for what I did.'

'Well, of course you are,' says Mae. The story of Nasim's ill-fated affair is well known. Within a few years, the strumpet he had married took the family jewellery and left him for a younger man. Who left her, soon after. Mae had lost interest in the story after that, although her sisters-in-law would have been more than happy to keep her up to date.

'I don't mean for me. I mean for you. I think it's just . . . well, look at you now! You've barely aged. People would think you were my daughter. They would never believe you were my wife. You were just too beautiful for me.'

'Well, you found someone who said that you were too beautiful for them, and you were stupid enough to believe it,' says Mae unrepentantly.

'Another middle-aged man having a crisis. You should have just bought another car.'

Jakie walks in and catches the end of the exchange. He gives Mae a warning look, mouthing, 'Be nice!' to her, as he crosses the room to shake Nasim's hand. The man who used to work for his father, whom he once called Uncle, and then called bhai. Neither seems appropriate now. 'Sir,' he says. 'How the devil are you?'

Nasim is obviously reluctant to take Jakie's hand, and grips his teacup more firmly with both of his, and this hypocrisy is what finally tests Mae's patience. He won't touch the son of the man whom he claims gave him everything, as though Jakie's inclination is something that's catching. Nasim is a doctor, just like Jakie; he should know better. She dismisses him abruptly, before he can come up with a response to Jakie's friendly greeting. She doesn't even want to hear whatever it is he might have to say.

'Well, thank you for your visit, Nasim. I'll tell my mother you paid your respects. And thank you for the car,' she adds. 'I mean that most sincerely.'

'It was good to see you, Mae,' Nasim says humbly, and gets up to leave, looking defeated. He puts down his tea and nods at Jakie, but he still doesn't shake his hand. Mae inclines her head from the winged armchair, like the Queen, like her mother, but doesn't smile, and doesn't get up. She doesn't look at him as he walks away. She pours more tea instead.

Jakie falls and sprawls into his father's old chair, looking exhausted, tossing his cane to the side, as though the effort of standing upright without using it is too much. 'Well, that was fun. It's not often you get to see the Ghost of Christmas Past. He's left his stink in the air,' and he breathes deeply to make a point. 'Tweed and body odour. Like damp dog sprayed in Old Spice. I love the smell of bigotry in the morning.'

Mae tries to look disapproving, but stifles a laugh instead. 'It's not morning, it's tea time,' she says, passing him a cup. 'It's always bloody tea time here.'

'You could have been nicer to him,' says Jakie. 'He looks awful. The next funeral you'll see him at will probably be his.'

'So what? He's just a bigot, like you say,' says Mae flatly.

'Well, this is Pakistan. This is the land of stiffly suited bigots. Fixing elections. Bribing officials. Shouting at the cricket. It would be odd if he wasn't,' says Jakie.

'Mummy said the same thing when he took a mistress,' says Mae. 'This is Pakistan, it would be odd if he didn't.' She sits up straight, and says, 'At a certain point, you have to stop blaming your country, and look at yourself.'

'At a certain point, you have to stop blaming your parents, and look at yourself,' replies Jakie.

Mae is about to scoff at the pat neatness of this, but then there is a soft creaking on the stairs. She and Jakie look at each other, and then at the door, as their mother appears, still swathed in white. She stops and looks at them in shock, as though catching sight of a pair of ghosts, and Mae follows her gaze to see themselves reflected in the glass over the black cloth hanging high on the wall. She sees what her mother sees. A straight-backed woman pouring tea. A friendly-looking man opposite her, accepting it. Those eyes, that mouth. The practical haircut of a family doctor. As though their mother has stepped into the living room of the past twenty years, and seen what she has lost; the tableau of herself and her husband, seated on their thrones. In the glass, in the flesh. As though Jakie and Mae are now the parents, discussing the whims and foolish faults of the errant child sulking upstairs. Mae stands up swiftly, aware that she is in her mother's chair. Jakie is slower than her, with his aching leg, but goes to his mother's side.

'Mummy . . .' he starts to say. His mother brushes off his kiss, and interrupts him impatiently.

'Your room is ready, Jakie,' she says. 'It would have been ready before, if you'd given me some notice. Don't think of touching me until you've washed yourself from whatever cesspit in the hills you've come from.' She warms to her theme, glad to have a chance to rant about this, grateful to Jakie for giving her the chance to complain. 'Look at all the dirt you have brought into my clean home!'

She looks like she'd slap him again if she could reach his face. It looks like she'd put all her brittle energy, her anguish of the last few days, into that slap. Jakie seems aware of this, and is suitably apologetic.

'Yes, Mummy, sorry about the mess, Mummy,' he says, with such a straight face that Mae has to suppress the urge to giggle; he walks carefully around his mother so that he doesn't touch her with his grubby clothes, and remains out of her reach. He winks at Mae as he leaves.

217

Pari appears in the doorway, and Mae warns her off with a subtle shake of her head before the poor girl gets the slap that is building up inside her mother. Pari understands, and scurries back, unseen and unheard, like a good servant.

'Well, Mae, is our guest gone?' says Mae's mother, her voice calm, but her whole ticking body on edge, humming with a slight vibration.

'Yes, Mummy,' says Mae.

'And why has he left . . . that thing he came in?' says her mother.

'Come with me, Mummy,' says Mae appeasingly. She's trying to sound nice. She's trying to sound kind. Her voice is gentle. 'It's for you.'

Mae and her mother stand outside, and inspect the Rolls-Royce, which appears to be in superb condition, polished to a mirror shine. Her mother approaches it, as though unable to believe that it still looks so gleamingly good, and runs her hand over it. She presses her fingertips to it, and pulls them back to see the prints marking the paint. She withdraws her hand, lifts it high, and hits the bonnet, hard. The slap unwound finally from her body, like a spring snapping back into place. Mae breathes with relief, thinking that her mother's fury has been released, unleashed and spent, with that single ringing smack of flesh on metal.

But then her mother hits it again. And again. And again. Harder and harder each time. As though it is exercise, something she has had to limber up for, the drumming rhythm of her blows becoming faster rather than slower. The spectacle is as disquieting as a public flogging. As difficult to witness. The loss of dignity of the old woman, who is unravelling into a spool of jumbled thread. The alarming nakedness of her anger.

The servants, who have been watching with curiosity, disappear, and find anything else to do. The security guard with his gun goes back to staring down unseen intruders past the gate. The bearer returns to the house. The gardener disappears to the vegetable patch, and the cook to the kitchen. No one wishes to be caught at the crime scene, and risk catching her mother's eye when she finally turns to face them. Only Pari remains, hovering in the shadows of the house, not far from Mae, as though unwilling to leave her alone with the sound of this lunatic violence. The cream-softened flesh striking the cream-veneered metal.

Mae remembers how her mother used to beat her brothers, when they were little boys, with a spitting strap, the spikes of a brush, in the name of discipline, and piety. She suspects that in England and America, mothers would be arrested for less these days. She listens to the sound of punishment, resounding around the courtyard as insistently as the leaden echo of a gong, the leather sting of a whip.

Mae stands back patiently, and lets her mother carry on. She doesn't offer soothing words, or pull her back. It doesn't matter if her mother seems mad, or if the servants gossip. Her mother is hurting no innocent, this time. The thing that she's hitting is a machine. It's already dead, like Daddy. It won't bleed. And she makes no dent in the thing, beyond smearing the paintwork. It's like punching a rock with bare knuckles. The only pain is her pain. Her palms must be bruising. Her joints must be aching. But she carries on. Her stamina is extraordinary. The white witch has hidden powers.

When she finally stops, she stands up stiff and straight, although everything about her tells Mae that she longs to collapse into the dry dirt of the courtyard. 'He died in that car. It was his coffin. My last son. I'd called him Choto, when I was carrying him. I was going to call him Khalil.'

'Choto Khalil,' says Mae. 'Little friend. That would have been a good name.'

'He was my only good son,' says her mother, presenting her rigid back to Mae, to her house.

Mae loses her patience, forgets her resolution to be kind. 'It's easy to be good when you're dead,' she snaps.

Her mother turns back furiously, and her face is a picture. White and almost ugly with emotion. 'You've never known what it was like, Mae. And if you did know, I don't think you cared. Do you think *I* don't know what you all think of me? It's taken Daddy's death to bring you back here.' She breathes, calms herself, and says in a more measured voice, 'You've never lost a child, Mae. I lost four. And I lost another one I never had.'

Mae's mother is not crying. She is holding herself up with determined firmness, her knees locked in place. She refuses to sit. She refuses to weep. If she does sit and weep, it will be where no one can see her. Mae understands this much about her.

'Khalil was my chance to make things right,' her mother says simply. 'And I lost him.'

Mae tries to imagine what it would have been like, to have come home in the summer of '71 after leaving her husband, to find a teenage boy called Khalil slouching in the house, as indulged as an only child. Her mother calling him down to dinner, nicknaming him Carl, or maybe Al, for Al Pacino. A merry mess of cricket bats and tennis racquets in the garden, schoolwork scattered upstairs among board games and puzzles, and kites collected on the roof. He would have been just a few years older than Sherry, and Mae feels a twinge of guilt, how she laughed when her mother tried to get Sherry to call her Buri Ammie. Older mother. Although Khalil wouldn't have called her this; he would have called her Mummy.

She tries to imagine Sherry giggling with her adolescent uncle at the dinner table, swinging the acorn weight from one side of the long table to the other, for Bhai Khalil to catch, while his parents, Sherry's bore-bore grandparents, ate and prayed, thanking the Almighty for their last child, their chance to make things right. She tries to imagine her mother smiling as this beautiful boy won all the prizes, and credited his mother in the school hall for all his grand achievements as he stood and accepted them at the end-of-year ceremony. The son who would find greatness abroad, and then return to Lahore and marry a pious local girl of good background. A son who would open a hospital in the city, and give it his mother's name. A son who would be a credit to her. A son who would stay.

Mae tries to imagine all this, and fails. It is painted too bright to be real; it is too blurred to be a true account – like Sherry's teenage Vaseline has been smeared all over the lens, and tinted rose. People don't change. And if they do, they rarely change for the better. But she can see the importance of this lost memory for her mother, this belief in what might-have-been, in the absence of her happily-ever-after. The weight of expectation on the poor little prawn, unborn Khalil or Carl or Al. He would have fitted neatly in a pickle jar, that's what Lana had said when she came back from the hospital. It seems he's preserved there for posterity.

'I never buried him,' says her mother. 'But I shall bury this car. It sickened me to see it paraded around the town, like a body dragged in the streets. I've wanted it buried for years.'

'I knew you wanted it,' says Mae. 'I didn't know why. Sherry's the one who had Nasim bring it over. Don't worry, you won't need to thank him for it. I've done that for you.'

Her mother is becoming herself again, controlled and imperious. 'Thank?' she says, as though she has never heard of anything so preposterous. She looks back at the house. 'Where's your brother? How long does it take him to get washed? Always so slow. Limping around in old clothes like a common labourer.'

'I'm here, Mummy,' says Jakie, appearing in a decent shirt and trousers. He's hastily shaved, too. Mae preferred how he looked before, when he was stained and stubbled, carelessly rakish rather than respectable.

'You're the man of the house today,' says their mother. They know she means until Sulaman arrives, the older brother. 'Do your duty. Take this . . . thing, and get rid of it. Bury it, crush it, throw it in the canal, I don't care how you do it. But don't just dump it in the slums for children to play in. I don't want to see it again. Get rid of it altogether.'

'Okay, Mummy,' says Jakie cheerfully, as though she has made a far more sensible request. Even with the cane, Jakie's better on his feet than he is sitting down; he's more dashing and impressive when he's in motion. Mae can see why he must find his desk job in general practice frustrating, even though the pay and hours are better. He calls the bearer, and the driver, and between them they manage to get the car on the handcart it arrived on. Mae watches with her mother as the driver and bearer push the enormous car down the street. Like the President being wheeled away on the back of a pushbike. A scattering of children divide in front of the car, and fall behind it, gathering and fluttering like sparrows, laughing at the spectacle. The enormous cream corpse of the car, drifting slowly down the street like a float in a carnival. It seems as though it is being lifted by the fragile hands of the children, in their brightly coloured tatters and rags.

Mae's mother turns back into the house as the car moves out of sight, nods briefly at Mae, and returns up the stairs. Mae wonders if she will cry in her room, whether she's looking forward to being alone, to do this. To bathe in the warm pool of her tears, to slide slowly into it, and feel her knotted muscles melt. The day is cooling, and Mae, standing in the shadows, feels a shiver.

'Madam,' says Pari shyly behind her, carrying a thick, expensive shawl she has unpacked from Mae's luggage. Mae would normally drape the piece decoratively on the shoulder, but she lets Pari wrap it around her, like a blanket. A thoughtful girl. A quick learner. Mae has already decided that she will ask her mother if Pari can come back to Karachi with her. She thinks Amma will probably agree, as Mae has got her back the car she asked for, and she dislikes feeling indebted. The old woman will probably think it is a good trade, that the machine is worth more than the maid. She'll happily exchange the warm living body for the cold metal corpse, and swap the stewed tea in a stained pot for the spilt blood on the seats. White witch, bleached bitch, black widow, thinks Mae with a cynical edge. Everyone seems to think that Mae is so mean, and sometimes she feels the rebellious urge to prove them right.

Be nice, Sherry said to her. Be kind, Mrs Kannon said to her. Be good, her mother has spent a lifetime telling her, and she has spent the last fifty years telling herself. Be good.

Again, Mae feels the battle has been won, and pulling the shawl tightly around her, like Athena with her Aegis, she feels like she is dressed for it, as she stands on the highest step and watches the last stragglers following the car down the street. Be nice. Be kind. Be good.

No, no, no, Mae says to these distant voices echoing down the line, the saints shining with the light behind them, the white witches reflected in mirrors. She doesn't need to listen to any of them. She answers to herself. She is Mae. The good daughter, sister, mother. She knows that she has already been all these things, and more.

Chapter Ten

Lana

LANA SOMETIMES DOESN'T KNOW WHAT TO SAY, AND SO SHE SAYS AS little as possible. She lets the stuff that surrounds her speak when she is silent. The powerful white air. The fat, syrup sun melting in the jalebi sky. A woman with puddles for eyes. Breathe, blink, reflect. Don't be sad, they say. She sees the man in a good suit, shaking, like a fault line about to split open with tremors. His silent mouth slit wide, a red curtain rising on a lit stage. His hidden body a theatre for distress. Don't be sad, she wants to say to her brother, to Sulaman, a man she hasn't seen in too many years. Fault lines between them. His fault and hers.

She wants to say, it's too late to be sad. He's already dead. It's too late to be sad, it already happened. Accept that. Except that. Except that she knows not to say this. And so she just says his name. Sulaman.

She offered him cool water once, when he was hot.

She let him go, when he didn't want to stay.

She promised to forgive him, when he wouldn't forgive himself.

And now she gives him his name, when he doesn't know who he is, when she feels that he feels that he might have forgotten what it ever was. This foreign man, from somewhere else, who belongs neither here, nor there. This man who has spent his life passing through, and passing off. Sully. Sulaman. Son. Their mother's firstborn. Her Adam. Her fallen angel.

'Sulaman,' she says to her brother, on the third day, the day of prayers for the dead and swiftly buried, limbs folded neatly, wrapped and packed for the next world. 'Sulaman,' she says. He's here. She's here. In a house of black mirrors, covered pictures, and frames of Qur'anic script.

Remember me, I will remember you is etched in Arabic, gleaming in gold. A prayer. A promise.

She loved him too. The man missing from their lives. Punched out of the world as suddenly as metal through cloth. A hole shot in the glass, with shards bleeding from it, sharp crystal tears, the cracks radiating outwards like threads of a spider's web.

But she does not feel what Sulaman feels, she knows that. She does not feel regret. She believes and she belongs, and she gives him the comfort that she does not need. Don't be sad, she says, it goes on. Life goes on. It must. She knows that there is another time, another place, another world. She cannot imagine the pain of loss for those who live without faith, bereaved without belief. She grieves for her brother's pain, for his loss, dragged behind him like lead weights. The heavy body of the dead. The powerful white air. Her white, hopeful words.

Don't be sad, Sulaman. He loved you. He loves you still. His life goes on. It must.

Lana knows what people think of her. What her family think of her. That she is some sort of savant. A woman wise beyond her years. That she is some sort of child, defective in her innocence, who has got away with it all her life because she is so very blameless, so very statutory. Even now, in middle age, with a thickening waist and greying hair. That her translucent little head is full of things unsaid. That her still waters run deep.

She sits waiting for her daughter in the café, a shiny branded franchise in the airport in Dubai, where they are forced to pass a few hours until their connecting flight to Lahore, and knows that these people are right and wrong. That they must be. She knows that she is special in every complicated way that word implies, gifted and dismissed. She knows, as she sips an indifferent latte in a fancy cup, that she is the centre of the café, of the airport, of the Middle Eastern country she has landed in for refuelling, of the whole spinning world, and that everything pauses and stops to take notice of this, and that as she moves, so moves the world. The waiters, the stewards, the duty-free shoppers and the steel and glass building spin around her like electrons, the marbled tiles under her feet like shifting tectonic plates. She knows that something else, something bigger than her, sees her on the tiny world like a bubble of bacteria on a slide, and could squash her and everything around her to a smudge and a stain, with a thumbprint on the glass.

Lana believes, and she belongs. She always has. And so she pulls all she knows within the small frame of her body, inside the flesh and bones, and makes sense of it for others. She is a quiet woman who earns her living caring for other people's loved ones, and who spends her spare time caring for her own. She cleans her windows with vinegar and newspaper; she watches the world with dedication though the glass of the television screen. Those who sit with her when she does – family and friends, patients and colleagues, those dying slow or dying fast – feel comforted by her presence, by the light she brings to a room. It is something to do with her faith, or her stillness; she is the centre of the storm. Even if they are watching news of bombshells and earthquakes, flying body parts and floods, acts of man and acts of God, they feel that as long as she is seated there, closing the cupboards with her keys, shaking out the tea leaves into a pot, using the scrunched newspaper to clean the glass, everything will be all right.

Lana knows she is special, and sometimes it feels like a burden.

Sometimes she is silent, because she simply doesn't know what to say.

Lana's daughter, Minnie, approaches her through the busy airport concourse, and divides the airy space as she passes. A kite in the sky. A paper boat causing ripples in a basin. People look at Minnie as she passes, in a way that people have never looked at Lana, even though they have almost the same face. The only difference between them is twenty-three years, and the slight sharpness of Minnie's father's bones, which gives something of a point to her shoulders, and a slight hook to her nose. On her father it looked predatory, and less appealing, but it suits Minnie, who is about movement, a bird-like energy, rather than stillness, who cuts air and water around her. Minnie's hair is dyed three shades, red and gold and chocolate brown, but she is dressed like someone who doesn't care too much about how she looks, and would be embarrassed if people saw her trying too hard. A grey sleeveless tunic, over dark jeans. She stands out among the dark-haired women in the airport in garish outfits the colours of jewels and boiled sweets. Her nails are painted, a fashionable shade of sky blue that came in a free sample bottle taped to the front of a magazine, but she doesn't have a scrap of make-up on her face.

'Mum, there's kick-ass duty-free in this place,' she says, sitting down beside her mother, taking up more than her allotted space at the table, as she bundles bags on the seats around her. 'Are you sure you don't want to look around?'

'Quite sure, sweetie,' says Lana. She is watching a news channel on the screen. There is trouble in Northern Ireland, in Frank's home town, and emotive pictures of messy-faced white children, looking bedraggled and helpless, against a scummy city street. The brown bejewelled people in the airport nod with sympathy, the white people in suits look disinterested. When the news of the latest flood in Bangladesh comes on, with messy-faced brown children, looking bedraggled and helpless, against a scum-coloured river, the white people nod with sympathy, and the brown people look disinterested. Lana isn't quite sure what to make of this; she supposes it is easier to show concern for other people's problems. Perhaps it is more comforting to feel sorry for people who look different than those you resemble.

Lana sees her daughter waving to the barista for a coffee as she shuffles through her purchases. She knows that Minnie is waiting for her to ask about them. It seems a little callous to turn from partisan fighting and rushing-river flooding to fashion, but Lana knows she can get away with it. She gets away with most things.

'So, did you have fun, sweetie? Did you get anything nice?' she asks generously.

'So much fun,' says Minnie. 'The French guy working at Ralph Lauren asked me where I was from, and said I had a *visage magnifique.*' She doesn't wait for her mother to respond, and pulls out the purchases. 'And he was so cute. Anyway, after that I couldn't buy anything from Ralph Lauren, even though there was this gorgeous little scarf, because he'd have thought I was flirting, and that any old line from a hottie with an accent could work on me.' Minnie stretches out her hand thoughtfully, and adds, 'It's a shame I didn't have Seamus's ring resized in time to wear. A ring really stops people hitting on you. It's a shame he couldn't have come along, to announce the engagement with me. It might have cheered everyone up.'

There is much that Lana could say to this; that Seamus's ring is from his grandmother, as he can't afford anything grander on his schoolteacher salary, and that the pinprick diamond is nothing to show off about, and that Minnie might well get sniggers from the Lahori ladies when she shows it to them, as they swing diamonds that could buy whole houses in the city's new developments from their ears like chandeliers in a ballroom. That it would have been completely inappropriate for Seamus to come along, as he isn't family, and never met Lana's father, Minnie's grandfather. That Uncle Sulaman isn't even bringing Radhika. Lana could say that it is even less appropriate to use a funeral, and the third day of prayers, to announce an engagement, because people don't want to be cheered up, they need to grieve, and that when Minnie does announce it, she'd be wise to do it when she is half the world away from Lana's mother, who is unlikely to think that Minnie, a divorced woman with two children, entering a second marriage with a white schoolteacher is anything to celebrate, and will howl down the phone like a persistent hound, calling, 'Disgrace, dishonour, disobedience' until the unreliable long-distance line mercifully cuts off. Lana doesn't say any of this. There is no need. There is no ring, and no Seamus, and she doesn't waste words, or say anything unnecessary. Lana doesn't lie either; she doesn't agree with her daughter that it is a shame, because in fact it is all great good luck, that the ring and the fiancé are unavailable.

'The ring you're wearing looks nice,' Lana says instead, nodding towards the Minnie Mouse ring on her finger, which Seamus bought for her in Euro Disney when they first started dating. Minnie smiles, and nods, because it does look nice, and suits her better than any pretty, little-old-lady diamond. It reminds her that she does have something of Seamus after all, and because she is in love, still in the stupid-soppy early days of the relationship, she almost tears up as she squeezes her mother's hand. As though unaware that she needed comfort, or needed this reminder of him, until her mother gave it to her.

'Oh, Mum,' she says. Her coffee arrives, and she beams at the waiter, who beams back at her in confusion. Her happiness is infectious. As though she's singing a cheerful tune that everyone will pick up from her and carry to the far ends of the airport, the far ends of the world. 'I did find another little scarf, though, at Hermès, for Nanu. And another one for Auntie Mae. Tanqueray gin and Jack Daniel's, for Uncle Jakie, and

227

me. And . . . I don't know what to get for the other uncle. The rich one. What do you buy someone who's got everything?'

'I think he'd like a coffee,' says Lana, as she finally sees the face in the crowd she's been waiting for, in the world beyond the screen. The good suit. A three-piece cage he doesn't seem to have stepped out from for years. His one bag appears to be all he possesses in the world. She stands up, and waves.

'What?' says Minnie. 'Is that Uncle Sully? What's he doing here?'

Lana doesn't bother to respond to this, as it is obvious what Sulaman is doing here. His father is dead, just as hers is. He was summoned to take a plane as soon as possible, and he is changing at the same airport, for the same connection to Lahore. It strikes her that Minnie can be a little dense sometimes, with her failure to see the obvious. The pig of a first husband she married, when Lana and everyone else could see that he wasn't any good for her. Lana supposes she must get that from her father, who was dense enough not to notice for a whole year that Lana had left him.

Instead she tells her daughter, 'He has it black, sweetie. No sugar.' Just like their mother. She wonders if Sulaman is aware of this, and whether he'd start adding cream and sugar, like he used to when he'd forgotten to eat, just to shrug away any clinging points of similarity. She sees that Sulaman has seen her, and he looks relieved and panicked all at once. He looks like someone who's just been saved out of a pit, who can finally allow himself to howl with the horror of what might have happened, to crumple with the fear. He's still a handsome man, his face rising carved out of his collar, like a cast-metal bust of himself, but his body seems to be made of trembling paper, stuffed into his clothes, held together by clever tailoring.

As Minnie shrugs and gets up, Lana adds, 'Better make it decaf, dear,' because her brother looks frayed, and stretched out. Minnie still seems annoyed, as though she has been caught out, and looks a little crossly at her mother for not warning her.

'Why didn't you tell me he was coming?' she stage-whispers as she passes her, although her uncle isn't close enough to hear her, not even close enough to read her lips.

'I didn't know that he was,' says Lana simply. Her brother has made many excuses over the years, has cancelled trips to London at the last minute because of his busy working schedule. His important research.

His work with government institutions. In war zones. The practical study and analysis of conflict and torture. This is Sulaman's bread and butter; it spreads him thin. His expertise has made him a wealthy man, and put his face on the back of books, and occasionally on television. She wasn't sure until she saw him that he would come. It would have been useless to ask him outright, 'So, are you really coming? Or are you just saying that you'll come, and then you'll find a way not to come?'

Lana suspects that he didn't know himself. That he didn't know at check-in, didn't know at passport control and didn't know until he made the decision to step past the wobbling stand of complimentary news-papers, past the inch of air between the moveable tunnel and the plane, and on to the plane itself. She can see that he still doesn't know whether he'll make it on to another plane to pray over a body that is already dead, and sleep in his old bed, and the reason he looks so dismayed is that seeing Lana has made it real. Seeing Lana has made it all the more difficult to turn back the way he came. The way he is holding his single bag, Lana knows that it is all he has carried. He hasn't checked in luggage, he hasn't sent any part of himself ahead. Not even spare socks and underwear in a case. He has made no promise.

Minnie huffs with impatience at her mother for this unsatisfying response, and goes and orders another round of coffees. Lana watches Sulaman approach, watches him look behind himself, as though hopeful that she is watching and waving at another person instead, and then finally he stands in front of her. She sees him with the critical and professional eyes of a career care-giver, and thinks, this poor man needs to sleep. She sees him as a sister, and thinks, this poor man needs a hug. She crosses the final inches between them, stopped by the cloth barrier to the coffee place, which hangs between waist-high posts. He is one side, and she is on the other.

'Lana,' he says inadequately. He doesn't say hello, or how are you, or any of the usual formulas, and Lana wonders why he is quite so afraid. Their father has died, and they are going home. That is all. It is sad, but it is simple. They will not go back for ever, just for a few days. There is no monster lurking in a cave, just their mother mourning in a house. They will be prayed over, not preyed upon. There will be holy words and halal food, shared out to each of them, and then they will stream back out like fish in a current towards their own lives, nourished for the journey, to repeat their usual scenes with their colleagues, friends and loved ones until they are dead. Nothing surprises Lana, and she is never afraid. She supposes that this is a fault of hers. She knows she is loved, and she knows she feels love, but she does not really grieve, or regret what is gone.

And here is Sulaman, like blood spraying out of a splintered body, bursting open like poppies on broken ground. Tattered, tangled, torn.

Lana does what a mother would do. She takes the broken pieces, and puts them together again. She puts her arms around her brother, and her cheek towards his cheek, and makes him whole. 'Sulaman,' she says, as though completing a circle. She doesn't say hello, or how are you, and she doesn't say that it's good he made it, as she's not sure that it is good for him, and it doesn't matter to her father, who is already in the ground. She tells him the selfish truth, because he is her big brother, and she loves him, and she wants him to know this, before he leaves again, and runs back to his real life, the one he began by himself a long time ago. 'I'm glad you came.'

Minnie has been chatting with the barista in the coffee place, and watching the hug between her mother and her uncle, has shrugged off her brief mood, her annoyance slipping away to fond exasperation, an indulgent Oh Mum expression, as she returns with a tray.

'Hi, Uncle Sully,' she says. 'Mum ordered your coffee already. Black, right, no sugar?' She puts the tray down, and leans over and pecks him on the cheek.

Sulaman starts slightly, and Lana sees him looking at Minnie as strangers must see her. Flaming hair, bare-faced and bare-armed, all her decoration painted on to her nails, and none on her blank clothes; she looks like a teenager, not a professional in her thirties. No one would believe that she has two almost grown-up boys. Lana likes this about Minnie; her effortless youth, which comes from a sense of not having been hurt by her life. Nothing clings to her. She doesn't even resent her ex-husband. She has all the freedom of a girl who grew up never being told what to do.

'That's right, thanks, Minnie,' Sulaman says, having finally located the formula. His body is stiffening, re-forming, and he knows who he needs to be now. Uncle Sully. It's an easier role to play than Sulaman, who he hasn't been in God-knows-how-many years.

Minnie notices that he is still on the wrong side of the barrier. 'Well, would you like it out there or in here?' she asks, and laughs a little. Sulaman smiles faintly, and walks around. He sits at the table, after Minnie repacks and pushes away her purchases, and sips his coffee with a hum of appreciation. Lana thinks his smile is so rare, it could cause walls to come tumbling down, the sunshine to break through clouds. She can't remember Sulaman laughing, not since he was a boy, flushing her coloured ribbons down the latrine. She can't imagine him crying. She thinks that she should be satisfied with the smile, but then it fades, and reappears upside-down

'Decaf?' he asks with a frown.

'You need to sleep,' says Lana. She doesn't say it bossily, she says it sensibly, and it is impossible to argue with her, because she's right. Sometimes Lana feels a little guilty for being almost always right. She knows that it is an unattractive quality. Minnie starts showing her uncle the presents, and people in the café are smiling in her direction. There is so little edge to Minnie; the only sharpness to her is in her shoulders, and her father's nose.

'I haven't got anything for you,' she complains. 'I would have done, but you turned up too soon.'

'I could go away again,' says Sulaman, and Minnie laughs like he's made a joke. Lana frowns at him, and he says, a little apologetically, 'So, Minnie, how are your boys?' Lana knows from the way he says this, the slight hesitation, that he can't quite remember their names.

'They're great,' says Minnie distractedly. She gives him no more details, because she knows he is just being polite, and doesn't want to bore him with the answer to his question. He doesn't want to know about how they are doing at school, their hobbies, their friends, their complicated relationship with their father, and with their mother's boyfriend. He doesn't want to know about what keeps them awake at night, and what they fear, and what they dream about when they fall asleep, their mother's lips brushing their foreheads, her hand on their hair. Lana understands this, and she gives her daughter an unreadable look; not because she feels Minnie is being rude, dismissing a question that did not require a real answer, but because she is surprised that her daughter, who usually talks enough for both parts of a conversation, has understood this. Minnie has more sensitivity than she realises.

Minnie's Euro Disney ring taps on her coffee cup, and she glances at it, and grins. 'You know, I've just thought of something. You both wait here,' she says, as though they really would go anywhere else. She picks up her purse, and dashes off.

'So her boys aren't coming?' Sulaman asks Lana. She winces slightly at 'her boys', and fills the gaps for him.

'No, Jamal and Frank Junior have school,' she says. She means to be helpful, but realises she sounds a little impatient with her brother, who is a world expert, with letters after his name. Lana's grandsons' names are easy enough to remember, as Minnie called her first son, Jamal, for Jakie, and named her second for Frank. Her uncles were her substitute fathers, as her actual father was so far away and never visited her when she was growing up. Uncle Jakie and Uncle Frank were the ones who came with Lana to Minnie's school plays, and watched her compete in netball and lacrosse on her school team; the ones who cooked her dinner with their own kids when her mum was working late, and who told her he wasn't worth it when she cried over a boy. They were the ones she casually introduced to her friends as *My Two Dads*, sincerity gleaming in the joke.

Minnie won't even see her real father on this trip to his home town, a few streets from his house, as he is in India on business. Lana suspects that Tariq, the man she had married all those years ago, and whom she had never got around to divorcing as it seemed like too much bother and paperwork, arranged the meeting across the border as soon as he heard of her father's death, to avoid a messy, distressing reunion. Tariq prefers having his daughter at a clean and comfortable distance; he keeps an attractive photograph of Minnie in his house, in her sober black and white graduation clothes, a tasselled cap on her hair, holding a scroll tied with ribbon. His family nose stamped on the face of his suitable first wife, the deceptively meek girl of good background from Gulberg. The one who behaved appropriately, never argued, went to visit her family abroad for a few months, remained with them to deliver her daughter as tradition recommended, and simply never returned. An apparently accidental, almost absent-minded separation, her forgetful failure to pack the baby in a buggy and get back on a plane. It was so casual, Lana's departure from her marriage, so lacking in malice or moment, that Tariq probably did not remember the last day he spent in her company; he is probably still unsure if he ever said goodbye. Lana got away with it; she was blameless, as always. After all, Tariq found a second wife easily enough, and there was little stigma in having a daughter raised abroad; if anything, there was a certain status.

Lana knows that Tariq likes talking about Minnie's achievements, and the education and professional training he has helped to finance. He tells his dinner guests that he sends his distant daughter, every birthday and Eid, a page of verses from the Qur'an, written out in his own hand, instead of a card with a cheque. As a teenager, Minnie began to frame his letters in unvarnished wooden frames from IKEA, preserving them like pressed flowers in an attic; she liked that they were reliable, and that they were rare. They were a conversation piece. This is what Minnie is to Tariq, something piously displayed in a formal frame. Something silent, that he can boast about.

Tariq would have no idea how to deal with a real Minnie, bursting into his house like a firework, putting her arms around him and kissing him warmly on the cheek. The hushed silence in his house, as everyone, retainers and relatives, stared at this bird of paradise, bare-armed, crop-haired, with lips that dared to kiss rather than murmur humble prayers and pious greetings.

'What?' Minnie would say to the offended gathering. 'What's wrong?' She'd look in confusion at the shell-shocked father she was embracing, and ask, 'Did I kiss the wrong man?' The shame. The excitement. Too much for Tariq, who had married a quiet girl like Lana for a reason. He would probably burst into flames himself.

'I see what you did there,' says Sulaman. 'You didn't need to. I know their names.'

'No, you didn't,' says Lana. Not unkindly.

'No, I didn't,' admits Sulaman. 'I'm a lousy liar. I guess I thought it politer to pretend.' He sips his coffee like he wants to complain about it, but then remembers that this is the coffee Lana ordered for him. Prescribed for him. He's drinking it from politeness, too. Lana is comfortable with the silence, but Sulaman isn't. 'Radhika sends the birthday cards from us. Or Buzz, these days. He's better at this than me.'

'This?' asks Lana. She thinks she should pull him up for it. She doesn't like being described as *this*. It feels insensitive. That she is something to be dealt with, and managed.

'Family,' says Sulaman. 'He's better at it.' Lana says nothing, as it is still insensitive, but it is true. Anyone and everyone must be better at family than Sulaman. She's seen Buzz, Sulaman's son, much more often than she's seen her brother over the years; Buzz even spent a summer before college in London. He's almost the same age as Minnie, and just a year younger than Jakie's adopted boy, Hari; they all went InterRailing in Europe together, with a group of student friends. They sent jokey postcards from Paris, Amsterdam, Rome and Madrid, which Lana took to work to cheer up her elderly charges. She still has a photo of them from that summer on her fridge; they are waving on a bridge like tourists, with Big Ben and the Houses of Parliament behind them.

But Sulaman has rarely visited London, only really when work shuttled him in and out on brief flying trips. And he hasn't visited Lahore since he left in the fifties. He's not bringing his wife to his father's funeral, and it doesn't even seem odd, as Lana knows that Radhika has just met their parents a few times in all the years she and Sulaman have been married, and then only briefly; just long enough for their mother to dislike her on sight, and dismiss her altogether on learning her unsuitable background. Lana doesn't know if Radhika decided not to come, or if their mother said outright that she wasn't invited. She supposes that it doesn't matter. Sulaman is here, and he is alone. He is always alone. If he smiles again, the walls will tumble down, and the sun will break through the clouds, and all the mist that separates them will dry up and clear. She'll accept his smile with her own; she will take what he can give, and let him know that it's enough. Instead, he glumly drinks his disappointing coffee, and taps his fingers on the table.

'Buzz's kids are in grade school now, and I don't remember their names either. Radhika writes them down for me before we visit. I mean, of course I remember what they're called, Sami and Dani, but I never know which is which. Which is the girl, and which is the boy.' His own grandchildren, thinks Lana, and he's describing them as the girl and the boy. Poor Sulaman. Poor silly man. So unaware of all the gifts he has been given.

'Samia's your granddaughter,' says Lana. 'Try thinking of her as Sweet Sami, for sugar and spice and all things nice, and then you'll remember that she's the girl.'

'Thanks,' says Sulaman. He seems surprised. Perhaps he expected Lana to tell him off; perhaps that's what he wanted from her, to feel better or worse about himself. Instead she offers a practical solution to his practical problem, without criticism or judgement. 'Thanks,' he repeats. 'You know, that helps.'

Minnie comes back with a bag from the Disney store. She passes it proudly to Sulaman. 'Is this something for my grandkids?' he asks. Lana thinks that would have been a good idea, if she'd had the wit to suggest it to Minnie. It seems obvious to her that the gifts which Sulaman, the rich uncle who has everything, most needs are the ones he's forgotten to buy for others. Something for Sami and Dani that hasn't been purchased pre-wrapped on his behalf and hidden in a cupboard by Buzz or his wife, so that he won't be as surprised as them when they tear it open. So he won't have to ask someone quietly what it is. Lana decides that she'll do this for him before the end of the trip. She'll buy him the whole damn set of Teenage Mutant Ninja Turtles for him to wrap himself and give to Buzz's kids, to Samia the girl, and Daniyal the boy, with love from Grandpa Sully.

'No, it's for you,' Minnie says proudly. 'Go on, you can open it now.'

'Sure, great . . . okay then,' says Sulaman, suddenly very American and uncertain, despite his positive-sounding words. He unwraps the little taped package in the garish bag and pulls out a matching set of Minnie and Mickey Mouse cufflinks. 'Oh, thanks,' he says, looking at them in confusion. Minnie is beaming, and clearly expecting more from him than this, and he says, 'Why thank you so much, Minnie,' a little more formally, and kisses her cheek because she leans forward and presents it like a child.

'They're great, aren't they?' says Minnie. 'Mum was just saying that she liked my ring, and then you turn up, and I realised you're probably the only guy I know who still wears his suits with shirts that need cufflinks.'

'Minnie Mouse ones?' says Lana to Minnie, with a slight sigh that brackets her words with *but* and *really*, without her needing to say them out loud. It seems more than a little self-centred; like a bumbling spouse buying something for a partner that they want for themselves. A football season ticket for her. A spa day for him. Well, if you won't use it I know someone who will. Sulaman seems to her like the last man in the world who would willingly wear comedy cufflinks.

'Well, of course,' says Minnie, aware of her mother's disapproval, and confused by it. 'Then he'll remember they're from me.' She looks at Sulaman. 'Do you like them, Uncle Sully?' She doesn't ask, don't you like them, as she won't ask a question that expects a no. Lana likes this about Minnie, she likes many things about her, and already her exasperation is sliding back to indulgence, back towards affection. Her own daughter, and this is the narrow gamut of emotions that Lana feels towards her: annoyance to tenderness, tempered with love, like cool milk in tea. Lana never feels hate, she has never felt alone; she can feel sorry for those who live with hate, or loneliness, the opposites of love, but she knows she can't really understand them. She feels sorry for Sulaman, successful Sulaman, falling apart as he falls from grace. Firstborn. Adam, alone in the Garden. The fallen angel, alone in the pit. A child, alone in the sandbox. It is as though the ones that came after to redeem him, Jakie and Mae and Lana herself, are just shadows dancing on the wall of his cave, and he can't ever be touched by them, even when they reach out to him. He can't be unburdened by them. Even when they hold him in their arms.

'They're great,' repeats Sulaman, and it doesn't escape Lana that he hasn't actually answered Minnie's question. Minnie doesn't notice this, and beams at her mother, with a flouncing little *so there* in the set of her shoulders. Sulaman catches Lana's eye, and hastily justifies his bland praise. 'Buzz's kids will love them. I'll wear them when I see them, and ask them to guess who gave them to me.'

'You wear a suit to see your grandkids?' asks Minnie tactlessly, sipping her coffee. She tosses her hair, and a group of three businessmen, in travel-rumpled suits, notice her as they walk past.

'Did you see that girl in grey?' one says to the others, and they glance back, and look away. Not a woman, not a lady, but a girl. They'll hum Minnie's happy song all the way to their meeting and beyond.

Minnie doesn't notice this either, and doesn't wait for an answer to her question as she looks around the airport. 'So where's Buzz? Is he still shopping?'

'No,' says Sulaman. 'He's not here. I mean, he's not coming.'

'Why ever not?' asks Minnie, suddenly very British and uppity. 'That's a bit rubbish of him. Tania can look after the kids.' She turns to her mother. 'I mean, they have *help*. They've got a full-time nanny. I've had to call in Uncle Frank, Asha, Hari and four sets of favours from the stay-at-home mums to get my boys taken care of for the week.'

'You know, Sherry's not coming either, sweetie,' says Lana, in a firm voice that tells Minnie to stop going on.

'Well, everyone knew that. She's Sherry. She's all about her. But Buzz . . .'

'I'm sure he'd come if he possibly could,' says Lana, and as subtlety is lost on her daughter, she adds, 'Your nanu loves chocolates. Those ones with crystallised violets. Do you think you could find some?'

'Christ, if you want me to shut up and go, just say so,' says Minnie. But she gets up anyway, and drops a kiss on top of her mother's head. 'You're right about those chocolates, though. I'll pick some up for her.' She admits this ruefully, a little proudly, that her mum always knows best and is even able to use a barefaced excuse to get rid of her to practical and useful effect. Minnie leaves, and heads turn, as the air ripples around her.

Sulaman sits back in his chair; it seems that just a few minutes with Minnie has exhausted him. Lana covers his tapping hand with both of her own. She has the hands of a working woman. Her nails are trimmed short, her palms have a reassuring toughness to them, her skin a little dry. They are practical hands that can change a light bulb, make a bed, fillet a fish, knead bread. He guesses she has to wash her hands several times a day, in her job, and that she doesn't bother to cream them at night. His daughter-in-law, Tania, sleeps with expensively creamed hands in special gloves, because she doesn't want Manhattan mommy hands; she says this without embarrassment. Lana is unembarrassed too.

'Why isn't Buzz coming?' she asks him, because she senses he wants to tell her. He's looking guilty. The boy in the sandbox wants to get something off his chest. He feels the need to confess. He stole the ball. He ate the pie. He painted on the wall. He can't tell a lie. I did it. It was I.

'I asked him not to come,' says Sulaman eventually. He sits up straighter, as though he can breathe properly for having admitted this. 'I asked him outright not to come, because I knew he wouldn't say no to me.'

'Are you ashamed of us?' asks Lana. She says it with no edge. She is simply asking a question.

'Of course I am,' says Sulaman. 'And I'm ashamed of myself.'

'Well, that makes sense,' says Lana mildly. 'You're one of us too.'

He fiddles with Minnie's cufflinks, and says, 'I don't want him to see what I'm like, at home, with Mummy. I don't want him to see that I can't cry at my own daddy's death. I don't want him to see that I'm dead inside. God help me, Lana, it's our father's funeral, and I don't want to go.'

Lana is a mother, and her brother is a child. Plaintive and whining. Stricken and struck. Lana thinks that she might have dismissed Sulaman in the past, just as she was dismissed, and feels a little guilty for this. Mum doesn't know best after all; Mum doesn't know everything. She didn't think of Sulaman as having wants and don't-wants, desires that couldn't be achieved and fears that couldn't be fixed. She thought that he would always bear, forbear and endure. Sulaman, her big brother built of brick, couldn't burn; Sulaman, tick tocking like a clock, couldn't just stop. Manufactured by their mother like Frankenstein's monster, like a machine; spun from her iron-soaked blood, carved from her bone, wired with nerves. The man of many parts, falling apart. Held together by his clothes and his mask.

She sees now what he doesn't; Sulaman, their Adam, their fallen angel, the first child. She sees the soft living part of him, exposed and humming with distress, naked on the floor, holding his knees and rocking in the corner.

'I know you don't,' says Lana. 'You don't have to go, Sulaman. You know that. You have a choice.'

She looks at him steadily; she is the centre of the café, the airport, the world, with a still light glowing inside her. He is her big brother, and she loves him. She has offered him a practical solution. A glass of cool water on a hot day. She is letting him go, because he doesn't want to stay. She will forgive him, if he won't forgive himself. She wants him to know this. She smiles. She smiles, and then he smiles. And the walls fall down.

When Lana first met Minnie's husband, the thing that struck her most was how much Zafar resembled Minnie's father. It bothered her. It bothered her enough to mention it to Jakie and Frank, while she was pouring tea for them.

'He could be Tariq's son,' she said. 'That's strange, isn't it? I'm not sure Minnie even sees it.' Her brother and his lover had dropped into her flat after work one soggy Wednesday; it was just a few streets from their house, on the way back from the local Chinese takeaway. As she was talking, Jakie was paged by the hospital, and said he had to leave, even though they had only just arrived.

'Sorry, Lana,' he said apologetically, kissing her goodbye just as warmly as he had kissed her hello. She leant her head briefly on his shoulder, as comfortably as though he was furniture. 'Save me some of the takeaway,' he said blithely to Frank, already walking past him towards the door.

'Don't count on it,' Frank replied.

'I'll see you at home,' Jakie called back as he left, a bit more contritely, realising from Frank's deadpan tone that he was annoyed that Jakie was ditching him again.

'Don't count on that either,' called back Frank. But Jakie was already gone, his footsteps echoing down the stairwell in Lana's building. 'Well, that was a quick date night,' Frank commented to Lana, settling himself on her sofa, stretching out his feet on her coffee table.

'He'll have better hours once he moves into general practice,' Lana said sympathetically, swatting Frank's feet back down again. It seemed to her that Jakie was always abandoning him. He'd said sorry to her, but not to Frank. She worried that Jakie was taking him for granted, and that Frank wouldn't keep putting up with it. That he shouldn't have to. Frank was family. She was thinking that if Jakie lost Frank, she and Minnie would lose him too.

'Don't worry about it, sweetheart,' Frank said blithely, sipping his tea, grimacing as though it was missing a shot of something stronger. Lana thought briefly about offering him the ceremonial bottle of champagne she had in the larder, a gift from work that needed using up, but Frank drank too much anyway. Especially now that Asha had moved out of the house, and little Hari had suddenly become old enough to share beers with him by the barbecue. She realised that Frank hadn't been talking about himself and Jakie, but Minnie and Zafar, when he added, 'It might seem strange, but it's perfectly normal to seek partners who resemble your parents.'

'Which part of your mother does Jakie resemble, then?' Lana asked. Whenever Frank talked about his mother, he cattily spoke of dyed red hair, Christmas Catholicism and a fake fur coat. He said she'd never go to hell, because animals didn't have one, and although he loved her, God he loved his mammy, she was a terrible bitch. It seemed to Lana that Frank's mother, with her careful grooming, public piety and look-at-me-clothing, improbably resembled Lana's own mother far more than her brother.

'He's got the Catholic guilt, for a start,' said Frank. 'Always trying to make things right, our Jakie.' Lana thought it was generous of him to say this, our Jakie, as though he wasn't Frank's or Lana's, but belonged equally to both of them. She'd owned Jakie as the boy, and Frank had him as the man. He'd raised two children with him. My Jakie. Your Jakie. The empty space on the sofa next to Frank.

Lana drank her own tea, while Frank complained animatedly about his day and the eejits he worked with, and the editor who compromised his copy, and when he paused for breath, she got up and pulled a photo album out of a drawer. She didn't display her wedding photos, but she hadn't thrown them away either, as she knew that Minnie liked looking at the old shots from the sixties. A young Lana, so highly painted as to be unrecognisable, and Minnie's absent father, dressed like an old-fashioned movie star.

'Look,' she said, showing Frank the formal portrait of herself and Tariq. 'Zafar doesn't look like Tariq now. He looks just like he was back then. With an outfit change and a haircut.'

'Christ,' said Frank, inspecting the picture. The resemblance was startling. 'That's creepy,' and he downed his tea like it really was something stronger. 'Not you, sweetheart, you look like a doll. Positively statutory. Practically jailbait. How old are you there?'

'You know I was twenty,' said Lana, a bit impatiently. 'It was the year I first came to London.' They had talked about it just the other day, when he was signing the photos for her passport renewal. Frank was so forgetful, lately, that sometimes Lana suspected him of doing it on purpose, to annoy Jakie or to get out of dull social events, claiming they had conveniently slipped his mind.

'You're right, so,' said Frank. 'Don't take it personally; you know I'd forget my own head if Jakie didn't hand it to me at the door in the morning.' He added gallantly, 'Besides, you're a much finer figure of a woman now than you were then.'

'Yes, now I'm like two twenty-year-olds,' said Lana, replacing the picture.

'Almost the same age as Minnie,' commented Frank. 'She's far too young to get married, in this day and age. You should say something.'

'But what?' asked Lana. 'That I'd rather she not marry a man who looks like her father? That I'd rather she not get married at all?' She sighed, as she knew that conversation wouldn't end well, and so it would never happen. 'You know Minnie, she's impulsive. I'd rather she just lived with him, but he's far too traditional for that. He doesn't believe in . . . that, before marriage.' Lana was embarrassed by her own coyness; she didn't know why she hesitated and substituted 'sex' with 'that' – fortunately, Frank understood her perfectly.

'God, imagine if I'd had to marry every person I ever shagged,' he laughed. Lana knew that he was trying to cheer her up with the joke, not dismiss her concerns.

'That would have been quite expensive,' she said. 'All those ceremonies. Time-consuming, too. All those in-laws.'

'I like my in-laws,' said Frank, putting down his cup and standing up, getting ready to leave. He kissed Lana on the cheek, with real affection, and put his arms around her. She briefly let her head rest on his shoulder, just as she had with Jakie. 'They're great gas.'

Lana stepped away, and looked for Frank's hat and briefcase, and the brown-bagged takeaway he and Jakie had bought for their date-night dinner, before he walked off without them.

'Thanks, you're an angel,' he said. He picked up his hat, and then put it down again. 'You're the one who should be getting married. Not Minnie. The foolish fellas out in town don't know what they're missing.'

'I'm already married,' said Lana, suppressing the urge to titter delightedly behind her hand at the compliment, like the waitresses and barmaids Frank was always flattering. 'And I'm really not looking for anyone else.'

'I've seen your ex. If I were you, I'd look for *anyone* else,' he said, and Lana let out a little bubble of laughter after all.

'I wish Minnie could have picked someone like you, if she was going for a daddy figure,' she said. She meant it quite seriously, but Frank took it as a joke, and grinned. He seemed to think that Lana was kinder and funnier than she really was; no one else teased her like this. No one else, apart from Jakie, really made her laugh.

'A Father Frank figure? But how would she ever find a devastatingly attractive Irishman with a devil-may-care attitude at accountancy college?' he said.

'Asleep on the steps in the morning, maybe,' said Lana. 'With the milk bottles.'

'God, I remember all that. At Minnie's age, I was out with the cats in the night, and back with the milk in the morning. Shouting drunken abuse at the haters and the starers at pub closing. I was always getting into fights. I'd wake up black and blue.'

'That all sounds horrible,' said Lana flatly.

'God, no, it was great. Good times,' said Frank. 'So you see, it's your fault she's marrying a strait-laced, straight-faced Asian accountant.' He picked up his briefcase in one hand, the takeaway in the other. 'You should have sent her to work at eighteen, pulling pints in some fleapit in Finchley. Then she'd have run with the fun crowd, and met fellas like me.'

He kissed Lana again, and left. He'd forgotten his hat after all, and she propped it up on the coat stand. She liked that he'd left something of himself; it was a promise that he'd come back. Her brother's lover. Her child's most present father. Her friend.

She went into Minnie's room and sat on her daughter's bed, looking at the picture of her and Zafar on the dresser, taken on the steps of their college. He was well scrubbed, with a shining cap of dark hair, wearing jeans and a checked shirt. He looked better than Tariq, simply because he was smiling, even though he showed too much gum. Zafar's looks were all in his colouring, his caramel skin and pearly teeth; in black and white, he'd just look like any other suitable boy, high-nosed, with a high-nosed mother behind him.

On the wall behind Minnie's bed were the framed pages of verses from the Qur'an, copied out in Tariq's determined hand. Lana remembered him signing the marriage papers, the careful seated position he took with the pen in his hand; no slapdash scribble with splashy ink, the way she had seen other people sign themselves away, but deliberately and firmly, sharp nib to soft paper, carving his name in rock. It was the same way he had made love to her later that evening. Carefully positioned. Sharp to soft. As though he was making his mark. Her blood, his ink. Irrevocable.

There were twenty-three frames on the wall, one for each year since Minnie was born. Whether Lana liked it or not, Minnie kept Tariq in her life. In a decorative box on the shelf, where other girls her age might keep jewellery or gum, condoms or cigarettes, she kept the stack of thousand-rupee notes that had been sent twice a year for Eid. A ceremonial payment, as Tariq had contributed fairly to Minnie's upkeep, and she was probably the least expensive of all his children, not requiring the inane fripperies of the wealthy Lahori sons and daughters he had with his second wife.

Lana would rather that Minnie hadn't kept all the notes so carefully; it gave them a sort of talismanic importance that she found disquieting. It was just cash. Perhaps Minnie simply didn't see the point of paying to change them to sterling; she was an accountant after all. Perhaps she was planning to take it all to Pakistan one day as holiday money, or to donate to an orphanage. Lana nursed a secret hope that Minnie was simply keeping the notes to throw back in her father's face one day, torn to confetti and scattered on his doorstep like petals, but she doubted that was the case. Minnie was like her mother. She took family seriously.

Lana wondered if it was the framed Qur'anic script, the writing on her bedroom wall, that had made Zafar propose to Minnie so quickly, on their fifth date or thereabouts, deciding he had finally found an independent career girl in London who was as pious as he was, despite her regrettably gay uncles. The Book proudly displayed above her pillow, not hidden in a drawer like a hotel bible, as embarrassed to be discovered as a gatecrasher at a party. Lana wondered what Zafar would say if she took him aside seriously one day, before the three-day event that his family were planning for the wedding, and pointed out that Minnie would just as happily have framed beer mats from pubs, or comically risqué postcards of animals in costume, or those prints of bare-chested beautiful black men holding white babies, if her father had sent those instead. What if he was really marrying her for her father's wall of words?

Lana left Minnie's room as she heard the front door open and her daughter rush in, her firm step on the wooden flooring. She found Minnie in the hall, experimenting with one of Lana's dupattas in front of the mirror, covering her hair with the scarf, tying it this way and that. The dupatta she had picked off the coat stand was the blue one that matched Lana's work clothes; it was too whispery and sheer, and didn't seem to do what Minnie wanted. She went from Pirate Pippa to Gypsy Jane, and looked like she did when she used to dress up for Halloween. It seemed unlikely that she had a fancy-dress party on a Wednesday night.

'What are you doing, sweetie?' asked Lana mildly. Minnie was dressed like every other student in the eighties, in leggings and a T-shirt from Gap. The T-shirt was a shade of dusty pink that suited her, and she looked perfectly lovely, but she seemed dissatisfied with her appearance, and dashed into her room, returning with a cardigan and sarong.

'I thought you were with Zafar today,' said Lana. 'Aren't you meeting some of his people?' She watched her daughter wrap the orange sarong around her hips, so that it fell to her ankles, and tuck it into the waistband of her leggings. She shrugged on the sand-coloured cardigan, a long and loose one in crumpled linen.

'I am,' said Minnie, wrapping the sheer scarf inexpertly over her hair again, back to Pirate Pippa, Gypsy Jane. 'How do I look?' She turned and presented herself to her mother, double-dressed, her long-sleeved, full-length costume over her day clothes.

'You look a bit warm, sweetie,' said Lana flatly. In fact, Minnie looked rather pretty, with the orange skirt, sandy top and blue scarf, like a topsy-turvy sunset on a beach, but Lana refused to show approval. 'Is this for Zafar's benefit? What's wrong with what you had on?'

'His grandmother is a bit traditional, and he wants her to like me,' said Minnie.

'If I were him, I'd be more worried about whether you like her,' said Lana. 'You don't need to cover your hair, sweetie. I don't. It's not like you're going to a funeral, or a mosque.'

'I know that,' said Minnie impatiently. 'But it's the colours; he thinks I don't look serious enough.' She pulled off the scarf, and ran her fingers through her tousled multicoloured bed-head, dyed for free by an Italian instructor called Gianluca at the Vidal Sassoon School in Bond Street, who asked Minnie back as a model every other month. Lana would swear he had a crush on her, if he wasn't so tight-trousered and flouncing. Minnie's natural friendliness was frequently mistaken for flirting.

'Does he?' said Lana, with more than an edge to her voice. 'But you love your hair, sweetie. That's what you said to Gianluca when he'd finished. You said it three times.'

Lana remembered the delighted look on the instructor's face when Minnie grinned and squealed this at the final reveal, the high polished mirror in his hands positioned to show front and back. Lana had been standing at the door, having just arrived to take Minnie to lunch, and had been ushered into the basement classroom by the receptionist, as Gianluca was running late. Minnie was his favourite model for his Japanese students, as he could show them how to strip the colour from her hair first, before dyeing it. The earnest-looking high fashion students were seated in a semicircle around Minnie, scribbling notes during the final blow-dry, taking photos for their course files.

'Did you hear that?' he exclaimed. '"Love, love, love it!" That's what you want your clients to say.' And he winked at Lana by the door. 'Not "that's nice, that's fine, that's okay". We don't want their consent to do what we do. We want passion. They have to love, love, love it!' And the students gave him a dutiful round of applause.

Lana looked at Minnie, waiting patiently for her to think about this, about what she was doing. Changing for a man. 'Maybe I shouldn't love it so much,' said Minnie, unabashed. 'I might stop dyeing my hair. It looks a little vain.'

'Well, I'm not lending you that scarf,' said Lana decisively. 'You look like a fortune-teller at a fair.'

'Oh,' said Minnie, as though her mother was being helpful rather than obstructive. 'You're right, that would be worse.' Lana suddenly wished she had a tarot deck and crystal ball to slip into Minnie's handbag, some signs of black magic that might scare Zafar's relatives away from her daughter. A voodoo doll stuck with pins. She sighed. She knew she was being childish and oversensitive. It was just an old woman who preferred baggy clothes on girls, just a comment about her hair.

There was an impatient honking from downstairs, and Lana glanced out of the window. Zafar was waiting in the street, leaning on his father's sensible, boxy-looking car. Minnie pulled off the scarf, and as she replaced it on the coat stand, she spotted Frank's hat. She slapped it on impulsively.

'I should have known Uncle Frank had been here; the stairwell stinks of fag ash,' she commented, tucking most of her hair away so that only some darker strands at the front were showing. 'Well, that'll do,' she said. 'Wish me luck.'

'Good luck,' said Lana, too surprised at the sight of her daughter's face with Frank's hat on to say anything else. It was like looking at her own face wearing the hat, as though she'd had the daring to try it on in front of the mirror, looking this way and that, deciding whether or not it suited her. Minnie kissed her, and clattered down the stairs.

Lana watched from the window as her daughter flew out of the front door from their building, and dived straight into Zafar's car, chattering apologetically as he got in himself, holding the hat on her head. Lana saw them side by side in the windscreen, below the haze of reflected light and smeared raindrops on the glass. Zafar didn't seem to be saying anything back, but he put his arm possessively around Minnie as he drove off.

Lana shuddered, thinking of her own wedding day to Tariq, his hand on hers, the knowing looks from his uncles and aunts as they were driven to his house. She remembered how she had remained smoothly stoical and expressionless, doll-like as Frank had aptly said. While everyone stared at her, and the older ones who knew what happened between men and women on their wedding nights nudged each other with vicarious delight. She had worn her unaccustomed make-up, her scarlet lips and black kohl, like a mask. A niqab under a burqa. A smooth blank space for a face. Blood and ink.

Lana told herself that Minnie's wedding would be less disquieting than her own. This was London, not Lahore. It was the eighties, not the sixties. Minnie hadn't simply consented to the marriage; she was passionate about it, and seemed to be giddily in love with her man. Without consulting Lana, she had even bought her mother a frivolously extravagant shalwar kameez in sky blue and silver, with underwear and heels to match, which Lana obediently wore, feeling like she was the one in fancy dress for Halloween. She hated heels, and had never really learned to wear them. Dressed by her mother as a girl, and by her daughter as a grown-up.

She couldn't shake the feeling during the wedding that although she had fled with her daughter from the messy, mixed-up world of two-faced tradition, the mother ship had just turned up, hovered overhead, and beamed her back home. She'd stolen her child from the Punjab, and it had reclaimed her. Frank had told her once about a woman in his old neighbourhood in Belfast who'd had an affair with a Catholic priest; her love child had been educated in a convent, and then chose to join the nunnery as soon as she finished school, going straight back to the God she'd been borrowed from. Apologetically returned like goods in a shop. It seemed unfairly inevitable, to Lana, that in the end everyone got returned. We all go back to where we belong.

Zafar's extended family had trekked down from Bradford and

Birmingham for the wedding. They were Punjabi too, but less affluent and pompous than Lana's people. Zafar, as a chartered accountant in training, represented the pinnacle of their achievement so far. They had jobs rather than professions, they worked in commercial enterprises rather than owned them; Zafar's parents and Lana wouldn't have mixed socially back in Pakistan.

Despite this, his relatives had been perfectly friendly and welcoming to Minnie, although they were much too earnest on the subject of religion. Lana had always believed and belonged, and was comfortable in her faith. She didn't have the zeal of a convert or a returning prodigal, and never pushed her religion on others. Not even on her daughter; she waited until Minnie asked her before she taught her prayers. Lana thought that her own mother's aggressive piety had alienated Mae and her brothers from faith, and that it was a great shame. Lana was the only one of them who still prayed, and kept her fasts, in a modest and unfussy manner. She invited family and friends to eat with her on Eid, making their old cook's spicy specialities alongside fish fingers and chips for the children, and she went to Jakie and Frank's to eat at Christmas, and left presents under their tree. She answered to herself; she was prepared to answer to God. She lived and let live.

So she was polite when she and Jakie's children, Asha and Hari, found themselves cornered by one of the bearded and snow-capped imams from Birmingham, who spoke about good works in his local community, and littered his story with aggressively holy phrases, like a salesman pushing for a deal, *Mashallah*. Thanks be. Praise be. Almighty Allah. All merciful. *Inshallah*.

'*Inshallah*, innit,' said Hari quietly to Asha, the teen mother who had been raised as his big sister, reducing them both to poorly suppressed giggles, until Lana told them both off for being snobs. She was relieved that no one else had heard. She looked around for Jakie and Frank, hoping they'd behave with the guests for Minnie's sake. She saw Jakie with Minnie, talking to her in-laws, looking terribly respectful and professional, but he grinned briefly when he caught Lana's eye, so she saw the silver flash of humour with the whiteness of his teeth, the rueful acknowledgement of the show he was putting on.

'Where's your dad?' she asked Hari, when she couldn't see Frank in the crowd; his red hair should have made him unmissable. She could imagine him getting bored enough at an alcohol-free party, the fruit juice served misleadingly in cocktail glasses, to start a heated political argument just for a bit of light entertainment.

'He's done another lap of the buffet, piled a paper plate high with chicken and lamb kebabs, and taken it to the car,' said Hari, looking as though he wished he could get away with doing that too. 'West Ham are playing; he's catching the second half on the radio.' He chewed a beef kofta from his own plate a bit glumly. 'I told Minnie that the date clashed with the football. She told me I was being silly. I bet you she'd have shifted it for Zafar's lot if it was the cricket instead.'

'Minnie's right, you *are* being silly,' said Asha impatiently. 'Bugger off and listen to the footie with Dad, if you're that bothered about it.' Lana appreciated the support, but privately thought that Hari had a point.

'Your daughter is a jewel,' one of Zafar's great-aunts started telling her, stopping like a ship coming in to moor, wrapped in several feet of shawl. 'All the girls these days are so modern. So greedy for money, only. With their careers. All flirting-shirting, and sales-shales. Shopping and shoes. Not Minnie. She's a good girl.' The great-aunt looked with disapproval at Asha, in her Western trouser suit and silk shirt, her ringless hand on her good handbag, as though unmarried working women in their mid thirties had no place at social events. Lana supposed disapproval was better than pity; they had advanced that far.

'She is. But Minnie likes shopping and shoes, too,' said Lana. She gestured down to her fancy-dress mother-of-the-bride outfit, determined not to be embarrassed by it. 'She bought me this, and the sandals.' The great-aunt looked stonily at Lana, as though she had let her down deliberately, and giving her a small nod, sailed off to join another group.

'Well, nobody's perfect, Auntie,' said Asha, and she put her arm through Lana's, in solidarity. Lana nodded, touched that Asha had seen how stricken she was. Not at the criticism of her clothes, but at the implication that Minnie shouldn't have got her them. That shopping and shoes were somehow not acceptable.

'Silly old Stone Age bitch,' whispered Hari on her other side, sounding just like Frank. 'Don't worry, Auntie. Our Minnie earns her own money. She can do all the flirting-shirting in the sales-shales that she wants.' He glanced at his watch, and put his plate down. 'You know, I'd better check in on Dad,' he said, 'just in case he's choked on a chicken kebab,' and walked swiftly out to catch the rest of the second half, as sweetly transparent as someone taking a sick day on a Friday, and returning on Monday with a tan and airport chocolates for the team.

Still, Lana was relieved when Zafar proudly told the gathering that his lovely and talented wife had got a job at one of the big five accounting firms; he hadn't seemed embarrassed by her professional success, which was what Lana had feared. Her success was his success, he said, hugging a blushing Minnie at his side.

Minnie kept her hair in more sober shades of red and brown as she started work in a highly corporate office, and seemed to enjoy married life. She enjoyed pregnancy, far too soon, but again, Lana could hardly tell her off about it, as that was what she had done herself; for Lana, the whole point of agreeing to her marriage had been to have a baby. But then Zafar wouldn't let Minnie go back to work after her maternity leave, insisting it was too soon to leave little Jamal, even though Lana would have happily adjusted her own hours to look after him. Minnie agreed; she loved her baby, of course she did, but sometimes Lana thought she loved being part of a traditional family even more: a child, a mummy, a daddy. A real daddy, providing, protecting, and most of all, present. The missing puzzle piece in her childhood, which Lana had refused to fill for her all those years; the hole in their little household, filled with verse in frames. A marriage was one thing, but the baby made it real and irreversible. Irrevocable. Their contract carved in flesh. Little Jamal had completed Minnie's dream of a proper family, and she spoiled him shamelessly.

'How could I leave this ickle wickle prince in nursery?' she said, blowing besotted bubbles on his tummy. 'Anyone else can audit; I'm the only one who can look after this little man.' And she positioned him, freshly washed, clothes pressed, in his highchair in the kitchen, facing the front door, so that the first thing Zafar would see when he turned the key was his winsome wife giving milk and rusks to his beautiful baby.

This was the only time that Lana felt sorry for him, walking into this forced performance, this glossy corporate ad; it was clear that he did not know how to play his part when he came back from work after a long day. He was the father in Minnie's little play, but he didn't know how the father should act, and it was sometimes painful to watch Minnie feed him his lines. Doesn't little Jamal look adorable in those new dungarees? Did you see how nicely he's eating? Isn't he a poppet, isn't he the loveliest thing in the world? Lana remembered her own mother doing something disturbingly similar, albeit without Minnie's wholesome and silly optimism.

Then Zafar got a promotion, and moved the family out of their apartment in town to a bigger house in the suburbs, nearer to where he worked, so he could get home sooner and help Minnie, he said. Minnie liked the garden, and having a swing and slide for baby Jamal. But it was too difficult for Lana to get there without a car. She became used to speaking to her daughter on the phone, and being restricted to occasional weekend visits, when Zafar collected her and dropped her off at the station. He had as little to say to her during these uncomfortable trips as she did to him. She would rather have called a cab, but Minnie always said she was being daft, that Zafar just adored her. Lana thought that if that was the case, he hadn't told his face; he always looked annoyed and dismayed to see her, before composing his features into a polite smile. She reminded herself that he was her daughter's choice, and composed a polite one back. Mask to mask.

Then when Minnie was barefoot and pregnant for a second time, with baby Jamal just fifteen months old, he hit her. For popping outside in her old student leggings and a stretch gym vest to pick up some milk from the corner shop. She was in her third trimester, sweaty and uncomfortable, so she'd dressed for comfort. Her sports vest was unusually tight over her swollen breasts. She had been pushing the buggy uphill. It was too hot to wear a cardigan, and so she had wrapped it around her waist. A couple of builders had wolf-whistled and cat-called her lewdly on the way home.

'For God's sake, you're disgusting. I've got a kid here, and one on the way,' she had told them crossly.

'I'll give you the next one, love,' said the younger builder, working shirtless in the summer heat.

Minnie had been relieved to see Zafar pull up beside her, on his way home from work. Rescued from the mean suburban streets by her knight in shining armour. Provider and protector. He had watched her pack the baby into the car, and fold the buggy, while she chattered obliviously to him. He ignored her as he drove home, until she eventually fell silent. He had hit her as soon as she was inside their closed front door. The disgrace. The dishonour. The disobedience. Walking the streets with her breasts on display, like a whore. Talking shamelessly to half-naked men, like a whore. Letting them proposition her, like a whore. She was disgusting, he said. He hit her again, while their baby dozed in his car seat in the hall. When Minnie's sobbing woke Baby Jamal, and he started wailing as fearfully as his mother, Zafar walked out of the house.

Minnie cried down the phone to Lana, and said that Zafar had cried too, when he had come home. She said that he was so, so sorry for what he had done. 'Will he get help?' Lana had asked, when Minnie had calmed down. Just those four words. Minnie's suburban house was detached, and the neighbours weren't close enough to hear what went on behind closed doors. If he'd kept hitting her daughter, no one would have stopped him. He'd claimed to have been a religious man; he had beaten his pregnant wife.

'Mum, he can't do that,' said Minnie, a little sharply. Already defending the man who beat her. Critical of the woman trying to protect her. Already falling into the pattern of it wasn't his fault – I made him do it – look at what I made him do. 'You know what it's like. He'd lose face.'

'Then get out,' said Lana, simply. Three words. The less she spoke, the more persuasive she would be.

'I'm not you,' said Minnie. 'I'm not going to walk out on the father of my children in a hissy fit. I want my kids to grow up *knowing* their father.' She sounded angrier at Lana than she had been at Zafar. 'Get out?' she repeated incredulously. 'That's your advice? That's what you think I should do? Just get out with the baby and a bag.'

'Yes, sweetie,' Lana said. Two words. It wouldn't have mattered if she'd said more, as Minnie had hung up on her. She hadn't called Lana again for weeks.

And then one morning, Lana woke to the sound of a baby crying. She pushed her feet into her slippers, and went to Minnie's room, and opening the door slightly, she saw that Minnie had arrived in the night and was asleep in her old bed, with her son beside her. There was no bag, after all. Nothing for Minnie, and no changing bag for Jamal. She hadn't even worn shoes. She had called a cab, and in the middle of the night, when Zafar was asleep, she had picked up her baby in her arms, and walked out of the door silently in her socks.

'What about all your things, sweetie?' Lana asked, fussing over her in the morning, wanting to fill her empty wardrobe.

'I didn't think to pack,' said Minnie. 'Anyway, it might have looked suspicious. He would have stopped me.' Lana could tell that Minnie was lying, but she didn't know why.

'I'll go over and get them,' said Lana, and when she saw the look in Minnie's eyes, she added hastily, 'Not on my own. I'll go with Uncle Jakie or Uncle Frank. And I'll get someone to stay with you too. I'll call Asha. Or Hari.'

'Look, there aren't any things to get. He cut up all my clothes,' said Minnie. She tried to say it sensibly, like it was no big deal. 'All my Western clothes. Except these pyjamas. Because I was wearing them.' Lana thought about what this meant. That the only clothes Minnie had left were the dressy sets of shalwar kameez, high-necked and long-sleeved, that she had worn at her wedding. They were just clothes, but she felt a pang, thinking that the outfits she associated with her daughter were gone: those leggings, that dusty pink T-shirt from Gap. Perhaps the orange sarong had survived, if he thought it was a scarf.

'Don't worry,' said Lana quickly. 'It's just stuff. We'll buy new ones.'

'How? He cut up my cards too!' howled Minnie, and she threw her head into the pillow of her arms, crying hot and messy tears. He had taken the money she had earned. Transferred it out of their joint account to his personal one, which had a better rate, he said. Her success was his success. 'You were right, Mum. God, I was so stupid.'

'It's not your fault, it's his,' said Lana. She put her arms around her daughter, the way her own mother had never put her arms around her when she had left her marriage. She had not gone to her mother, because Lana knew she would have sent her back. She had gone to her brother. It was her brother, Jakie, who had held her instead. 'It's all right, sweetie,' she murmured to Minnie. 'It's going to be all right.'

It's going to be all right. A promise. A prayer. She knew her daughter would believe her if she said it. She knew that if she said it, it would become true.

Lana is shaking out her clothes, preparing for the third day of prayers after her father's death. She is in her old bedroom, her polished four-poster bed with the high carved headboard on one side of the room, and Mae's matching bed on the other. Minnie has been put in the old nursery, where Mae once learned dressmaking and trained in domestic affairs, which her mother has had made up as a guest room for her.

'Well, it seems the flying monkeys that she sent out did their job,' says Mae, coming into the room and sitting on the edge of Lana's bed. 'We're all here. Except Sulaman. And he's on his way.' Lana doesn't reply to this. She hasn't told anyone what she said to him, or even that she saw him. She's not lying. She hasn't been asked the question.

'You know, I could sleep down there,' Mae says in an offhand way. 'If you'd rather share with Minnie.' Lana smiles at the familiar careless tone, which she knows means that Mae cares very much indeed.

'No, I'd rather share with you,' says Lana. 'I see Minnie all the time.' Mae seems pleased. She gives Lana a long, appraising look from head to toe.

'You're looking very well,' she admits grudgingly. Lana doesn't return the compliment, as she doubts that Mae needs it. With all her facials and massages and hairstyling, Mae must be aware of how good she looks, as she knows how hard she works to maintain it. 'What shampoo are you using?'

'Oh, I don't know, a blue and white one,' says Lana. 'It was on offer at Boots.' She has no interest in this sort of stuff, in toiletries or cosmetics. The question is as pointless as asking her what car Minnie drives. A red one.

'Head and Shoulders,' says Mae. 'I thought so.' She starts to help Lana shake out her clothes and place them in the cupboard. And then she effortlessly takes over, and practically pushes her sister out of the way, pulling out Lana's shalwars and shirts, trousers and tunics, arranging them into outfits.

As Mae rearranges her wardrobe, Lana remembers how she rearranged her furniture when she first visited her flat in London, tugging an armchair into a far corner, pushing the sofa against the wall, complaining that Lana didn't have any staff to help her. Lana didn't show she was annoyed then, and doesn't show it now. She will always be the little sister, even in her fifties. She lets Mae carry on.

'So, are you seeing anyone?' Mae asks casually. Lana is tempted to pretend to misunderstand the question, and say something facetious: why yes, I'm seeing you, Mae, I can see you right now, with your hands digging in my clothes, like a security-wallah at the airport. She is beginning to wonder if Mae really is seeking contraband, evidence of

Lana's secret life, under the pretext of being helpful. Lana's too old for birth control pills, too grown-up to have hidden a love letter or photo there. She should have put some modern mousetraps in her luggage instead, to snap on Mae's hand. No could argue that they wouldn't be useful here in Lahore; she'd have got away with it if she had. She pauses long enough for Mae to get impatient, and realises that this is the sort of thing her mother would do, use a pause to get attention. Lana doesn't want attention. It's a straightforward question, with a simple answer.

'No,' she says. This doesn't seem quite enough to satisfy Mae, and she adds, 'Sorry.' She even means it. She suspects it would have made Mae's day if she had a torrid love affair to confess, and they would have giggled over the details in the night, like schoolgirls discussing their crushes, while helping themselves to the violet-tipped chocolates that Minnie has bought for their mother. It would have helped them to forget, however briefly, why they were back together again, in their old room.

'Oh, don't apologise to me,' says Mae. 'It just seems such a waste. You're living in London, you could get away with it. Here, I have to marry someone if I want to live with them.'

'We noticed,' says Lana. Mae had remarried twice. Both times quietly, in Karachi, with an embarrassed note afterwards. Followed by another embarrassed note a few years later, announcing the divorce. It's true that if Mae were living in London, she'd have probably just dated or moved in with the men she had married since Nasim, and saved herself a lot of tedious paperwork.

'Well, I've had enough of all that now,' says Mae. 'It was more trouble than it was worth. Now I just have a massage a couple of times a week. And an electric toothbrush.'

'Mae!' says Lana, shocked. Mae looks at her with amusement.

'You knew what I meant? So you're not such an innocent after all, little Lana,' she says. She seems satisfied with her organisation of Lana's clothes, and sits back on the bed, smoothing out the material of her shalwar over her legs. 'Sometimes I think you stayed married to Tariq because you didn't want to find someone else. It gave you an excuse. Who needs a lover when you're already a wife and a mother? Tariq served his purpose, didn't he? He gave you his name, and knocked you up. And then you threw that poor man away like an empty seed packet.'

To someone else, this might seem a little unfair. After all, Tariq, like

254

Nasim, had had a mistress. He had taken one within a month of their marriage. When Lana had asked to visit her family abroad, he had been happy to let her go, happy to have the extra time with his other woman, whom he kept openly in another part of the house. He had generously said that Lana could stay away as long as she wanted; he did not realise that she would take him at his word. She left with his baby in her belly, and an old-fashioned trunk that had been her father's.

When their relatives had worked out that she had left him altogether, after Minnie was born in London, after Lana had moved out of Jakie's house and into her own flat, few people asked her why. Lana had always been so transparent. They assumed it was because of the mistress. They thought that she was hopelessly naïve not to realise that this was what men did. They had wives for children, and other women for pleasure; only those who paid for whores or boys would bother to keep it secret. A strong wife would have thrown out the other woman, or at least waited her out, until she was retired with a bribe to another family and another man. It was considered a measure of Lana's weakness, rather than her strength, that she left; that she was too cowardly to return.

But Mae grew up with Lana, she shared this room with her until she married, and she knows her better than anyone else. That poor man, Mae said, and Lana knows she's right. It was an arranged marriage, and it was considered a good match. Tariq had high hopes of Lana; he was several years older than her, and he had watched her turn from adolescent to adult. He had seen her calm competence at Mae's wedding, as she took care of her bleeding mother. He had seen her at college, as she finished her education with a modest Bachelor of Arts degree, putting off proposals from interested parties, year after year. She was considered shy and serious, and despite her education, a little simple; all of these were attractive qualities. Tariq's patrician family weren't as wealthy as Lana's, and Tariq wasn't considered handsome; his mother shrewdly made an offer for Lana when she was twenty, guessing that her parents were keen to marry her off before she got a reputation for being an eccentric old maid, a sweet-eating child who had never grown up. Lana doesn't remember if anyone actually asked her if she wanted to get married, while all the arrangements were being made. She had never noticed Tariq before, although she knew of him vaguely, and met him officially for the first time at the wedding. Mae had held her hand, and told her not to be scared; she told her that a man would be much easier to manage than their mother.

Lana remembers Tariq's ardent determination on their wedding night, his ambition for their new life, as husband and wife. She could feel the anticipation building in him, from the signature on the page, stretching his body until he was twanging like an elastic band, waiting to release himself into her with a snap and a sting. To pour into her, and fill her completely. His lawful vessel. The mother-to-be of his children. The dirty, impatient act he had indulged in in the past to be washed clean by marriage and the purity of his intent. When he walked into the bedroom where she had already been led to wait for him, he made a great effort to be polite, to avoid offending her with his quaking eagerness.

'I hope I'm not disturbing you, my dearest,' he said. He wanted to use soft words with her. He was willing to love his wife. He waited nervously for her response.

'No, you're not disturbing me,' Lana said. And he sat beside her on the bed, pretending to read. He was trembling, and the pages of the newspaper he had brought with him trembled too as he turned them distractedly. He took a deeper breath, as though he had a pain in his gut, and then he folded the newspaper, *The Pakistan Times*, and moved towards her. She was still fully clothed.

'Excuse me, my dearest,' he asked, 'if you consent,' and she turned with polite enquiry towards him, which he optimistically interpreted as the answer he wanted. Consent, if not passion. He took that careful position on top of her, just as he had with his pen at the desk, ready to sign his name, and claim his property. He hastily loosened his clothing with clumsy tugging, and then pulled aside hers, more carefully, a little apologetically. When he first pushed himself into her, he was trying very hard to be gentle, keeping his weight on his arms, to avoid pinning her to the bed.

'Are you all right?' he asked, struggling uncomfortably to control his rapid panting. She said neither no nor yes, and just let him continue, until the gentleness dissolved, and he plunged himself more urgently into her, stamping his name on to her soft-fleshed walls, while she failed to react altogether, beyond breathing a little more sharply through the pounding movement and the brief moment of pain.

When he had finished, he groaned like he was the one who had been hurt. He pressed his face against her hair on the pillow, and looked at her neat profile in the dim light. Dismayed by her distance. Her indifference. It was as though she remained untouched, as though the undignified suck and squirt of their organs had happened somewhere else, to someone else. He would have better understood her disgust or her tears; if she had cried, he could have comforted her. Instead he felt as though he had fucked a dress-shop dummy, defiled a doll, and he couldn't bring himself to kiss her smooth doll's cheek, her still doll's lips, to touch the porcelain of her flesh. Their married mouths never met. If she had shown him some kindness, he would have opened to her like a flower. Lana knew that. But she didn't want his affection, or his tenderness. She didn't want anything more from him than what he had given her. The seeds scattered on fertile earth.

'Excuse me, dearest,' he said as he left her, as though he was asking her forgiveness.

He said it again when he came to her room the next night, and all the nights that followed during the first few weeks of marriage, each time hoping that this time it would be different. That the story her body told would offer a different ending, the happy-ever-after of fairy tales. That she would open her mouth to taste him, open her eyes to look at him, put her warm arms around him, whisper soft words of encouragement and pat the pillow for him to sleep by her side. But the story was the same each time he folded the newspaper to begin it again. He still asked if she consented, before he fed her his flesh every night, and she still failed to reply.

He began to visit her later and later in the night, when she was already half asleep, and if she was on her belly, he would not disturb her or turn her over, but simply mount her quietly and quickly from behind, like a dog in the bazaar. She knew it was easier for him if he didn't have to see her face; it was easier for her too. She preferred him to think that she wasn't really there, so she didn't have to maintain her blank expression, and she could bite the pillow silently if she felt more during these moments than she wanted to show.

It didn't hurt. It wasn't unpleasant. And each time was quicker and less meaningful than the one before. It was a duty. Painless and perfunctory. A signature on a page. It seemed possible that he respected and resented her mastery of herself in equal measure. She was perfected by her lack of passion; it implied a sort of piety, a pureness on her part.

A married virgin. A virgin mother. Sometimes Lana thought he wrote all those letters to Minnie, those pages of Qur'anic verse, simply to impress her; to show that he had become a pious and pure man too.

Lana was relieved when he took a mistress; a plump and smiling maidservant, bribed with baubles, who yelped with noisy pleasure as he grunted on top of her in the night, who giggled and fluttered about him by day. The maidservant, like Lana, was found for him by his concerned mother, and installed in the household. She was worried that Lana was not meeting her son's natural needs, and Tariq was clearly grateful to his mother, and even more grateful to the maid, who was older than Lana, and more experienced than Tariq. The whole household heard their amorous antics, and the older servants were a little embarrassed by the public nature of the spectacle.

Lana herself once saw Tariq bending the girl over the dining table, his face in the back of her neck, warming his hands inside her sari blouse while he squeezed her breasts like the cook choosing fruit from a stall, rubbing himself against her buttocks. It was like a pornographic postcard, a square from a salacious strip; even now, Lana can't think of the scene without a satirical line scribbled beneath it. A comical caption. How much for these mangos? Is this where I left the keys? Gloves might be more practical. Guess what we're having for dinner? Tart for dessert.

The girl was moaning with apparent pleasure, but her eyes were open, and she caught Lana's eye as she passed, and laughed at her, while she widened her mouth with an ecstatically exaggerated O, showing the intimate pink gum, her string of white teeth. Perhaps she thought Lana would feel mocked, shocked, humiliated. Instead Lana kept her face serenely blank, and carried on walking past the open door in her slippered feet. She nodded politely at the scandalised sweeper, who saw what she had seen, and apologetically raced to shut the door quietly on the coupling pair, who had begun grunting and yelping. Dogs in the bazaar.

Lana tried not to smile, for the servants' sake; she stopped herself from humming a tune. She made a mental note to make sure that she changed her usual seat for one at the other end of the table – after all, she ate there. She was relieved that between his mother and his mistress, Tariq would have no reason to ask her to stay, or miss her when she left. It was true that she had used him. But she had been careful not to hurt him. Unlike the mistress, and the woman who took her place, and probably the next one after that, she had never pretended affection that she would later withdraw. He took a second wife, some years later, who behaved with more decorum; she gave him four children, whom Minnie had never been invited to meet.

'It wasn't like that, exactly,' says Lana, as Mae raises her perfectly plucked brows at her. 'I didn't divorce him, because he never asked me to. And I never needed to ask him. Because I never met another man I wanted to marry.' She pauses, and then says, 'You're right. I guess it was never important enough to me to go looking for one.' Lana goes to her case, and pulls out a small Qur'an, which she puts on her bedside table. 'Minnie didn't need a father figure; she had Jakie . . . and she had Frank.'

'You mean you had Jakie . . . and you had Frank,' says Mae, mimicking the pause Lana left before she said Frank's name, as though it is somehow significant. 'I used to wonder if you were just waiting for him. Waiting for him to get drunker than usual one day and forget that he likes boys.'

Lana looks at Mae carefully, and realises that she isn't being spiteful, or witty. This is what she thinks. That Lana is in love with Frank, and has been all these years. She realises that her sister is concerned for her, and only now, when someone has died, does she feel brave enough to say this out loud, because the living are more important than the dead.

'Oh Mae,' she says. 'Of course I love Frank. Like a brother.'

'If I looked at Jakie or Sulaman the way I've seen you look at him, you'd be the one worried about me,' says Mae.

'It's fine,' Lana says. 'I'm fine. I'm not waiting for him. I would never do that to Jakie.' She smiles mildly, a virgin mother in blue, and goes to leave the room. 'I'm going to check on Minnie. Mummy was picking outfits for her; she's found a new doll.' She says this firmly, to show that the conversation is over.

Mae thinks otherwise. 'You know you'd get away with it, if you did,' she says. She looks at Lana's serene, chaste face, and says, as though considering this possibility for the first time, 'For all I know, you might have got away with it already.'

Lana goes downstairs, and finds Minnie in the old nursery, with piles of her mother's vintage clothing around her. Her daughter playing dressing-up again. Her mother is supervising, with a smile carved deep into her cheeks; it looks odd, because it is unfamiliar. She wonders if it is uncomfortable for her mother to do this, to sustain the slack, rarely exercised muscles that hold the smile in place. Minnie has been dressed in a sari, one of her mother's more daring ones from the fifties, with a sleeveless blouse that shows inches of her belly, the smooth skin rippled with silver creases from her pregnancies. She looks like an actress, and the pleats of silk hang firmly in the wide skirt.

'Like this on the shoulder,' says Lana's mother to Minnie, pulling the embroidered end of the fabric over Minnie's shoulder to hang down her back, almost to her ankles. The silk slides off her skin as Minnie turns to look at it in the mirror, and she holds her elbow up awkwardly to stop it falling off altogether. Lana's mother tuts. 'That won't do. You think you can walk around all evening like that? You'll poke people's eyes out. Silly girl.' She begins rummaging in the triple-tiered leather-trimmed jewellery box beside her. 'You need a brooch to fix it in place, if you're not used to wearing one of these. Less elegant, but practical. It's what foreigners do.'

'The newsreader on the evening round-up was wearing a brooch on her sari,' says Minnie conversationally, and Lana's mother nods as though Minnie has proved her point. She finds the piece she is looking for: a butterfly pin, encrusted with semi-precious gems on the wings, with diamonds set down the body. She blows on it as a blessing, before fastening it firmly on the shoulder of Minnie's blouse, digging the blunt pin through the pleats of sari fabric. Minnie lets her arm fall, and looks a little surprised at her reflection. She looks like a local; from Londoner to Lahori with a simple length of silk.

'Thank you, Nanu,' she says softly, touching the brooch. 'It's beautiful.'

'Your mother could never carry this sari off,' her grandmother replies, 'and your Auntie Mae has enough of her own clothes. These are for you. Pick your favourites, and Sherry can have the others, when she visits.' She taps the brooch in a businesslike way. 'Take care of this,' she says. 'It's gold, and the diamonds are real.'

Minnie is touched, probably more by the impulsive nature of the gift-giving than by the extravagance. She leans down a few inches – she is taller than her grandmother in the borrowed heels she is wearing – and puts her arms around her. Lana watches her mother stiffen, as though this isn't something she was expecting, and tentatively pat Minnie on the back. She doesn't seem displeased. Lana tries to think whether she ever spontaneously hugged her mother, if she wasn't being hugged first. She must have done as a child, but she can't remember a single instance. She remembers hugs with her mother being more about a calculated display of affection to someone who was watching, or else a sign of control, a cage of arms.

Her mother sees Lana in the doorway, and straightens herself hurriedly out of the embrace. Lana suddenly feels guilty for not announcing her presence, for simply standing there watching through the open door. She thinks it's even possible that her mother is embarrassed to have been seen in this way, as though she has been caught out. It seems that Lana is always looking through doors, through windows, through the glass of the television screen; standing at a safe distance, while she watches other people's lives and loves. She has never really noticed this about herself before, but what Mae just said about Tariq, about Jakie and Frank, her vicarious way of living, has started her wondering. Lana had thought there was something admirable about her restraint, about her tacit decision to forbear. But now she feels less generous; selfish rather than selfless, refusing to share herself or share her life. Parasitic even; a spy in the homes of the people she loves.

'We'll try the rest later,' her mother says to Minnie. 'I'm tired. Go get your old Nanu some tea.' Minnie smiles and nods, and walks swiftly off, the material swishing around her heels giving her an unusual elegance, as she is forced to walk tall and straight to stop it sweeping the floor. She squeezes Lana's waist briefly as she passes her in the corridor. She doesn't do this to warn Lana to be nice to the old lady; it is simply affection. Minnie thinks the best of Lana; she expects her to be nice, as looking after lonely old ladies is what she does all day in the care home. She has a talent for it.

When Minnie is gone, Lana sees that her mother's face has darkened to grey, and the carved smile has faded like a rainbow in a sudden downpour. Her muscles have relaxed to their usual position of disappointment and disapproval. Lana isn't afraid of her mother's moods: the scowling, the scolding, the scalding words that burn and slaps that sting; she lived with them longer than any of her siblings. She stayed in this house with her mother for seven years after they had all left, running away like rodents in the same dry season; first Mae to another house in town, then Jakie to England, then Sulaman to America.

Lana supposes that familiarity usurps fear, and she alone knows that her mother is not the monster of her sister's and brothers' memories; a creature roaring with rage, trapped in the tower of their town house, with the bridges burned around her. Lana saw her become a frail, damaged woman after Mae's marriage, and the public miscarriage. She saw her slap on different masks when she went out into the corridor, into the courtyard, and into the city, like a child during the Basant festival with too many kites in the air. She saw her mother cover her arms, wear her scarf over her hair, retreat into religion, bear and forbear. She watched her withdraw and diminish, as motherhood was lifted from her, one child at a time; sometimes she regretted the loss of the fearsome woman she had been. They were not the only ones who had grown up, and grown old; their mother had too. Lana knows it is impossible to hold on to anger across a lifetime, to keep the storm seething and the thunder rolling and the lightning flashing, just as it is impossible to remain madly in love. In time, the storm ends, and the rainwater drains away, or gathers in still pools.

Still, she wishes she hadn't been the cause of this new burst of wrath; did she really deserve it, simply because she had remained outside, looking in? She hadn't done it on purpose; she had been enjoying the rare beauty of this family moment, her mother and her daughter in the old nursery, surrounded by fabrics and jewellery like Aladdin's cave. The smiling girl accepting magical gifts from the wise old woman, a story-book scene from the *Thousand and One Nights*. But it was another stolen moment, belonging to someone else, to Minnie and her mother. She should have walked in, through the door, across the burning bridge, and made it her moment too. Or else she should have walked away.

'Minnie looks lovely in that sari,' she says. It is intended as an uncomplicated compliment, a thank-you for the gifts. Her way of calling back the cheerful presence of her daughter, even though her mother has deliberately sent her away. Her mother takes her words as an apology which she refuses to accept.

'With that face, figure and complexion, Minnie looks lovely in anything,' she says brusquely. 'Even the rags she flew here in.' She snaps shut the jewellery box, closes the metal clasps tightly, turns the little copper key. 'She has a proper Punjabi nose; she gets that from her father. Not your Disney princess nothing little nose.' Lana doesn't reply; she is used to this, a compliment followed by a criticism. If her mother were angry with Minnie, instead of her, she would turn her comment the other way.

'Come for tea, Mummy,' she says kindly, but as she steps forward, her mother steps back, guarding the battle line she has drawn between them.

The old woman in white breathes hard, and attacks, raising her rifle with the bayonet attached, stabbing Lana with a look that is as sharp as a blade in the guts, as intimate as hot breath spraying in her face as the knife twists. 'Why didn't you tell me that you saw Sulaman at the airport? Why isn't he here?'

So this is why her mother is angry, and Lana wonders how she managed to pack away her emotion like a bomb in a box while Minnie chattered about bumping into Uncle Sully. How she kept herself calm on hearing this news, and continued turning those neat pleats in the silk fabric on her hand; how she was able to make small talk, select jewellery, accept an embrace.

Lana is watching the delayed explosion now, controlled and operatic; she still feels distant, as though she is observing the detonation, the destruction, from a far-off place of safety. Her mother is trembling in her white cloth, and the fury briefly makes her seem bigger and more alive, more glowing and brilliant, a flame roaring with a final breath of air before it is blown out altogether. A white star swallowing the space around it before it shrinks to black rock. Lana is witnessing the nuclear echo of the monstrous, magnificent woman that her mother once was. The woman who commanded duty, deference and despair. She who must be obeyed, rising up from the past, a ghost banging her fist on a seer's spinning table.

'So,' her mother spits out, 'where is he? Is he still there?'

Lana wonders why her mother doesn't ask the real question: is he coming? And then she realises that she doesn't have to ask this question, because she already knows the answer. It was answered by his absence, the moment Minnie let slip that they had seen him in Dubai. Her mother doesn't want to hear the no; saying it out loud makes it real, and something that can't be taken back. As to where Sulaman is now, it doesn't really matter. Lana imagines him still wandering around Dubai airport with his single bag, like a soul in purgatory, drifting from plane to plane, departure gate to departure gate, unable to choose where in the world he will go. Perhaps he thinks that all the planes will remain on the runways, because in his unbeliever's heart, beyond where he already is there is no other destination.

'I don't know,' she says, simply. Her mother looks at her as though she is simple, as though remembering that Lana is the child of hers that never grew up. Remembering that she can say what she wants to Lana; it is like confessing a crime to an infant, whispering to a wall.

'Well, I won't wait for him,' says her mother. 'Not any more. I've waited forty years for Sulaman to come back to me. The rest of you came back, you visited. But not Sulaman, not for all this time. Not once.'

'You saw him in America. You never asked him to come back,' says Lana. It's not a question. She says it gently. Her mother slaps the air with irritation, snapping her hand as though swatting Lana's stupid comment away.

'The excuses I've had to make for him. Year after year. Sulaman's so busy. So important. So good.' She begins to fade, to shrink back and diminish, and she takes a step towards Lana, and then another, becoming smaller as she approaches. 'They all believed me. They repeated it back. Such a celebrated son. Such a credit to you. Such a good boy . . .' She is now standing in front of Lana, and she has to raise her head to look Lana in the face as she speaks. Lana doesn't remember her mother ever seeming this small.

'I don't know what you said to him. I don't know what you've said or haven't said, at the airport, across all these years. But I won't wait. Not a day longer.' She goes to leave the room, and rather than brushing against her daughter, pushing her into the door frame, she waits imperiously for Lana to get out of the way altogether, before sweeping past. 'You should have persuaded him, Lana. He would have listened to you.'

He did listen to me, Lana thinks. Perhaps she should have used her words more wisely. Her mother is upset. Of course she is upset. Sulaman is absent. Lana promised to forgive Sulaman, but he's not her son to forgive.

'His own daddy's funeral,' says her mother, turning in the corridor as though she has realised that she has a bullet left, and she wants to empty it into the person she has already finished off. A waste of her words, thinks Lana, feeling sorry for her. She's already made her point; she'll harm herself more with the effort than the defeated body in front of her.

'Mummy, don't,' she says. 'You'll upset yourself.' Her mother ignores her again. She is not used to obeying someone else, even if they are right. Even if they are telling the truth, and speaking from concern.

'You know what I thought when your daddy died? I thought, at least this will bring Sulaman home. At least Daddy's death will do this for us.' Her mother's eyes are brightening, filling like puddles. The storm is over, and the rainwater flattens into still pools. 'His own daddy's funeral, and he's not here. Does he really hate me so much?'

Her mother turns away again, and starts walking swiftly towards her room, her back straight, her head held high. She does not raise her hand or her sleeve to her eyes. She is crying, but she does not want this to be seen. She does not want to be exposed, to be shown as weak and unguarded, even in the corridor of her own house; it is still a place where a servant might stray and see something they ought not, or Minnie might stroll by, humming her happy tune, clumsily carrying the tea tray. Lana knows that if her mother must cry, she will cry alone. She will hide the evidence and emerge with a face of solid stone.

She wonders if her mother would weep the same way over her own absence, or Mae's or Jakie's. Of course she would, she realises. She would cry for them all, if they were missing for all those years. She is crying for what has been taken from her; by his extraordinary absence, he is too distant to despise. She is crying for him as she cried over the child in heaven, who never lived to dishonour or disobey her, the child who is as good as he is dead. Her mother is crying for the missing. Those too distant to touch. Those who refuse to return.

The house is prepared. It is full of pious women, who cover the pictures with pillowcases. There is a scent of rose water. Lana and Minnie stand together, their heads covered by their scarves. Mae comes to stand with them, after having given final instructions to the servants regarding the slicing and grating of vegetables, the soaking of the precious strands of saffron, the food to be fried, steeped and served. Jakie has gone with the men, the room separated by deep lengths of cotton cloth, their long shadows thrown on the makeshift walls between them. Her mother is hunched over, half of herself, at the front of the room, shaking her head at the comforting words offered by the guests, by the kindly man from the mosque with a neat grey beard, a clean white cap.

Their father's former colleagues, in their dark suits, do not recognise her mother at first. They must think she is an elderly aunt until they see where she is sitting, and marvel at what despair and death have done to her. A ghost of herself, her echo in the room. She doesn't seem to care, her indifference keeps them at a distance; a cool shadow is around her, a moat that can't be crossed.

Another hired car comes into the drive, and no one takes any notice. Another mourner, another man in a dark suit. It is Lana, her light still and burning, who sees the face in the crowd. The middle-aged man held together by his clothes; a fearful man who is outside, looking in.

'Mummy,' she calls out urgently. 'Mummy, he's here.'

There is a ripple of confusion, of concern, as her mother rises from the cloth puddle. She sees her firstborn son, and her face gives nothing away. He sees her, as she was, as she is. The monster of his memories, a small widow in white.

He steps over the threshold, through the door and across the burning bridge, and the bustling crowd falls away until he is by her side. The ladders of years collapse as he crouches towards her, and she touches him briefly on his shoulder, and blows on him, as a blessing, murmuring an indistinct prayer. She stands up with dignity, her back straight, her head high. She is blazing with white light as she nods that he should join Jakie, and stand with the men. Her children are all with her, and she has been vindicated. Her firstborn son has returned on the burying of the dead, to add his voice to the prayers for his father, who is resting in peace in the family plot. Her Adam, her fallen angel, has returned home.

Lana sees what it has cost Sulaman to come, to play this part. He is on one side of the cloth wall, and she is on the other. Her stretched shadow lapping over his. She knows that he is still shaking, his eyes cracked and dry, his brother's arm around him, keeping him from falling face down on the covered ground, kissing the sheet, dirt against his teeth. She knows that she needs to speak to him. You should have persuaded him, her mother said. He would have listened to you.

This time, Lana will be wiser with her words. She will not say too little, and she will not say too much. She will say only the truth, because she has seen what no one else has. She has seen grief for the living overshadow grief for the dead. Lana doesn't feel what the others feel; she does not feel regret for those who are dead, who are already at peace, her father asleep in the family plot, her younger brother, unborn, among the company of angels in heaven. She grieves for the living; those who are falling apart, their pieces shattering on the ground, scattering with the wind. For those who do not believe, or belong. For those who have lived with the opposites of love, with hate and with loneliness. The blood bursting from their open wounds like poppies springing from broken ground. Mummy, don't. Sulaman, don't. Don't give up. Don't be sad. Because it goes on. Life goes on. It must.

'She loved you, Sulaman,' she will say to him, with cheap white hope.

Perhaps it changes nothing, but it is still the truth, and she will be brave enough to step forward, and share what she has witnessed. She will stop watching and listening; she will play her part, and find her voice. The living deserve the truth; the dead have already discovered it for themselves.

'She loved you. She loved you best of all.'

PART 3

GOOD FATHERS, GOOD MOTHERS, 1961–2009

Chapter Eleven
Sully

I'M AN OLD MAN PACKING A BAG. IT'S A NICE APARTMENT ON THE Upper West Side, and my son and daughter-in-law live a dozen blocks away in another brownstone. Their kids are in college. The phone rings, and I know who it is. 'I'm doing it, I'm packing,' I tell the phone in annoyance. I press the loudspeaker button, and say it again as I move about.

'If you could get in the habit of opening your laptop, I could see you,' says Jakie, 'and you could see me, and then I'd know if you were lying.'

'You know I don't lie,' I say. I feel affection now, rather than annoyance. 'And nobody wants to look at this old face anyhow.'

'You should tell your publishers that,' says Jakie. 'If you had me on screen, you'd see me pointing to the back cover of your last book. Very dignified.' He pauses and adds, 'Nice suit. Ralph Lauren? Giorgio Armani? Calvin Klein?' He says the brand names like they're dirty jokes. Ivor Biggun. Ben Dover. Buster Pants. He and Frank used to come out with this schoolyard stuff over dinner like it was hilarious.

'Stop that,' I say.

'Stop what?' he asks innocently.

'Making fun of me.'

'It's the only vice I'm allowed these days,' says Jakie. 'Like yours is not lying. That's a bit of a personality flaw, too.' He pauses again. 'Well, I've finished my packing already. Not that there's much to pack here.' Jakie has spent the last couple of weeks working in a refugee camp, in the north of Pakistan, doing his usual annual stint for the aid agencies. 'You'll probably get to Lahore before I do.'

'I guess I will,' I say. 'So how's Frank?' I don't know why I bother asking this. It's almost insensitive. Frank's always the same, and has been for some time now. And he won't care if I asked after him.

Jakie just replies, 'He's okay. He's good. We just spoke. He's . . . well, you know,' and trails off, much as I expected, but then I know exactly why I said it, as he asks almost the same question back: 'So how's Radhika?'

I'm not sure why I manipulated him into this, as I don't have anything new to report about Radhika. I guess I just like hearing someone say her name. Even my own boy barely mentions her in front of me, and if he does, he calls her 'mom' like that's all the name she needs. I guess I just like an excuse to say her name myself, after all these years. It makes me feel that something survived of us.

'Radhika's good, too. She's still working, supervising doctoral candidates part time.' I pause and admit what he already knows. 'I don't see her so much these days. Just family occasions. Christmas. Birthdays. Thanksgiving too, sometimes.'

It feels like the words flutter about us, and don't really settle, and maybe Jakie feels this too, as he says, with a touch of reproach, 'How long has it been, Sulaman?' It feels like many questions rolled into one, a rubber-band ball, or a handful of marbles thrown in my direction, rattling on the polished floorboards with a glittering, brittle menace. How long since Radhika, since our mother, since us? How long since we found love or lost it? How long since we discovered that it was easier to leave than stay, and that we were so easy to leave ourselves? I answer the least disquieting question, although given the nature of the trip we're both going on, back to Lahore, perhaps it doesn't reflect too well on me.

'Since I last saw Mummy? Really saw her, to touch her? I don't know, not for years.' I think about it, and realise that I'm not so senile that I can't answer when it was me who decided the question. 'It was a few years after Daddy's funeral. Just after September 11. We took Buzz's kids with us. His wife wanted us to get Sami and Dani out of New York. We changed planes twice. Once in Berlin, to see Radhika's mother. Once in Lahore, to see mine. And then we went to Singapore for a beach holiday on Sentosa Island.' I pause, and add with a little embarrassment, 'We were meant to stay the whole week in Lahore; that's what Buzz and Tania arranged when they booked our flights. We changed our tickets the day after we arrived, and left two days after that.'

'We?' asks Jakie, in a curious tone. It seems he is accusing me of lying after all.

'I,' I correct myself. 'I changed the tickets.'

'Well, I guess I better go,' says Jakie lightly. Perhaps he's feeling guilty for coaxing this admission from me. 'I don't want to miss my mule train over the mountain pass.'

I laugh, like I'm expected to, but I'm not sure if he's joking or not. I'm thinking of our mother, either dying or not dying, alone in her hospital bed, in the town in which we grew up. I think of Buzz's kids playing in my childhood home with Radhika, in rooms I never played in myself, and my mother drifting around the house, covered in cloth, like a mistreated ghost. She was pleased to see my grandkids; she dressed them up and gave them extravagant gifts, watches and jewellery worth a college scholarship, and she didn't even criticise their nut-brown complexions. But she ignored Radhika, and she avoided me.

Amma tried not to remain alone in the same room as me, and if we found that we were, at the start of breakfast, at the end of dinner, sometimes we would both leave so hurriedly, we would almost bump into each other at the door, before walking in separate directions down the corridor. It was as though something embarrassing and untoward had happened between us; like ex-lovers thrown together during a conference, making stilted small talk by the coffee machine, unsure whether to shake hands, or brush cheeks. I knew she was offended when we left early; I blamed work, I'd had a meeting at the National University of Singapore brought forward as an excuse. But as my mother complained about our departure, more animatedly than she'd spoken since our arrival, I knew she was also relieved.

I wonder if Radhika would come with me again, if I asked her. If I begged. I don't dare test her in this way. I don't dare test myself. It's not as though I'll be on my own with Amma. Jakie and Lana will be there, and Mae has already gone over from Karachi. But I'm terrified that Jakie is right, and I'll get there before him, and find myself alone in a room with her, and the door shut behind me. I've gone back just twice before. Once to pray over the dead, my father in the family plot, with his father and grandfather before him. Once to hide from screaming ghosts free-falling from downtown towers, from the bodies melting like snow into the ashen pavement below.

I've dealt with the dead. I don't know how I'm going to deal with the living; a woman who is dying from the inside out. Our mother's cells washed clear, and held up to catch the light like crystal. Her brain like coral, living stone, layered in lovely strata of stiff lace, with thoughts straying in and out like darting coloured fish. I daren't show my weakness to Buzz, and Radhika already knows how weak I am. How weakly human. How inhuman. I should be better at this, by now. The work that has made me famous, in a modest academic way, has had me squirming like a maggot into the heads of the cruel and criminally inclined, chewing at their wiring; the collaborators, the torturers, the terrorists. This is who I am. This is what I do.

I pack my bag more slowly, and more slowly still, and then eventually I stop, like a clockwork toy that has just wound down. A beautiful robot, Radhika called me once. A wooden boy, still wishing on a star, still waiting for something magical to happen. It's as though this bag is all that I own, and this body is all that's left of me. And I'm wrapped up in my memories like an old hag in winter, fearful of the future, fearful of the frost. My daughter-in-law lives in the now, that's how she puts it. Tania works in technology, and she talks about it like fashion, changing every season; she won't live in the past, as she is all for the now. She says this at her weekend brunch parties as though she's supporting a political party, wearing their button on her lapel. But my memories are throbbing in the hollow box of my chest, in the cavity that holds my heart, and I try to remember that I loved her.

I say this out loud, as I hold my single bag, for my journey to the other side of the world. I loved her. The more I repeat it, the weaker it sounds. An actor with a script, in an empty room, trying out an unconvincing line.

'I like cars,' said Radhika, just as she had said the first time I picked her up in one. She wasn't looking at me, and she wasn't checking whether I remembered this. Perhaps she didn't care, or didn't even remember it herself. Her hand was dreamily fluttering out of the open window, as though trailing her fingers through cool water. 'I like that we're not here, or there. That we're in between things.'

When Radhika talked about the things that she liked and didn't like, she became a simpler person; a child skipping barefoot in a dusty backyard, a hermit proclaiming from a hilltop. Sometimes I agreed with her, and there was nothing more to say, and the silence would gather about us, not unpleasantly; two bodies, casting shadows, breathing in the shared space, and looking at the same view from slightly different angles. Sometimes I disagreed, and we would argue, and I would try not to look at her with wonder, as though she had just walked into a crowded place, and everything had stopped around her. If I'm honest, I hated that I felt this intense need to impress her, but that she didn't feel the same way. That she could casually say how she liked cars, and why, and not worry what I thought about it. I could never say something like that, not without agonising whether I was being banal or a bore. It was as though we both knew that I loved her more than she loved me. I was the one who had asked her to love me, that first night, and she was the one who answered.

I was driving, and doing a better job than usual. We were on the interstate, so I just had to point the lump of tin in the right direction, and keep my foot on the gas. I let other drivers overtake me, and stayed out of the way of the truckers. I drove with one hand, wearing the single glove I'd found in the glove compartment; it was as though someone had left it there for a joke. And it fitted, like a glove. My other hand was in Radhika's lap, gently resting on her thigh, and sometimes she took it, and sometimes she didn't. This wasn't the car that we didn't have sex in; it was one that I'd bought for this particular trip, and that I'd have to sell the other end, as I couldn't afford it in the first place. Radhika glanced at me, and I couldn't decide if she would rather simply be heard, or whether she'd rather I replied. I couldn't decide if silence was considerate, or impolite. She took my hand in hers, and turned, watching me make the decision. And when I made it, she smiled.

'So, is that where we are?' I asked. 'In between things?'

'I guess so,' she said. 'That's what being engaged is. That's what we are.'

I glanced down at her hand. 'You're still not wearing the ring.' I tried to say it in a practical way, like it was just a matter of fact, but I was afraid I'd sounded reproachful, or whining, and so I stupidly carried on.

'It's not like I blame you. I know it's not such a great ring, huh?'

I think I was trying to sound casual, and not make a big deal of it. The fact that my fiancée didn't want to wear the ring I'd bought her. It wasn't a cheap ring; it was the best one I could find at short notice, and afford on my academic's salary. It cost more than the car. It sounded like I was trying to make a joke of it, even. Huh? Who said huh? I must have heard it on the television.

'What are you doing?' she asked sharply.

'I have no idea,' I said humbly, and indicated to get into lane, even though no one was behind me, because there was a sign telling me that I should.

'And I am wearing the ring,' she added, a little curtly.

'Really, honey?' and I started to grin, because I didn't think she was lying to make me feel better.

'Really, Sully,' she said.

'Where?' I asked.

'I guess that's for me to know, and you to find out,' she said, stretching her arm out again, and letting the wind ripple through her ringless fingers, her sleeve flapping. She was laughing at me, but I really didn't mind.

I watched the road, and the signs told us we had another two hours until our gas and rest stop. I knew I was getting tired when I started to see a series of freeway signs posted along the roadside telling me everything I'd done and should be doing, all my little life. Be Good, Study Hard, Go to College, Study Hard, Become a Doctor, Be Good. But flashing up between these was a sign with Radhika's question, What Are You Doing? Like it was contradicting all the others, a reality check. I felt like I was on trial in Wonderland, swiping at the pointed playing cards flapping over me, beating them back, waiting to wake up in the real world on the riverbank.

A little while later, once it had got dark, I saw that Radhika had fallen asleep. I was touched that she trusted me enough to do this. That she trusted me not to crash the car in an accident as bright as our meeting, because I was so tired, I didn't quite trust myself. The phantom signs on the roadside were sucked up by a blinding light, and I realised that it was just a trucker, headlights full beam in my rear-view mirror, impatiently trying to overtake. I swerved over, and soon the real sign, smeared with dirt, came up, and pointed to our exit.

Radhika was still asleep while I got the gas, and still asleep while I pulled into the motel, a dingy box of plastered bricks that looked like it could just be loaded on to the back of a lorry and driven away.

'Honey,' I said, and gave her a gentle shake, pulling her upright slightly. She didn't loll like a doll; she slept with a certain dignity, the way people do in the movies, with her jaw firm and her face soft and serene. She could have been lying in her bed at home, and I forgot for that moment that neither of us had one. That we were in between things, on the way from one life into another.

She looked like a girl who had briefly closed her eyes, waiting for a kiss, and so I kissed her like the prince in the fairy tale, thinking how perfect the moment would be if she woke and kissed me back, but she still didn't wake up. Kissing a sleeping body now seemed creepy rather than romantic, and I shook her a bit more firmly.

'Honey, we're here,' I said, too loudly. There must have been something unconvincing in my voice, as the guy who'd been after me at the gas pump gave me a strange look as he parked up too, like I'd transported a shop window dummy in my passenger seat, and was trying to pass it off as my girlfriend.

She still didn't wake up, and I was beginning to get worried that she wasn't well. I leaned over and pulled her lids open gently, one at a time. Her eyes were moving, a little, but not too rapidly, and she didn't see me. I wondered what she was seeing, so deep in her own world.

I got out of the car, and pulled her out, carrying her in my arms, and she nestled against me like a child, or a small, soft animal. Something in the way she needed me at that moment touched me terribly; it troubled me too, as it seemed unlike her to need me at all. It was like her dreaming self was briefly someone else, someone I couldn't really touch even while I held her in my arms. I carried her straight into the motel, where a scratching man in a vest slapped dead a fly on the counter and handed me a key, in a single gesture. Like a magic trick, or something that he had got better at with practice, a dead fly and a key.

'She sick?' he asked, without interest. To be fair, he asked it without any judgement either; he might as easily have been asking 'She drunk?' or 'She dead?' Like it really wasn't any of his business, and he was just making an idle comment to pass the time, before he killed another fly and handed over another key.

'Just tuckered out, I guess,' I said. 'It's been a long drive. We're on

277

our way to New York now.' He wasn't interested in the explanation either, and didn't care whether this woman in his motel was sick or tired. I suppose, thinking about it now, it would have been more surprising to him if his guests weren't sick or tired.

'Our bags are out front,' I added, and realised that he wasn't going to offer to help, even though I obviously couldn't carry them. 'Would you get them for me, please?' I asked, astonished at my bravery. I wished Radhika would wake up, just so that she could have witnessed this. The truth was, I wouldn't have bothered if it had just been my bag. I didn't care if my bag got stolen. I cared if Radhika's did. She had made me a braver, better person, just by sleeping in my arms. The man grunted, and peeled himself reluctantly from his stool, and pulled his shirt from the hook behind him, as though aware of social niceties. He could welcome guests in his vest, but he needed a shirt to go out to the dirt yard. Besides, it was cold, now that the sun had gone down. 'I'll pay you for your trouble,' I said, suddenly less brave, thinking that he might spit in our coffee in the morning, or put a dent in the car. It wasn't like he had to worry about repeat business.

I thought I'd better leave the light off when I got to the room, so Radhika could carry on sleeping, and stumbled to the bed with her in the dark. Just as I managed to lay her on top of the covers, she woke up. Her head had barely touched the stiff pillow. It was maddening; like she'd planned it.

I started to say, 'Hey, sleepyhead,' and was going to add something banal and affectionate, about how she had got me worried. But she just swung her legs straight off the bed, and looked around the shadowy motel room, and then at me, with something approaching annoyance.

'Why are we here already?' she asked, rubbing her eyes. 'Why are we sitting in the dark? Aren't we going to eat?' The unfairness of her accusation left me momentarily speechless, as though I'd been planning on skipping dinner to seduce her while she slept. I was almost as tired as her, and definitely hungrier. She never ate a damn thing.

'You were out cold,' I said shortly. 'It was like you'd taken three Valium. I even pulled your eyes open.' I thought about this, and said, 'Is there something you want to tell me?' It occurred to me that perhaps she had taken something; she had access to all sorts of drugs. Perhaps she'd thought she'd get the drive over with faster if she didn't have to speak to me.

'Jeez, calm down, Sully,' she said. 'I'm starving. Let's go.' She stood up, stretching her arms, taking in the view of the dimly lit dirt access road from the window. The man at the front desk was looking at our car, and called someone else from inside the motel to look at it too. 'What are they looking at?' she asked. 'It's a car, it's like they've never seen one before.'

'I don't know,' I said, suddenly not wanting to admit that I'd asked him to bring up our bags, and had possibly got him mad with us. For all I knew, they were planning to crap in the car, and blame it on local wildlife, or steal the tyres, and blame it on local louts. 'I guess that when you live a long way from anywhere, you make your own fun.' I swatted a fly on the windowsill instinctively, and the firm slap sounded like I was making a point. I was briefly horrified at what I'd done.

Radhika didn't notice any of this, and didn't look at me like I'd suddenly become a sweaty motel guy in a vest, slapping flies for target practice. 'I hope they've got honey-fried chicken,' she said. 'Or maybe some eggplant in marinara sauce.'

I realised that now I was the one looking at her with accusation – first passing out in the car, and then this. It was wholly unlike her to care about what she ate. 'It's like I don't even know you any more,' I said as a joke, and followed her out of the door. Radhika just gave me this look, as though it was presumptuous of me to assume I'd ever known who she was.

I still didn't quite believe that she was hungry, even as I watched her order macaroni and cheese, with garlic bread, and a milkshake. Even when she asked for extra parmesan, and extra butter. I started worrying about the cost, and just ordered a sandwich, assuming I'd finish her leftovers. I wanted to pay our way, and it was humiliating to think that I probably couldn't; my research stipend barely covered basics, unlike Radhika's generous tobacco-funded grant. When it came to attracting money from the medical community, cancer trumped torture. Sick bodies trumped sick minds. I was trying not to imagine a time in the near future when Radhika would become my meal ticket and I'd be her kept man. She was careful with her money, it bought her independence. I wondered whether she'd stop me buying candy on the streets from the scouts, because I could get the same stuff for less in the store. Whether she'd give me a weekly allowance, and an occasional few extra dollars to treat myself to something nice.

'This place is okay,' Radhika said cheerfully, determined to make the best of a bad thing. She'd picked the rest stop, not me. The waitress was quite pretty, and Radhika looked at her with sympathy, as though she was thinking that it must be hard to be so pretty with no place to go. Once she'd served us, the waitress went outside to smoke; she'd done her hair and her make-up, but her hands were chapped and raw, with bitten nails. It was like she had to dress up to put on a show each day, with no idea whether there'd be an audience. If the diner was shut, she didn't need to bother getting dressed at all. That night she had seven of us: Radhika and me, another couple with a child, and a couple of truckers. Her cigarette break took a couple of minutes, and she stared out towards the road in silence. Intermission. She came back in, and put on her party face.

'Just look how nicely you cleared your plate,' she said to the child. 'Well, you must be your daddy's darling. You want another slice, honey?'

'She ain't mine,' said the man, pleasantly, and the woman he was with glared at him. She ignored the waitress, and put her hand protectively over her stomach. She was quite pregnant, and obviously embarrassed, that the whole diner knew that she was a woman who would soon have two children by two different fathers. 'But she'll have that slice,' added the man hastily, aware that he had to make up for something, even though he didn't seem to have worked out what he had done wrong.

The little girl was digging into her hair with her nails, like she had eczema or nits. She had a complicated smile while she did it, as though the scratching hurt, but made her happy at the same time. As though happiness hurt. She didn't care about the extra slice of pizza, but when it was put in front of her, she ate it. In a methodical way, as though it was a dull duty, rather than a pleasure. Obedience rather than appetite. I remembered my sisters, when they were little, eating their sweet treats and fried pastries from my mother in exactly the same dead-eyed way.

'We should come here for breakfast,' said Radhika, as though she was now someone who ate breakfast. Perhaps she thought that I was staring too much at the other people in the diner. Perhaps she thought I ought to be paying her more attention, instead of looking at scabby children, pregnant women, and pretty waitresses. Although she had been paying her plate more attention than me, and was still mopping up the smears of cheese sauce with the double-buttered garlic bread.

'We'd have to, there's no place else to go,' I replied. I looked out of the window, and now the motel owner, and his friend, and one of the truckers were staring at our car. I still had no idea why. It wasn't a particularly impressive or ugly car; it was a black Ford, about ten years old. Their interest was unnerving; I didn't know how I was going to turn on the engine in the morning. I imagined the thing exploding like in a gangster movie.

'It's places like this that breed serial killers,' I said.

'Because you have to make your own fun?' she asked, finishing her garlic bread with a final wipe around the plate; the dish looked as clean as though a cat had licked it.

'Yes,' I said, as though she'd asked a serious question, drawing on my professional expertise.

'I can think of another way,' she said, 'of making our own fun.' She was smiling, and I was about to ask her what she meant when I got it, and shut up. She was teasing me. Propositioning me. Since my proposal, I was the one who usually asked, and she was the one who said yes. It was as though that first night had set out the way things were going to be between us. 'My God, Sully, are you blushing?' she asked. 'I didn't know you could.'

'It's hot in here,' I protested. I grabbed my jacket, getting ready to rush Radhika back to the room, but then she waved to the waitress, and ordered the last slice of cheesecake. I put my jacket back down, feeling a bit foolish; I decided I must have misunderstood. Perhaps she had been talking about Scrabble, which she usually won. Or chess, where we were more evenly matched. I waited until she said she was ready to go. She hadn't left a thing on her plate, and I was still hungry. Still, I was relieved that she let me pay, without a fuss, or offering to pay her share.

I braced myself as we walked past the fly-swatting motel owner, waiting for him to say something about the car, to say that all the tyres needed replacing and he knew someone who'd do it, but he was looking with slack-jawed curiosity at Radhika. Perhaps she was more interesting to him now that she was conscious.

'You Mexican?' he asked her. She just smiled, bobbing her head to the side, an ambiguous gesture that was neither a shake nor a nod. 'Your room's up the stairs,' he said, pointing to them. 'Stairs,' he repeated, as though teaching her the word. 'You need anything, miss, you just holler.'

He looked at me with suspicion, as though I was a prom date with bad intentions.

'I brought your bags in,' he said to me, adding significantly, 'from your car.'

'Thanks,' she said for both of us, and I saw that she was trying not to laugh as she walked up to our room. I presented her with the key on the flat of my palm, and she opened the door, and looked around it with a sigh, the bubble of laughter sinking back down. In the harsh electric light, it was even more dismal than it had been in the dark, and she flicked the light off almost immediately, and walked across in the moonlight to turn on the bedside lamp instead. Our cases had been left on the bed, and I started pulling them off.

'So, do you still like being in between things?' I asked. It felt like since leaving the campus for our road trip, on our roundabout way to another one in another state, we had fallen down some sort of rabbit hole, into a joke world of interstate in-between America. I couldn't wait to leave this place and get back on the road, to get to where we were going that much faster. I was hoping she'd say the same thing.

'I suppose this place has character,' she said, not admitting that she'd chosen a lousy spot to stop. She'd just stuck a pin halfway down the route I'd marked up, on the free map we'd got from the gas station. I'd have picked one of the shiny new Holiday Inns. 'And characters.'

'Yeah, they come free with the fleas,' I said sourly. Instead of being annoyed, she laughed. I wondered if she was managing me, to stop me getting in a mood.

'I don't think I'm going to sleep too well here,' she admitted, but she began undressing all the same, untying her cardigan from around her neck, and kicking off her shoes.

'Me neither,' I said, sitting beside her on the bed, trying to bounce it, and feeling hard metal knots in the mattress. No wonder she had woken up when I laid her there.

'Well, no one says we need to sleep,' she said. I must have started blushing again, as she asked, 'Are you still hot, Sully?' and began pushing off my jacket, and unknotting my tie.

For a moment I still wasn't sure if she was just being practical. That she was undressing me simply because I looked warm. That she was about to offer me a glass of cool water. But when her hand slid inside my shirt, and she started kissing my neck, pressing her face against me,

I was finally sure what she wanted, and started to respond. And then I got nervous all over again, at her expectation. I tried to remember that I was the guy; that I'd marked up the map and driven the car, that I'd pumped the gas and paid for dinner, and that I could do this, and get it right. The truth was that the sex we'd had that first night, when I'd tumbled her to the floor and practically broken into her, had been the best and worst sex we'd ever had. After that time, whenever I asked her if she wanted to, she never said no, but nothing we'd done since had compared. It was the fear of losing her that had made it so first-and-last-time, so desperate and passionate, and I was worried that unless I started to do better with her, I'd lose her all over again.

I turned into her to kiss her back; to kiss her hair and her forehead, and then her nose, her lips, her throat. As I unbuttoned the top of her blouse, I tasted metal, sour and warm, in the hollow of her throat between her collarbones.

'You're wearing it after all,' I said, pressing the thick golden ring against my mouth while I tasted her skin, feeling the sharpness of the small cut stone, and the texture of the thin chain that held it around her neck, which used to hold the little Ganesha instead. I don't know why I hadn't guessed; it seemed so obvious now, it was the only place she ever wore jewellery. Perhaps the ring was too heavy for her hand, and bothered her when she worked. Radhika wrote with her left hand. I wondered where she'd put the familiar charm, and I felt a little sorry to think of Ganesha, remover of obstacles, in an envelope in her case somewhere, or taped to her brother's ashes.

'I said I was,' she said.

'It's hidden,' I replied, with an edge of criticism. I realised that she didn't usually button her blouses so high.

'It's safe,' she said, dismissing the complaint. 'If no one can see it, no one can steal it.' She added lightly, 'And right there, it's closer to my heart,' as though it was something funny but true. Something she was worried about admitting.

She was right, I could feel her heart beating, against my face. I carried on unbuttoning her blouse. I still wasn't sure how much Radhika really enjoyed sex; whether like the child eating her pizza, like attending the dance, it was a frivolous sort of duty. I wasn't sure how much I really enjoyed it either; it had been more about release, relief, and the complicated proof of possession. But it was that night, in that horrible motel, that I remember how she opened up to me like a flower. How I opened up to her. She made me feel that I was someone breakable and beautiful. That I was a real boy after all. The most private and poisonous parts of me felt washed by her touch; her fingers on my flesh, her cleansing kitten mouth lapping at my skin. Her tongue, and her teeth. Sucking, and snapping. It was wonderful to be wanted. To be tasted and drunk from. Her sharp edges felt blurred, and her body felt softer and more heated as her damp skin swam over me, marking me as her possession too.

'Will you marry me now?' I asked her again, afterwards. I could feel her flesh on mine, cooling slightly under the scratchy sheet, as she lay easily along the length of my body, like I was sand on the beach. I could feel the metal of the mattress digging into my back. I could feel the biteable gold of the ring between us, warmed where the blood pulsed in the soft flesh of her throat. I had my arms around her, and traced the smooth curve of her spine, feeling the delicate bumps under my fingertips.

'I've already said yes,' she replied, breathing in and exhaling deeply, as though she was about to fall asleep again, my chest for her pillow. I couldn't see her face.

'I mean right now,' I said, glancing at the clock on the counter, which was quietly ticking away the seconds. It was past midnight. 'Will you marry me right now?' I kissed the top of her head. 'I mean, not literally now. Not this precise instant. That would be crazy. But today, sometime.'

'I didn't think you knew,' she said. She slid off me abruptly, and lay beside me instead, staring up at the ceiling.

'Knew what?' I said stupidly. I'd missed the signs, again. You don't see what's closest to you. You don't see what's under your nose or between your eyes, or inside your head or heart. You don't see the body that's lying on your own. I didn't know what she meant, and my only fleeting thought was that she had been planning to leave me all over again, which was why she had treated me with such tenderness. That she thought I'd guessed she was leaving, and that was why I wanted to bundle her into marriage like a body in a trunk, so she'd be locked away safely with me, and I could drive all night knowing she couldn't get away.

'That I'm pregnant, Sully. But it's okay. We don't have to get married today. Or tomorrow. We can wait.'

'You're pregnant?' I said stupidly, again. 'You're pregnant!' and I jumped up, tugging my underwear back on. I stuffed all the things back into our cases, which were lying open on the floor with their innards hanging out, and slammed them shut. I dragged them to the door, before rushing back and kissing her swiftly, kneeling to put my arms around her waist, as she sat bemused and naked, with the sheet up about her breasts.

'Are you okay?' I asked urgently, thinking about my mother's last pregnancy. How her baby had practically poisoned her. The vomiting, the flu-like fatigue. The symptoms that hadn't let up until the week it died inside her. 'You're not feeling sick?'

'I'm okay,' she said. 'I think I'm about ten weeks in. I'm hardly sick, not even in the mornings. Just really tired. And hungry. And a little horny,' she added as a joke.

I buried my face briefly in her lap, in the sour-stiff sheet, against her flat belly where our baby was growing. Hidden and safe. A secret. Her hand was warm against my neck, and when I lifted my head, I realised that I'd been crying. That happiness hurt.

'What are you doing, Sully?' asked Radhika, nodding towards our bags by the door. She asked it without any criticism this time. She seemed genuinely interested.

'We're going,' I said. 'Let's go right now. If I drive all night, we'll get to New York, and we can be queuing up at City Hall in the morning.' I realised that if Radhika said no, I'd feel like an idiot. She didn't say no. She never said no. She gave me a smile that lit the room brighter than the moonlight.

'Okay,' she said. 'Sure.' And as I dragged our cases out to the car, I don't think I'd ever been as happy as I was in that moment. A young man in love, with a bride, and a baby on the way. A wife, a life. A place plotted out on the planet. A free gas station map marked with You Are Here. A roadside sign saying, You've Arrived.

I guess when something is perfect, it can only get worse. Radhika was my chance to make things right, and I think I really did love her. I know I did. But in the end, it wasn't enough. I failed her just like I failed everyone else.

I try saying it again, nervously, to the window overlooking the city lights, as though there is a persistent director staring at me impatiently from the chair. I try saying it once more, with feeling. I loved her. Such a flawed and fragile line. A working week story that gets less interesting each time it's told, until the dinner guests start to fidget, and cut across it, hinting for dessert or coffee. I loved her. How past and final it seems. My case is packed. I've dragged it to the door.

I look back from the grilled lift into my apartment. My blank bachelor apartment. At the open doors leading off the corridor. What should be a guest room is my office, as I have no guests in that sleepless cell. Instead I have hundred of files chronicling terrible acts of violence, committed by the people it is my job to understand, and in some way excuse. Some years ago, I stopped using paper, and paid a research assistant to scan it all. I keep the hard-copy files locked away, and just leave a neat row of little black box hard drives on the open shelves. Smooth and sinless. Me and my machines. No one else knows what's in them.

The office is the same size as my student room when I was at Yale, and has a box with the same clippings from the wall, from my first doctorate. When I sit there late at night, I keep it brightly lit, to stop myself talking to the ghosts, the condemned and dead whose testimonies I studied, some of whom I met, across a glass-partitioned table, or through the bars of high-security prisons. I even met that Lithuanian soldier, a former policeman, who shot people in a pit for the Nazis. I interviewed him in the nineties, just before he was released. He had told the court that one of the other collaborators, who was condemned to death on his testimony, told an old Jew to take off his coat and shoes before he shot him, because it was a nice coat, and they were good shoes.

'He was happy,' the soldier had said. 'He said, I'm lucky that old man was here today. Tonight, I'm going to go out dancing in his shoes.'

I asked him about this story, across an ordinary table in the regular visitors' room in the provincial prison; the same place where his family came to see him. I didn't need a lie detector to see his old eyelids flicker, and to catch the moment he missed a breath.

'It was tragedy,' said the soldier emphatically, unable to look at my local translator, and suddenly speaking to me directly in his halting, heavily accented English, as though he had seen something in my face that reflected what he had betrayed in his own. He said it urgently. He said it as an excuse. 'It was *big* tragedy.'

He had no bigger word than big, to describe the loss. He had served his thirty years, and he would leave prison as a man in his sixties, and live with his mother, who was still alive, and help her to tend the grave of his father, who had died. He was looking forward to meeting his daughter's children, who lived abroad, for the first time. But I knew that he was the one who had gone dancing that night. He was the one who wore the dead man's clothes.

I stand at the door, and lift my case, feeling the weight of it. Resisting the urge to take it back to my bedroom and shake it out again. It's about the same size, but of course it's not the same one. God knows what happened to those old cases we dragged from Yale all those years ago; me to Columbia, and Radhika to Barnard, in a black Ford that had blood spatter on the front grille. I didn't find out about it until I tried to sell it; I just thought it was rust. It was probably why I got the car so cheap. I hope it was just a hit-and-run deer. I can't imagine what the motel guy thought when he saw we'd disappeared in the night, cash for the room and the tip for bringing in our baggage left in an envelope like a bribe. I suppose our old cases were taken to the dump, or given away in one of the yard sales we used to have every year when we lived in Long Island. Radhika was diligent about getting rid of all the baby stuff, as Buzz got older, and then all the paraphernalia from the hobbies that he outgrew. She never held on to baggage.

This new case is already several years old, and was a present from Buzz and my daughter-in-law, Tania. They gave it to me when I took their kids on holiday for them, with Radhika, that September the towers came down. When Tania's mother died, she sent the kids to Disneyland for two days, so they wouldn't have to be at Grandma's funeral. I think that if she died herself, she'd leave instructions for Buzz to do the same thing; when someone's unpleasant, leave the room. When something horrible happens, leave town. She lives in the now. Not in the past. I'm embarrassed by the ostentatious Louis Vuitton branding, I guess that Buzz chose it so that I'd know how much he spent on it. I appreciate the generosity, his touching try-hard extravagance, but all the same, I hope that people assume it's a fake.

I realise what I must look like, to any oddballs scanning the lit Manhattan windows with their telescopes; an old guy in a good suit, standing indecisively at his doorway with an overpriced case. Like an old lady in pearls fussing with the flowers on her table. I pull out my cell, and say a name. I like to have an excuse to say it out loud. To be obliged to repeat it, more slowly and clearly. For once the technology works first time. The phone repeats the name correctly back to me, and dials.

'Won't you meet me? I'm getting a plane tonight.' I say it in a defeated way, to let her know I'm already expecting the no, to let her off. I don't want her to feel too bad about it. It's my problem, not hers. I'm the one who's calling, from way across the burned-out bridge. She shouldn't have to hear me, and she doesn't have to see me.

Won't. Don't. I know I won't persevere, when I get the no that I've already accepted. I'm not a young man any more. I won't even ask why. I already know why. So I wait, in the empty space that my question has opened. A ballroom with just two gilt chairs, facing each other. I sit there with her. Alone in a room.

'Okay,' says Radhika. 'I'll meet you at the airport. You're leaving from JFK, right?'

'Oh, that's right, JFK,' I stammer, too surprised to sound grateful. 'I didn't think you knew.'

'Okay,' she says again, as though I had simply said yes, like I should have done. 'I'll see you there.' She sounds both breezy, and businesslike, and I imagine her putting down her wine glass, and her papers, and snapping her glasses into a case. I imagine her picking up her car keys, and cancelling her takeaway. I imagine her walking to the door of her apartment, and standing there, just as I am standing here.

I put my bare hand to my heart, and feel the solid gold ring that I still wear, on a chain; under my shirt, next to my skin. It's my secret. It's hidden, and it's safe.

She didn't say no. She knew that I was going to call.

Chapter Twelve

Jakie

I WOULD RATHER STAY THAN LEAVE. I DON'T TELL MY KIDS THIS, AS I know it would upset them. I don't tell the other aid workers and medical volunteers, but I know it would surprise them. That I'd rather be among strangers than my family; it probably seems selfish rather than selfless. Like I'm running away.

The truth is that I feel I'm doing some good here, and I know I won't be doing anything nearly as helpful back home in London, or in Lahore. In general practice, in my clean office and white coat, I've rarely saved a life. I just got people better faster, or slowed down the spread of their disease. It's all or nothing here; I save people, and know that without me to save them, they'd die. I can treat lots of people, rather than just one at a time, spaced out at twenty-minute intervals during a working day, like street lamps in a line. I can help strangers as distant as statistics, all ticked off my list as they get their vitamins, shots and polio drops. I can give them what they need to survive.

I can help strangers. But back in London and Lahore, the ones closest to me, close enough for them to have been inside me, or me to have been inside them – my lover, my mother – I can't help at all.

It's cleaner in the hills, even here in the camp, with the dirt and the stench of the open latrines. I haven't dared to shave for the last couple of weeks, because my only razor's blunt and I can't risk an open cut and an infection; antibiotics are too precious here to waste on people like me, who are just passing through. Even with all of that, it's cleaner. I still have a few minutes with the internet connection working, and so I open

289

the laptop, and call Mae. I told her that I would if I could. When she answers, she is sitting composed and elegant in front of her own computer, and I imagine that she has smoothed her hair, and the fold of her high-fashion monochrome sari over her shoulder, before she clicked to accept the call.

'*Asalaam alaikum*, Dr Jamal Kamal Saddeq,' she says with mocking formality.

'Salutations, gracious lady of Lahore,' I reply, and she gives a sideways nod, as though undecided whether or not I have said something funny.

'So, is he really coming?' she asks.

'He says he is.'

'Of course he says he is. It doesn't mean a thing until he gets off the plane,' she says. 'And are you really coming?' she asks, more sharply.

'God, I don't know, Mae,' I say honestly. 'I told Sulaman I was, but I'm a better liar than him. I'm busy here. They could use me for another week. I could help people. I can't do a thing for Mummy, can I? I don't know what I'd be coming back for.'

'What rubbish,' she says. 'You'll come, Jakie. And if you don't, I'll come out there on a plane, train, bus and bloody mule, and drag you back here myself. St Jakie. Charity junkie. You're too old for such nonsense.'

'Well we all are, aren't we?' I say. 'I already said goodbye to Mummy. I've said goodbye to her every year for the last ten years, just in case. And you'll have Sulaman and Lana.'

'Lana I'd let off,' says Mae briskly. 'She's the one insisting on coming. If I were her, I'd stay looking after Frank until you got back from your little escapade. The living take priority over the dead.'

'Mummy's not dead yet,' I reply.

'And she never will be, without you and Sulaman to sign the consent forms. She'll just sit there like a piece of meat on a counter, plugged into the wall.' She adds accusingly, 'You're keeping her from heaven.'

'I'm surprised you didn't just pay off some orderly to cut the power to her room,' I snap. 'Or accidentally inject some air into her carotid artery.'

'I don't know what those words mean,' retorts Mae. 'You think it's so easy, that you can make your clever doctor jokes from way out there, vaccinating your messy-faced little orphans, sprinkling polio drops in the villages like Tinker Bell shaking fairy dust out of your faggot fanny.' She becomes prettier the crosser and coarser she gets; she's always had that sort of face. She's still a very handsome woman; people still think that she's her daughter's sister, when she goes around Singapore with Sherry, doing the sales on Orchard Road.

'I think I prefer Tinker Bell to St Jakie,' I say, but she doesn't calm down or laugh.

'You know, all the time she was ill, before that last stroke and the coma, she was . . . God, she was awful. She had a mouth like a sewer, and all this filth kept pouring out, about all of us, about Daddy. How disgusting we were, how shameful we were. Disgrace, Dishonour, Disobedience. How we'd filled her heart with darkness, how she wished she'd never fucked our father, and had drowned us all at birth. Divorcees for daughters, sons who slept with sodomites and half-breed Hindu whores. How her only good child was the unborn one that was waiting for her in heaven.' Mae takes a breath. 'The doctors said it was the drugs. They said they couldn't do anything about it. And so I just prayed. I just prayed for it to stop.'

'You were praying for her to get better,' I say. And I don't realise that I'm asking a question, until she answers it for me.

'You know, I'm fairly certain I was praying that she'd get to heaven faster.' There is a pause, and a crackle. 'I think I was just praying that she'd die.' The screen fizzles for a second, and then dims, as the electricity cuts out, and the computer is now working on failing battery alone.

'I'm sorry,' I say eventually. Inadequately. 'I know how hard it must have been for you.'

'I don't think you've ever known, Jakie,' she says crossly. 'You and Sulaman, out there in the world. With your paid-for education, your medical degrees and your noble works and published books. Your houses in Notting Hill and the Hamptons. Your annual fortnight of foreign aid. And if you knew, I don't think you cared.' She pauses, and then smooths her hands across her face, pushing back her hair. She sits up straight, and composes herself. '*Uff, Allah*, I'm beginning to sound like her.' She says it more to herself than to me.

'Enough of this nonsense, old man,' she says then, signing me off in the same familiar way she'd speak to the jeweller who melted her wedding gift bracelets to pay for her divorce, or the cantankerous family cook she left her daughter with while she went to the clinic for her discreet abortions. 'No more chatter. No more excuses. I'll see you soon.'

'I love you, Mae,' I say. I'm not sure I've ever said it to her before. I'm not sure why I'm saying it now. 'You're a good sister.'

'I know that,' says Mae impatiently. 'And I know that too.' She hesitates, and then replies quickly, 'And I love you, old man. Now get on that damn mule.' And she slams her computer shut before I can coax any further embarrassing admissions from her.

Frank was pretending to work, sitting across from Asha at the kitchen table in our hastily rented terraced house in Notting Hill. William Godfrey and his girlfriend lived nearby; they'd moved into her white mother's house, they paid her rent between them, and were practically engaged. Asha was wearing a school uniform, and had cut a foot off her long braid; with her treacle-slick hair, so shiny that it seemed wet, she looked like a miniature Mary Quant. She ruined the effect with a pink plastic hairband from the market, with purple butterflies printed on it, and in her school uniform she looked exactly her age. She was still thirteen.

Frank claimed to be writing copy for the paper that he had reluctantly started working for again, to help pay the bills, but was really helping Asha with her homework. He was chattering to her while he tested her on her times tables. She laughed with him while she wrote them out, her numbers as neat and precise as a grocer's assistant. As soon as she had finished with her maths, she started revising her spellings, shushing him because she found them so much harder. Her fierce concentration was infectious, and Frank abandoned his own work, and did the daily crossword with the same look on his face.

For a moment, studying their profiles, bowed over the table, they looked like father and daughter. Frank was almost old enough to be her dad, had he got some girl in trouble when he was fifteen. Neither of them were looking at me, and neither of them were looking at the baby, who was lying flat on his back in his Silver Cross pram, staring in my direction as I made up his formula at the sink. He was playing with his hands, sucking at them, and I wasn't sure if he was hungry, or if he had just decided that he should be, because he could smell the cookie-sweet Nestlé formula.

Caitlin waved to me from the kitchen window, in her familiar green coat, and knocked on the door out of habit before she opened it, even though she knew I'd seen her so she didn't have to. She laughed when she found me shaking the baby bottle, an apron over my work clothes.

'Oh, Jakie, bless you,' she said, as though I was too funny for words. She was loaded down with plastic bags from major department stores, although it was too early in the day for anyone to have been shopping.

'I know,' I said grimly, nodding in the direction of Asha and Frank, who grinned and waved hello at Caitlin's entrance, but were otherwise competing for who could finish their task first in our little kitchen. 'Why do I have to be the girl?'

Caitlin laughed again as she kissed me chastely on the cheek. She pulled off her coat and picked up baby Hari with one smooth gesture. He was delighted to see her, and giggled in rolling bubbles. 'Shall I be mother instead?' she said, and took the bottle, efficiently dashing a splash inside her wrist, and licking it off, before feeding Hari. He gripped the bottle with both hands, and his intense face was quickly replaced by one of dopey dreaming; he looked like he was in love.

Asha glanced up at the clock, ticking quietly in the room, and yelped, 'Focking hell,' in her sweetly accented English, as she gathered her exercise books and stuffed them in her satchel.

'For Christ's sake, language, Asha,' I said, and then corrected myself as I could see Frank's mouth twist with amusement. 'I mean, language, Asha,' I said more firmly.

'But Frank says focking hell when he's late,' she said in confusion.

'No, focking hell is what you should say when something breaks,' said Frank unrepentantly. 'Come on, sweetheart, I'll walk you in,' and he stood up, folded the paper and went towards the door. Asha flew over to me, pecked me on the cheek, fluttered another wave at Caitlin, and followed him out.

Caitlin walked through to the lounge with Hari, and sat on the sofa. It had sagging cushions and stiff wooden arms, but was still the most comfortable thing in the room. All the rickety furniture had come with the house. I put the kettle on for her, and rifled through the plastic bags that she had brought, pulling out the contents.

'Thanks for these, Caitlin,' I said, as I put folded cloth nappies, baby clothes and knitted booties beside her on the sofa, admiring the little cardigans with careful stitching.

'Thank my sister,' replied Caitlin. 'She'll want them back when she has her next one.' She looked at me wryly. 'I'm guessing that you're not planning any others?'

I barked out a laugh with a bit too much enthusiasm, so much so that snot ran out of my nose. I hastily wiped it away, hoping that she hadn't noticed, and knowing that she had. Hari had already finished, and fallen asleep, lolling drunkenly in her arms. She took one of the baby blankets she had brought, embroidered with flowers and appliquéd bunnies, and spread it on the floor, laying him carefully down. He immediately stretched out, and raised his chubby hands above his head, his fists as tight as flower buds.

'They're going to take them away,' I blurted out. I looked guiltily at the kitchen, in case Asha might have come back for something, as though she might be staring at me through the doorway with slow comprehension. Betrayed again, by the people meant to protect her. 'That's what they've said.' I stared at my hands, at the half-moons on my nails. 'I've had letters from Social Services. I've been ignoring them, and avoiding them, but I can't do that for ever. They'll both end up going into care.'

'Oh, Jakie,' she said again, looking down at little Hari. Our Christmas pudding baby. Brown and plump. Edible and adorable. She straightened her skirt over her knees, and I noticed that she was wearing shiny new stockings, and that she'd gone to some trouble with her hair, which was shining like Doris Day's in her latest movie poster. Sulaman and I weren't watching the same movies any more; he didn't tell me about the films that he'd been seeing. He just told me about his wife, and the progress of his unborn child, and a little about the disquieting nature of his research; with every word he wrote, it became clearer that he'd started a new life. We'd been separated for so long, and I was happy he wasn't on his own. I knew it was a good thing that he didn't need me to look after him any more, but then I wondered who was going to look out for me. Caitlin, who I'd only known for a few months, suddenly meant more to me than my own brother, because at least she was here. She was sitting in this room, and she was close enough to touch.

I saw her looking around the room. We'd only lived in the house for a little while, barely long enough for the dust to settle, but I guessed that it had, as she brushed it off the sofa arm surreptitiously with her petrol-blue sleeve, gathered at the wrist, just like her skirt was gathered at the knees. I knew that this little gesture was made with sympathy rather than criticism, but suddenly I wondered what she was really thinking. Whether she thought that it was stupid of us to try to play house with a teenager and her rape baby, whether she thought that they'd really do better in care than with a couple of faggots. And because she was close enough to touch, I didn't resist the urge, and I touched her hand, which was now gently resting on the dusted mahogany arm of the sunken sofa; as though by touching her skin, I could read her mind.

'I never ask about you,' I said humbly. 'I never ask how you're doing.'

'Oh Lord, Jakie, I'm fine,' she said impatiently. 'I'm not pining for you, if that's what you're thinking. I'm seeing a bloke I met in a dance hall. He works in a garage.' But she didn't reject my hand, and patted it with hers; she seemed pleased to have been given the opportunity to tell me this. 'Is there anything you can do?' she asked. She said this kindly rather than helpfully; it was as though she knew there probably wasn't, but just wanted to let me talk. It was a gift that she had, knowing when to offer comfort, when there was no solution to offer instead.

I shook my head. 'I'm beginning to think I've done enough.' I got up, and started to walk restlessly around the barely furnished room, picking up things, and putting them back down again. I wasn't good at sitting still. I'd have felt more comfortable if we were already at the hospital, and walking down a long corridor, on our urgent way somewhere, as though the conversation was just part of a journey, rather than some end in itself. 'I don't know what I was thinking. I'm a doctor, not a social worker. I just wanted to help them, and now I've messed them around more than ever. I've made them part of a family, just to take it all away.'

I picked up a book from the shelf. It was H. Rider Haggard's *She*, and when I opened it, a photograph fluttered out. It was a posed family shot, taken at Mae's wedding, just an hour before Amma was taken to the hospital. I didn't have the heart to put it back in the book, and so I propped it up on the mantelpiece, beside the tooth glass full of dead flowering weeds that Asha picked from the garden, which smelled of camomile and cat pee. I didn't have the heart to throw those out either.

'You're not the one who's taking it all away,' said Caitlin sensibly. 'You're the one who took them in.' She stood up, and put the photograph properly in place at the centre of the mantelpiece, in a safer spot beside the mirror, where it couldn't fall into the grate and burn to a melodramatic cinder. She took the tooth glass full of weeds to the kitchen, and threw them in the bin, washing up the glass, drying it, and replacing it in the cupboard. As simple as that. Another patient's dead flowers to be dealt with. I didn't think she could have any idea how much I admired her at that moment, how much I wished I were the sort who could have kissed her in that hospital corridor on Christmas Day, and watched her make our house into a home.

'It's going to kill Frank, too,' I said. 'He doesn't think they'll really take them. He's in denial. He loves Asha and Hari. He loves them already. I never realised how much he was a father at heart. I think he'd always just assumed he'd never be able to have kids.'

Caitlin squeezed out the cloth she had washed the glass with, and started wiping down the furniture. She seemed content to let me ramble on, as long as she could do something useful while the baby was sleeping, and Frank and Asha were out of the house. 'You boys need a wife,' she said shrewdly.

'That's exactly what we need,' I agreed. I wasn't actually joking. Frank and I both knew that if one of us had a wife, they'd let us keep the children. 'That's just what I wrote to my little sister,' and I nodded towards the photo. Lana was thirteen at Mae's wedding, just like Asha. In the shot, you could see that she was insistently holding on to her childhood, with her braided hair and un-made-up face; she was looking at the camera with a careless indifference, smiling only because someone had told her to say cheese. It was me, not the photographer, I had whispered, 'Cheeese, pleeeze,' in her ear, in a mock-British accent, and had started humming 'God Save the Queen' as Amma sat regally on the bench, covered in cloth of gold that just happened to match her sari. Lana and I had exploded in giggles after the photo was taken, and were sent away in disgrace so that the happy couple could be photographed with their parents, and with each other, in various stiff poses.

'Lana's older than that now,' I explained to Caitlin, in case it wasn't obvious. 'She got married recently. It was just after Christmas.'

'I can see why you wanted to look after Asha,' said Caitlin, looking at the photograph closely, and then looking at me, smiling as though she saw the resemblance. She stooped to pick up Hari, who had started mewing like a kitten. Frank came back in the door, and took him gently from her arms, as though having dealt with one child, he was ready to focus on the next one.

'Are you staying for breakfast, Caitlin?' he asked, kissing her belatedly
 her lily-of-the-valley-scented cheek.

l people have breakfast,' she

'Just give me five minutes.' I
e. When I came back, I saw
able, while the little creature
, that he looked like he was
l of milk on to Frank's shirt;
n his vest while Caitlin fussed
's life would have been like if
ead. If he had chosen to be a
ce made by lots of homos in
em announced an engagement,
vere dead and gone; we used to
cattering their ashes out to sea.
or them, and that they weren't
at moment, as I watched Frank
the kitchen table, with a pretty
ned them so much any more. I

Jakie,' said Frank, still making
jealous of the baby; the way he
hing made me suspect that he

m, and kissing Hari on the top
with giggles, and he poked a
ecause it was shiny. I hadn't
s, at the thought of losing Asha
Frank and I might not survive
at it was like to be a father. It
in the world could compete

had turned briefly away from
me on the lips. Softly and
quickly, behind her back, so as not to embarrass her. It was a magic
trick kiss; now you see it, now you don't. It felt sweeter because it was
stolen, like the ripe pomegranates scrumped from our garden by the

swallow-swift orphans in Lahore, flying over the wall when the servants weren't posted there to keep them away. I felt choked up instead of comforted. I was thinking that he was everything to me.

'Well stop it,' he said. 'When you're an old black woman with a limp, living in a mud hut in some Third World country, scraping up maggots for your supper, then you can feel sorry for yourself.'

Caitlin laughed out loud, and I managed a ghost of a smile before following her out of the door.

'So tell me about this best boy of yours,' I said, because I didn't have anything better to say as I drove through Notting Hill. There were roadworks, and I ended up going past Whiteleys, and along the park, following a big red bus diverted along the same route.

'Do you really want to know?' asked Caitlin.

'Of course I do,' I lied, protesting a heartbeat too late to be convincing.

'Well, I'll tell you anyway,' she said, amused at my discomfort. 'He's called Tom, and his mum's gypsy, although she pretends she's not, and his dad's an East End fruit and veg man. And he dances like a dream.'

'And he likes you?' I asked, going past Marble Arch, and jostling for space with the cabs that were turning down Oxford Street.

'Would've been faster down Piccadilly,' said Caitlin unhelpfully. 'That's the way the bus goes.' Then she beamed at me as she added, 'And I think he fancies me rotten. He asks to see me every time I have a day off, and whenever I'm going to the dance, he calls for me first. He takes me out for fish and chips and buys me a shandy.'

'Smart boy,' I said, trying to sound ironic rather than wistful. It seemed she lived a beautifully simple life. 'But he'd be smarter to make an honest woman of you, before some other Tom, Dick or Harry catches your eye.'

'You know married sisters aren't allowed on the ward,' said Caitlin. 'So he'll have to wait. And don't tell the ward sister, or the night sister, and for Gawd's sake never tell Matron, or they'll throw me out on my ear before I'm done with my training.' I looked at her as I pulled up at the hospital to let her out before I parked the car, as I usually did. I realised that I wasn't the only one who had to do what I was told or suffer the consequences. That I wasn't the only one with secrets to keep.

I was thinking of what Frank had said, about that old black woman with the limp and the mud hut, and of Mae and Lana held hostage at home in their gilded cages, as I watched Caitlin climb out of the car and tug down her skirt.

'I've been dying to tell you about Tom,' she grinned, 'but promise me you'll keep it to yourself.' She didn't wait for an answer, and began clicking swiftly up the street towards the hospital, where the senior sisters watched over the junior nurses like dragons with their eggs; where she would have to stand up if a doctor came in the room, and accept instructions without even being looked in the face. It was easier to be a man than a woman almost anywhere. Frank was right. I had no business feeling sorry for myself.

'Don't worry, I'll be good,' I called after her. Someone beeped me, and began swearing when he saw that I was brown.

'That's what I said to the ward sister,' said Caitlin over her shoulder, before waving and calling back loudly, 'Thank you, Doctor, that was very kind of you,' for the benefit of the curious visitors and staff who were walking in her direction. People were watching her, in her green coat, with her shining red hair, and her shapely legs in stockings, and I think she even got a wolf whistle from across the street. She looked as appealing as a photograph in a glossy magazine. I wondered why the pretty white women in the hospital all turned fat, frumpy and forbidding the moment they gained any kind of authority; as though prettiness was the same as silliness or giddiness, and was something they were encouraged to shed like poor elocution.

I was still being beeped, and as I pushed the car into gear, and turned to raise an apologetic hand, I saw a middle-aged man in the car behind me turning purple with rage. It was the way I'd looked at Caitlin, of course. It was because she had stepped out of my car. He looked just like the man who'd refused to sell me rubbers. Just like the man who had walked out of the tea shop in disgust that day. As though he had been following me around with the express intention of being outraged.

I knew his sort, and I'd met him again and again. I'm not saying that I thought all white men looked alike, like babies and sheep; God knows I'd had enough of being mistaken for the other brown doctor, and being known as 'that one' or 'the other one'. This was just another one of the old duffers who had won the war but were now whining through the peace; who led disappointing lives and disappointed their wives, and whose children had turned into fashionable spivs or Teddy boys who disgusted them, or sweet young daughters who felt sorry for them. He'd have called someone like me a wog or a coolie twenty years ago. He'd have called my father a coolie to his face, even while he was bandaging him up in an army field hospital and saving his life.

I didn't grin insolently back at him; I didn't wave and move off. It turned out that I'd been feeling so sorry for myself that suddenly I was feeling sorry for everyone. I got out of the car, and watched the man turn an even more interesting shade as I approached. Puce, I think they'd have called it. Not violent violet, or prosaic purple, but puce like puke. He really looked like he was going to be sick.

'Sir,' I said to him quietly, 'I'm a doctor at this hospital, and I'm very worried about your blood pressure. Please come with me.' And he surprised me, because he got out of his car as meekly as a lamb. Like someone who had fought against something all his life, and just wanted to stop. Someone who wanted the chance to say yes rather than no.

'Yes, Doctor,' he said. Defeated. Relieved.

In the hospital, I left him with one of the nurses, and discovered that his blood pressure really was dangerously high. I might have saved that man's life. I was being congratulated on my miracle street-side diagnosis by William Godfrey when the ward sister came to tell me that there was a woman waiting to see me. She didn't try to hide her disdain.

'Is it a social worker?' I asked, making no attempt to sound calm, even though I'd known this was going to happen, and there was no point to panicking. I'd been wondering whether they'd go straight to the house, to pull Hari out of Frank's arms.

'I doubt it,' she sniffed, and her eyes were round and cold as marbles, in a shade of blue that would have been pretty in a prettier woman. Her scrubbed face looked slightly chapped, and a network of fine lines fanned out from her eyes and her pursed mouth. I wondered how she had aged so badly, and at the frailty of her parchment skin. Like Caitlin, she gave off a faint scent of lily of the valley, and I wondered if there was an offer on talc in the local pharmacy.

'She's an Indian lady,' she finally clarified. As though I should have already guessed that much from the eloquence of her sniff. She was forced to look at me, as otherwise she would have had to look at William Godfrey, who was smiling broadly at her in a way that would make anyone uncomfortable. He had blindingly white teeth, and it was hard to tell whether he admired her, or found her amusing. His crocodile smile faded as he and I both worked out what this could mean. An Indian lady. It seemed that Asha's people had finally found her, and decided to claim her. The distant relatives who had taken her from her widowed mother, and smuggled her here to work for them. I was surprised they had turned up after this long. I had hoped they would stay away from her, to avoid investigation and prosecution for the statutory rape.

'What does she look like?' I asked. I wasn't sure what I was asking: whether the woman was angry, or tearful, or repentant for what she had let happen to the child in her charge. Whether she was dripping with jewels and new merchant money, or dowdy and destitute. Whether she looked like Asha, who had already become part of our family; whether she wore our new daughter's face.

The ward sister looked at me impatiently, as though it was a stupid question. 'Well, she's Indian. She looks just like you,' she said. William Godfrey glanced at me significantly, and rolled his eyes. I tried not to sigh. The Indian lady looked just like me. Of course she did. She was one of my lot. That one, or the other one. We all looked the same. Like babies. And sheep.

The ward sister didn't notice any of this, and checked the time on the little watch pinned below her left shoulder. She was waiting for me to make a more appropriate response, and I knew there was a set phrase that I should use, but I couldn't think of it for a moment. Something as obvious as congratulations for an engagement, or get well soon for an illness, or many happy returns for a birthday.

'I'm afraid that she'll need to make an appointment,' I said, finally locating the correct formula for this particular situation, a stranger turning up without warning. 'Could you please ask that she leave her name and state her business, and if I can't help her, we'll direct her enquiry to the appropriate department.'

'Yes, Doctor,' said the ward sister promptly, as though this was all she had been waiting for; she would have done it herself, if etiquette hadn't required her to come to me first.

'Nicely done, man,' said William Godfrey. He slapped me on the back so heartily that I staggered. He was trying to make me feel better, because he knew that this small victory was all I had. That I could put it off for a little bit, for a few days, but I wouldn't win this thing. 'Come out for a smoke,' he added. Like I really was a condemned man.

'Fine,' I said glumly. I was due a break, and happened to have some of the boldly branded cigarettes from America that Sulaman had sent me; his wife got them for free as part of her research, from some tobacco conglomerate. She was researching safer cigarettes. Which seemed as illogical as safer cyanide. Oxymoronic. Moronic. I didn't say any of this to Sulaman; he was in love with his girl, and they were having a child. Amma hadn't yet found out she was a Hindu, because he suspected she'd disown him as soon as she did. Besides, his wife would probably end up saving thousands more lives than I would, just by recommending they put a little less poison in their pretty white death sticks.

People stared at William Godfrey and me as we came out, as they always did. William Godfrey was terribly good-looking, so nice they named him twice, as Frank used to say, but I didn't think that was why they stopped and gawped. I admit it made me feel better when I pulled out the American cigarettes, and offered the pack to William Godfrey to admire. I admit that holding them in my hand made me momentarily less nervous of the future, and look briefly urbane and knowing. A couple came up to us casually, as though about to ask for the time, or directions. She was too smartly dressed, and he was wearing a tie and a bowler hat; I should have noticed them sooner, and walked away.

'Can I help you?' I asked, pulling out a lighter. I'd had to buy one from the tobacconist on our street corner. We went to fewer bars these days, and had fewer matchbooks. Since we'd brought Asha and Hari home, there had been no more anonymous numbers or golden-brown hairs hidden in Frank's jacket.

'Dr Saddeq,' said the man. 'You haven't responded to our letters regarding the female minor and her child who are currently living in your residence.'

'We'll need to rehouse them. We'll place the children in foster care while we conduct an investigation,' said the woman briskly. 'You can't just pick up stray people like kittens in a cardboard box. Not in this country, anyhow.'

'I don't know what . . .' I started to say, and realised that there was absolutely no good way to finish the sentence. I was about to deny it, but there was no point. William Godfrey nudged me; an Asian woman was standing on the steps with the ward sister and Caitlin, and being directed towards me. She was wearing a sky-coloured shalwar kameez, unjewelled and barely embroidered, which would have been considered everyday-plain in Lahore. Here it was so vivid against the grey stone steps of the building that she might have been a Technicolor star who had been spun off her reel and strayed into a black and white film. She wore flat shoes, and had a coat over her arm. Her face was modestly powdered, but otherwise unmade-up. She looked like the sort of girl who wore glasses, even though she wasn't, and her hair was pulled back and pinned up. Like Asha, she had cut off her long braids.

She wasn't the girl on the mantelpiece any more. She had grown up. I hadn't seen her for seven years, and I was never so grateful to see someone in my life. If I could have called out for anyone to get me and Frank out of a fix, I wouldn't have called for the father who had paid for my education, or the mother who had beaten it into me. I wouldn't have called for the big brother who had looked out for me, or for Mae, who'd been forced to look out for herself. Seeing her standing there made all those faces from the wedding photo spin before me, on a one-armed bandit, and however many times I played, only one face came up.

'Lana,' I called out, desperately. 'Lana!'

I thought she'd run to me laughing, or crying, throwing her arms around me, like the dramatic reconciliations in the movies. Instead she walked smartly down the steps, still with a schoolgirl's briskness, in her sensible shoes. No simpering or sashaying.

'Hello,' she said, not to me, but to the official-looking couple, who were pulling a clipboard out of one bag and a dossier out of another. 'My brother's helping me look after my daughter,' she added, as though she was just making conversation, and it had nothing to do with what they had been saying to me.

'Your daughter?' said the woman, looking in disbelief at Lana, who even with her grown-up hair and outfit still looked younger than me. 'The girl is your daughter?'

'My stepdaughter,' said Lana.

'And where's her father?' questioned the man.

'In Pakistan,' she said. 'We had to send her away.' She said nothing more, but the expression on her face was innocent and blank.

'I'm sure it was a delicate situation, with her pregnancy,' said the woman sympathetically, disarmed by Lana's quietness, filling the silence. 'A baby out of wedlock. The dishonour. It must have been difficult for your family.'

Lana nodded, as though she and the woman understood each other perfectly. 'I knew my brother would look after them.' She smiled slightly as she said this, and the man and woman both started nodding and smiling at her too, before they realised what they were doing.

'But I'm afraid I don't understand, madam,' said the man. 'The hospital didn't have her paperwork . . .'

'I have it,' said Lana. She had a guileless expression, and everything about her – the sensible shoes, the pinned-up hair, her softly spoken English – said that she was a woman you could trust.

'Well, if you have her full paperwork, would you be so good as to send it to us?' said the man officiously. 'So we can close the file.'

'Yes,' said Lana. 'Of course.' The couple beamed at her, and glared at me, as though they suspected me of simply not having bothered to open my mail. Lana hadn't made the mistake of apologising, so they believed that she had nothing to apologise for. She had a face that could lick chocolates and put them back in the box; she could spit in coffee and serve it, and give nothing away. Blameless in every situation. Her duplicity was sweet and effortless; it was as though she didn't even think she was lying. She believed herself utterly. I think she'd have passed a lie detector test in exactly the same way a child would, saying that fairies existed because she'd seen them at the bottom of the garden.

She was nodding again, and so the man and woman nodded again too, and William Godfrey nodded along with all of them, until the woman said, 'That would be most helpful, madam. Apologies for the misunderstanding.'

'Shall I see you to your car?' said William Godfrey courteously, with that nuclear crocodile grin that made people want to cover their eyes from the glare, and back away.

'No, that won't be necessary, sir. Good day, Dr Saddeq,' the man said to me, as though I was the one who had done the talking. As though we all recognised that I should have done.

'Good day, sir, madam,' I said, pretending that I had.

Lana took me by the arm and led me inside the hospital, where even with all the noise and bustle, and the echoing footsteps around us, it suddenly felt that we were quite alone.

'I'm so glad to see you,' I said, and I was the one who threw my arms around her, and I was the one who was laughing and then crying. She submitted to this outrageous display of affection like a stoical child, one who had either been hugged too much, and learned how to put up with it, or one who had never been hugged at all, and wasn't sure how to react. She didn't kiss me, but put her arms around me, closing a circle, and pressed her cheek gently against mine, her skin on my skin. It melted against me, as sweetly soft as Baby Hari's. 'How are you even here?'

'Well, you wrote that you needed a wife,' she said. 'That's exactly what I am. These days. You all made sure of that.' She didn't say it with any particular resentment. It was true.

'How long can you stay?' I asked.

'The visa is for six months, but I can stay as long as you want,' she said practically. 'Tariq's not going to miss me, between his mistress and his mother.' She smiled at me, and patted her flat stomach as she said, 'Your Asha and I have got something in common. We've both run away from home, and have taken the baby with us.'

'Lana,' I said. 'Oh Lana.' Little Lana, all grown up. Little Lana with her pigtail cut off, and striding down the steps like the cavalry. Little Lana, saving herself, and saving me.

I don't need to speak to Lana now, because she was the one I called first. She's been looking after Frank for me while I've been away. I tried to speak to Frank too, but he just chatted to me idly like I was an interesting stranger he'd bumped into on the street, and then he told me a story I'd already heard, like old people do. He's only a few years older than me, but he's recently begun to age that fragile way of certain white men, palely creasing around the edges like the skin on hot milk. Lana steered him firmly towards the armchair, and put him in front of the television. It was a rerun of *Father Ted*, I think, and he laughed out loud. I heard him say, 'It's like a focking French farce,' not once, but three times, as Lana spoke to me in the calming tones of a career care-giver.

'Well, it's been a good day for him,' she said, reporting to me on my loved one, pleased to give me good news. 'Much better than usual.'

'That's great,' I replied. I was pleased to hear this, but I was looking at her face. She was looking tired. 'How are you? Are you okay too?'

'Oh, I'm fine,' she said, smiling to reassure me. 'I'm okay when Frank's okay.' I wanted to believe her. She shrugged, as though to dismiss any concerns, and I saw the fabric of the plain cotton shirt she was wearing lift to her ears. I could almost hear it rustle, although that might have been static. 'Asha's popped over after work when she can. Hari's come over a lot.' She paused before she mentioned her own daughter, as though it were a little tactless to point out that her child was helping more than mine were. 'And Minnie, she'll be moving in first thing tomorrow, when I leave. She's taken the whole week off, so she can stay with him until we get back.' She paused. 'Until you get back, I mean,' as though reminding us both that Frank was my responsibility, not hers. That he was my Frank, not her Frank.

'We can't ask her to do that,' I protested.

'I didn't ask,' said Lana, almost offended. 'She offered.' She peered into the screen. 'I can barely see you. Can you see me?'

It made me realise her age, the way she squinted and distrusted the technology; all of our long-distance conversations include her can-you-hear-me if we're on the phone, can-you-see-me if we're on the screen. She is so well preserved and unlined on the outside, her guiltless life having taken little toll on her, that I forget she's almost as old inside as the rest of us. That sometimes she walks into a room for something, and can't remember why. Sometimes she calls someone, and doesn't know what she wanted to say to them.

'Not when you do that,' I said; all the camera was now picking up was the divide of her hair, so that the pale line of her parting gleamed briefly between her smoothly brushed salt-and-pepper strands. Lana doesn't dye her hair, and cuts it herself, which bothers Mae hugely. She thinks it's Lana's way of showing her up. It's absolutely possible that Lana keeps her natural colour and unstyled look specifically to annoy Mae. She's always shown her aggression in these passive, blameless ways, so that her accusers would feel foolish saying anything, even when they know they are right. It took her husband the best part of a year to be certain that she had left him; everyone seemed to believe that she had simply gone to England to help me set up home. Nobody ever believed she had it in her to leave her marriage. Or lick chocolates. Or spit in drinks. I wonder at the complicated crimes she could have got away with, had she wanted to.

She leaned back, so I could see her again, and then turned briefly, as though she thought that Frank was calling for her, but he was just talking to the television.

'You know, I'd rather be here with him than out there with you,' she said. And I knew she wasn't talking about the refugee camp, but about the trip we're taking to Lahore, with Mae and Sulaman, to see our mother. 'I'd rather stay than leave.'

'You don't have to come, you know,' I said.

'I know,' she replied simply. 'But Mummy needs me to come.' She didn't say any more, and I knew that she was thinking in practical terms. Lana is the only one of us who practises our mother's faith. She is the one who will make sure that the prayers are said. She is the one who will wash her body, and prepare it for wrapping in white. She is the one who will pray at the Qul, with the small Qur'an from her handbag, while the rest of us make small talk with the mourners about politics and property prices.

Lana looked over her shoulder at Frank. I could see his agitated movement behind her, her face creasing with concern. 'I wasn't sure if you'd be able to speak to me today,' she said. 'I sent you an email.' Frank was getting upset about something he was watching. 'Focking animals,' he started complaining. 'Focking animals!' He sounded annoyed on the way to angry. Lana got up to go to him, smoothing out the surfaces around her, preparing to calm him gently back in his chair. Lana, the practical provider of care, watching over my neglected man with the same tender attention she would give her child. My man, her child. My Frank, her Frank. It feels that he now belongs to her as much as I always have. She owns us both, as men and boys. I've accepted this now, though it took me a while. I don't know what we'd have been without her.

Frank jumped up with his easy energy, before she could go across to him, and wandered back towards the computer screen. He seemed to have already shrugged off whatever it was that had made him cross. He put his arm warmly around Lana, and she tipped her head against his shoulder, surprised and pleased by the sudden affection. 'You asked me if I was all right,' he told me, looking down at the screen, as though we'd been in the middle of a conversation.

'Did I?' I asked. I wasn't sure I had. While I'd been away, that was the sort of thing I'd ask Lana, rather than put to him directly.

'You did, so. You said, are you all right, sir? It was the first thing you ever said to me. Outside the café.'

Frank was smiling at me. He said it like it was no big deal, that he remembered this, when so much else was gone. In fact, it wasn't the very first thing I'd said to him; I'd actually asked to share his table the moment before, but he'd been asleep, so I guess it didn't count. Not so long after that, he'd told me he loved me, after we'd banged for an hour in my sunlit student room. And I'd told him, you know I do too, but that didn't count either, because I'd said it while he slept in my bed, speaking quietly against the pillow.

'The first thing you ever said to me was fock off,' I replied. I was grinning back at him, but I had a lump in my throat.

'Sounds just like me,' said Frank. There was a gleam of humour in his dry delivery, as though he might have just been being sarcastic about my terrible attempt at his accent. He wandered back towards the television.

Lana watched him until he sat back down. She was looking at him with love. There's no other word for it. She turned and she was looking at me the same soft way, her expression as clear as rainwater. I didn't know what she saw in my face. I didn't know how well she could see me, after all. But she felt the need to comfort me.

'It's going to be all right, Jakie,' she promised. I wasn't sure if she was talking about Frank, or if we were still talking about our mother. The people closest to me, the bodies I've been inside, who I can't help at all. 'I'll see you tomorrow.'

She closed the laptop on me, as gently as closing the door on one of her elderly patients' rooms. As though she'd been checking up on me, instead of the other way around. As though she'd taken my temperature, my pulse, and made sure that I was okay. That I'd last another day.

I feel guilty about having left Lana with Frank for my trip this year. She's taken time off from the care home, so it's been a busman's holiday for her, spending it tending to yet another batty old person. She said she was happy to move into our house and look after him while I was away. I didn't ask her. She offered. If it wasn't for her, I wouldn't have been able to come out at all. Asha and Hari couldn't stay with him full time, and I wouldn't hire a stranger. I'm not ready to do that yet. And Frank's her family too.

I feel guilty for having left Frank with Lana, too. Running away for weeks to the hills on the other side of the world. Another annual adventure. A little escapade, putting strangers before family. St Jakie, charity junkie. Asha and Hari would never say this to me, but they think I'm out here because I need a break from him. As though I'm abandoning him because he isn't fun any more. An obsolete toy I no longer want to play with. The going's got tough, so I've got going. I've ditched him with my sister, so I can forget about him for a bit, like he's forgotten about me, just for a fortnight of foreign aid. Perhaps they think it's understandable. And because they don't say this out loud, because they wouldn't dream of accusing me, I can't defend myself. I can't tell them that I don't forget him. He's always on my mind. I think about him all the time.

But I know Frank doesn't think about me, and he hasn't missed me while I've been gone. Not like I've missed him. Every day, for years now. Even in the same house, and for a long time in the same bed. We've had to stop sharing a room, as it began to bother him to wake up with a stranger, and after a while, it began to trouble me too. I remember the first time it happened, when I woke to find him staring at me. Not in an unfriendly way.

'So how are you?' he said. And without letting me answer, he asked, 'So who are you?' It was as though he was making a joke to a stranger he didn't remember picking up. Like I was a one-night stand he was surprised to find was still there in the morning. It's not like that all the time, though. He gets better as the day goes on, around familiar things.

When they asked me to come back out here, I knew that I would if I possibly could. Frank's the same, with me, or without me. His is a life I can't save. I watch him drift a little further from me every day, and it kills me. Out here, it doesn't just feel that I'm saving the lives of strangers. It feels that I can save myself. I wanted to do something good for the both of us. I want to make it mean something. What happened to us. What we lost.

It's like whatever we once were has died, but there are no bodies to bury. Maybe Mae's right. The living take priority over the dead.

I haven't eaten my lunch as yet, and I look into the tin cup of drinking water, which is brown and cloudy. I don't bother to pick the bugs out of the rice sludge in the plastic bowl, as they're a free source of protein, and the only one available here apart from the vermin that the children catch for fun, and the milk powder that we save for the babies and infants.

While I eat, I open Lana's email, and there's a link to a photo of me, from an article printed in a national newspaper, surrounded by grinning brown children. The press coverage must have been organised by the international charity that sent me here. I wouldn't recognise myself, skinny and sunburnt in my stained local clothes, if it wasn't for the caption. I'm described as a British doctor in the article, and as an angel of mercy to be doing this work for so many years, especially given my age, but the comments below from the online readers aren't exactly complimentary. Some say that I've got a funny sort of name and a funny sort of face for a man they're claiming to be British. At least two others say that I'm abandoning the NHS, which trained me, at the British taxpayers' expense, to help support the families of terrorists. Some others say good riddance, I'm back where I belong.

Lana's note on her email is brief: 'Bags packed. Leaving first thing. Minnie's staying with Frank. Jamal sent this link to me. We're proud of you. But you know that. Love from Frank, Asha, Hari, Minnie, Jamal, Frank Junior and me.' I don't know why she always puts herself last, on the notes that she writes, or the cards that she sends. As though she's still the youngest child.

I remember what Frank said to me, all those years ago: that I shouldn't feel sorry for myself, that I didn't have the right, unless I was an old black woman with a limp, in a Third World hut with infested food. It seems almost funny, how apt this now is; I'm impressed yet again by his wit. I'm old, sunburnt black, and the arthritis I've had for years means I can limp along with the worst of them. I'm sitting in a shack with an earth floor and a tin roof, chewing on the bodies of insects that have drowned in wet rice.

'Well, Frank,' I say to him. I talk to him all the time out here. I feel he can hear me better from the other side of the world than if we're connected by wires, or even in the same room. I speak to him like other people speak to their deceased children, or to God; like he's everywhere. Like he's not locked in his body, a memory box buried under a building, just occasionally leaking out through the vents, but is here with me now. I'm thinking of his face, the edge of laughter that clings to him, even when he's sad. I try to say it with humour, like he would. 'Can I feel sorry for myself now?'

Chapter Thirteen
Sully

I THINK I MADE PRETTY GOOD TIME, BUT RADHIKA IS AT THE AIRPORT before me. I guess she didn't have to wait for a cab, and she's an efficient driver, if a lousy parker. She got her licence when she was pregnant with Buzz, and failed four times on parking, ramming the car into the sidewalk each time. It's how she habitually parks now, if she's not in a space; she runs impatiently over the kerb, and then lets the tyres drop into place, barely in the road. When I used to complain about the wear to the tyre rubber, she said she'd rather wreck the wheels than replace a wing mirror again. I always pulled in like you're meant to and parked a few inches further out than her, and the wing mirror once got sheared off in the city by someone who didn't leave their details. Radhika had to order the replacement from out of state, and she got stopped by traffic cops twice for driving without one while we waited for it to arrive, once on the school run with Buzz, the other time car-pooling to campus from Long Island.

Radhika stopped letting me drive a few years into our marriage; she took the wheel because she said I drove like an old lady. She said it with affection, in the early days, and with annoyance, at the end. I did a lot of things like an old lady, it seemed. I wonder if she still uses that as a criticism, now that she's one herself. I don't know why I'm thinking about all this stuff, as though our marriage was defined by car repairs, as I look at my phone, and read her brief message. She is just letting me know which bar she's in. I'm surprised she picked a bar rather than a coffee shop. Especially as when I find her, she's drinking a coffee, while tapping at her phone. It's an uninspiring, dated-looking place, a pastiche diner with a fifties theme; I guess it must have a good internet connection.

'Hi, Sully,' she says, standing up politely, and for a terrible moment I think she's about to shake my hand. Perhaps she's afraid that I'll do the same, as she sits down hurriedly, just as I am leaning over to kiss her, and my mouth brushes the smooth surface of her hair in a clumsy accident. It's so awkward that she laughs, and after a moment I find myself laughing too, with a rueful exhalation. The walls come tumbling down. 'God, Sully, you'd think that we'd have got better at this by now,' she says, putting aside her phone, picking up her coffee.

'You're looking well,' I say. It's a polite understatement, because she's looking great. She used to be sharply beautiful, rather than conventionally pretty, and now she's sharply elegant, rather than apple-cheeked elderly. She is wearing cream slacks, and a skinny dark sweater, a tailored jacket over her shoulders. Her glasses are propped on top of her head, like sunglasses, pushing back her hair, which is several shades lighter than it used to be.

I can't believe that she bothered to change for me. This is how she looks these days. Collected and casually professional. And just like in the old days, her hair is short, her shoes are flats, and she isn't showing any more skin than her hands, and her face. Her face. I don't want to stare, but close up I can see a scattering of pores, under her dusting of powder, on the sides of her nose, a network of fine lines fanning out from her eyes, the brackets of amusement drawn around her mouth. I remember how I used to look for her flaws as she slept, and I'm grateful for these flaws now. I want to reach out and touch them, to check they're real. I want to hide them from others, under my palms, and make them mine. Safe, and secret.

'You're looking well too,' she says. 'Considering.' She says this last word carefully, as though she is considering it herself. I don't look well, and I know that she is lying to be polite. Now we're not married any more, she thinks about my feelings, and is as polite to me as she would be to any stranger on the street. She puts kindness over honesty.

She sits back and waits for me to speak, like she's in no rush. I'm the one who asked her here, after all. I'm the one who dragged her out to the airport, even if I'm not the one who picked the kitsch neon-lit bar. After having wanted to see her so much, I suddenly have nothing to say, at least nothing that I haven't already said in my head. She's right: you'd think that after all these years, I'd have got better at this. I think we're both grateful when the waiter comes up to us, and tells us that it'll be his pleasure to serve us this evening, and points out the specials on the board. It seems far too late to eat. I order black coffee, and a slice of Dutch apple pie, which I don't want. All I really want is a glass of iced water. But I can't take up a table without ordering something.

'I'll have a refill,' says Radhika, 'and a slice of the cherry pie.' The waiter nods and moves off.

'No please or thank you,' I comment. 'You'll get a side of spit with that.' I say it as a joke, because she's never said please or thank you, and I guess that people don't change. It would be more surprising if they did. I say it hoping she'll feel a sort of affection for me, for showing that I remember this about her. Sometimes you miss what's wrong with people, as much as what's right. But Radhika just looks annoyed, as though I've caught her out. A bit embarrassed even. As though she suspected I always thought she had bad manners, but that I didn't have the guts to call her out for it.

'If you want a please or thank you, move to Canada,' she says, defensively. 'Or join Jakie out in England.' I'm about to point out that Jakie's in Pakistan at the moment, to introduce it gently, because that's why we're here. I'm going back to Pakistan, on my own. This time there isn't even a body that's been buried over there. There aren't bodies to raise up through the rubble over here. There is just a white-sheeted piece of meat, wearing one of my mother's many masks; peeing into a bag, beeping into a monitor, plugged into a wall.

I don't get the chance to say this, as Radhika is distracted by her phone, which is flashing silently; it then starts buzzing rather than ringing, and I can see a picture of our son, Buzz, gleaming on it. I can tell right away that he's the one who loaded the picture on, he's the one who chose the buzzing ringtone, and that he's the one who must have given her the fancy-looking phone, insisting she needed one like this for emergencies. For whatever emergencies semi-retired college professors consulting on long-term research projects might expect. The photo is the same one that appears on his various social networking sites, on his office ID card, and in the glossy programmes when he's talking at out-of-town sales conferences; he's grinning like an all-American dentist who spends his weekends playing golf, and the only giveaway that he's almost all-Asian is his thickly shining cap of espresso-dark hair. His paleness doesn't seem to have affected him being nominated for the third year running as the local South Indian American Businessman of the year; his wife is properly and fiercely brown, and he has bred the brown back into his children. He maintains the darkness of his hair stubbornly; I'm not sure if he dyes it, or if he has so few greys that his wife could pluck them out for him, one by one, as delicately as Cook used to pick stones out of the rice and lentils.

Radhika sighs, as though she resents being checked up on, but answers it anyway. When she speaks, she switches instinctively into her mom voice; it's like she's a different person, speaking a whole different language. Her sharp edges soften and blur; her tone is warm and reassuring, and every word has a Mommy's Proud subtext. 'Hey, Buzz. Yes, honey, I heard. Yes, I know. I guess not, I'm with him now. We're at the airport. That's nice of you, honey, you have a great night. Well, you can tell him yourself.'

I try to stop myself shaking my head; the last thing I want to have is a hearty valedictory conversation with my son, and possibly Tania, wishing me a safe journey, and telling me about anti-allergy pillows and hand sanitisers for the Third World country I'm visiting. It seems that this is the last thing Buzz wants too, because then I feel disappointed when Radhika says, 'Sure, honey, I'll let him know,' and hangs up. I would have liked the chance to shake my head ruefully, and sigh like Radhika, while I patiently take his call. I would have liked the chance to pretend to resent his buzzing, bumble-bee attention, swatting him away with an irritated hand, while he dutifully waves me off. Perhaps I've now done this too many times. If Buzz says he wants to see me, I'll just call him instead. If he calls me, I email him back. If he emails me, I text him a brief reply. If he texts me, I drop him a note on his social networking site. If he posts a reply for me there, I click Like, and do nothing more. With each interaction, I slide further down the greasy pole of communications; it's because the lower I go, the less of myself I show, like a monkey in a zoo climbing down the tree until his bright red ass is no longer on display, his private parts safely concealed by the dirt as he sits on the ground. I keep sinking, until there's nowhere left to go, and no reply to be made. No way to clamber back up. Buzz has finally done what he should have done years ago; he's left it to his mother to say goodbye on his behalf.

'Nice of him to call,' I say. I try to say it flatly, without an edge. I try to mean it. 'But there was really no need, I'll be back in a week. Less, if I can manage it.'

She looks at me like she knows me too well, probably remembering the September when the world changed, and how I rebooked our tickets the day after we arrived in Pakistan. 'Less than a week? Seriously? How long do you think that conversation's going to take?' she says. 'You're not a college kid breaking up with someone in the corridor during a party because you've seen someone else you'd like to bang. You think it's that easy, just to wander in, sign a death warrant, and wander out again?'

So this is why she turned up, I realise. To criticise me. It surprises me, but I like the surprise; I'm encouraged rather than disappointed. Perhaps she's missed me after all. Perhaps she's missed trying to make me a better man, and a little bit less of a self-centred jerk. I only indulge myself for a few moments, before I realise that I'm a bit too old for this sort of vanity. I'm probably just another long-term research project for Radhika; the experiment she proposed in her basement room, years ago on Christmas Eve, and which she checks in on periodically, at the stages of life cycle significance.

'Maybe it's just that easy. Like Eichmann in his office, signing off on all those Jews,' I say. Eichmann was on my mind the first day I met Radhika in the cafeteria; he was on the news. I guess at the end, it's comforting to remember the beginning. Like him, I'm sitting in a bulletproof glass box, and I don't really think I can be hurt any more. I don't think I can be touched, either.

'She's not a faceless stranger,' says Radhika, patiently pointing out the obvious. 'She's your mom, Sully.'

'I know who she is,' I say, less patiently. 'But she doesn't know who I am any more.' I don't tell Radhika this, but I'm not sure I will know my mother, when I see her. She's been disappearing since I left, and the woman I've met in Lahore doesn't match my memories. So much is missing, and I don't know if it feels like a loss. I don't know if I sound stricken, or simply whining. My mother has already gone; she's just a body in a bed.

'You know, that damaged thing you've got going on worked a lot better when you were younger,' says Radhika. It seems that I still amuse her, at least. 'You only get away with being broken if you're beautiful.'

Her smile is dug deep, scoring the brackets around her mouth, and it makes me realise her age, and mine. I am showing no more of myself than her; my face, my hands. I'm glad that the mirror is high above the bar and I don't have to look at myself, the way she has to look at me. She once told me I was beautiful, but I don't think I've ever seen the-me-that-she-sees. Whenever I pass my reflection, accidentally in car windows and glass store fronts, I just want to put a bag over my head.

I find myself glancing at my hands on the table, the skin as thick and raw-looking as a plucked bird, the trimmed nails as tough and riveted as claws. I'm embarrassed by them. I wish I could withdraw them into the linked cuffs of my shirt. Mickey and Minnie Mouse are beaming there in gleaming enamel, bright and ageless; the cheapest cufflinks I own are also the most precious to me. I'm not sure that Lana and Minnie believe me when I say that I wear them all the time now. Minnie was right: there's no way I'd forget they were from her. Here in the States, people smile at me when they see them, like they misjudged me. Foreigners smile at me when they see them, like I'm just another dumb American, anodyne and sanitised, and I smile back, because I know I'm one too.

'Anyone can be beautiful these days,' I say, to hide my discomfort, fiddling with the cufflinks, and then pushing my hands in my pockets. I nod towards a group of girls at the bar. They look almost alike, a set of plastic dolls distinguished by their outfits alone, and are woo-hooing, and downing cocktails vacuously as they flip their Barbie hair. There's something quite horrid about their happiness; it seems as fake as them. Real happiness hurts.

Radhika doesn't even glance at them. 'As it happens, Buzz wasn't actually calling for you. He was calling to tell me that he finally won South Indian American Businessman of the year. I already knew, though. Tania was live-tweeting through the ceremony.' She taps her fancy phone with her trimmed nail.

'Oh,' I say. Perhaps I was wrong about the bulletproof box. Perhaps I could still be hurt. I'd forgotten about Buzz's big night, in a swanky downtown hotel. And he'd forgotten about mine. 'I didn't think he was brown enough to win,' I add a bit stupidly.

'I didn't think Obama was black enough, but it didn't hurt his chances either,' shrugs Radhika. 'Just coloured enough. And just on the outside, where it doesn't really matter.'

Our coffee arrives, and she takes off her jacket. 'It's warm here, isn't it?' she says apologetically, and then she pulls off her hair like a hat, and puts it with the jacket on the spare seat. Her hair never really grew back properly after her last set of chemo treatments, and it is trimmed to a few millimetres all over, a soft brown-grey shadow against her pale scalp. Show me yours, I'll show you mine.

'It is warm,' I agree, and unbutton and pull off my own jacket. I push up my shirt sleeves, showing not just my ugly old hands, but my ugly old scars, parallel lines up the wrist and a long one down the vein, inexpertly stitched up into a railroad track by an intern at a prison hospital. Sick bodies trump sick minds. Cancer trumps torture, especially if it's self-inflicted. She wins, again.

'So who's funding the research into tobacco these days?' I ask, mentioning another one of her long-term projects.

'The American Cancer Society,' she says. I don't know why this surprises me. The tobacco companies used to fund her research into cancer, in the old days, and now it's the other way around. She says it seriously. She says it so seriously that it feels like a joke.

When we got married, and had Buzz, it's fair to say that I left Radhika holding the baby. I threw myself into my work when we got to New York. I started off wanting to prove something to her: that I could support her and a family. But then I ended up wanting to prove something to myself. I wanted to believe that she had made the right choice all the times she'd said yes to me, all the times she'd given her consent to my outlandish demands. Say you do too. Say yes. Marry me. Marry me right now.

I wanted to make Radhika proud, but I never felt that I was good enough for her, and so I kept trying to fill the gap with professional success. I worked long and crazy hours. I just came home to eat and sleep, and even then barely slept by her side. I was habitually at my desk until midnight, and up again at 5 a.m. It seemed to pay off; I was fast becoming one of the most prolific and best-known experts in my field. I thought I was doing it for her, and for us. But the truth was, having bundled Radhika into marriage and motherhood, I abandoned her to it.

I didn't realise how much it affected her, until a few months after Buzz was born. I got back from work one night, and heard him squalling in his room. It was long past his bedtime, and I assumed that Radhika was out on the patio and couldn't hear him. She went out there to smoke sometimes; more frequently since he'd come along.

'Honey,' I called. 'Are you out back?' She didn't reply, and she wasn't there. It seemed unlikely that she'd leave him to get the laundry from the basement or anything like that, but I couldn't see her anywhere else in the little faculty apartment. I found her in his room. Sitting in the armchair, with him sprawled across her lap, but she wasn't hugging him, or comforting him. It was like she wasn't even there; like she was asleep, with wide-open eyes.

I took him from her knees awkwardly. 'Hey there, big guy. Hey there, little man.' Buzz calmed down straight away as I held him. He'd seemed frightened. It was as though he thought his mother had died while he lay across her, that she'd frozen to furniture.

'Did you fall asleep, honey?' I asked. She stayed in the chair, looking at the blank wall. And then she got up and left the room. Left the apartment. I heard the door click behind her. I wasn't sure if she was even wearing shoes. She certainly wasn't wearing a coat.

I realised, when she didn't come straight back, that I'd never been alone with my son for an evening. That I'd never changed a diaper, or made up his formula. I worked it out, but the first diaper took me twenty minutes, and three pins. The formula was too hot, so I had to walk him around, sucking a knuckle, until it cooled down. I didn't know where we kept the pacifiers, and when I found one on the floor, I wasn't sure how to sterilise it. Or even if it needed sterilising. I was all ready to apologise to Radhika when she came back in, but she said it first.

'Sorry,' she said. 'I'll be good. I promise,' and she took Buzz out of my arms, and left me sitting alone on the couch, the television flickering in the darkness.

And she was. She was a good wife, and a good mother. She made sure that there was food on the table, and she made sure that the house was clean. She worked long hours too, and when we moved to Long Island, she paid for and organised the help. She cheered at Buzz's sporting events, with all the soccer moms, and turned up to his school science fairs. She made sure that she never needed me again, after that one night. She let me get away with it. She still never said no. It's like she had made a private vow, that she would end every argument before it began, by agreeing. Perhaps that's why I remember the broken wing mirror and the bumped tyres; it's because that sort of discord was so rare.

She never talked about having another baby. Sometimes I thought she would, when the PTA moms turned up to school events with another bundle wrapped in baby blue or candy pink, and when Buzz's buddies all seemed to be cooing over or complaining about their little brothers or sisters. Buzz asked himself once, for a baby, but seemed just as happy with the hamster she got him instead. I don't remember being disappointed that she didn't seem to want another kid. I think I was relieved.

I didn't think we were doing so badly, at least compared to the other couples we knew. We had a marriage, successful jobs, a family house and a sweet, smart kid who didn't give us any trouble. Ticks in every box. When I bumped into old university colleagues, I had a good story to tell, while everyone else complained about their divorces and funding frustrations. I trotted it out with casual competence when I caught up with one of the academics I'd worked with during my Yale days. Dr James M. Garrison. Jim-Just-Jim to his friends. We met over dinner after a conference at his West Coast university, where I'd been the keynote speaker. My latest book had crossed over to the mainstream, and was reviewed in the book pages of the national press, as well as the academic journals. The conference hall was full. They filmed my lecture, and took my photo at the lectern like I was a celebrity.

'You're a lucky man, Sully,' said Jim-Just-Jim, as sitting there, a few thousand miles away from my family, I showed him the attractive photograph of us all in my wallet, on the trimmed and raked front lawn of my sprawling Long Island home. He bought my tall tale of domestic success. He fell for it hook, line and sinker. He was so convinced, I could almost believe it myself.

It was when I got back, and saw myself through more familiar eyes, that the soft rose-shaded haze cleared. I saw what I was in a sharper, unflattering light. My pale face in the shaving mirror in the white and steel bathroom. The morning sun streaked in the window and spotlit all the deep cracks in the new plaster that I hadn't seen when I'd brushed my teeth in the early hours.

I'd arrived late, long after midnight, and Radhika had been asleep on the far side of the bed. I slipped under the covers, careful not to wake her. She was so far over that when I stretched out my arms, I barely brushed her shoulder. I don't know why we owned such a damn big bed; it was wide enough for a decorative third pillow between hers and mine. The Berlin Wall down the middle of the headboard. Still, I was relieved she was there at all. While I was away, she often slept in the little guest room next to Buzz's, which doubled as her office. I didn't risk kissing her good night, even though I knew that I could without waking her. Just like at the motel, ten years ago, it seemed creepy rather than romantic. I told myself that I'd kiss her in the morning. I saw a glass of water by her bedside and a packet of Tylenol. It wasn't like her to take over-the-counter drugs; I guessed she must have had a rough day.

When I woke up, she wasn't there, and I could hear sounds of activity in the kitchen. I was the one who'd overslept. I washed briefly, looking at my face, the fine lines around my mouth, the deep cracks on the walls, and went downstairs. The kitchen was full. Mae was visiting with Sherry; she must have arrived the day before. Radhika was already in her work clothes, inexpertly trying to work a waffle iron, while Mae was chatting to Buzz as he ate his cereal. He gazed back at her with that faintly besotted look that all kids get around very pretty women, stopping only to shoot annoyed looks at Sherry. Mae looked like something from a fairy tale, in her jewel-coloured shalwar and pretty sparkling sandals. Her hair was swinging in a fringed, fashionable cut, and she was already wearing make-up, with pale pink lips and a powdered nose. Sherry was ignoring everyone, slouched over a magazine that took up too much of the table.

'Hi,' said Radhika, stopping to kiss me so briefly she might as well have been kissing me off. She was pissed with me but she wasn't going to show it in front of company. 'Good trip?' She didn't wait for an answer. 'If you want coffee, honey, you better make it. I've kind of got my hands full.'

'Hey, buddy,' I said to Buzz, who stopped eating his cereal and glared at me instead of beaming awkwardly at Mae.

'It's not fair, Dad,' he said. He was nine and his whole body was full of the sense of injustice, like he was still too small to hold more than one complicated emotion at a time. 'How come SHE gets waffles?' He shot a furious look at Sherry, who indifferently turned a page. She tossed her head with a sharp gesture, as though shaking off an annoying bug.

'Um,' I said, as I didn't know why, and I was trying to imagine the conference hall of two hundred academics who had applauded me last night looking at me now, blundering like a hapless stranger into the kitchen of the house I was meant to call my home. 'Hey, Mae, hey . . . Sherry,' and I saw Mae's eyelids flicker and her lip curl with amusement at the hesitation. As though I really had forgotten her daughter's name. I hadn't, but I couldn't remember if she preferred Scheherazade these days. She looked so grown up, but she couldn't have been more than twelve. She was wearing white jeans and a long jewelled T-shirt. She even seemed to be wearing lip gloss. I went to kiss Mae hesitantly, and she kissed me firmly back with confidence, as though my squeamish uncertainty was annoying her.

'You're looking well, Sulaman,' she said, and I smiled gratefully, even though we both knew that she was the one who was looking well. Sherry accepted my kiss stoically with a nod and a dignified wave, like the Queen of England. Her manner reminded me disconcertingly of my mother.

'How come, Dad?' insisted Buzz, reminding me that 'Um' wasn't really any sort of answer at all.

'*Uff!* Because you're a boy, and you're a baby, and I'm the GUEST,' Sherry said. 'I need juice, Auntie Radhika,' she added, waving her empty cup, looking around as though there might be a maid to leap into action to take it from her with a deferential nod.

'Sure, honey,' said Radhika, and I wondered if only I could hear the caustic edge.

'*Please*, sweetie,' admonished Mae.

'Please what, Mummy?' asked Sherry, looking at her with genuine confusion.

'I'll get it,' I said swiftly. I took her glass, and went to the fridge. I couldn't see any juice there, and began rifling through the cupboards.

'You're meant to say *please*,' said Buzz to her. 'When you ask for stuff. Everyone knows that. Even boys. Even babies.' He ate the rest of his cereal defiantly. He watched me struggle for a few moments, before saying, 'It's the top one, Dad.'

'Oh, thanks,' I said, finally locating the juice boxes.

'You live here, right?' joked Mae. She knew how to deliver a line. Radhika and Buzz laughed along with her. I suppose it was quite funny. I was mortified, but tried not to show it.

'You know, I thought you were coming tomorrow,' I said, a bit defensively.

'That's what you told me,' said Radhika breezily to me.

Mae shook her head. 'It was always Sunday,' she said. 'We spoke about it. I called you from Jakie's, remember?'

'Oh, sorry,' I said to both of them. My annoyed wife. My amused sister. I poured Sherry's juice.

'It's not fresh,' she sniffed. I saw the hollow orange rinds by the garbage disposal, and realised that Radhika must have actually had to squeeze fresh juice for her. No wonder she was pissed.

'Oh, sorry,' I repeated. I said it to Sherry, but was really looking at Radhika. Her back was turned to me. Her shoulders were stiff and about two inches too high in her jacket.

'*Thank you*,' hissed Mae to Sherry, beginning to look a bit embarrassed about her daughter. She sat up straight, and put her teacup down firmly. 'Sherry, sweetie, just have some cereal. Auntie Radhika isn't your waffle-wallah. She's got to get to work.'

'She works?' said Sherry. She sounded disapproving, and gave me a critical look, as though it was my fault. As though I couldn't afford to keep a wife and feed my family, and was sending my long-suffering spouse down the mines, or out to dance for dimes. 'Why?'

'*Uff, Allah*, have some damned cornflakes, sweetie,' snapped Mae.

'No,' snapped Sherry back, adding an acid '*Thank you*.'

'I wouldn't be allowed to get away with it,' complained Buzz to the room at large. He pushed himself away from the table, and diligently put his bowl and spoon in the sink.

'Have a good day, honey,' said Radhika, going to give him a kiss. It was brief, but it was still affectionate. Perhaps she hadn't been kissing me off after all. 'Remember, Eric's mom is dropping you back for me tonight.'

'See you, buddy,' I said, as he closed up his school bag. I felt the urge to make something right. To promise him waffles for the next day. But I couldn't make a promise I couldn't keep. I didn't know how to make waffles. I hadn't even known we owned a waffle iron until that morning. It was probably one of those unwanted Christmas presents we never got round to returning. 'Do you want to do something after school today? I've got a meeting, but I could rearrange it.'

'I've got baseball practice,' said Buzz.

'Oh, right,' I said. Of course. That was why Eric's mother was dropping him off; otherwise he'd just get the school bus.

'See you, Dad,' said Buzz, and as he hauled his bag on to his shoulder, he came over and gave me a little hug. I realised that he was the one who felt bad for me. He always called me Dad. When he was little, I'd taught him to call me Abbu, but I was never around enough to make sure it stuck, and everyone else would say, 'Where's your dad?' or 'How's your dad?' I was someone referred to by other people, so that's what he thought I was called. Even Radhika got into the habit. So I was landed with yet another American nickname. Dad. I didn't wear the name particularly well. Dad wasn't really me; he was the guy who sorted out the bathroom cracks, and knew where the juice was kept. A guy who remembered which day his kid had baseball practice.

'See you, Auntie Mae, have a nice day,' Buzz said politely to her. He didn't say anything to Sherry, but she was ignoring him in any case. He went out to wait for the bus.

Radhika flipped out the waffles, and she and I were both surprised at how well they turned out. She'd made them from a packet mix; she must have run out and got it from the store last night, or first thing that morning. Or borrowed it from a neighbour. The empty packet was still there, beside the glass bowl, the milk carton and the egg box. Radhika looked almost annoyed that she was effortlessly so good at the mom stuff. I think she'd rather have served them to Sherry burnt to a crisp.

'Thank you, Auntie Radhika,' said Sherry sweetly, squeezing over syrup, and cutting into them daintily. Mae looked relieved that she hadn't shown her up again. She sipped her strong tea.

'I'll make the coffee,' I said. I didn't particularly want coffee, and I knew that Mae didn't drink it, and that Radhika wouldn't have time to wait for it and would get a cup when she got to work. But I wanted to show Mae that I knew my way around my own kitchen; at least enough to work the percolator. To prove to her, and to me, that I wasn't a stranger in my own home.

Radhika left shortly afterwards. I wasn't going into work for another hour, and then it was just Mae and me, with Sherry watching television in the den. I hadn't seen her for years, and realised that I didn't really have anything to say to her. We'd caught up on the phone a couple of weeks before, when she'd arrived at Jakie's and given me her schedule. She'd told me her story, and I'd told her mine, and now I felt that I'd been caught out in a lie. A tall tale of ticked boxes. Wife, kid, job, house. Tick, tick, tick, tick.

'Do you mind if I smoke?' she asked.

'Sure, go ahead,' I said, even though I did mind. Radhika always went outside to smoke. Mae lit her cigarette, inhaling and exhaling deeply. She sat wreathed in curling blue vapour, like a glamorous genie in a bottle. 'How is everyone?' I asked. 'How were Jakie and Lana, and all the kids?'

'They're great,' she said. 'Asha's busy with law college. Hari and Minnie have great Little England accents. And they're all so polite. I was hoping it was just a British thing. But Buzz is the same.' She grinned at me ruefully. 'I'm sorry about Sherry.'

I didn't pretend not to know what she was talking about it. 'She'll grow out of it,' I said.

'I didn't,' shrugged Mae. 'When we were at Jakie's, I caught Frank calling her Princess Pain-in-the-Arse. I told him it takes one to know one. He wasn't even embarrassed. He just laughed and told me to stop flirting with him.' She was laughing a bit herself as she remembered this. 'He's such a bitch,' she added, and she seemed to be saying it with approval. I looked at her, as I wasn't sure what she wanted me to say to this. 'I guess it does take one to know one,' she said. 'Is that what you were thinking, Sulaman?'

'Of course not,' I protested, shaking my head. I wasn't as witty as either Mae or Frank, to come up with something like that. 'He's good value, Frank,' I added. 'He's passing through New York again next month. Doing some series on neo-Nazism in America. Radhika loves him.'

'Everyone loves Frank,' complained Mae. 'Lana's like a smitten kitten around him.' She tapped her cigarette ash neatly on her saucer. 'And you, Sulaman? How are you?'

'Me? Oh, I'm great,' I said. I realised that I wasn't smiling while I said this. I wasn't sure if that made me look more or less sincere. Mae looked at me closely, unconvinced in any case.

'We'll get out of your hair tomorrow,' she said. 'I've booked us into the American Hotel. Sherry's too much trouble for Radhika, and keeps winding Buzz up. I'm going to have to do some serious gift-shopping to make them like us again.'

'You don't have to do that,' I said.

'Believe me, it'll help,' said Mae. 'I've done this before. Sherry's hard work. And nothing says sorry like a bit of damn good Gucci.'

She stubbed out her cigarette and got up a bit restlessly. She glanced towards the den, where Sherry had turned up the volume so the television was blaring with canned laughter. Mae spoke to me more quietly. 'You know, the other day Sherry asked me outright if I loved her father. I was complaining about him to Lana. I wasn't even saying anything untrue.'

'What were you saying?' I asked. I wondered if Radhika complained about me in front of Buzz. It didn't seem likely, although God knows she had enough to complain about. It wasn't her style.

'He wants more kids,' said Mae. 'That's what he says. What he means is that he wants a boy. He doesn't know that I've already got rid of two of his.' She said this casually, like it was no big deal. As though abortion was a perfectly practical form of birth control. 'Neither does Sherry. Mummy did, but she's like a witch – she's got eyes and ears everywhere. It was the chauffeur who gave me away. The one I hired to go to the clinic turned out to be her bearer's brother-in-law.'

'What did you tell Sherry?' I asked. 'Did you answer the question?'

'I had to, she put me on the spot,' complained Mae. 'I told her that of course I loved her daddy. I loved the fact that he'd paid for us to see my family, and had the good manners to stay home.' She added unrepentantly, 'I said I loved the fact that he wasn't there.'

'Oh,' I said. She looked at me significantly, and I knew that she wasn't confessing something to me about herself, but telling me something about myself, instead. 'That's kind of harsh.'

'So what?' said Mae. 'She asked a direct question, and I gave her a direct answer. People shouldn't ask questions if they don't want the answers.'

'Even kids?' I asked.

'Especially kids,' she said.

'And you really don't want any more?' I asked her. 'You're still so young.' Mae was just past thirty, and she looked ten years younger. She was unusual in Lahore for just having the one child.

'Once is enough, for me,' she said. 'I know I'm not a great mother. It's not my gift, is it? Lana really showed me up in London, with her perfect little Minnie-me. But I'll get there. I'll try.'

She smiled, and went to hug me, just like Buzz had done. As though she thought I needed one. As though, again, she had been talking about me, and not about herself.

325

Later that evening, I came back from work, and saw that Radhika was helping Buzz at the kitchen table with his Spanish homework. Her brown head was against his, turned away from me. I could just see her creamy cheek and the tip of her nose, as she helped him with his spelling and pronunciation. I stood by the counter and watched them, acutely aware of all the wonderful words that he was learning to say. *Niños*. *Helado*. *Pastel*. Children, ice cream, cake. All his work seemed to have a celebratory theme. *Fiesta*. *Amigos*. *Piñata*. I didn't feel able to sit at the table and join them. I felt that I'd have been interrupting, gatecrashing a private party. They didn't notice me until I went to the fridge and poured myself a glass of water.

'Hey,' said Radhika. She smiled as she looked up, and I felt hopeful that I'd been forgiven for screwing up her weekend and getting the dates wrong. For dumping her with my sister and her obnoxious brat for a whole day without me, without warning.

'Hey, Dad,' said Buzz distractedly, copying out the line that Radhika had written for him. His handwriting was extraordinarily neat. I was unbearably touched as I saw him carefully join his letters as he wrote *fiesta*, and then dot the i and cross the t. I couldn't remember when he started with cursive writing, but it couldn't have been that long ago. My last birthday card from him had been school-made and printed by him with the same careful hand.

'Where are Sherry and Mae?' I asked, still hesitating on the edges, putting my glass on the granite counter instead of their table.

'Princess Pain-in-the-Ass is still out shopping with Mommy,' said Radhika sweetly.

'Have you been speaking to Frank?' I asked. 'That's his line.'

Radhika nodded. 'I called Jakie's. Just to double-check we had the right dates for Frank's visit next month.' She said it practically, without any reproachful edge. I guess she wouldn't have said it at all if I hadn't asked her. 'Mae said they'll be back for dinner. She said she'll bring dessert.'

'Great,' I said. I didn't dare ask what was for dinner. I didn't dare suggest that we just order takeout, to make it easier on her, in case it sounded like criticism rather than concern. 'So how's your Spanish?' I asked her.

'Coming on. You should learn, too,' said Radhika. 'It would help when you need to talk to Maribel.'

'Maribel?' I asked, and immediately regretted it. I should have nodded, as though I knew who she was.

'The cleaning lady,' Buzz told me kindly.

Of course I knew our cleaning lady. A friendly Mexican woman who wore colourful scarves and thick glasses. I just didn't know she called herself Maribel. I called her Maria-Isabella, because that's what was written on the contract they sent over from her agency, with our signed schedule. I had the depressing vision of a Spanish class devoted to teaching the privileged local kids the words for 'soap powder' and 'floor wax' and 'that's dry clean only'.

It bothered me that neither of them seemed surprised at how hopeless I was. That they didn't really expect me to try. I leaned back and sipped my water.

'You know, there are a few cracks in the upstairs bathroom,' I said. 'Didn't notice before this morning.'

'They've been there for ever,' said Radhika. 'If it bothers you, I'll pick up some spackle from the store. Get a guy to fix them.'

'I'm a guy,' I said. 'I could fix them.' Buzz glanced up at me, and let out a puff of laughter.

'Good one, Dad,' he said. He beamed at me like it really was a good one, and carried on working.

It was too much. The dates, the juice, the baseball practice, the cleaner's given name and the cracks in the wall. Everything I hadn't got right, all the real boxes that built up our life left empty and unticked. Perhaps Radhika saw how stricken I looked; she stood up and, leaving Buzz at the table, came over to me.

'You okay, Sully?' she asked.

I looked at her cream-coloured face, her brown eyes and her brown hair. I wondered if she knew how beautiful she was to me, scrubbed clean in her moth-plain clothes. I know I'm not great at this, I wanted to say, and I'm sorry. Maybe I'm just not made for this stuff, it's not my gift, and when I try it comes out like I'm kidding.

I reached for her hand, the words bubbling up inside me, like soup in a pan. Her dry fingers in my damp palm, cool from the condensation around my glass. But please forgive me, I wanted to say, and tell me you love me. I know that you did once, but I don't know it now. You've never told me you love me. Not really. I asked, and you answered. And if that's what you can give, that's what I'll take.

Say you do too. Say yes. Say it again. Please.

I didn't say any of it. I couldn't. Instead I asked quietly, 'Have you ever thought about having another kid? Maybe trying for a girl?'

This time Radhika was the one who looked at me like I was making a joke. A bad one. She pulled her hand away from me. 'Like Sherry?' she asked, sarcastically.

'God, no,' I said quickly. 'I mean, Buzz is amazing. Don't you ever think about it?'

'Buzz *is* amazing,' agreed Radhika, and she looked back at the table thoughtfully, and then at me. She tilted her head, considering me as she had done that first time, in the cafeteria. She had worn a too-long lab coat then, in brilliant white. Now she was wearing a dark work jacket that fitted her small frame perfectly. I was waiting for her to point out that I was never there. That I had never really raised him. That she had a busy job and couldn't do the baby stuff again. She didn't say any of that. She never argued with me, and she still didn't say no. She squeezed my hand briefly, her slim fingers with a firm pressure against my palm. A gesture that was decisive more than affectionate. 'He's amazing. And you know what, Sully, he's enough.'

I didn't push it. I didn't know who I was trying to fool. Even if she picked up the damn spackle to fill the deepening cracks, I wouldn't have had a clue what to do with it. I wasn't really Dad; that was just the name other people had given me. I'd already got lucky once; perhaps it was greedy to want more. Everyone else thought I was lucky. Apart from the ones who really knew me, like Mae, who could see past the chocolate-box photo in my wallet, as she walked into my house, and into my head. Tick tocking like a clock. Ticks in every box.

The next morning, I woke to find Radhika looking at me. Her hair was messed up, and she was wearing an old T-shirt. It was too big for her; it had to have been one of mine. It was the same grey, cold colour as the early morning light. She was on one side of the bed, and I was on the other, with that middle pillow between us. I think she was feeling bad for dismissing the conversation so easily. Perhaps I'd accepted her answer too readily for her to believe that I was really okay with it.

'Hey,' I said, sitting up.

'Hey,' she replied, and she shifted over to the middle pillow, and brushed the back of her hand over my face, across the angles of my cheekbones, and the day-old stubble. No one else ever saw me like that apart from her, not even Buzz. I was always clean-shaven by the time I made it downstairs. She looked at me ruefully, and sighed, like I was still someone to sigh over. A troublesome boyfriend. A beautiful boy. She looked solemn as she traced her fingers down my neck, to the old chickenpox scar that stretched the skin in the dent between my collarbones. She bent down, and kissed it, washed in the grey light. Like she understood something about me. Like she'd been scarred too. There was such tenderness in her touch.

I was thinking that Radhika was the most intelligent woman I'd ever met, that her work saved people's lives, and that she wasn't made for this stuff either. She was good at it simply because she was good at everything she did. She was good at making things work; she'd done it with us, she'd done it with me. I was sure then that I really was relieved, more than disappointed, that she didn't want more children.

I went to put my arms around her, to pull her towards me, but then she got up, too swiftly, swinging her legs off the bed. She was worried I'd misunderstood her. That I'd interpreted her moment of tenderness as a change of heart, as though I'd stupidly thought she was ready to start trying for another straight away. I hadn't misunderstood at all, but before I had a chance to tell her this, we heard Buzz and Sherry arguing, and then Buzz started yelling from downstairs.

'Mom! Sherry's in my bathroom. And she's locked the door. And I need my toothbrush.' Radhika sighed, but she grinned at me. I think she was relieved at the diversion. She went out of the room, padding downstairs on her bare feet.

I threw myself back on the pillow. I had a too-big bed, in a too-big room in a too-big house, and all these stupid trappings of success simply meant that I didn't get laid in the mornings, because I could barely reach my wife. She didn't want to have any more of my kids. And I didn't want her to, either. I wasn't going to push it. Even when I heard from Mae the following year that she and Nasim were getting divorced, that she was taking her daughter and leaving him, I still didn't push it.

Radhika wasn't going anywhere. I told myself this as I heard her calmly reasoning with Buzz while he bickered with his obnoxious cousin through the bathroom door. One child tied her to me as much as a dozen. We didn't need to Band-Aid our marriage together with babies. But then, Buzz wasn't a kid any more. He was in college. And then she met Anton.

'So, you seeing anyone, Sully?' Radhika asks, conversationally. I look at her quickly, in the dim light of the diner, but realise that she's just being polite.

'Not really. I think I'm better off on my own,' I say eventually. I know that she's living alone, like me. We always had so much in common. 'It's a funny sort of thing to work out about yourself, at this late stage of the game.'

'It's better to have worked it out than not,' says Radhika, unsurprised, as though she knew this all along. As patient as a mother, letting a child make his own mistakes, so that he can learn from them. 'You know, I'm actually not on my own,' she adds, and seeing how startled I look, she explains wryly, 'I got landed with the neighbour's cat. She went into a retirement village, and asked me to look after it for her. Until her daughter flies over from Florida to pick it up. Like that's ever going to happen.'

'So, you're finally a batty old cat lady,' I say with humour, and she shrugs her shoulders at the joke, as though she knows what's coming. 'Do I have permission to shoot you?'

'I'd rather you shot the cat,' she says. It feels so good to hear the silver thread of laughter in her voice. I don't want to leave; I can feel myself starting to work again, the rusted cogs turning, the coiled springs releasing.

'Would the world end if I didn't go to Pakistan tonight?' I ask her, quite seriously. 'I mean, if I had a heart attack, right here and now, they'd manage without me, wouldn't they? Jakie, Mae and Lana. If my plane crashed, they'd manage.'

'Well that's not going to happen, is it?' says Radhika sensibly. 'And you shouldn't wish for it. No mother should have to outlive her child.'

She runs her hand over her scalp, and I feel like stroking it too, as one might a kitten, the soft newborn down of our own baby Buzz, of our two grandkids. Her shaved head makes her look both vulnerable and solemn.

'And when the world really ends,' she says, draining her second cup of coffee, 'you're going to have to think of a better line than that.'

The world already ended once, and as it turned out, I didn't have a better line. I had nothing to say about it at all. It happened with Anton, and with what came afterwards. But I didn't blame him, or her, or even her illness. We were already broken by then. It had just taken me a while to notice. Like I said, I wasn't great at this. It wasn't my gift.

Anton wasn't anything special to begin with, just a junior colleague who helped with Radhika's research. He was a doctoral candidate from Zurich, and worked in the lab. They spoke in German, because it was more comfortable for him, and Radhika's was rusty, so she liked getting practice. She was a bit embarrassed that she had lost so much of her first language, the language her mother still spoke to her. She'd taught some Hindi to Buzz, but hadn't persisted with German, beyond counting games and a few songs. She didn't like the way people looked at her in public when she spoke German to him, as though she was being somehow pretentious or else insincere.

Radhika was aware of Anton's admiration, of course she was. When she smiled encouragingly at him while he was making a point, he stopped and smiled back before finishing it. She smiled, then he smiled. He practically glowed. She'd been there before, but she knew it was just a harmless crush, the sort any dull student might have on a dashing professor, or a faded professor on his star student. She was married, and had an almost grown-up kid, and was fourteen years older than him. It didn't make her feel uncomfortable; she genuinely liked his company, and if she was honest with herself, she liked being liked.

Then one day, sitting opposite each other in a busy lab, she laughed at a joke he'd made. It wasn't a very good joke, and she probably hadn't understood it, but the fact that she laughed encouraged him. Why else would you laugh at an unfunny joke? Why else would you agree with an absurd opinion? Why else would you smile at someone as though there was no one else in the room? It was more than kindness. And he blurted out, in thickly accented English, as though he wanted to be certain that she did understand completely, even at the risk of being overheard, 'I think about you all the time.'

She stared at him, shocked, and saw how distressed he looked. It was a crazy thing to say, and she knew that he had said it because their time was limited. His work on the project was ending, and he would never see her again, except by chance.

'I don't understand,' she said quickly, before the silence could get too thick to cut up with small talk. A colleague walked over, sensing some discomfort between them, and asked her a helpful question, rescuing her from the funny foreigner. She smiled gratefully as she responded, and tried not to notice Anton's face. How dismayed, betrayed. She didn't mean to be cruel, and she certainly hadn't been mocking his English, but she'd wanted to give him a way to take the words back. The understanding between them had evaporated in seconds; the temperature had dropped.

He nodded curtly, and went to leave the room. She should have left well enough alone. But she couldn't bear the thought of this young man walking stiffly down the corridor, his whole body bowed with disappointment. He was as transparent as the glass slides that lay backlit under the microscope. She excused herself from her colleague, walking towards the door to stop him before he left.

'Look, I'm sorry,' she said, and he suddenly looked hopeful. It was the way she said it. She wasn't dismissing him after all. It seemed that she was apologising for lying, because she had understood perfectly. 'I've just no idea what you expect me to say.'

'What I want you to say?' he said in German, now too emotional to speak in English. 'I want you to say you think of me too. I want you to say you'll see me after this. Please, Professor.'

Radhika doesn't know even now why she found it so impossible to say no to this clumsy request. Perhaps it was because of that pleading please. She thought of the last time someone had felt so passionately for her that they were willing to make a fool of themselves. It was compelling to be so admired. She liked to be liked. She said to him, then, what she had once said to me.

I do too. Yes.

Another colleague was approaching, and she briskly told Anton her office hours, and moved off.

The next day she was at her office half an hour early, a paper cup of coffee in her hand, a briefcase stuffed with papers under her arm. She was wearing a long, dark coat, like a modern nun, un-made-up as usual, because it was an ordinary working day. He was sitting on the floor outside her office, and she thought to herself that this was what twenty-somethings did. They sat on the floor, when there wasn't a chair. He had a coffee too, and it was finished, the paper cup beside him. He wasn't reading a book, or looking at papers; he was just sitting there, with his eyes closed, as though he could dream her into appearing faster. He jumped up as she approached.

Radhika told herself to look reserved and professional, perhaps a little apologetic, as though late for a meeting they had arranged. Instead she walked straight into his arms as she approached her door, spilling her coffee all over her dark coat, like one of those women who are charmingly clumsy. She struggled to find her key as he kissed her, and she kissed him back, and they managed to make it into her office, and slam the door behind them, just as the cleaner turned the corner of the corridor, dragging the humming hoover, tutting at the coffee cups left outside on the floor. Radhika remembered afterwards that her main regret about that first time was that she had worn quite so many clothes.

She saw this guy for three years, until her first cancer diagnosis. She figured that he didn't deserve to go through all of that with her. She figured I was the one who deserved it, and that I'd manage it better, because she didn't think I loved her like he did. She thought it would hurt me less. Snow White in her clear coffin. Me in my bulletproof box.

Radhika told me about Anton when she was in hospital, when her uterus had been removed, and the aggressive chemotherapy had left her as thin as a kitten, and more hairless than the cadavers she used to work on; they at least still had their eyebrows and lashes. Buzz was in his last year of college by then, dating a blonde cheerleader with great teeth, and didn't have to see her at her worst. She didn't tell me about Anton out of spite, or anger, or even as a confession. She was just being practical; she thought it likely that he'd turn up at the hospital, or at her funeral, and if that was the case, she wanted me to be warned. And she wanted me to be kind to him.

She hadn't told Anton about her illness; she'd tried to keep it as quiet as possible, but it had become public knowledge. The scandal had just broken at the university, about the tobacco funding of her research into cancer, and her results were being discredited, as being tainted by big business. There were photos of Radhika in the papers, looking like a shaved Auschwitz victim, taken as we walked to the hospital from the cab, but with 'Collaborator' emblazoned across her portrait in thick black letters, like a sign hung around her neck. A traitor, not a martyr. The shaved heads of the local girls who were punished for sleeping with the Nazi occupying forces during the war. As though some vigilante Resistance group had come up to her in the night, and shorn her hair to publicise the shame of being in bed with the murderers, the multinationals. The universities that had collaborated on the project, an unfortunately accurate phrase, announced a revision of funding policy. Radhika couldn't be fired, as she was on indefinite leave in any case.

And she was right to tell me, because Anton did come one day, when the press interest had died down. He was carrying flowers, extraordinarily extravagant ones, like someone who'd never been to a hospital before, and when he saw me in the waiting area, getting a snack from the vending machine, he broke down and cried. He held on to me like he was my brother or my son.

I was taken aback by how deeply he seemed to know me, when I knew so little of him. I could only imagine what it had been like for him to stare at the framed photos of me on Radhika's desk, or the family snapshots on the fridge in our summer house in the Hamptons, or my press portrait in the books sections in the national newspapers, all those years he was sleeping with my wife. I didn't know whether he had pitied, or envied me. He was ranting with anger about the headlines, about the racism in the editorials when they had dug up Radhika's half-German heritage, about the bald photo of her that had been briefly everywhere and had made a photographer for the *New York Times* briefly as notorious as she was. He said all the things that Radhika and I had tacitly agreed to ignore, and failed to discuss altogether.

Anton's passion was infectious, and as he hung on to me, sobbing and raging incoherently, I just let his words and tears splash over me. I ignored the people who stared at us. I shook my head at the security officer, who was approaching to detach the clinging madman from me. I understood why she had slept with him. I understood why he still loved her. I tried not to imagine what they had done when they were alone, her breath connected to his, or the life they might have had together if I wasn't in the way. I said nothing to him. I had nothing to say. But I held him, as I hadn't held Radhika in a long time, or my own brother, or my own son. I held my wife's former lover, and let him rave in my arms.

'We're going to be all right,' I told Radhika later, by her bedside. Forgiving her for the affair, as though she wanted or needed my forgiveness. I didn't ask if there had been others. It didn't matter, now that I knew that she would live, and we were going to stay together. I knew I wasn't going to leave her; I didn't work without her. 'We're going to make it.'

'Oh Sully,' she said. 'I thought you already knew. We didn't make it. We've been over for a long time.' She paused, and said it again. 'I thought you knew. I'm so sorry, Sully.' I couldn't bear her kindness. She really meant it. She was letting me down gently.

Sorry, Sully. Sorry, Sully. You say it enough times, it sounds like a joke.

It feels that there should be more to say. I guess it's always felt that way.

'Do you ever hear from Anton?' I ask eventually. I know that it's none of my business, but I would like to think that he's all right, somewhere.

'He got in touch a few years ago,' says Radhika. 'He emailed through the university. He got married, twice as a matter of fact. He's got two kids from the first marriage. His second wife was divorced with one of her own, so he's got a stepdaughter too. No grandkids yet, though. He started late.' She pauses, and then adds, as though it's something she doesn't want to say, but feels she can't leave out, 'He's divorced again now.'

'Maybe he's still waiting for you,' I say lightly. 'Maybe you should meet up with him.'

'Why? So I could have this exact same conversation with him about you instead?' she says shrewdly. 'I'm an old lady now. And he's almost an old man. And I think I'm better off as I am.' She adds with humour, 'At least I will be once you kill that damn cat for me.'

'Would it be weird if I asked you to come with me again?' I finally manage to say it. I asked her once before. When the towers fell, she came with me to Pakistan, with the grandkids. She agreed, as long as we took them to see her mother on the way. And everyone else – the grandkids, our estranged and distant families – we let them think that we were still together, because they never asked or assumed that we were not. We'd been separated for years; even when we lived in the same sprawling house in Long Island, with the Berlin Wall down the middle of our bed, and the brownstone in the city, we were separated.

I told myself that everyone broke apart, sooner or later, and the ones who said they weren't were just fooling themselves. I told myself this as Buzz and his wife celebrated their twentieth wedding anniversary with a lavish party in the Hamptons, forcing all the other guests to drive out and act like happy couples too, holding hands on the beach as they sipped their margaritas and peach Bellinis. Maybe I resented the blonde prettiness of the much younger colleague who'd offered herself as a date, resented Radhika for turning up with a dignified guy who looked like a clean-cut Clint Eastwood in a suit. Maybe I just resented having to drive. I really am a jerk.

'It wouldn't be weird,' she says, as though she is proud of me for having the guts to ask her. As though it is what she expected, always that step ahead of me, all of our shared and separate lives. 'But I'm not coming.'

I finally realise why she picked the cheesy diner. The late fifties style with the neon, and the coffee, and the pie. I see her looking out of the window, on to the lit interior of the airport, and then back at me. This is where we got on. The night I called her beautiful. The night I kissed her. Two lifetimes ago. Two scarred people, one with a body to bury. This is where she gets off. It seems we'll end right here, where we began.

'You know, Sully, that I loved you,' she says. 'I don't think I said it enough, when we were married.'

'I don't think you ever said it at all,' I reply. I'm just being honest, but it comes out like a criticism.

She scoffs a little, and tilts her head to the side. Neither agreeing nor disagreeing, not a nod or a shake. I've missed that little gesture. 'I didn't think you'd notice,' she says. 'I thought I'd finally get up the nerve to say it one day, and you'd be distracted with your hands full of papers, and leave the room, leave the house and get in a cab to another damn conference, without replying.' I feel terribly sad, as I know that this was entirely possible. 'I didn't really know, back then, if I did love you. I think I felt I ought to, because you wanted me to so much. It was always easier for me to say yes than no. Easier to agree than to argue.'

'It's not just you,' I say. 'It's easier for everyone. There've been papers on it. I wrote one. I got that award.'

'You and your damned awards,' she says. 'The men who ask me out these days don't want me for the sex. They want me for my ex. Like you're a rock star. They want to ask what it was like to be with you.'

'What was it like?' I ask. 'I mean, what do you tell them?'

'That it wasn't easy. You were never there. Maybe that's why I didn't know it then. But I know it now. I loved you.'

'Will you come with me?' I ask, as directly as I did that first night. I feel like a young man again, as I raise my face to look at her, full of hope. 'Say you will. Say yes.'

The gold band hanging at my throat is hidden, safe and secret. The line of scars on my arm is exposed. I scored them into my flesh when I was investigating abuse in the prison system, after she left me. I cleaned and bandaged the wounds myself, cut after cut, day after day, and covered them with my sleeve when I left the prison in the evening. Hidden, safe and secret. And then one night I couldn't stop myself, and cut a long line down the vein, and watched the blood pour out of me until I was found, passed out in the room.

I said it was a cry for help, that I just wanted to get my wife back, to get her attention. But the truth was that I hadn't cried out for help; I had just sat there, in clinical silence. In a clean room, mopped and swabbed. It was more of an experiment; I wanted to check that it would hurt, to check that I really did bleed. That I was a man, and not a machine; someone, and not something. That I wasn't a hollow box, but someone who had loved and been loved. Digging deep in myself. Excavating. Searching for proof, with my body, my blood.

Radhika smiles. She takes my hand in hers, and shakes her head. 'No,' she says. The shape of her lips as she forms the word like a smoke ring, her breath in the air of the room. 'No.' Her fingers brushing the scars on my wrist. There is such tenderness in her touch.

She's finally telling me no. She's finally telling me now. She loved me.

Chapter Fourteen

Jakie

THE ELECTRICITY CUTS OUT AGAIN, AND I SWEAR AS MY LAPTOP DULLS and dies. I hope the back-up generators have switched on, to run the fridges for the medication that needs to stay cool. I go outside and see that the guide has arrived early, and is waiting patiently in the shade. He will take me to the nearest village with a bus stop. The bus will take me to the train. And the train will get me to the airport, and then I can fly to Lahore.

The guide, a nice old man called Hanif, will not be taking me on a mule, for all my jokes. He'll be driving a battered old 4x4, which has a curious mechanical fault where you have to switch the engine off to change gear. He's doing a supplies run at the same time, and delivering post and paperwork; they're not wasting the petrol just on me. Although they are giving me and my bag space in the car, so that's enough. I start complaining to Hanif about the electricity, just to make conversation, and he nods mildly but looks faintly baffled. He lives in a hut with a stove and an oil lamp, and I guess it must be difficult for him to understand the importance of electricity in other people's lives, especially out here.

I used to find it just as difficult to understand the importance of television in other people's lives. Frank and Hari always in front of the football. Lana and Asha and Minnie watching any old rubbish that came up on the box. It seemed to me that there wasn't a piece of furniture in my house that wasn't pointed at one. I used to watch them all from the kitchen table, reading the paper, and felt a bit rueful and superior, dismissing what I didn't understand.

I'm better these days. I've stopped making fun of Lana's dedication to the soaps. I sit on the reupholstered old sofa where we once fed my baby son, my arms around Asha and Minnie's shoulders, when they visit, and watch their shiny American sitcoms. I take the third bar stool in the kitchen, the one between Frank and Hari, and try to care about the game. Every show or match is the same; it's about a happy ending. And if it's not happy, the show's just not over yet. There'll be another episode. Another match. And that's fine, because I've finally got that it's not about what's on, but who you're sitting with. Just like when I went to the Ratan Talkies with Sulaman and my sisters when we were teenagers. Just like the dark and sticky cinemas I'd sit in with Frank. We could just as easily be lying on our backs on a rooftop, staring at the stars.

I used to do that on the hottest nights in Lahore, with Sulaman, when we were kids. I used to sky-gaze at home in Notting Hill with Frank, up on the roof extension with a fag or a joint, when our own kids were growing up. Sometimes I still go out there alone, when Frank's settled in his bed. I stare at the stars, and feel that I can reach out and touch them. I join the dots and frame the moon in my fingers. I remember that I used to want my kids to be astronauts. I feel like one myself. As though I fell from space. From heaven. That part of me is still out there, rather than down here.

Sometimes when I sit with my family in front of the telly, when I lie out there at night, looking up, I remember what Mae said, and I can even believe it. That the best is still ahead of us. The best of us is still to come.

Hanif is stuffing the final bags of papers into the car, and casually picks up my own bag and throws it on the top, where it is most likely to fall off. It doesn't bother me, as my belongings are the least important, and the most replaceable. Just a couple of changes of clothes, and some of my medication. And my brother's latest book, in fat paperback. *Collaborators* is written in large, menacing text across the cover. In smaller text, the subtitle is placed far below, *How Good People Do Bad Things*. It's another book on the psychology of the authorised executioners, torturers and abusers in the military and prison systems. It's cited on the cover as a stimulating summer read. Sulaman looks dignified, carved out on the back cover like a statue of himself, all his little flecks and flaws polished off – although the smile looks fake, like they borrowed it from somewhere else, and Photoshopped it in. I'm not worried about losing it. It's not like it's a signed copy, with a personal dedication from him. If it gets lost, I can probably pick up another one at the airport.

I'm getting into the 4x4 when the camp administrator, Omar, comes up to me, wearing stained beige slacks and a tattered Drink Coca-Cola T-shirt that came with the last lot of donations. I didn't think that my departure would attract much notice, but he shakes my hand with crushing determination before saying, 'Dr Saddeq, you will be coming back, won't you?'

He's telling me rather than asking me. He's looking me in the eye. He needs every doctor he can get, and he doesn't have time to mess around with social niceties; he has to bully to get the funding and staff he needs. There are few people who could do what he does and still sleep at nights. So intimidating an arthritic old bloke into returning to a refugee camp is easy for him. I don't mind; I don't need to be persuaded. I've been volunteering in the camps for years.

'I'll keep coming back,' I say. 'If I possibly can. I'll probably come until they have to ship me here in a box.'

He relaxes, the intensity around his eyes clears, and his stiff shoulders soften. He even laughs at my dark little joke. 'Good,' he says, clapping me on the back, more gently than when he gripped my hand. 'We can always use more boxes.'

I sit in the 4x4 beside Hanif. He starts the engine, and the old motor sputters into life. It must have done a couple of hundred thousand miles. When he moves off, the radio starts playing. He can't actually switch it off. He fiddles with the dial until the song is clearer; it's a modern sort of pop ballad from an Indian movie. The children, who have been playing a complicated game with sticks and stones and a clear plastic bottle, hear the music, and come flying after the car like a flock of birds.

While the air ripples through my fingers like warm water, I think of the starlings I watched one day on Parliament Hill. It was the day after an argument, the day after Frank came back from New York. I'd screwed up. I got called into the hospital; I'd abandoned him at the airport and messed up our dinner plans.

Frank was scribbling over his notes. He'd ditched work to spend the day with me, but still had to deliver his copy to deadline. He was leaning against a tree, and I was lying on his lap, watching the birds up in the sky. He was looking down, and I was looking up. I remember that he was wearing his hair long, like me, and my sunglasses were tinted blue; it was the early seventies. I remember feeling guilty that he'd forgiven me so easily. I remember the way the hundreds of hollow bird-bodies moved the air as a single fluid figure, forming and re-forming like a shoal of fish while they drew deep circles around us, following the flowing currents, staining the sky, the spinning-swimming sense of them. They made me feel like I was on my back on the soft seabed, looking up at the ocean. The birds flapping-splashing in the blue mirrors of my shades, which polished the glass-green eyes of my lover to aquamarine jewels. Sunken treasure. I felt like I was breathing underwater then. I feel like I'm underwater now; I feel the soft heaviness of it around me. The children wave us off while they can still hear the song, making us look briefly popular, and then scatter like sparrows behind us.

Hanif bobs his head sideways to the music, left to right, right to left. When the car has enough momentum, he efficiently switches off the engine with one hand, and shifts the car into second gear with the other while it is still moving, and then switches the engine back on. The music stops and starts. When we reach the straight dirt road, he switches off the engine again, wrenches the stiff gearstick from second straight into fourth, and then twists the key neatly back into place, the engine refiring with a muffled roar. His movements are as co-ordinated and elegant as a set of Indian dance moves, the engine killed and kindled in the silent beats between the music, stopping and starting again with just the roughly rolling tyres as his accompaniment. He smiles at me, still waving his head, pleased to be able to demonstrate his prowess to someone for a change. Pleased to show that he is a man in charge of his machine. He generously pats the back of my seat.

'Rest,' he says in English, as though I am a guest in his house, and he'll soon call his wife or daughter to serve me samosas and lemonade. I wonder if I'll be able to get something to eat at the bus station, and maybe a cold drink. I wonder when I'll be able to sit down to shit, on a toilet, rather than squat in a pit. The old world, the dusty roadside with bits of stray metal glinting in the sunshine, is being left behind. As we approach the villages, there will be men with turbans pulling handcarts loaded with vegetables, and women driving goats or bullocks, carrying baskets neatly on their heads. As I approach the modern world, with the car, bus, train and plane, there will be stalls, sodas, sanitation and eventually a sterile hospital.

There will be a door opening on a clean white room, a widowed woman lying under clean white sheets, her children by her bedside. My brother, my sisters and me. And then the door will close behind us, briefly illuminated around the edges. We'll all be there to shepherd her out of the dark.

'So, how's my big brother?' I asked Frank, when he turned up at the hospital, fresh off his flight from New York. He'd walked straight in and found me in the corridor outside the ward. I didn't ask what he was doing there, or where his suitcase was. I supposed he'd left it in the cab.

'I've been away for a week,' said Frank. 'You want to try that again?'

'How are you?' I said apologetically. I went to hug him, even though a couple of passing patients were staring, but he stepped back.

'I'm hacked off,' he said flatly. 'I'm knackered and starving, because airline food is shite, and I've been drinking hard spirits for a week because the Yank beer tastes like cold piss.' He carried on complaining without stopping for breath. 'You said you'd meet me at the airport. I've been sat there for a bloody hour with the unclaimed baggage.'

'Sorry,' I said, gesturing sheepishly at the bustle around me, the staff moving swiftly, as though the fact of all this activity would be more eloquent than I was. I moved to the side for a patient being wheeled along on a trolley, a nurse holding his drip and speaking to him in a reassuring tone. I hadn't exactly forgotten about going to the airport, but I hadn't thought about it until I was already at the hospital. Perhaps I wasn't as bothered about it as I should have been. After all, Frank was a big enough boy to get a cab. And he was so impatient, it didn't occur to me that he'd wait for even five minutes if I wasn't already there. I never thought that he'd hang around the airport, and be the one worried about letting me down instead. 'Got called in.'

'No shit,' said Frank, giving me a withering look. I clearly didn't seem sorry enough. 'So who's with Hari?' he asked abruptly, as though I'd have forgotten about him too. 'You didn't drag Asha out from college, did you? She's got exams.'

'Lana switched shifts and picked him up from school with Minnie,' I said. 'I'll get him later.'

'No, I'll get him now,' said Frank. 'I'll take them all to dinner instead. No use wasting a perfectly good reservation. I bet Lana would have picked me up from the airport.'

'Christ, Frank, stop bitching. You just had to grab a cab,' I snapped defensively. 'Is it your time of the month or something?' I wasn't proud of myself for this, but I was upset because he was right. I knew we relied on Lana, and I loved her, but sometimes it annoyed me. More than I liked to admit. Sometimes when Lana and Frank talked about Minnie and Hari, it was like they were talking about their children, not hers and ours.

Just before Frank had gone to New York, the religious education teacher at their school gave both the kids a hard time for not making the sign of the cross during an Easter assembly. Hari wouldn't because he'd decided he didn't believe in God, thanks to Frank's infectious atheism, and Minnie didn't because she was Muslim. Mrs Liddle had dragged them out of the school hall to tell them off in the corridor. When they reported this to us, Frank was ready to storm down there and have it out with the head. I didn't think it was such a big deal, and thought Lana would back me up, because she was normally so calm about things. She was good at smoothing out situations.

But instead Lana nodded to Frank, complicitly, and their eyes met with agreement over their coffee cups in the kitchen. For a moment, it was as though Frank and Lana were the real couple, rather than him and me. She touched him reassuringly on his shoulder, as though she would sort out this little problem with their upset kids, and walked back into the living room with juice and biscuits on a tray.

'Meenu, Hari,' she said solemnly, 'I'll talk to the head about Mrs Liddle.' She added practically, 'Don't worry about her. She doesn't know what she's talking about. She's not one of the good ones.' And I could see how all the anxiety was mopped out of the children with these well-chosen words. It wasn't their fault. The bigoted teacher wasn't one of the good ones. They were.

I remembered how we all remained quiet for a moment, gathered in the still pool that surrounded Lana. Frank was leaning in the doorway with his coffee cup; he was looking at Lana with love, there was no other word for it. And Minnie knew that her mother was serious, that she wasn't just fobbing off her complaint, as she had used her real name, Meenu; it was the name on her passport, but no one else ever called her that. Lana's choice of phrase had the precision of poetry, and the simplicity of a psalm: 'Not one of the good ones.'

'Thanks, Mum,' said Minnie gratefully, and Hari nodded, looking a little jealous that only she got to call Lana that. I remembered how much I admired and resented my sister at that moment. I understood what Mae meant, when she visited with spoilt little Sherry and said that Lana always showed her up. I remembered wishing, disloyally, that Lana wasn't quite so helpful, and that she didn't live quite so near.

A nurse was tapping my shoulder, handing me a chart. Frank's expression was scathing, his mouth a hard, tight line. I think he was surprised by my aggression, as though he expected me just to keep apologising. 'It's not like I'm playing pool in a pub. I'm working,' I said in a calmer tone, scanning the chart distractedly, trying to remember what I was looking for in it. 'You're acting like I forgot your birthday.'

'Patient's waiting, Doctor, the surgical consultant's in there too,' the nurse said to me, both businesslike and critical. It was a patient with advanced appendicitis. I was worried that she was showing signs of peritonitis, that the obsolete organ might have already ruptured. She was in pain and I needed to get her booked into surgery.

'I don't mind you forgetting my birthday, Dr Dick,' said Frank. 'I mind you forgetting me.' And he walked off.

'We could do something tomorrow,' I called after him guiltily. 'I've got a day off.'

'Well I haven't,' he said, not turning back. 'I work too, you know.'

'Dr Saddeq, they're waiting,' said the nurse, glancing primly at the watch pinned to her chest.

When I got back, Hari was already in his room. It was a school night, and he usually took himself to bed just before 9 p.m. I opened his door gently. He wasn't asleep yet. He was reading the first book of *The Lord of the Rings* with his torch.

'Night, son,' I said, kneeling by his bed to kiss him on his spiky hair. 'Did you have fun with Auntie Lana and Minnie and your dad tonight?'

He nodded. 'We went to a posh seafood place in South Kensington. I pretended Auntie Lana was my mum, and Minnie pretended Dad was her dad.'

'Really,' I said, trying to sound amused. Trying to keep any telltale stiffness from my voice. 'They must have loved that.'

'Not sure they noticed,' said Hari. 'I ordered in French. Salmon puffs. *Feuilleté au saumon, s'il vous plaît.*'

'Show-off,' I said.

'That's what Dad said,' grinned Hari, his teeth very white in the smooth brown of his face. 'He's well pissed off with you.'

'Language, Hari,' I said.

'That's what we all said to him,' said Hari blithely. 'Night, night, Abbu,' he added sweetly, putting his arms around me. I was touched that he was still hugging me at ten years old. I kept waiting for him to get embarrassed by us, by his two bickering dads, but it still hadn't happened. It probably helped that we were hardly ever at his school together; it was usually just one or the other, most often Frank, whose schedule was more flexible. Sometimes Lana went with him, if it was a parents' evening, seeing as Minnie was at the same school. Hari snuggled back under his duvet, and picked up his unwieldy doorstop of a book.

'Is that any good?' I asked.

'Most of it is,' he said, 'and I just skip the bits that aren't.'

'Sounds like cheating,' I commented, leaving the room.

'It's not, Abbu,' said Hari. 'Everything's better without the boring bits.'

I looked around the house, but couldn't find Frank. He wasn't in bed, or in the garden. I stood outside, and looked up at the stars, and the half-moon on a clear night. There were faint traces of smoke drifting from the top of the house, so I climbed up the metal fire escape, and saw Frank lying on his back on the flat bit of the roof extension, a cigarette in his hand. I went and lay beside him. He didn't say anything, but he dragged deeply on the cigarette, and passed it to me.

'Could we skip the argument, please?' I suggested. 'Hari's idea. He said to skip the boring bits.'

Frank exhaled carefully. 'He's a smart kid,' he said. 'Last thing I feel up to now is having a hissy fit about how you only notice me when I'm not there for the childcare.' He took the cigarette back from me. 'Besides, I did that in the snotty restaurant already. In front of Lana, Minnie and

Hari. And a faggoty French waiter who tried to blow me in the gents'. It would be exhausting to do it again.'

'He tried to what?' I said. I was laughing with the shock of it, the casual way Frank said it, but I was furious.

'Maybe I'm irresistible when I'm angry. Maybe he thought I'd tip him better if he cheered me up,' shrugged Frank. 'You're not jealous, are you, Jakie?' He didn't seem pleased, or even amused. 'You've hardly got the right. Did you even notice you were sleeping alone at night, this last week? I bloody did.'

'How was your trip?' I asked, avoiding the question, annoyed that he'd asked it. I watched him blowing thoughtful smoke rings above us, which expanded to circle the stars and then dissolved in the air. I accepted the cigarette when he offered it to me again, inhaling deeply myself. I remembered smoking out of the window that sunny morning in my student flat beside the river, the church bells chiming. The leaden rings pealing with dogged persistence and dissolving in the air. I'd just made love to Frank, knowing that he'd been with someone else the night before. I was thinking of Frank on his own in New York for a week, sleeping alone in a hotel. It hadn't occurred to me that he'd cheat on me. Now I was trying to think of a reason why he wouldn't.

'Hilarious. Deluded ravings of neo-Nazis. Good fit with my Mosley British Fascist work. The monsters among us. The paper's delighted with it,' said Frank. 'Throw in a bit about sinister ministers in the church establishment, and the bishops banging little boys, and I'll have a real crowd-pleaser on my hands.'

'That's great,' I said, without irony. 'So they kept you busy then.' I couldn't ask outright if he'd found the time in between doing all that to go out and take someone home. At least we were speaking. The good thing about Frank was that he could never sit in aggrieved silence for more than a moment or two. He liked talking too much.

'And then some. Had to see my sisters, too,' he complained. 'God, Maggie's kids are whining little eejits. Worse than Sherry. At least she's entertaining. And Niamh's got pious as hell. Her lot all go to Mass on Sundays. She told me off for swearing. Expected me to say grace.' He shook his head. 'As though our sainted mother ever said grace in her life.'

'How about Sulaman?' I asked. 'You saw him, right?'

'Just for dinner. He's fine, I suppose,' said Frank. 'He doesn't give too much away. Not one of the fun ones, is he?'

'I guess not,' I said.

Frank could tell that this bland assessment of my brilliant big brother had disappointed me. 'He brightened up when I asked if he had any research to help with my piece, dug out some useful stuff. And Buzz is a sweetheart.' He paused for a moment, and then turned to me. 'You know, I don't think Sully and Radhika have banged in an age.'

'How could you tell that?' I asked.

'Journalistic instinct. Muck-raker's radar. Bar-goer's gaydar,' he said. 'I'm used to digging out people's dirty little secrets. Who's up for it and who isn't. Who has and who hasn't. The dirty laundry. I can tell when people have been shagging. It's a gift.'

'Wish I had it,' I said, turning on my side to look at him, leaning my elbow on the hard tiles. I'd never thought to check our laundry basket for dirty sheets. Although I was almost sure Frank would never bring anyone else home, not to our house, not to our bed. If he went out to play, like he did in the old days, he'd play away. He looked back at me steadily, and he was like a black and white portrait of himself in the moonlight. A disturbingly similar stranger. His eyes were dark grey instead of bright green.

'What's that supposed to mean?' said Frank. 'I'm the one hacked off with you, remember?'

'Am I enough for you?' I asked him straight out. I felt stupidly brave asking a question this direct. I'd have felt gutless if I hadn't. But as soon as I had, I didn't want the reply. It was a game-changer. I knew it might destroy everything, bring the sky down upon us. I just kept talking, to soften the effect of what I'd asked, to distract him into an argument. 'Before Hari and Asha came along, I wasn't.'

'I'm the one that's not enough for you, Dr Dick,' snapped Frank. 'It's all work, work, work with you. And the rest of us are just a close-run second. You're just not interested in people you can't *fix*.'

'That's not true,' I protested. 'You're everything to me.'

'Really?' said Frank. 'So tell me. If someone had been shot, dying, on their way to dead, but the fella who shot him was bleeding out, who'd you treat first?'

'The one who was bleeding out,' I said promptly. It was obvious. I thought he was trying to catch me out with the morality of it. Doctors didn't always prioritise fairly, and there were a few I knew who would treat the policeman before the criminal who shot him, but we were meant to act on clinical need. We weren't meant to decide who was guilty or innocent before there'd been a trial.

'And if I was the one who was shot dead,' he said calmly, 'and someone else was bleeding out, who'd you go to first?'

'You,' I said, shocked that he'd ask this. 'I'd go to you.'

'Liar,' Frank said. He said it again, sadly and almost affectionately. 'Liar. Like hell you would. You'd go to the one you could save.' I felt terrible that he thought so little of me. And that he knew me so well. My dirty little secret. My dirty laundry stuffed deep in the basket. We were back to when we first met; all those blokes he messed around with while we were together, because he was sure I was going to let him go one day. Betraying me before I betrayed him.

'Look, I'm sorry,' I said. 'I really am. About today. I screwed up. I'll make it up to you. I promise.' I felt like I might cry. I wasn't just talking about abandoning him at the airport and ditching him for dinner. We'd been together ten years, and now we'd come to this. I was certain he was thinking about leaving me; that he'd spent the week in New York deciding whether he would. Trying on another life, his old life, and seeing if it suited him better. I wasn't sure I could blame him.

'I should bloody well hope so,' said Frank. He looked cynically at me, as though he didn't quite believe me, however upset I seemed. 'Well, you are who you are, Jakie,' he said. 'We're neither of us going to change, are we?' His tone wasn't kind. It was barbed. Sharpened to a stinging point. But it gave me hope that he wasn't going to let me down gently. That he wasn't going to let me down at all. I kept myself from snivelling and swallowed it all back.

'Did you? When you were away? I mean, have you, ever?' I asked. 'I won't say anything about it. I just want to know.' Another direct question. It was like I couldn't help myself. It was like the moonlight had stripped all subtlety from us both along with our colour, and we were just black and white all the way through.

'After we got Asha and Hari,' Frank admitted, 'a few times. It didn't mean anything. It was just a habit I had to break.' He rolled over, and looked down at me, leaning on his arms. 'You?'

'Caitlin . . .' I started to say.

'That cockney hussy,' spat out Frank furiously, flinging himself back on the tiles. 'I knew it! The focking flame-haired, big-boobed, back-stabbing strumpet!'

'I just kissed her,' I said, laughing at how cross he was. I was so glad that he still cared. 'Once. For like half an hour. Years ago.'

'That's worse,' he complained.

'It's not worse,' I said. 'Shagging trumps snogging.'

'Snogging means it meant something,' insisted Frank. 'She ate your face for half a bloody hour, and has the nerve to look me in the eye! When she gets back from her timeshare in the Costa del Slut, I'll give her a damn good slapping.'

'Don't,' I said. 'Please. She brings us the good sangria.' It was an impressively feeble excuse for my mild-mannered infidelity. Frank looked at me, and then he laughed. He watched as I stubbed out the cigarette, which had burnt down to the butt while we were talking, and then he pulled a joint out of his top pocket instead. He re-rolled it, tapped it down, and lit it with a matchbook from a bar. I turned away while he did, looked up at the sky. It didn't matter if there was a number scribbled inside. Frank was here, beside me. He wasn't anywhere else.

'You know, I did think about hooking up with someone last week,' said Frank, drawing on the roll-up. 'I thought, what the hell. You wouldn't even notice if I did or not. But every time a bloke bought me a beer, I thought of you. And every time I bought someone a beer back, I saw your face.' He offered the joint to me but I didn't take it. I wanted to keep my head clear, to hear what he had to say. He shrugged. 'I realised that I was only chatting up blokes with curly hair. Like yours.'

He pushed his hand through my hair, which was too long, like everyone else's in the seventies. The style didn't suit me really; even if I brushed it back brutally, it never stayed tidy, and fell in my face when I was working. Frank's fingers scraped my scalp as he tugged a chunk of my hair, not too gently, twisting the curls around his fingers. Like he was annoyed with my hair, not with me.

'So I walked back through the streets to my hotel room alone every night, right up to the fifteenth focking floor. I sat on the bed, and looked across the Manhattan skyline, and I missed you. I worked out something. I'd rather be lonely with you than without you.'

I felt something in me unknot as he spoke. 'I think I only kissed Caitlin because she's as ginger as you,' I admitted. 'And I see your face every time I buy anything at all.' I added with perfect sincerity, 'But it's hard not to. I've got your picture in my wallet.'

Frank laughed again, and rolled towards me. He kissed me, hard, biting my lower lip, and I knew I'd been forgiven. I felt glad and bad and sad that he'd done it so easily. I felt like I'd tricked him. That I'd got away with it, again.

'Let's go out tomorrow,' he said. 'When Hari's at school. Somewhere high. With fifteen floors of view.'

'That's a tough one. London's a bit squat compared to New York,' I said. 'Thought you had to work?'

'Well, it's not all work, work, work,' said Frank. 'I'll call in sick. I'll phone in my copy. They'll think I'm a hero, getting it in while I'm dying.' He coughed dramatically on the joint. 'You can vouch for me. Let's get some use out of that damn medical degree.'

'Will do. I'll tell them you're dying of a fake smoker's cough,' I said, grinning.

'Well, try not to sound so cheerful about it,' said Frank. 'You'll give me away.'

'How about Parliament Hill?' I suggested. 'That must be fifteen floors' worth of view.'

'Done. We'll drink your ginger slut's sangria in the park,' said Frank. 'Watch a movie. A perfect day. Like the song.'

'What do you want to watch?' I asked. I hadn't been to a film since he'd dragged me to see *Midnight Cowboy*, a year or so before.

'Oh, I don't focking care,' he said, looking straight at me. 'I won't be watching the screen.' He dragged me on top of him, nibbling my ear lobe, and then stuck his tongue in my ear, just like he had in the cinema ten years ago. I started to laugh, and tugged out his shirt.

'God, I love you, you bugger,' said Frank, a little ruefully, his mouth against my neck, his teeth digging into my skin. I felt the neat hinges of his hip bones beneath me, and guessed that he'd lost a little weight while he'd been away. That he hadn't been looking after himself, and had lived on fags and joints and booze. I slid my hands over his sharp ribs and down past his stomach, feeling protective as I cupped the soft flesh of his cock. He was the one I wanted to save, except he didn't need me to save him at all. Frank was right: he didn't need fixing.

'But?' I asked. He still used those three little words freely, and always with the but. He had used them just the other week about Mae, during her visit. 'God, I love Mae, but her kid's Princess Pain-in-the-Arse.' Frank didn't say anything more, so I filled in for him. 'But I'm a stranger-saving workaholic.'

'No,' said Frank, 'there's no but.' I raised my head to look at him and saw the half-moon and stars reflected in his eyes, his pupils dilating with the joint and the chemical rush of arousal as he hardened under my hand, shining with grey light. He looked strange and beautiful. Sky-coloured. Sad. It was a question he wasn't asking. A game-changer. I felt his hands tearing into my hair as he tugged me back down impatiently towards him. My whole body was trembling, tender, as open as a wound. Like he'd been drawing my blood with his teeth. I remembered that I used to want my kids to be astronauts. I'd just worked out why I never wanted this for myself. I didn't need to fly to the moon. It had come down to me instead. It swam in my stoned lover's eyes as we lay on our rooftop.

I answered the question he didn't ask. I'd said it before, when he slept. This time I needed it to count. I pulled back just for a moment, to make sure that he could hear me. I watched him watch me as I spoke, the sky in his eyes, the sky on his skin.

'You know I do too,' I said.

Hanif and I arrive in the village. He drops me by the market stalls where the bus usually comes, once a day. Discharging people from the train station in the local town, and collecting others. It arrives around midday, and nothing seems untoward, but Hanif looks around with concern, at the other people squatting on their haunches.

'You wait, sir,' he says in English, and goes and chatters to a stallholder in the local dialect. I'm looking at the stalls, and have an urgent desire to buy something, anything; it's been so long since I passed change warm from my hand to someone else.

I dig into the bright plastic purse where I've stashed my cash; it looks like something a child would keep her sweets or crayons in, chosen deliberately at another stall just like this, for that very reason. My actual wallet is almost empty now; it just holds a few old receipts I never got around to throwing away, but which provide a convincing and misleading bulk, and photos of the family. I've left it in my bag, which is still on the 4x4, and indulge in a sudden urge to get them out.

My favourite shot is the one I see first. It's of Frank and our kids sitting with Minnie and Lana. Asha and Hari are holding on to Lana's shoulders as they smile. It's as though Lana is their niece, instead of their auntie. Lana is submitting to the embrace with a resigned air, looking frankly at the camera as though to say, 'See what I have to put up with?' Frank is laughing uproariously beside Minnie, his arm around her, as he looks at them all, his grin grooved deep into his cheeks. He's holding a joke mug I bought him on a family day trip to the seaside, which says, 'I was fantastic last night, just ask your boyfriend'.

This is the photo I wanted to see. I remember the Saturday afternoon when I took it. I needed to check that everything I remember about us is true.

'Sir,' calls Hanif. 'Bus delayed. We go.' He has been pulling some of the deliveries out of the car, organising them into efficient piles, and talking to the stallholder, with whom he seems to have an understanding. He waits a little impatiently for me to replace my wallet in my bag, and then throws it back in the 4x4. He gestures to me politely to get in too.

'Back to the camp?' I ask, closing my plastic purse. I'm not sure how disappointed I feel. The stallholder's face closes too, and I realise how I have been teasing him, standing there with an open purse around my neck, not making any purchase at all. I open the purse again hastily, and point to several items, and he beams. I get that slightly grubby feeling that I've just made someone's day, and that I've bought their happiness with my cold, hard cash. I haven't felt that for a while; in the camp, money is fairly useless because you can't eat or drink it, or clean a wound with it. Like gold nuggets in the wilderness.

The stallholder has a luxurious moustache and beard, which must be itchy, but which hides most of the scarring that ravages his face, probably the result of childhood smallpox. He has the frail frame and good teeth of someone who cannot afford to eat his own wares. He passes me two plastic combs, a lighter, the coconut hair oil that I've noticed Hanif uses and a sensationalist magazine featuring a busty sari-clad actress striding through a river. I pass these items to Hanif. He thinks I just want him to carry them for me, and it takes him a moment to realise that these small gifts are for him and his family. He looks embarrassed, and bows briefly, like a man who has never had to accept a gift before, or a compliment, and is embarrassed that he is being forced to do this now.

I buy a stale-looking packet of pastries too, for us to share, and a cola for the sugar. I'm a little light-headed from the journey, and think it won't do to turn up at my mother's deathbed looking like I'm the one who's dying, especially if I'm to be a day late due to the delayed bus. I'd look as comical as a husband fainting in the hospital room where his wife is giving birth. Charity junkie Jakie, upstaging our poor mother. Just like she upstaged Mae at her wedding.

'We will go to the town,' says Hanif decisively, inspecting the comb for broken or bent prongs, carefully enunciating each English syllable.

'You don't need to take me,' I protest, but Hanif holds his gifts out towards me, in a talk-to-the-hand gesture that seems strangely American and out of place at this little village bus stop.

'We will go to the town,' he says, even more firmly. 'I will do this for you. Come, my friend.' I realise belatedly that he thinks the gifts are a bribe. Or that he now feels he is in my debt, and desperately wants to pay it back, because he is not the sort of man who wishes to be in debt to anyone. My impulsive gesture has cost him something, and I feel a bit grubby all over again.

'I'll wait for the bus,' I say, but Hanif pretends he hasn't heard me. I say it again, louder, and follow him to the tea stall, where he is given two cups, and passes one to me. He doesn't pay, but I see someone from the stall add a package to the 4x4, so perhaps he is delivering as payment in kind.

'My friend,' Hanif says kindly, gesturing towards the tea, as though I am not his client but his charge, someone for whom he has a duty of care. He looks sympathetically at my feet, and I realise that my cracked brown heels are indistinguishable from the cracked brown leather of my sandals. The sight of them pulls at my memory: the heels of the pedalling driver who took us to the sweet shop, and slept under his rickshaw. I remember how I envied him. 'You cannot wait here. The bus will not come today. I will take you to the town.'

He taps his heart with his hand as he says 'I', and I realise that I need to let him do this. He looks on approvingly as I drink my tea, stewed strong enough to stand the tin teaspoon up in, and throws back his own with a curiously continental gesture, like an Italian playboy downing an espresso at a beachside bar. I follow him back to the car with resignation. As I sit in the front seat, I wish I'd got my bag back out and kept it with me, to look at that photo again. I suppose I'll have time enough to do that later. I'm a man on a journey. I have all the time in the world.

'Why was the bus delayed?' I ask Hanif, and the music starts blaring as we move off. He jerks the engine on and off as he moves up through the gears, shaking his head, either in time to the music, or to indicate that he is unsure.

'Terrorists,' he suggests eventually, as casually as another driver might say, 'Traffic.' He doesn't specify what sort of terrorists: the ones who blow themselves up, or the ones who blow up other people; the ones who support the extremists with Kalashnikovs, or the ones who kidnap foreigners and film the executions. It seems to be of little interest to him, despite their having directly inconvenienced him.

I shrug, as though this is the sort of thing that happens here all the time, public transport delayed by terrorists, as common as a power cut. Hanif shrugs back, as though he knows this is true.

I took that photo at one of our usual family get-togethers, on the first Saturday of each month. Lana had arrived first, still wearing the Western clothes she wore to work, as she'd done the night shift at the care home: comfortable trousers with an elasticated waist, and a long silky shirt in a sober shade of blue. She'd bought her clothes from the new Hennes on the high street, but she could have worn the same outfit in Lahore without turning any heads. Something about Lana made everything she wore look like traditional dress. She had kicked off her shoes, and her unvarnished toenails were gleaming in the flickering light of the television. She was watching the soaps, and carefully drinking the tea I'd made her. She sometimes slurped, and complained that she'd inherited the family slack jaw from our father's side, that it was coming out with age.

Asha sat beside her on the sofa, still wearing her office heels with determination, as her suit didn't look right without the shoes. She'd been working through the weekend again; she'd just been made a partner at her law firm. She was watching with disapproval as Minnie sat on the armchair and painted her nails in bright violet. Minnie was wearing her second husband's faded denim shirt, and complaining about how he'd buggered off to the football again.

'You bought him the season ticket, sweetie,' said Lana reasonably.

'You could do that at home, you know,' Asha commented about the nail varnish.

Minnie ignored them both and carried on. 'And since the boys went to college, and he doesn't have to be a good example, he's always out on the lash. He went into work hung-over yesterday. He's shameless.'

'Shameless Seamus,' laughed Asha, pleased with her joke. 'It's weird, it's like you're married to my dad,' she added. 'He's almost as ginger, even.'

'He's nothing like Uncle Frank,' said Minnie crossly. 'He's a teacher, not a journalist. He works out. And he's so much better-looking.'

'I can hear you, you know,' said Frank, calling out to them from the kitchen, where he was watching the football and I was rifling through the weekend papers. 'I can hear every focking word you're saying.' He grinned at me over his coffee cup.

'You know, I even thought he was gay when you first brought him round,' commented Asha. 'Anyone that good-looking is usually gay.'

'Great, we've raised a bigot,' I said to Frank. The shocking red of his hair had faded with the grey, but it suited him. Sometimes I wondered if he still fancied me, after all these years. He'd never been keen on older men. He never talked about his illness, the countdown that had started just before my father died. I'd told Mae, at our father's funeral, that Frank had years and years. I couldn't tell her the number; it felt too final. Irrevocable. Like a kidnapper asking you to put a price on your life, to write it on the ransom note. The number was fourteen. No patient of mine had lasted longer than that. He had fourteen years, from his diagnosis, and half of those had already gone. Frank had never been scared of death. He used to point out carelessly that we were all dying, and that any one of us could fall under a car tomorrow. As though that was meant to be a comfort.

'Not every gorgeous Irishman is gay, you know,' he said, joining the girls in the sitting room, heading for the drinks cabinet.

'Well, you all look the same to us,' I said, and Lana stifled a laugh.

Hari was the last to arrive at the house. He let himself in, and called us from the hallway. He had a large square package wrapped in brown paper and tied with string under his arm.

'Happy anniversary,' he said to Frank and me. He gave us both a brief, manly hug. 'Is the telly working, Dad?' he asked Frank. 'The second half's just started, and there's a bloody great gull outside tugging on the aerial.'

'Oh focking hell, not again,' said Frank, and dashed back into the kitchen, just in time to watch the screen turn to fuzz. 'Those bloody buzzards will be the death of me.'

'It's because you've never put in insulation,' said Hari wisely. 'They perch there because it's warmer than the other roofs on the street. You're haemorrhaging heat,' and he looked around our ramshackle house, as though he'd suddenly become a handyman and was thinking of plugging cracks with Polyfilla and hammering up plasterboard partitions. It made me smile, because little Hari, neat in his pale chinos and striped sweater, with his raven-black hair spiked up like a footballer, was not the type to get his hands dirty. He worked for the BBC and had the cleanest nails I'd ever seen on a man. Both Frank and I suspected him of getting manicures.

Asha looked at him stiffly, annoyed with his lateness, and so he went to kiss her first, his very brown smooth cheek against hers. They didn't even bother to say hello to each other, with the casual rudeness reserved for siblings.

'Hey, Auntie Lana,' he said, going to kiss her too.

'Hello, sweetie,' she replied, submitting politely to kisses as she always did. Hari finally went towards Minnie, who just swatted him away with an impatient hand. He ruffled Minnie's many-coloured hair instead of kissing her, as though there was something funny about it. Minnie's boys, Jamal and Frank Junior, weren't there. It was term time, so they were out of town.

In the next room, Frank had been banging the TV, uselessly. He shouted out to me, louder than he needed to, 'I'm going out there.'

'You're not to mess with the aerial,' I called after him, just before the kitchen door banged shut behind him. 'Or it really will be the death of you.'

'Rod Hull and Emu,' called out Asha. 'He died fixing his TV aerial. Poor nutter.'

'And that bloke from *EastEnders*,' said Minnie. 'Or *Coronation Street*. Or it might have been the other one.'

'You should get cable, Jakie,' said Lana sensibly. 'We have cable at the hospice. I'm saving up for it at home.' She turned to Asha. 'Your Uncle Sully has cable in Manhattan.'

'Buzz and Tania have it too,' replied Asha.

'Auntie Mae is talking about getting it in Karachi,' added Minnie, and I sensed that they had planned some version of this conversation. I suspected Frank of putting them up to it, because he wanted to get the extra sports channels.

356

'Aren't any of you going after him?' said Hari, looking outside with concern.

'Of course not,' I said. 'You know your dad: if you tell him not to do something, he only wants to do it more.'

'You're managing him,' said Hari, and it sounded like an accusation. 'You're managing each other.' As though it was something that dishonest couples did; fifties housewives asking for a new washing machine or an easy-steam iron as a favour after sex.

Frank came back in, and the TV was working again. 'I threw one of next door's cats at the gull,' he said calmly. 'Seemed to work.' He nodded towards me. 'I think we should get cable, Jakie.'

'Honestly,' I said, exasperated.

'The neighbours won't mind,' he said, deliberately misinterpreting my annoyance. 'Tiddles was the spare.' He turned to Hari. 'What's this about an anniversary? We don't have one, son. We're gay, we're not girls.'

Hari grinned, his teeth very white, his spikes of hair shining in the spotted sunlight through the glass. 'I thought it was about time you did. It's the anniversary of buying this house, give or take a few weeks.' Frank and I glanced at each other. He was right. The landlord had agreed to sell it to us when Hari started school.

'I've been thinking it was time we sold up and moved out to somewhere bigger,' I said idly. Asha and Hari looked shocked, that I could talk so casually about abandoning our family home. Frank didn't say anything, but he gave me a sharp look, as though he could see right through me.

'Why on earth would you need to do that?' said Asha. 'It's just the two of you now.'

'Well, the house always feels too small when we have visitors, and it's falling to bits,' I said defensively. 'And the area's changed; it's full of braying middle-class professionals now. You don't see a brown face here these days.'

'I don't know,' said Frank drily. 'Seems to me that I see brown faces everywhere I look.' Lana and Minnie burst out laughing. And Asha and Hari laughed too after a moment, relieved that he'd dismissed my mad ravings so easily. That he'd managed me.

'Where's Tishy? I thought she was coming back with you,' I said. Hari had started dating his childhood friend Latisha, William Godfrey's

357

daughter. She'd become a doctor too. I remembered when she was a toddler, I'd looked after her for an afternoon in Kensington Gardens with Caitlin, while William Godfrey took his wife out for her birthday. Tishy had held Hari's hand, and looked like a sweet edible treat, with her plump cheeks and neat cornrowed hair; we'd nicknamed her Little Tishy on a Little Dishy. Caitlin had brought her red-headed baby, in our old Silver Cross pram. People in the park had thought we were a couple, with our own rainbow tribe.

'I feel just like a film star,' she had said, when she saw how everyone stared. It was with much less hostility than we used to get in the tea shops; they mainly looked with genuine admiration at Caitlin, who was wearing an extraordinarily short skirt, and had really lovely legs. Hippies were smoking under the trees; they greeted us with 'Peace' as we passed, and gave flowers to the kids, dandelions and daisy chains. Indian doctors were less unusual by then; they had been called in by the NHS in the mid sixties, and it seemed that there was one in every inner-city practice.

'Latisha apologised, but she got called in,' Hari said. 'You know how it is. One of her tumour patients. I don't know how she does it.'

'Bollocks, you're just embarrassed by us,' said Frank blithely, putting his coffee mug down to untwist the cap from the whisky bottle. 'Can't think why. And making up a tumour patient is a little bit distasteful.'

'Can't think why either,' I said ironically. 'There's nothing embarrassing about us at all.' I was watching Frank add a substantial glug to his comedy mug. I'd bought it for him as a joke; I didn't expect him to use it all the time, especially not in company. 'Is there even any coffee in that cup?'

'God, no,' said Frank. 'I'm cutting down on coffee. That stuff's poison.'

'Anyway, Abbu,' said Hari, deciding that I was once again the more sensible father in the room, 'we got you a present. Latisha found it clearing out her granny's attic.'

Hari handed me the package with ceremony, and as Frank had wandered back to the kitchen to watch the game, we followed him in there. Hari took the bar stool next to Frank, accepted a beer, and they both shouted, 'No! No! Yes!' at the television, as Spurs missed a penalty against Man City. I was actually unsure who they were supporting, as they both followed West Ham. It was something complicated to do with points in the league.

I ripped open the brown paper, and cut the twisted string with the kitchen scissors, and saw a grubby painted sign, framed beautifully in shining steel. It was the sign that Frank, William Godfrey and I had nicked on a drunken night out in the sixties. It had been nailed outside a boarding house that had refused lodgings to Frank when he first moved to London; it said, 'No Irish, No Gypsies, No Blacks'. When Frank had shown it to me, I had gone back, and painted on, as a joke, 'And No Pakis Either'. We had noticed with amusement that the owners never bothered to wash that bit off, as though they had agreed with it.

Then one night, not content with petty vandalism, we stole it altogether. It had been one of Frank's bright ideas. We'd all been out to celebrate Caitlin's engagement to Tom, her half-gypsy boy, and in the early hours Frank decided that the sign would be a focking fantastic wedding present. When we were sober, we worked out that Tom didn't know us well enough to get the joke, and Caitlin might not think it funny in the first place. We got her a dinner service instead. William Godfrey had taken the sign home, and hidden it in his mother-in-law's attic.

I wondered if Tom ever found out that I had kissed his wife in the park that afternoon, under a willow tree, while the three rainbow children in our charge were napping. It was one of those white, hopeful days when the sun bleached everything so clean that we were both a little drunk with it. And Caitlin was such a pretty girl, in such a pretty dress, that I really didn't think it mattered at all if I kissed her. She looked like Frank's little sister, with her luminously lovely hair, and she tasted sweet, like the cherries we'd been picnicking on. She didn't mind at all, and she kissed me back, her arms innocently around me, and mine around her. We lay there for half an hour, rolling on the dry grass, snogging like teenagers, until Tishy woke up and asked us what we were doing.

Frank was right. It meant something. He'd never have kissed any of the fellows he fucked like that. I didn't think he'd have kissed them at all. It was just for half an hour, but Caitlin and I both tried on another life, briefly, as easily as trying on a new outfit in a clothes shop, and looked at ourselves uncritically in the mirror. We liked what we saw, but we knew it wasn't us. We both loved our men. But it was naughty, and it was nice, to lie under that willow tree, with three dozing children in shades of black, white and brown, and imagine that she was my adorable wife. That she made my house a home. That we walked in the park on Sundays.

'Would you look at that?' said Frank in wonder, finally noticing the sign. He looked at me and grinned, and I felt guilty because I knew I wasn't thinking what he was thinking. I had been remembering the cherry sweetness of Caitlin's kisses. I was thinking that I missed her since she and Tom had moved to Majorca. She still wrote to me, funny notes about expat life, saying things like, 'Well, Jakie, I'm only here for the weather,' and I was glad she wrote, but it wasn't the same. I was thinking that I'd chosen Frank, picked him up from a café as easily as a penny from a pavement, and told him that I wanted to everything with him. That he was everything to me. I'd only almost-cheated on him that one time, and thought I was so bloody admirable because I spent all my time fixing people and had never fucked around.

But now we were middle-aged men with grown-up children, our years together were counting down and I couldn't tell you the last time we'd made love. I knew I'd taken him for granted. And he'd let me, because he loved me. I'd spent so much of my working life ditching him for my patients. It was selfish, rather than selfless.

'There's this as well,' said Hari. Taped to the back of the frame was a manila envelope, with a faded black and white photo of three young men standing next to the sign, outside the south London boarding house. William Godfrey, Frank and me. Darkie, Paddy, Paki. 'It was in Latisha's dad's house; he let me copy it.'

'Would you look at that?' Frank said again. He put his hand comfortably on the back on my neck, studying the photo, the grinning young men pointing ironically at the sign, pulling faces. The shot had been taken on William Godfrey's box Brownie by a good-natured workman in overalls who had been passing by. 'I remember those fellas.'

'Yeah, I remember them too,' I said. I felt the familiar warmth of Frank's hand on my skin, and felt so sad. So stuffed with regret. I looked at the photo, at the adventurous men we'd once been. Passionate and reckless. I felt that I had something to say to them, to young Frank and young Jakie, some advice to give, if only they could hear me.

I wanted to remember what we were, Frank and I, surrounded by our family, before anything more of us was lost.

'You're a good boy, Hari,' said Frank. He propped the frame and the photo on the mantelpiece, and the two of them settled back to shout at the rest of the match. I waited for it to finish, and then I called Lana and the girls into the kitchen, and got them all to pose together for the shot. My children holding on to their Auntie Lana. Frank with his arm around my niece. I didn't mind that I wasn't in the shot. I was the one who had brought us together. I'd bought the mug that Frank always used. I was there.

Later that night, the house was eerily calm. Our family had spun back to their homes like streamers across the capital, and the place felt too big rather than too small. Frank was sitting at the patio table with his laptop, working on an article, chain-smoking to keep the flying insects from splatting into his lit screen. I just put the dishwasher on and went to bed early. I didn't go out to him to say good night. I thought about it, but the neighbour's bloody cats were screeching, and I felt so tired. Like parts of me had spun away across London too; like I was something spread too thin.

When Frank eventually came in, with his familiar scent of fag ash and whisky, I'm not sure why I pretended to be asleep, but I did. Frank wasn't fooled in any case. He knew what I sounded like when I slept, after all our years together. He didn't even bother to ask if I was awake.

'Have you really been thinking about selling the house, Jakie?' he asked. He said it seriously, as though apologising for having been so dismissive of the idea before, for making a joke about it.

'No, not really,' I said, after breathing deeply, as though he'd disturbed me.

'Are you all right?' he asked after a moment, and I could hear him undressing. He went to the bathroom to pee, and then wandered back in again. 'I mean, are you feeling all right?' I'd never been comfortable with people asking me that question. I don't know why.

'God, Frank, are you really asking me about my feelings?' I said. 'We're gay, not girls.'

Frank laughed, and sat on the edge of the bed. I could feel his weight shift from side to side as he pulled off his socks. 'I'm glad we're not selling the house,' he said. 'I know it's falling to bits. I know it's old, and it's cracked, and full of crap and baggage and piss and wind. But it still works, doesn't it?' I realised he wasn't just talking about the house, and I realised I hadn't been talking about it either.

'Well, bits of it work,' I said. 'The TV reception could be better. I'm wondering whether we should get cable.'

'Good idea,' said Frank, nodding at me with approval, as though the idea was all mine, and had come to me out of the blue.

'We should get cable installed for Lana, at her place, while we're at it. As an early birthday present. She said she was saving up for it,' I added.

'She'd like that,' said Frank. 'Another good idea. You're on fire tonight, Jakie,' he added with a perfectly straight face.

'Did you throw birdseed up on the aerial?' I asked him.

'Something like that,' he shrugged. 'Well, you know what you're like. If I'd just talked to you about it, you'd have bored everyone's tits off about how we already watch too much telly.'

'Hari's right,' I said. 'We do manage each other.' I almost sighed.

Frank hesitated before getting into bed. For a moment I thought he was just going to say good night and switch off the light, but then he rolled into me, and held me in his arms, and kissed me fiercely, like the young man in the photo would have done.

'We've had a beautiful life, Jakie. Here, in this house. And I don't regret any of it. Not for a moment. And I'm sorry if I've ever given you cause to think that I did. Or to regret it yourself.'

'You say that like it's over already,' I said.

I could never stop thinking about his diagnosis, but he preferred to pretend it hadn't happened. I felt the weight of it, like water around me. Whenever I tried to bring it up, he said I talked too much. He'd started drinking more and more, so that when he forgot things, he could say that was why. My clumsy alcoholic. My catch.

'Well, we're getting on a bit,' he said, 'but we're not dead yet, are we?' And he kissed me again, and I kissed him back, stunned at how much he understood my need for comfort. Humbled, as well. He'd pulled me to the surface, and reminded me how to open my mouth and breathe. He'd reminded me of what we still had, not of what we had lost.

He was right, we had built a beautiful life. He was wrong, because we didn't yet know that it was already almost over. That I would regret forever what I missed. Every day that had passed when I didn't appreciate what I'd had. While we still worked, old and cracked, and full of crap and baggage and piss and wind. As we kissed, for the first time in a long time, rolling on the bed and snogging like teenagers, I realised that he tasted almost sweet. I held him back for a moment.

'You brushed your teeth,' I said to him, accusingly. It was a joke. Of course he had. He always did before he went to bed. I said it because I remembered something. I really didn't expect him to remember too. But it seemed he did.

'You talk too much, Jakie,' he said, tugging my vest over my head.

It was just a few weeks later that I got a cross call from Asha, left on the answering machine at the surgery, while I was in the consulting room with a patient. 'Abbu, could you call me? I know you're working but I'm trying to get hold of Dad. We've been here for an *hour* now. He's not answering at home, he's not on his mobile. I'll have to go back to work in a bit. Look, call me, or get him to call me. Okay? Thanks . . .' I played the message in the main office, and deleted it with a sigh. I switched on my mobile to ring her back. It rang straight away. It was Lana.

'Where's Frank? He's meant to be having lunch with Asha and Minnie today, but he didn't show up.' I tried not to show my annoyance. They knew better than to bother me during surgery hours. I was already running late, and I saw patients giving me disapproving looks through the glass partition, for taking a personal call.

'He's actually in the office today,' I said loudly and officiously, walking briskly back to the consulting room, as though it was to do with work. I sat down in the room, and shut the door behind me.

'On a Monday?' asked Lana. She knew his schedule as well as I did. Frank usually refused to work Mondays on principle. He kept a desk at the office for Thursday and Friday. He called them Lunchday and Drinkday.

'Well, he wasn't meant to be,' I said in my normal voice, 'but he forgot he had a meeting. They chased him up this morning.'

I remembered getting ready to leave for work, Frank still in his vest and pyjama bottoms at the kitchen table, drinking his coffee, doing the crossword, and then hearing the call and the message on the home phone. They'd called his mobile first, thinking he was stuck in traffic, but he hadn't charged it. Frank had looked at me, and I had looked at him, and picked it up.

'He left a while ago,' I lied to the unlucky intern who had landed the job of chasing their highly respected but highly eccentric contributor. One of the advantages of Frank having been so unreliable and irreverent over the years was that no one suspected anything untoward in his behaviour now. Before, missing deadlines and meetings, missing the point of the question he'd been asked, had been his bloody-minded choice. 'Yeah, maybe he's stuck in traffic,' I agreed with her.

While I was talking, Frank had left the room, and returned tugging on trousers, and buttoning a shirt over the vest he had slept in. He splashed water on his face, slicked back his hair, and was ready to go by the time I'd hung up.

'Don't look at me like that, Jakie,' he said. 'I've just missed a bloody meeting. I'm not dying.'

I didn't know what my face looked like to him. I couldn't see myself. I think I looked reproachful rather than sad. I was thinking, you're going to leave me behind, you selfish bugger. You demented bastard. You're going to leave me on my own. You'll forget me, and I'll remember you, and I'll have to live with that every day until one of us dies.

'You haven't missed it,' I said. 'They've had to postpone it for you. You're chairing it.' I rummaged in my wallet, and found a twenty-pound note. 'Here, you better take a cab.'

'Sod that,' said Frank, taking the note from me with a flourish and tucking it into my top pocket, like a handkerchief or an indiscreet bribe. 'You go buy yourself something pretty instead.' He walked out of the door.

'Shoes,' I called after him, and he returned just as swiftly, with comic reassurance. He picked up a pair of shoes from the rack by the kitchen door, and walked back out, still in his slippers. I didn't get a chance to tell him that he'd forgotten his phone too; it was flashing with the orange charging light in the kitchen.

I wondered if Lana knew all this, and could picture the exact scene in my house that morning, just with those two little words, which had become so familiar that I tried not to say them any more. He forgot. He forgot. He forgot. It became less meaningful each time.

'I guess he couldn't make lunch, and didn't think to tell them.' He hadn't even mentioned the lunch to me. I thought of Frank's phone in our kitchen, buzzing with the tension of Asha's and Minnie's and Lana's unanswered calls.

I was trying to sound patient, but I was tapping my fingers, looking at the clock. It was after 1 p.m., and I was already forty-five minutes behind. I hadn't had a chance to have the sandwich the receptionist had picked up for me. I was feeling coffee-fuelled and irritable. Every patient who came through the door of the consulting room complained about the wait before they complained about their illness. As though waiting was the real reason for their pain. There was a baby I wasn't due to see for three more appointments, who I'd spotted as I opened the door to let my last patient out. There was something that bothered me about the floppy way she was lying in her father's arms, about her stillness and silence. She wasn't even whimpering. I'd wanted to call her straight in, never mind the grumbling of the others with their colds and sniffles and sore throats, but then the nurse had come up to me to say that my daughter had left me a message. It was unusual for Asha to call me at work, so I went to listen to the call instead.

'I'll call Frank's office in a bit,' I said to Lana. A little too casually. As though to say, yes, he had dementia, and it was only going to get worse, but I had to try and live with it. I couldn't treat him like a toddler who needed constant supervision, and track every missed meeting or lunch. Frank wouldn't let me. I knew he'd be furious if he suspected that I'd started checking up on him, like the office intern with the Frank-chasing job. He'd pick a fight and piss off to the pub until closing time.

'No, don't worry. I'll call now,' said Lana. 'I'll call Asha too. I know you're working.' She sounded apologetic for bothering me, and I suddenly felt guilty. As though I was too busy and important to speak to my daughter. To take a call from my sister. To check that my partner was all right. 'I wouldn't have called you, but I'd already tried the office. He didn't pick up. And he didn't call back.'

'Look, he'll be all right. He's just missed lunch,' I said testily. I resented the fact that she seemed more worried about him than I did. He wasn't hers. He was mine. 'It's not like he's fallen under a car or in the river. He does this all the time. He's Frank.' I knew it sounded like I was just making excuses, for him and for me. I was furious with Frank for doing this again, and for not even letting me talk about it. I knew that if I tried to mention over dinner that evening how everyone had called me at work that day because of him, he'd shrug like I was making a big deal about nothing. Like I was being an anxious bore.

'Are you all right, Jakie?' asked Lana. I wasn't. That was why I didn't like that question. People only asked it when they knew you weren't. I suddenly felt like crying on someone's shoulder. I couldn't do this. People needed me.

'I'm fine,' I said briskly. 'I better get on.' I looked at the missed calls on my mobile. There were twelve of them. Lana, Asha, Minnie, Unknown. I snapped it off with irritation, and went to call the next patient.

'Dr Saddeq,' said the receptionist, as I went through, 'there's another call for you about Mr McAdam.'

'Sorry about that, Beverly,' I apologised. 'Just delete them.'

'Jakie,' she said quietly, 'listen to it.'

I went over impatiently, aware of the roomful of patients rolling their eyes at me again. Checking their watches. Coughs and sneezes and city diseases. Asthma and eczema. Renewals and repeats. The poor rag-doll baby in her dad's arms. I listened to the message from the intern with the Frank-chasing job, telling me she'd left a few calls on my mobile. Telling me that Frank had fallen down the stairs in the office. That he'd been found bleeding and unconscious on the landing. That he was on his way to the hospital in an ambulance.

He's Frank. Cheerfully drinking from the bottle stashed in his filing cabinet. Too impatient to wait for the lift. Too bloody-minded to change out of his slippers. Dashing down the stairs with his easy energy, because he was late for lunch with the girls. He's my Frank. Not your Frank. My clumsy alcoholic. My catch.

Keep calm and carry on. That was the line that was printed on Beverley's mug; it was the first thing my patients saw when they came into the surgery, and checked in with her. That was what to do when a bomb fell from the sky. When your friends and neighbours were blown to bits, and the body parts flew into the back gardens of England, where people played cricket and croquet in straw hats. Make a cuppa. Pass the port. Do your job. Because that was what servants did, and that was what we were. We were people who served, and people who obeyed. There were rules for these sorts of things.

I didn't remember the last thing I might have said to my kids, to Asha and Hari, when I kissed them goodbye that Saturday as they left the house. I suppose it was bye then, see you soon, or take care. It might even have been I love you. I knew that the last thing I said to Frank, my lover, my love, was 'Shoes.'

I asked Beverley to call Lana, to tell her where Frank was being taken. I stepped out into the centre of the waiting room, in a daze, my phone still in my hand. I just had to walk through the double doors, and get in a cab. And then I'd breathe again. But I saw the limp baby, and found myself looking at every other person there, while they all stared back at me, like extras waiting for an audition. As though I could diagnose on sight whether they'd survive another day. My lover was in an ambulance. My lover was bleeding my body's blood. And I still couldn't walk out of the door.

'Come with me, please,' I told the father of the baby, who looked surprised, and grateful. He started fiddling with the buggy, which I realised wouldn't fit through the consulting room door without being folded. Precious seconds were ticking by, on the clock on the waiting room wall. 'Please leave that here, sir,' I said, and I told the other patients, 'Everyone else has to rebook with a different doctor, or for a different day. I have to leave after this patient for a family emergency.'

I could hear the patients groaning. I ignored them all, and ushered the man and his child into the consulting room. I took the baby girl from her father's arms. His nails were dirty, and he wore no wedding ring. His face was washed but he wasn't clean-shaved, and his hair was roughly slicked back and otherwise unkempt; not so different from how Frank had left the house that morning.

I didn't ask him why he had brought the child, as that much was obvious. 'How long has she been like this?' I asked, unbuttoning her faded dungarees, and listening to her breathing. The man was white, but his daughter was mixed race, and her dark skin made the symptoms harder to read. She was warm enough, but floppy, and her hands and feet, where they poked out of her clothes, were cooler. She still didn't whimper, or complain, not even when I put her down on my knees and pulled off the rest of her clothing to look at her skin. She was about five months old. And I was looking at the child, and I was thinking of Frank, and I told myself that it was important that I keep calm and carry on. Do my job. Just for this moment. Just for these few minutes. That I didn't shake the father, or shout at him, that I didn't dissolve into a maddened mess.

'Since this morning. I went to get her up at eight, but she didn't want to wake up,' said the man, nervously, sure that he had done something wrong. 'Her mum would have put her down at ten-ish. She left for work at five a.m.' He added, as though this needed explanation, 'She works at the bakery in Tesco's.'

'Does she normally sleep through until eight?'

'No. I mean, not often,' he said, guiltily. I'd guessed he'd enjoyed the lie-in that morning; that for once he hadn't had to walk around with a squalling baby in the early hours.

'So she might have been poorly since last night,' I said. 'Her mum probably thought she was just sleepy.' I couldn't see any spots. It wasn't so long after one o'clock. They'd come just in time.

'Has she had anything from her bottle today?' I asked.

The man shook his head. 'Like an ounce; it just kept dribbling out. And then she kept sleeping. I called my girlfriend, and she said I should bring her here. We're an emergency appointment.' He said it apologetically, as though worried that he was wasting my time.

'You did the right thing,' I said. If I hadn't seen him in the waiting room, I might have left before looking at the baby. And the man and his girlfriend might have waited another day, rather than make a fuss. And the countdown had already started. The hours ticking away before it was too late to do anything.

I knew that another doctor in the practice, the locums we regularly called in, might not have recognised the signs, if they weren't used to coloured babies; they might have sent the man home with some minor infant medication, and told him to come back if it got worse. To be fair, it was what I usually said myself, since I'd gone into general practice: go home and wait a few days, and see if it'll get better by itself. It almost always did.

I typed in rapid capitals, and felt that I was sitting next to myself, tapping my fingers and looking at myself impatiently, complaining to people over my shoulder that I was writing a novel, like a passenger at a slow check-in desk at the airport. I printed out the sheet for the man.

'Please take this, Mr Fernandez, and take your baby straight to the hospital.' I tapped the address on the sheet. 'I suspect infant meningitis; do you know what that is?' He nodded dumbly, and then shook his head, as though aware that he was lying.

As I rifled through the paperwork, scattering leaflets, I realised that my hands were shaking. It had been almost ten minutes since I'd hung up on Lana, and heard the intern's message. In the ten minutes that I was making the diagnosis that was saving this baby's life, Frank could have had a heart attack and died. He could have had a bleed in the brain and died. And I wasn't by his side. He wasn't afraid of dying, and he didn't even believe in God, not any more, so he would just pull the flowered earth over him like a blanket, and fall asleep in the ground, and leave me utterly alone.

I finally found the leaflet on meningitis, and gave it to the father, and watched him start to button up the baby with painful slowness, his own hands trembling, while I told him how urgent it was that he get to the hospital so that they could do the tests and start treatment. I was trying to be calm, trying not to panic him, while still trying to get across the gravity of the situation. I don't think I cared about his baby once I had diagnosed her. I just wanted to get away and find Frank.

'Do you have money for a cab?' I asked. I pulled out the twenty-pound note that Frank had tucked in my top pocket, and passed it to him as I went to the door. He still hadn't finished dressing the baby. 'The nurse will see you out, Mr Fernandez,' I said. I was walking so fast that I was practically running.

'Dr Saddeq?' asked Beverley, as I reached the swinging doors. I knew she couldn't believe that I was still there. A servant doing his job. Making a cuppa. Passing the port.

'Bev, could you direct Mr Fernandez to the hospital, suspected infant meningitis, it's written up on screen,' I said, as I left.

I called Lana from the cab, and broke down. Dissolved into a maddened mess, sobbing down the line to her as soon as I heard her voice. I didn't even manage to speak.

'It's going to be all right, Jakie,' Lana said. She said it like it was a promise, or a prayer. It was as though saying it would make it true. It was something she knew. Something she meant.

When I'd told Lana that Frank would be all right, I hadn't known it. I hadn't meant it. Frank was the most important thing, but at that moment, I had dismissed him. I was the one who'd forgotten him. Again. And again.

In that brief cab journey, it felt like I was the one who was bleeding out, and it wasn't my life that was flashing before my eyes, but our life.

I remembered him asleep on a newspaper, on a café table in Temple.

I remembered a sticky cinema, with melting ice cream and his tongue in my ear.

I remembered making love in the sunlight, after he called me a bore, and I called him a whore.

I remembered going to work with a hair wrapped around my finger, from another man he'd fucked the night before.

I remembered fighting with him near a bridge at midnight.

I remembered kissing him outside the Savoy on Christmas morning.

I remembered telling him that we made a great team.

I remembered feeding our baby boy, while he helped our daughter with her homework.

I remembered lying on our rooftop with him, under the stars.

I remembered leaving him with my sister and a takeaway, while I was paged into work.

I remembered promising to get him cable TV for the extra sports channels.

And I remembered the first time we did it indoors with all our clothes off, and him standing at the door, getting ready to leave the morning after the night before. I remembered what I told him.

Remember me, I will remember you. Chapter 2, verse 152.

A promise. A prayer.

Well, that's just bloody lovely, he'd said.

When I got to the hospital, Lana, Asha and Minnie were already there. They had told them to wait. They couldn't tell us if he was alive or dead. Asha started to cry when she saw me, as though she'd managed to keep it together until I ran in and made it real, as though I'd cracked open the calm that Lana had created around them. I held my daughter in my arms, and shouted at the nurse.

'I'm his partner,' I said, 'and I'm a doctor,' as though that made a difference.

'You have to wait, sir,' she said patiently, as though she thought I ought to know better. 'Someone will come out as soon as they can.'

I grabbed the sheet from behind the desk to see which room he was in, then tossed it back and walked fast down the corridors. I saw him through the glass, his head bandaged, his eyes shut, and I pushed my way into the room.

A nurse pulled me back to the door. 'You need to stay outside, sir,' she said firmly. But I couldn't move. I was staring at Frank's paper-white hand, freckled and bony, hanging to the side. I had never noticed what fragile hands he now had. These most breakable parts of him had escaped any damage. I couldn't bear the thought that I might never touch him again, that he'd never touch me, and that my hands were probably as bony and breakable as his, but we'd never got round to noticing this change in each other.

'Frank,' I called out, helplessly.

He looked across, and found me. And oh God, his green, green eyes, staring out at me above the mask over his mouth and nose, and he didn't look frightened, and I knew I wasn't upset for him, but for me, because the bastard was leaving me behind.

A male nurse came to help shuffle me out, and Frank ripped off his mask, and said with a great effort and a greater gasp, 'For fock's sake, you eejits leave him be. He stays.' And I stood to the side of him as the nurse took the mask to fix it back on.

'You need to stop talking, sir,' she said.

'Fock off,' said Frank. 'I might be dying, but I'm not dead yet.'

'You're not dying,' she said. 'You're stable.'

'Could someone go and tell our family that,' I said. I was trying not to cry. 'Now, please.' I was still wearing my white coat. I'd already caused a scene. I looked like the type to make another. The nurses looked at each other, and one of them stomped out.

'You look like hell, Jakie,' Frank told me.

'You're no prize yourself,' I said. It didn't look good. He'd been lying in the stairwell for a long time. He'd lost a lot of blood. He had a head injury. He'd broken his arm and his hip, too.

'So, are you okay?' he asked with difficulty, and I couldn't believe he was saying that to me while he was smashed up in a hospital bed. It took me a moment to realise he was making a joke.

'I'll survive,' I replied. 'How about you?'

'I will if you will,' he said. The staff moved aside, and I was able to sit next to him, to hold his fragile hand.

'I screwed up,' Frank said, finally. 'It's my fault. I'm sorry.'

'No, I'm sorry,' I said. I didn't tell him what I was apologising for. 'You're everything to me.'

I saw Lana, with Asha and Minnie, coming to the glass outside. I saw Hari, arriving in a panic, and hugging them in relief. I held my lover's hand, and looked at our loved ones through the square window of the room. I watched them, watching us through the glass, like our story was on the screen, and it was one with a happy ending.

I came clean after the accident, and admitted to Frank that I'd stayed to diagnose a patient before coming to the hospital. That I'd betrayed him like he always knew I would. I hadn't gone to him first, but to the one I could save. I sat beside his curtained bed in the ward he'd been moved to, held his hand, and apologised for every time I'd ditched him in the past, and put my patients before him.

'God almighty, don't say you're sorry,' said Frank. 'You're not. You saved a baby's life between hanging up the phone and coming here. You'd do it again in a heartbeat. You're not going to change, and you know what, I don't want you to. You look after people. You save people. It's who you are.'

'You're the one I want to save,' I said.

'You already did,' said Frank. 'The day I met you. I looked up from that café table, hung-over as hell, and you were standing there asking me if I was all right. You were as wrecked as me, but you still looked like a bloody angel. It's like there was music playing.'

'I didn't think you'd remember that,' I said, trying to swallow down the lump in my throat.

'I remember what's important,' said Frank. 'If it weren't for you, I'd have been long dead by now. Don't think I don't know it. Riddled with AIDS or drowned drunk in a ditch. You saved Asha and Hari. All of us.'

'I'll miss you. I'll miss us. I don't know how I'll go on when I lose you.' I finally said it out loud. 'I don't know how I'll get up in the morning, and go to bed at night.' This was the conversation Frank never wanted to have. I waited for him to tell me that I talked too much, and change the subject. Comment on the weather or the hospital food, or complain that he hadn't had a drink in a week, and that his liver was recovering.

'You'll go on,' he said. 'You don't live in the past. You live with it.' He put his hand on the back of my neck, warmly rubbing it, as though easing an ache. 'Be proud of who you are, Jakie. I am. There's a kindness to you. A selflessness. It annoys me like hell sometimes, but it's what I love about you. I always have.'

I looked up, and saw that tears were running down the sides of his face. I was crying too, and I wasn't sure who had started first. 'Christ, Frank, we're gay, not girls,' I said.

'It's the focking pain medication these eejits keep stabbing me with,' complained Frank. He brushed the tears away brusquely, and grinned at me. 'You're a good man, Jakie.'

'No, you're the good man,' I said. 'You're a bloody saint for having put up with me. You know it's your family nickname. Mae came up with it. St Francis of Assisi.'

'You mean Frank the Sissy,' he laughed. 'God, I love Mae, but she's a terrible bitch. Witty, though. Reminds me of my mother.' He looked at me more solemnly, the edge of laughter still clinging to him, and said, 'Turns out we're both good men. We must make a great team.'

I remember hoping as I sat beside him that day that this might still be a story with a happy ending.

That it was going to be all right.

'It wasn't a story with a happy ending,' I say to Hanif, who has been nodding enthusiastically to a Korean pop song that has come on his radio. I'm amazed he gets reception, as it feels that we're truly in the wilderness now, and there is nothing but the long road, and dry scrub in various shades of yellow and brown, and the intense blue of the sky, which has the brittle, sparkling menace of cheap jewellery. And even with the cheerful music, perhaps even more because of it, it feels like something terrible will happen. Again.

'Maybe the only stories with happy endings in real life are the ones that haven't finished,' I add. 'The accident wasn't the end of it. We were never really the same after it happened.' Hanif nods again, and I know that he isn't listening, and is just being polite. I'm hot and thirsty and I'm just talking to myself. I glance in the rear-view mirror, and think that I see a shifting of dust flying up in the road far behind us. It's probably my imagination. I definitely see, as real as Hanif, myself and Frank sitting in the back, and we look like young men. The two of them are watching me gravely, as though to say that they're listening, if no one else is, and that they want to know what happened next.

'Frank recovered, but he couldn't go back to work, and then he began to slip away. His memory had been off and on for years, but after the head injury it began to go altogether.'

I look back, and see that young Jakie and young Frank are nodding with sympathy, and that they are leaning into each other, just slightly. Not for support, but to remind each other that they are there. I miss that. The ease of that casual contact. It's been a couple of weeks since someone held me in their arms. It was Asha, at the airport. She drove me there.

'I didn't look after him. All those years, I was so busy looking after everyone else, instead. He let me get away with it. He let me off. But I've made up for it. Now, looking after him is all I do.'

I'm surprised how bitter I sound, and let out an involuntary noise somewhere between a sob and a laugh. Hanif is surprised too; he looks at me with sudden concern, as though I might be delirious, and takes his foot off the gas long enough to slow the car. He does his usual trick of changing gear and switching off the engine, but this time the engine doesn't fire up again, and we grind slowly to a halt.

'I'm sorry,' I say. 'I really am.' I feel I should say this again to someone, and mean it. It does feel that it's my fault that we're both stuck by a roadside in the middle of nowhere.

'No problem,' says Hanif, his missing teeth showing when he flashes a reassuring smile towards me. He is used to the car, and takes out a plastic bottle with the remains of a peeling paper label and grey smears of adhesive, half full of a mucky brown water. He pours it into the radiator. 'We wait,' he says kindly, gesturing towards the back of the 4x4 like it is his home, and makes a comfortable area among the packages for me to lie down. Young Frank and young me are no longer there, and I do feel genuinely ill. I pull the photos out of my wallet, and protecting them safely inside my rarely used Pakistani passport, I put them in my neck purse, inside my kameez. The photos are the most precious things that I have. I can leave everything else but these.

I think of Lana in the photo, looking directly at the camera. I think of Mae, all those years ago, turning to Lana in a rickshaw, and saying, 'Oh, it speaks.' Lana found her voice, and she had an authority that the rest of us had lost along the way; her blameless life, looking after other people's lost loved ones with the same care as her own.

She was the mother we all wished we'd had. A good mother, who still loved us when we'd been bad. A Muslim Madonna in blue silk, framed by her family. The pool of light that surrounded her. She watched television with quiet dedication and cleaned her windows with vinegar and newspaper. She slurped a little when she drank her tea. She spoke with the precision of poetry, the simplicity of a psalm. I sometimes resented her blamelessness, how poorly I compared to her, with Frank and with my family, but I always trusted her.

Lana had told me that it was going to be all right. She had wanted to comfort me. I had wanted to believe her. But she made me a promise she couldn't possibly keep.

I sit in the back, and see that Hanif isn't looking at me, he's looking at the puff of dust rising more strongly on the horizon, in the direction we've come from.

'The bus?' I say hopefully. He shakes his head, and of course, the bus would be coming the other way. 'Maybe they can help us,' I say.

Hanif smiles mildly, as though I am a child who has said something well-meaning but nonsensical, and squats down on his haunches, producing a cigarette. He offers it to me, and when I shake my head, he lights it with his new lighter, beaming again with gratitude.

'Those things will kill you,' I say with a little irony, as we wait. A flatbed truck is approaching, with more than a few men inside, and Hanif gets up sharply, and gestures for me to lie down. He stamps out the newly lit cigarette, and this spectacular waste makes me realise the urgency of the situation, as he covers me with the thin, grubby blanket that lies in the back. He touches my chin with an appreciative look, as though he thinks it is fortunate that I have failed to shave for so long.

I realise that these men, patrolling the roads with ancient weapons slung across their chests, are the reason why the bus was stopped. I remain lying there, looking as sickly and old and harmless as Hanif intends, and they stop, and shout sharply at Hanif, but he falls back from the truck so they have no excuse for violence. I don't understand the local language, but their intentions are clear enough. They look in the back, and when Hanif tells them to leave me resting, they laugh as though he has told a good joke, and tell me to get out. I only understand the word for uncle, but their meaning is clear enough. Uncle, get out.

I stumble out of the back, still wrapped in the blanket, with my bare heels overhanging my old leather sandals, and they pay little attention to me as they pull out all the packages and parcels from the back, emptying them on the ground. They take supplies and ignore paperwork. They almost pass over my bag altogether, but the hard bulk of something inside makes them stop and shake it, as if they think it might be money. Instead it is Sulaman's book. They toss it aside. They find my British passport, but after a small start of panic, I realise that they don't think it's me. I look nothing like the prosperous family doctor of eight years ago who is in the picture. I'm just a limping man in a stained kameez travelling in the truck from the refugee camp; Hanif looks more prosperous than I do, in his beige slacks and short-sleeved shirt. They don't find the photos that would give me away, as they are next to my heart, in my plastic child's purse. I realise that my sudden urge to keep my family close to me may well have saved my life. Foreigners have been kidnapped in the hills. Bodies have been found on the bus routes, shot or beheaded. The men have taken what they want, and seem satisfied.

'Sit, Uncle,' says one of the men, seeing me swaying by the side with my cane. I sit in the back of the 4x4 with relief, and lean against the mess of packages. The man has a severe skin disease, an infection spattered across his face in spiral clusters like dotted targets. It looks like eczema herpeticum, and is approaching his eye. Eventually, he'll lose his sight. If untreated, his organs will fail. There are acyclovir tablets lying on the ground that will help him, and I can't help myself. I'm looking at them, and I'm looking at him.

I could let him die, or I could let myself live. And I think of the man I've lost already, and realise that I have nothing left to lose. Frank told me to be proud of who I was, of what I do, and so I give myself away. I stand up and make my choice. I point to the tablets, and as no one pays me any attention, I reach down to the pile of littered goods and pick them up. I walk over and pass the tablets to the man with the infected face. He looks at them suspiciously.

'Medicine,' I say in Punjabi. 'Five times a day. For a month.'

The man is actually quite young, probably just in his mid twenties, although he has the skin of someone twenty years older, and without the medication he will probably never become the ravaged forty-year-old that he already resembles. He will never see his children grow up.

I can see him working out that the passport is mine, and I don't even care. I don't care that I'm painting a target on my own face. Every life is precious to me. Now, more than ever. Even that of a man with a gun, stopping me on the road. Every life I can save for the one that I lost.

Hanif reluctantly steps forward, and translates. The man takes the medication. Barks to the other men. He looks at me, up and down, as though searching for something. He makes a decision, and leaves me there. 'Uncle.' He nods to me as they drive off.

I work something out too. He was looking for a British doctor, but he didn't see one. He didn't see me as a foreigner. Even though there is a British passport in the bag they have stolen along with the supplies. I've discovered, back here in the place where I once belonged, that I'm still a Pakistani after all.

'Sir,' says Hanif urgently; he has tried the engine, and it is working again. He has recovered the cigarette he ground into the dust. I didn't behave as he expected, I didn't stay quiet and hidden as he asked me to, and he wants to get going before the men change their minds. He's still afraid for me. He sees that I'm not. I'm grinning. I feel as brave and defiant as a child shouting *No!* to his parents in public. I feel the same reckless exhilaration. I don't know if he thinks what I did was kind, or just plain foolish. Selfless, or selfish.

'My friend,' he says, and he gestures for me to take my seat.

Chapter Fifteen

Sully

I REMEMBER THE BEGINNING AT THE END. I'M SITTING IN THE CAR THAT Mae sent to meet me at the airport, and although it is air-conditioned, I am drenched with sweat, under my arms, from my neck down to my chest, and it is dripping and catching on the line of hairs that run to my navel. The salty-sweet scent of the deodorant that I rolled over myself at the airport is overpowering, and I don't dare take my jacket off again. I wear my shirt like a damp skin, like I'm a piece of proving dough wrapped in wet cloth.

The sweating didn't start when it should have done, when I walked out of the cool plane and into the smack of sizzling air, when I shuffled with the others down the wheeled staircase under the blazing blue sky. It happened long before that. It was when I looked out of the window, with a proper linen napkin folded on my tray, and saw the shadow of the plane. It was clear as a kid's drawing, a crude block of black moving across the pale yellow of the desert. And I thought, my shadow is in that shadow. I'm a shadow on the earth. It was like I was already dead, that I'd been dead for years, and no one had bothered to tell me, or else they had all been too polite.

I wanted to leap out of the plane, and fly like a bird towards that scudding shadow that shifted in the sand like a cloud in the sky, and bite the ground and make a dent in it, like a tooth mark in gold. Something that said to the earth, I was here. I was. I am.

The air stewardess asked if I was all right. That was when I noticed how much I'd suddenly begun to sweat. Dirty water was escaping from

378

my body through every possible pore, fissure and runnel. Everywhere except my eyes. I felt clear, elastic snot drip from my nose. I wiped it with the linen napkin, and was embarrassed that someone would have to collect this for laundry, rather than throw it away. My bodily fluids. Left for someone to inspect like blood in a toilet bowl.

I asked the stewardess for some of the cheap napkins that they fling indifferently to the economy passengers along with their crackers and peanuts. Her make-up was so thick that I could see the edge of it, like a geisha's, around her hairline and jawline, and it was a shade paler than the skin beneath. She had a constellation of spots, a congested area around her nose and chin, and it was this imperfection in her mask that made me believe her kindness when she asked me again, 'Are you all right, sir?' even though I knew she was paid to be kind. Paid to be helpful when I needed something, and invisible when I didn't.

I looked at the shadow of the plane, and thought briefly about boring her with the truth, but I knew that I would stay quiet, so everyone in the seats in front and behind could rest easy, and the anxious ripple caused by her concern could flatten and the surface become smooth again. She didn't need to know that there was a dead man on her plane, who wanted to kiss his shade that was floating on the ground. I thought of the Lithuanian soldier, tending his father's grave once he left prison, who'd gone dancing in a dead man's clothes.

I danced with my mother at Mae's wedding, before her miscarriage, and then I drove us to this same hospital, where I am just arriving now, although the car park has been updated, and the bays are clearly marked. I remember the beginning at the end.

I don't expect to see Mae as I walk into the hospital, and so I almost walk past her. 'Sulaman,' she says sharply. Everyone else in the crowded area looks at me in surprise, that I should be walking past such a pretty, imperious-looking woman. She is wearing an embroidered shalwar kameez in a youthful rosy shade, her hair is dyed several shades of chocolate, and her make-up is perfect; even her forehead seems frozen into smoothness. I think of a dragonfly in amber, preserved in a golden glow, and she isn't really herself until she opens her mouth again.

'So, you made it,' she says, and I realise that she's made a decision to be kind, because if we're playing the little game that people always do when they meet up after a long absence, she's won, and I've lost. She sounds a little tired, and I remember that there is an old woman under those pretty clothes and frozen forehead, and I notice that she has draped her scarf artfully to hide the crêpe skin of her neck. She dressed up for us, for Jakie, Lana and me, and I find it touching that she went to the trouble, and actually cares what we think of her. I feel bad for disappointing her, and letting the side down. I'm normally more presentable.

'You look great,' I say, and step forward to kiss her, a little hesitantly. She impatiently waves away my awkwardness, and kisses me twice, once on each cheek, like a practised socialite. She takes my arm and starts walking me down the corridor.

'Oh, this old thing,' she says, with a sweeping downwards gesture, so it's not clear whether she's talking about her clothes, or herself. 'I don't always look like this. I'm usually a hag on the wards. People think I'm the one who's in here to get better.' She looks at me as though straining to find a compliment, as she can't say I look great too without sounding like she's mocking me. 'Nice suit,' she says eventually. 'Armani?'

'Something like that,' I say, not taking responsibility for it. She looks a bit impatiently at me again, for pretending not to know, as though I've never chanced to look at the label stitched into the lining.

'I'm starting a men's label at Gracious Ladies of Lahore,' she says. 'We're doing designer knock-offs, copying suits like yours.'

'Are you calling it Gracious Lords of Lahore?' I say as a joke, and then realise that it isn't funny because it's probably true.

'Something like that,' she says, letting me off. 'Jakie's not here yet, his plane won't come in for a bit. About the same time as Lana's. I'll send the driver back for them both. Do you want to go to the house to freshen up?'

'No, I'll wait,' I say. I realise that I didn't tell her I've booked a hotel. It's obvious now that she assumed I'd stay at the house, but it didn't even occur to me. It's as though I'd briefly forgotten the house was still there; as though it was just something that existed in memory. Impossible to imagine it without our mother. A shell without its host.

'Are you sure?' she asks, looking me up and down, sweating in my suit, with the critical familiarity reserved for siblings, spouses and sons. 'Well, I guess you just came from the airport, so you won't mind going back there,' she says. I follow her into the lift, and she stabs a button. She lets go of my arm when the doors slide shut, as though she had only been holding it in case I tried to walk swiftly back in the direction I came from. As though I was still a flight risk.

'What do you mean?' I ask; I'd nodded but realise I didn't actually understand what she was talking about. It seems unlikely that she is going to send me back in the car I've just arrived in, to collect Jakie and Lana. Nurses and medical students all smile and nod at Mae, and she smiles and nods back at them with friendly formality, just enough to acknowledge them, and not enough to invite conversation. It occurs to me that Mae is probably wonderful with her staff, just like her first mother-in-law, Mrs Kannon.

The doors open, and she takes my arm again, gesturing towards the sign for the terminal patients. 'It's what I call this ward,' she says. 'Welcome to the departure lounge.'

I walk beside her, making sure that my longer stride matches her quick pace, listening to the percussive click of the little heels on her sparkling sandals. We come to one of the private rooms, and I see the frame with black cloth stretched across the wall before I see her. It is hung above the bed like a black hole to fall into, or a tunnel out of a prison. Through the looking glass, down the rabbit hole. A verse from the Qur'an is written in gold Arabic script in another frame, by her bed, where the pictures of loved ones might normally be found, or a spray of flowers. It sits as the only decoration, like a plain woman wearing a plain wedding band, beside the jug of water with a napkin covering it, and a glass sitting on one small paper disc, with another balanced neatly on its rim. There is a packet of sponges in plastic wrapping, the kind used for coma patients to moisten their lips.

The verse says, *Remember me, I will remember you.*

I say nothing, and look helplessly at the little body in the bed, which once held mine inside it like a cage, and which kept me in her house like an insect trapped in a web. I look at the blank face and the wispy hair, far too thin to braid, parted neatly on each side of her head like a schoolgirl's. Mae steps forward like the hostess at a dinner party, and makes introductions.

'Mummy, this is Sulaman. He's come to see you. All the way from America. And Jakie and Lana are coming too. You'll be home soon. Sulaman's here, and the others are coming.'

I don't know what to say or do. I don't know how a son should behave in this situation. I try to think of what my own son would do, and Mae nudges me forward, like a director pushing a reluctant actor on to a stage, and gives me my line.

'Say hello, Sulaman,' she whispers.

'Hello, Mummy,' I say obediently, and I walk forward a few steps, and stand by the bed. I'm aware of the smell of my deodorant and sweat, and Amma's nose wrinkles imperceptibly, like a twitch or a wink, so briefly that I'm not sure if I imagined it. 'I'm here.'

She does not remember me. I do not remember her. And so I imagine. I blaspheme. Before she fades like a flower and crumbles into the dust, before she freezes to stone with her hands folded over her chest and becomes her own tomb, I make up the memories that we might have shared.

Mummy, when I didn't like what Cook had made for dinner, you mashed it up on your plate, and made it into little balls, and told me that he had made me eggs, which were my favourite. And when I asked what sort of eggs, you said they were magic eggs, and I could decide, and so I ate unicorn and dragon eggs that night.

Mummy, when Jakie and I had chickenpox, you covered us with cream, and gave us mittens so we couldn't scratch at night, and you sang us songs from your imported Elvis Presley records, and we forgot we were ill, and we danced to 'Blue Suede Shoes'.

Mummy, you didn't send me to bed without dinner, where I cried myself to sleep, and was so hungry in the morning that I drank three glasses of milk straight away, and vomited over my plate, and you were so disgusted by me that you just left the table and didn't look back. And Baby Jamal Kamal was sitting in his high chair, and trying to copy me. He spat out his milk and made me laugh, and that was when I realised that the baby would become my best friend.

Mummy, you didn't leave the house for three whole days, to visit your relatives, because you weren't going to risk catching chickenpox yourself, and see your lovely face ravaged and mined like those of your children. I still have the scars, one in my hairline, another on the side of my nose, a deep one in my throat that looks like a vaccination wound, and which catches the light because the skin is stretched and thinner there. You didn't know that sometimes my wife would trace that scar at my throat with her finger, with a solemn look in the early morning light, as though she had scars too, and kiss it.

But I do remember dancing with you, Mummy, at Mae's wedding. I remember the way you lost your looks beforehand, and then put your face back on for the party, as though beauty was an outfit you could choose to wear when it pleased you. I remember watching you as you stepped out of the cream-coloured car, with your head held so high and proud it was as though you had a crown on your head.

I remember sitting at my desk in my room, staring at my schoolwork, and hearing you say, your icy hand like a ghost at my shoulder, 'Be good, Sulaman. Good children do what they're told.'

And I'm sitting here, with my mother, at the end of all things, and they are expecting me to kill her. To send her flying out of this room to touch the face of God. Through the glass, into the night, towards the light. It seems that she was right all along. She knows that I will do what I'm told. It seems that she has won, again.

Tell me I'm good, Mummy. Tell me I'm good.

'What are you doing, Sulaman?' asks Mae, who has come back into the room, accompanied by her assistant, with a tray of tea and pastries. The assistant, who introduces herself with formal politeness as Pari, stands respectfully outside. I remember she was once one of Amma's maids. The light from the corridor softens Mae's edges, a halo around her hair.

'Nothing, just talking, and thinking, and talking,' I say. 'You look like an angel,' I add, and realise that I'm not even joking. It's not funny when it's true.

'Come out and have some tea,' she says. 'Mummy needs some privacy.' The nurse comes in, with a fresh drip, and a new bag for our mother's catheter. I nod, and get up slowly, and I want to leave the room, but feel too sluggish and heavy. I feel that I've been pulled back into Amma's orbit like some gas giant around the sun, and that unless I walk quicker, I'll fall into her altogether. I try to copy Mae's quick steps, keeping pace with her as I follow her out.

There is a little room further down the corridor, equipped with wipe-clean furniture, and magazines. Mae sits down, and rewards Pari with a smile when she asks if madam would like anything more, before dismissing her gracefully. I can't imagine any of the staff I've hired over the years asking if I want anything more; some of the research assistants

I've had might have done, but only because they were considering sleeping with me, or expecting me to further their careers.

Without any embarrassment, Mae picks up the magazine with the most garish cover, one with a busty actress wading through a river in a sari. 'I've done the same thing,' she says, looking critically at the sensationalist magazine. I reach for my tea, and pretend I don't know what she's talking about. 'My daughter has a great phrase for it. A *Yentl* breakdown. Do you remember the movie? All that time I wanted her to see me, or hear me. I've felt like shaking her, sitting alone in that room, day after day, night after night. I've wanted to pull open her eyelids and shout: so, Mummy, do you see me now? Do you hear me now?'

'I'm sorry,' I say, and Mae shrugs.

'You and Jakie are suddenly so apologetic. Send your apologies back to when it all started, and when I could have used the support.' She watches with some amusement as I blow across my tea, and sip gingerly from it. 'Have you had a bad experience with a cup of tea in the past? Do they make tea too hot in *Amreeka*?' she teases, having forgotten her previous resolution to be kind, and just deciding to be herself. She finishes her own cup in a single gulp, like a student finishing a shot, and pours herself another. 'You know, I think she did it on purpose.'

I'm not sure if she's just talking about the drinks-wallah who made the tea so hot, and I don't say anything. Mae raises an eyebrow at this, and so I ask, 'Who?'

'Who do you think?' she says irritably. 'The person we're all here for. All that mad stuff she spewed out before the coma, all the disgusting things she said about Daddy, and about us. And the way she is now. It's like she did it on purpose. That's she's doing this on purpose. To get her own back.'

'That's a little crazy,' I say quietly. I say it with authority. It's my area of expertise, after all.

'Are you telling me she's not?' says Mae. 'That she wasn't? I bet Jakie would agree. Why else was he always so kind to her? Year after year he went back to see her. She certainly didn't appreciate it.'

'I guess he felt sorry for her,' I say.

I don't think Jakie was ever really afraid of her, even when we were tiny. He shrugged off the beatings, and carried on being himself. I think about Amma being so wrapped up in her sense of what was honourable that she felt forced to reject the only child of hers who regularly returned. She respected him less for returning, even.

I think about our mother dissolving into shadow, all the years I was absent, until it was only her wrappings, the trappings of honour and obedience, that were left. The ghost of some monster from mythology; she who must be obeyed. I don't think I ever saw our mother the way that Jakie did. As someone to be pitied, looked after like the rest of us. As a little widow woman in white, with feelings like the rest of us. With hopes and fears, wants and don't-wants.

'I think you're right,' says Mae, looking at me as though surprised by my insight. 'She must have hated that. To have seemed so weak to him.'

'Where is he?' I ask; it seems to me that her driver went to the airport to meet his plane some time ago. As if in reply, her mobile rings, despite the large sign in all the rooms that phones are to be switched off as they interfere with equipment. Mae doesn't turn it off apologetically, but answers promptly. It's obviously not Jakie, and the excitement that it might have been bubbles back down in my stomach like acid. She speaks in a Punjabi so rapid that I struggle to follow, and think that it's wrong to feel like a foreigner in my own country.

'Nah, haan ji, okay,' she says eventually, and I wait for her to say, 'Khuda hafiz,' but she just snaps off her phone with an annoyed gesture, not bothering to say goodbye. 'That was the driver. Jakie wasn't on the plane. Or if he was on the plane, he didn't go up to the driver.'

'Well, where is he?' I ask, with a mounting panic that he's done what I should have done, and decided not to come after all. I'm wondering whether this time coming was more cowardly than staying away. I didn't have the balls to refuse; I didn't have it in me to say no.

'For all I know, he's walking barefoot from the airport with a loincloth and cane,' she snaps, 'like bloody Gandhi with his staff.' She drinks her second cup of tea, and gets up, smoothing out her clothes. 'I'm going to the office to get in touch with that camp of his. Find out if he really left. There was probably someone dying, so he stayed.'

'There's always someone dying, if you're a doctor,' I say, as an excuse for Jakie, as a sort of solidarity with her. As she tugs up her heavy handbag, easing it over her shoulder, her assistant, Pari, comes in.

'Madam,' she says, beaming.

'I feel we've been here before, Mae,' says Jakie, limping into the room behind Pari. He's sunburnt, unshaven and underweight. 'You know, I was thinking on the way here, it's a shame that someone has to die to get us all to visit.'

'Oh, Jakie,' she says, and she puts her arms around him, around his filthy clothes. 'You made the mule train, old man.'

'Do I look that bad?' he says with amusement, holding her with both arms, lifting the cane from the ground to let her support him instead. 'Do I look like I need a hug?'

'You do,' says Mae. 'Humour me.' She sees me looking at them, and steps back, a little embarrassed that she didn't hug me like that. I'm embarrassed that I didn't hug her either. I feel caged in my smart suit. Like no one can get close to me.

'Sulaman,' says Jakie, stepping back to look me up and down. 'Nice suit. Nice shoes, too.'

I want to retort something in kind: nice rags, nice beard, too. But the words dissolve as I face him. He looks dreadful. His stained kameez is hanging off him. His weight loss has made his cheekbones pop. My cheeky little brother is looking ravaged. Like an emaciated Christ on a cross.

I have to remind myself that I'm the older brother here; I feel the urge to take Jakie's elbow and lead him gently to a chair, as though he's a fragile old man. He is leaning heavily on his cane, like he'd tumble to the ground without it. As though he has hips that might break, and hollow bird bones that might crack with too firm an embrace.

My first thought is that Frank hasn't been looking after him. And then I think that of course he hasn't. Jakie is looking after Frank, instead, and has been for a long time. Since I last saw them, Frank has gone from hearty to helpless. And as though that isn't enough credit on his soul's account, Jakie has spent weeks in the hills looking after strangers, too. Changing his partner's pissy sheets in Notting Hill, vaccinating orphans in the northern hills. For a moment, I feel jealous of him. He's needed, in a way that I have never been needed, beyond a single night with my infant son. The toll that love has taken on Jakie is his badge of honour. He wears his loved one like a medal. Real love costs something. Real happiness hurts.

'Jakie,' I finally say, far too inadequately. I'm trying to say 'It's so good to see you.' But the words evaporate into a sort of strangled whimper, like I'm wetly clearing my throat, because I'm thinking that his looks and health and husband have all been stolen from him as abruptly as a highway robbery, and it's a tragic sight. I find it so hard to lie.

'Jakie,' I say again, and step forward to hold him, just as he steps forward to hold me. He claps his arms around my back, as though I'm the one who's had the tough journey.

'Are you okay, Sulaman?' he asks with concern, always a doctor with or without his white coat, 'Are you still jet-lagged or something? You look dreadful. Like you've seen a ghost.' He's seen the way I looked at him, and he doesn't even mind. He's laughing at me again, laughing at himself. Jakie the Joker, the gold that gleams in everything he says.

'Tea, Jakie?' asks Mae.

'God, no, I'd like something stronger than that,' he says. 'I had bugs for breakfast yesterday. Then the bus was stopped. Then the car got held up and my bag was stolen. I'll say hello to Mummy, and then we can go out somewhere.'

He moves off, swinging his cane with his game leg like a clumsy dancer, tapping out an uneven rhythm with the jittery energy of a man who's thinner than he used to be.

Mae's not amused. 'Honestly, Jakie,' she says. '*Uff, Allah*. Look at you! You're like free housing for fleas. Don't even think of saying hello to Mummy until you've washed off whatever cowpotty place you've come from.'

'You were right yesterday,' says Jakie. 'You do sound like her.' He says it without an edge, almost admiringly, but Mae looks uncomfortable. Jakie and I look at her. We are all suddenly aware that with our mother fading, Mae is filling the space left by her absence. The mistress of the manor. The lady of the house. As though with our mother gone, we are all aware that someone else has to tell us what to do, and the election among us will be uncontested. I don't have the guts to do it, Jakie would refuse, and Lana would never step forward.

'Oh shut up,' she says. 'Fine, go say hello, but then get washed. And changed. You can't go anywhere decent looking like that.'

'I've got no clothes,' shrugs Jakie. 'Nothing except what I'm standing up in. I lost my bag. And my British passport. Everything.' He seems rather too proud of this.

'Careless, aren't you?' Mae retorts, and she pulls out her phone. 'I'll get them to send some of Daddy's old clothes from the house. You're the same size.'

'Daddy's clothes are still there?' I ask.

'They're still in the wardrobe, even,' says Jakie, surprised that I don't know this. As though I'd have gone into my mother's room that last time I visited, and rummaged through her smalls.

'My daughter-in-law organised and bagged all her mother's clothes the week she died,' I say, as though I'm just making idle conversation. 'Chose her coffin outfit, and then divided the rest of them between Goodwill and the family.' I add with an edge, 'She says she lives in the now, not in the past.'

Mae nods, as though she approves of this. Treating the practicalities of death like any other domestic chore. A yard sale. A house clearance. 'I like Tania,' she says, with a bit too much emphasis, as though picking up that I don't, really.

'Well, there's a fine line between living in the past and living with it,' says Jakie. He's looking straight at me. He smiles.

He limps over to the room where our mother is lying, as though he is familiar with this place. Jakie is comfortable in hospitals. I guess he's comfortable with death. For him, it's like just another disease to be diagnosed and dealt with. He hesitates at the door.

'I was meant to come after you all. I made an earlier flight because the driver took me all the way to town when the bus was cancelled,' he explains. 'All the way here, I imagined the rest of you sitting in there waiting for me when I arrived.' He looks at us and shrugs, as though he knows it shouldn't matter. 'I thought I'd be last.'

'Looks like Lana will be the one to make the entrance,' Mae says. 'She'll be here soon. I've asked the driver to bring her straight over.'

Jakie seems pleased with this. 'Well, it's about time, isn't it?' he says. 'It's about time that Lana got to make the entrance.'

He pushes the door open. The room is dark, and he doesn't switch on the light, or draw the curtain. I think about feeding him the line, just as Mae did for me. I think about saying, 'Say hello, Jakie,' in case he is as tongue-tied as I was. I'm ready if he needs me. I'm the big brother.

'Oh, Mummy,' I hear him say, just as Mae said, 'Oh, Jakie.' I hear the same pity mixed with rueful affection in his voice. I can imagine the coral form of our mother closing like a statue, seizing up with anger, at this. The last living part of her, buried deep inside, that might still hear him. He closes the door behind him. I find it hard to picture him just sitting there, beside her, in the dark.

A little later, Jakie goes to clean himself up in the hospital washroom, borrowing my disposable razor. Mae sends me to him with some of our father's clothes, and a few pairs of his chappals, to try for size. I knock.

'Shall I leave these outside?' I ask.

'No, come in,' calls Jakie.

He seems to think nothing of the fact that he is stark naked at the sink. He is soaping himself all over with a plastic-wrapped bar he must have picked up from the plane, from toes to crown in efficient circles. I haven't seen him naked since we were teenagers. His hands and feet and face are several shades darker than the rest of him, like he's been dipped in something.

I'm embarrassed. The sight of all his slight flesh. I can see his ribs, and skinny flanks, and his soft cock hanging between his legs. I feel just like I did when I walked through a park in Munich after a conference, and saw all the topless locals and naked children frolicking by the water. Old women casually doing the crossword and cutting fruit for their grandkids with their withered breasts bared. For a moment, it's like Jakie isn't my brother at all; he's just another shameless European, and I'm just another prudish American.

'They've got showers, you know,' I say.

'They're for patients, not visitors,' says Jakie. 'This is fine. This is luxury. I've been bathing out of half a bucket of mud for the last few weeks.' He does his hair too, which has just grown long enough to start curling, and then starts washing the soap off, top to bottom. 'What?' he says, and I realise that I'm staring. He's being careful around his creases. I work out with a twinge of disgust that he's checking for bites and parasites.

'A photo will last longer, Sulaman,' he says, casually, as he starts lathering his face with the same bar of soap.

I sigh, and take off my jacket. I stand there looking at myself in the stiff shirt with the sweat circles under the arms. And then I take off my shirt too, and stand there in my vest. 'I haven't washed since the plane stopped for refuelling. Business-class lounge at Abu Dhabi. I haven't got changed since I got on the plane at JFK.' With a final burst of effort, I take off my vest, and my suit pants, and my shoes and my socks. I'm standing there in my underwear.

Jakie tosses me another plastic-wrapped bar of soap, and I catch it clumsily. I never played catch with Buzz. I didn't know how to play catch with Sami and Dani. My grandkids would drag me out to Buzz's manicured back yard, with a catcher's mask and a mitt, and expect me to do what other grandpas did. They used to get frustrated at how little I knew how to play. Not just baseball, but almost everything, apart from Scrabble or chess. It feels that I've come this far, so I can go a little further. I feel that I should stand beside my brother. I pull off my underwear, and I'm standing naked at the sink with Jakie. Wetting the cream-coloured bar, and soaping my skin all over, like him. I see him look at the scars up my arm, but he doesn't say anything. I see him look at the gold ring hanging on a chain around my neck, and then he does.

'How's Radhika?' he says.

'You asked me that yesterday,' I reply. He splashes me. My grown-up brother, a naked man washing himself in front of a sink, splashes me.

'I didn't know you still wore your wedding ring,' he says. He looks satisfied with his lathered face; testing the blade on the razor with his finger, he starts to shave. 'I don't claim to know everything about you, Sulaman. In fact, I'm sure all the things I don't know about you would make a bewilderingly long list. But I'm surprised that I didn't know that.'

'What's to know?' I say. 'I'm the guy who lives in the past. Not with it.' I look at myself, at my skin. At my scars. The blood pumping just beneath them. I remember watching as I scored the deepest cut, with my surgeon's skill, in that clean, swabbed room in the prison. The blood flooding from my pale flesh like it had been excavated from stone. 'The guy who's held together by his suit.'

'You're not wearing it now,' says Jakie. 'You're holding together just fine.' He turns, and looks at me appraisingly.

'A photo will last longer, Jakie,' I say, as embarrassed to be seen as I was to look myself.

'You're still a fine figure of a man, Sulaman,' he says, not slightly put off. 'You're a catch, for the right woman. You don't drink, don't smoke, don't swear, don't lie. You even come from money.'

'Shut up, Jakie,' I say, washing under my arms. I'm not smiling. I'm waiting for him to scold me now, to tell me to lighten up and take a joke.

'Shit,' he says, nicking himself, and bright blood drips into the sink, from the mess of the lather and beard. I wince, seeing the petal-red stains on the ceramic. But then I realise that Jakie's been having trouble standing at the sink and shaving, as he needs to hold himself up with the cane, too. I realise that the weeks of tough growth are defeating the disposable razor. It's painful to watch him drag it inexpertly, one-handed, across his face, ignoring the dripping blood, while he hums something cheerful and tuneless.

'Give that to me,' I say impatiently, and I take the razor, and start to shave him. He holds himself up, both arms on the sink, and lets me. He stands as meekly as a child. I forget that I can't stand touching people. That I don't like flesh and blood and mess. Jakie seems surprised at my skill; perhaps he had forgotten how good I was with my hands. I am struggling to think of the last time I did something like this for him, or for anybody. I guess Jakie does this every other day for Frank. I'm trying to think of when I last helped someone, or someone asked me for help. I think how much better a person I might have been if I had stayed with Jakie, and had him in my life. The other half of me. My brother half of me.

'You should have specialised in surgery,' says Jakie, looking impressed, running his hand over his smooth chin. 'Now that's some nice work. That's why you're the big brother.'

'Do you ever think about what would have happened if we'd stayed?' I ask him, running the water over the razor, tapping out the hairs. 'Do you think it would have been better for us?'

'Of course not,' says Jakie. 'Then I wouldn't have had Frank, and you wouldn't have had Radhika.'

'I don't have Radhika now,' I say, talking about her despite myself.

'No, Sulaman,' says Jakie firmly. 'I don't have Frank. But you've still got Radhika. She's still there, the mother of your child. She's living alone in the same town as you.' He sounds a little angry with me. I can't imagine how hard it's been on him since Frank got sick. 'Radhika's not lost; you just haven't tried to find her. You still wear your damn ring, and you hide it where no one can see.'

'I asked her to come with me,' I say. I want him to know that I'm not as gutless as he thinks. 'I asked her. She said no.'

'Of course she said no,' snaps Jakie. 'Mummy hated her. What the hell's wrong with you? Don't ask her to a deathbed. Ask her to dinner. Don't ask her to Pakistan. Ask her to Paris. Buy her a sodding big bunch of flowers, and make a fool of yourself for once.' He looks at me like I'm not the big brother after all. Like I'm someone hiding in the past. A damaged little boy with a struck, stricken face.

'I can't do that,' I say. 'You're being ridiculous.'

'Oh for God's sake,' he says, and he's not Jakie the Joker any more. There's something explosive and powerful about his fury, because it's so unexpected coming from him; he's usually so funny and kind. I feel the fierce passion in him that I have so rarely felt in myself. In a basement room after a dance. In a fleapit motel after a dinner. 'You know what I'd give to get back what you still could? Be a man, Sulaman! Be a fucking man.'

I don't say anything else. I wish I hadn't got drawn into this. I feel ridiculous, standing there naked, washing at the sink. I feel exposed. Not just my skin, but everything else. My moist tissues, the fluids bubbling inside of me. I wish I could just sit down. I wish I could hug my knees and rock on the floor in the corner. I'm thinking of my shadow in the plane's shadow, scudding on the sandy ground. Jakie looks at me in the mirror above the sink. We both see that I look struck, and stricken. His voice softens.

'Oh, Sulaman,' says Jakie. 'What have you been so scared of all these years?' He dries himself off, and begins to shrug on the kameez and loose pants that used to belong to our father. He's wearing a dead man's clothes, and he feels no disquiet. I'm surprised that I feel no disquiet looking at him. It seems like the natural order of things. They haven't been stolen from an old man shot in a pit. They have been passed down, father to son, like everything else that makes us. I watch Jakie dress, and now that he is shaved, and clean, and has lost so much weight, I notice a resemblance between us that I haven't seen since we were very young. Our cheekbones have the same hollow angles. His brown eyes, still clear and delicately veined, fringed with fine lashes, are like mine.

'Of her?' says Jakie, and he jerks his head towards the door. 'Poor Mummy, she's already gone.' He puts his roughened hands on my bare shoulders. 'Of losing? Because you've got nothing to lose that hasn't already been lost.'

'Stop telling me what to do, Jakie,' I say quietly. I say it like I've been betrayed, because Jakie is the one person I thought would never do this to me. I pull my underwear back on, because I can't be naked when he is not. Undressing and dressing again. Getting back into my glass box, where I can't be touched. Hiding my scars, and the ring around my neck.

'I'm not. I'm telling you the truth,' he says. 'You have something most people on the planet would give up everything for. You know who the love of your life is. You even know her number.'

I'm leaning defeated over the sink, and Jakie is fully dressed, and disconcertingly like a thinner version of our father. There's something almost dashing about his gauntness now, with the costume change. He looks like a local. I see him shaking out some of the other clothes I brought.

'What do you think of these ones?' he asks, pulling out another kameez, lightly embroidered, another pair of loose pants. He inspects a pair of chappals, slightly bigger than the ones he's stepped into.

'You look fine in what you're wearing,' I say. I turn to get the rest of my clothes, but Jakie has swiftly gathered them up, with my shoes, along with his own stained and torn outfit, and is walking out the door.

'I meant for you,' he says. 'I can't stand to see you sweating in that suit any more. It's like you're buttoned into a designer dungeon.'

He leaves me in my underwear in the bathroom. I look at myself, the biteable gold at my throat, and try to see the-me-that-he-sees. I look at my arms, my chest, my face. I try to see someone who wasn't just loved in the past, but who could be loved still. I try to see someone who can be a fucking man.

Lana has already arrived by the time I step sheepishly out of the washroom, dressed in the clothes of my father, his chappals on my feet. The footwear is too small, but I had no other choice. I waited there for ten minutes, certain that Jakie would return, but he didn't. When I heard him chatting outside to Lana, I knew that he wouldn't.

'So handsome, Sulaman,' says Mae, like an auntie at a wedding, and I don't know if she means it or is mocking me. I'm not sure she knows herself any more.

Lana hugs me. 'I'm glad you're here,' she says simply. She doesn't waste words. She didn't make an entrance, after all, and I guess it's never been her style. Instead she has slid into our circle like liquid mercury, a pool of light that shines and fills the spaces we have left. She will do what we have forgotten. Lana is holding a small Qur'an, which she has taken out of her handbag. She takes it into our mother's room, and reads quietly beside her. Jakie goes to sit with them, and watches Lana praying softly by our mother's bedside. She pats him on the hand after a while, releasing him with a whisper. Jakie leaves, kissing her on the top of her head. Like she's his child as much as Amma's.

'Come on,' he says to me. 'Lana wants to be alone with Mummy. Mae's conference-calling or nagging her accountants or doing something busy and important. Let's get out of here and go to a bar for a bit. And you can tell me about everything. Tell me about Buzz and Tania, Sami and Dani. Work. Everything.'

It seems that he might be apologising for yelling at me. He doesn't mention Radhika's name again, and part of me wishes he would. He walks ahead of me like he knows the hospital well, as though if it wasn't for his inconvenient arthritis, he would move along the corridors just as comfortably as all the other fast-talking and fast-walking Lahori staff.

'A bar?' I ask, aware of how disapproving I sound as soon as I do.

'Yes, a bar,' says Jakie. 'Do you want to notify the village elders?'

I follow him out of the hospital, and into a rickshaw. He chats easily with the driver; like Mae, he speaks colloquial Punjabi so rapidly I find it hard to follow. Jakie's been coming back here every year, since before Abbu died. In some ways it seems like he's never left. He gets us dropped off at a hotel bar, and I look at the clientele with their sparkling drinks with disapproval, like I really am a prudish American. Dressed as I am, perhaps they simply think I'm a good Muslim.

'A bit early for me,' I say, as I do think it's way too early for hard liquor, and I never drink at all really. Champagne at a wedding, just to be polite. At dinner parties and work events I'll drink soda or tonic water with a slice instead, so it looks like I'm having vodka or gin. A closet teetotaller, although I suppose everyone has something embarrassing to hide. Jakie never told me he was gay, all the years we were growing up. He still didn't tell me he was gay even when he wrote to me that he'd moved in with a man, and was raising a family with him. There was no need, I suppose, as telling me would have been as redundant as telling himself. We had never given each other presents, as children or as men, for the same reason. It would have been like giving something to yourself; wrapping your own box with a foil label to go under the tree, sending yourself flowers.

Jakie looks exasperated, but only briefly. I guess he realises how uncomfortable I am, and decides to put me at ease. 'Same old Sulaman,' he says, and I have no idea what he means by that. He orders two coffees, holding up his two fingers in a sign that could mean victory, and that could mean peace. Like they are buttons on his embroidered collar.

'You still know Lahore so well,' I say, trying too hard to pay him a compliment. Trying to apologise to him for who I am and have always been. Same old Sulaman. Defeated instead of victorious. At war instead of peace.

'I guess we all go back to the place we once belonged,' says Jakie. 'If only to bury the dead.' He's looking at me and I shift with discomfort; he puts his arm around my shoulder, sorry for criticising me like this. Jakie is always generous with his hands, with his hugs. He doesn't hold himself back. 'Next time, we'll meet up in Paris,' he says. 'I'll take a day off to catch up with you guys.' He's still smiling, but he isn't really looking at me. He's looking out the window, as though it's a private joke. As though he knows there might not be a next time for a long while. When he says a day off, I know that he's not talking about work, but a day off from Frank. When he says 'you guys', there's a gleam, as though he really thinks I'll be there with Radhika.

He downs his coffee like Mae, half the cup in one swallow, and begins working his way through the little platters of salted biscuits. 'Did you want some?' he says, noticing me glancing askance at them. I don't even eat peanuts at parties; I can't stand to think of all the unwashed hands rummaging in the bowl.

'No, I'm fine, thank you, Jakie,' I say, a bit too formally.

'Thank you, Sulaman,' says Jakie. 'For the razor. For the shave.'

'You know, no one else ever calls me Sulaman,' I say. 'Just you, and Mae, and Lana.'

'I guess we're the ones who know who you really are. That's who you are to us, at least,' he says. 'Serious Sulaman, Sulaman the Wise, our brilliant big brother.' He finishes his coffee with a second gulp, and orders himself a whisky. It's not until then that I realise I'm still blowing over the surface of my cup, just like a little old lady all over again. I drink it properly. It's so hot it hurts my mouth.

Jakie grins at me, and pours the whisky into his empty coffee cup when it arrives, as though he's been served at an old-fashioned speakeasy.

'This is how Frank has Irish coffee,' he tells me. 'He tells them to hold the coffee.'

'Why does he do that?' I ask. He knows I mean why doesn't he just order a whisky, but Jakie deliberately misunderstands me.

'Well, that stuff's poison,' he says. He smiles, and I know he's thinking about the love of his life. The man that he was and that he is.

'That's kind of how I have a vodka and tonic,' I say. 'I ask them to hold the vodka.'

When it's time for us to go back to the hospital, I wave for the bill, but the staff hand it to Jakie instead of me.

'So, that's a little offensive,' I say, looking down at myself, in my traditional outfit. 'Do they think I look like I can't afford it?'

'It's because they think you're foreign,' says Jakie. 'I'll get it.'

'I'll get it,' I say firmly. A foreigner in my own country, even with the costume change. I guess it's true, but I don't know how they can tell. I don't know if it's my haircut or my accent. 'I'm the big brother.'

I peel the notes out of my wallet, and as we stand up, Jakie hugs me impulsively. 'I'll always be here for you, Sulaman,' he says. 'You know that, don't you? I'll always look after you.'

I realise then that Jakie will never have a day off, even if he comes and meets me in Paris. It won't be a day off his usual duties with the people for whom he cares: his partner, his patients. It'll be just another working day, because I'm on his list too. Like Mummy and Mae and Lana. Like Frank. I'm one of the medals that he wears.

I wish I could let him off, and tell him not to worry about me. I wish I could tell him that I haven't been sad. But I can't lie. I don't even try.

I am in our mother's room. The doctor is waiting outside, talking with my brother and sisters. Discussing the practicalities of dealing with death. The Do Not Resuscitate form is completed and approved. The prayers have been said. The machinery and equipment that keeps Amma breathing, that keeps her tissues moist, that removes her waste into neat plastic packets, is still humming, beeping, dripping.

I'm looking at her profile, the fine hairs that are straying from her nostrils, the way her face has fallen back, toothless. A large section of her hair has been shaved behind her ear, because of a spattering of infected insect bites. She has already said goodbye to herself; she does not need to say goodbye to us.

She breathes more deeply, and I wonder whether, if I tap her empty head, she will ring like a bell. I stare at my hands, and worry at a piece of dry skin, until underneath it is raw and new, and stings when I press the oily pad of my fingertip against it.

'Mummy,' I say. 'Can you hear me?' I can feel the pulse in my temple. I can feel the beating of my heart. I talk to the body in the bed, to the undamaged parts deep inside that stubbornly persist when everything else is breaking down. I talk to the living marrow in her bones. 'Mummy, is this what you want?'

There is no answer in the room, just the rustle of my clothes as I shift in the chair. Amma has been brain-dead for some time now. She is just the machine of her body, plugged into the wall.

Mae comes in, and she has refreshed her make-up and fixed her hair. As though Amma would complain about how sloppy she looked if she didn't. Mae puts her corpse-cold hand on my shoulder, just as Amma did when I was a child. She inherited her poor circulation from our mother. Mother to daughter. I don't shiver or cringe. I cover her hand with mine. Jakie comes in, with his arm around Lana's shoulder, dressed like me in our father's old clothes. A clean white kameez. Father to son.

I know that Mae has made arrangements. That there will be a burial in hours. That the house will be scented with rose water, and filled with mourners who will not cry. With pious women who will cover their hair, and cover pictures with pillowcases.

I know Lana is prepared to wash our mother's body, with her own hands. To do her last daughter's duty, and prepare our mother for wrapping in white. No one has asked that she do this, but she will. I know that our mother will have a stone for a pillow, and be pointed towards the holy land.

But I do not know if she can hear me. I do not know if this is what she wants. I do not know if she will forgive us for her death.

Mae sits beside me, and I am comforted by the ice of her fingers in my sticky palm. Lana slips her fingers into our mother's hand instead, squeezing gently, the warm inside the dead. Jakie sits beside Lana, and she leans her head into his shoulder. They are so easy with each other.

I understand now why they are all so unafraid. They are already free of this slight body in the bed. They have been free of her for a long time. There is just a machine to switch off. They are not losing their mother. She is no longer here. There is no one else to forgive us, unless we forgive each other, forgive ourselves. My sisters kiss our mother's parchment face. Jakie kisses her too.

I'm the eldest son. They think it should be me. We have never discussed this, but they think it should be me. I'm the man of the house, today.

She loved you, Lana once told me. She loved you best of all.

Mae sits back, and breathes. She has started to cry a little, but I know she is relieved. She's been chained to our mother's living meat for too long.

Lana's ready, and she has no fears for the dead. Her sympathies lie with the living. For those who live with loneliness or fear. For those who are still seeking the truth.

Jakie nods to me. He is looking at me, not our mother. He is worried about me. She will feel nothing, as her organs fail. There will be no pain. There will be no cry from the stone body in the bed. No protest as her heart stops beating.

The protest comes from me, and it's deep inside my body. It's my heart. It's troubling me, I'm telling you. It's my heart.

I'm the eldest son, and I know what I need to do. They are all waiting for me to make the decision. I know that I don't have to do this. I know that I have a choice.

The hospital doctor stands at the door, to record the time of death. I see Mae's impatience, and wonder if she will push me aside and do it for me, should I blunder or hesitate. A mother watching her child make a mess of a specific and simple job, giving him only so much time to get it right before stepping in and doing it herself. I wonder if Mae and Lana are aware of how much they resemble the different masks of our mother, on this final day. The sharp-edged butterfly. The pious observer of faith. It is as though the pawns have reached the end of the chessboard, at the game's end, and each has slid into a final chequered square to become the queen.

I make the decision, and I stand. I switch off the machines, one after another. We wait for the final shuddering of breath. I wait to grasp it, this expiration. I want to hear her for a final time. I want her to say that she wants to leave.

I want her consent.

I kiss her, and so her final breath is mine, an elongated hiss like air being let out of a tyre, a snake sliding from the shadows of a tree, and if I imagine, if I blaspheme, it could be a yes. Yes, Sulaman. Yes, son. Yes. I feel the breath leave her body a few grams lighter. The weight of a human soul.

I look at the white walls, and the steel machines, and the nodding man in the white coat, and realise that I have never left this room. I've been sitting here from the very beginning.

And as we sit around the body of the woman who bore us, so small and defeated, I know it's time for me to leave this cage behind.

I didn't cry for my father, but I cry for her. The soft, living part of me, wimpled in my soft white clothes, rocking in the chair. I'm strong enough to weep, and as I finally split open, it feels that the tears of years are released. The walls of this white room come tumbling, crumbling down; they flatten and fall. The glass box breaks, and I can finally be touched. I'm free.

'Sulaman,' Lana says, as she sees me cry, her working woman's hand warm on my face. 'She loved you. She loved you best of all.' She says, with the luminous hope of someone who has always believed, 'She loves you still.'

I see what the others see. I can pity her at last, washed clean by my grief. I'm not afraid any more. I push myself forward, to hold in my arms those I love. My sisters, and my brother. To hold those who, like me, will go on.

Three days after her burial, there are prayers for the dead. We gather in my mother's bedroom early that morning, before the mourners arrive. Her clothes are spread on the bed, strewn on clean sheets across the floor. Our father's clothes too. The jewellery has been spilled out to be divided.

'It feels a bit wrong, doing this so soon,' says Jakie.

'We can't do it next week,' Mae says practically, matching up saris with blouses, selecting with her professional eye ones that she thinks

Sherry might like. 'I have to go back to Karachi. I've got a business to run. You and Lana have to get back to London for Frank. Sulaman has to go back too.'

'I'll stay if you need me to,' I say, surprising myself. 'I don't have to go straight back to New York.'

'Yes,' says Jakie, firmly. He's looking at me. Not in the eye. He's looking at my throat, where my gold band lies. Exposed on my skin by the open neck of my father's embroidered kameez. My loved one worn as a medal, where everyone can see. The best of me. 'Yes, you do.'

'You don't have to go back either,' says Lana to Jakie. 'Not just yet. I can take care of Frank for you.'

'I know I don't,' says Jakie. 'I know you can. But I will, I've missed him, and the kids.'

'You'll come to Karachi, won't you, Jakie?' says Mae. 'When you do your do-gooding stint next year.'

'Of course I will,' says Jakie. He pauses, and says, 'I was actually thinking I could come back in a few months or so.' He looks at Lana. 'If you're sure you can manage. They need me in the refugee camps. They need all the doctors they can get.'

'I can manage. I'm proud of what you do here,' says Lana. 'You know that. Frank's proud too.'

'So am I,' I say. 'So's Buzz. I called him this morning. You're the Doctors Without Borders uncle. You're like the family trophy.'

'Charity junkie Jakie,' says Mae acidly. I know that she's covering up how pleased she is that she'll see him sooner rather than later.

I stand beside Jakie at the Qul for our mother, and he holds me, giving me support, rather than taking it himself. His arm around my shoulder. Jakie's like that. He gives what he most needs. I remember how I trembled at my father's funeral, how I could barely stand. How afraid I was, to be here in this house. I stand tall, and put my arm around him too, and feel completed by him. My brother half of me.

I see Mae, marching to and from the kitchen, organising the food, while the mourners pick like gannets at the buffet, and gossip about house prices in Gulberg and Defence, and complain about the cricket, while their children silently crouch over hand-held games in the corner.

I see Lana, with her Qur'an, praying softly. People glance at her, and feel at peace. It is as though she has stepped into a dark place, carrying a light.

'You know, I didn't expect you to cry,' says Jakie. He's looking at me like he's the one who's proud of me. 'You're a good man, Sulaman.' He's been crying himself, but he smiles through his tears.

Be a man. Be a fucking man. That's what he told me. That's what I am. My name is Sulaman Saddeq, and on the day my mother died, I cried. I blamed no one else for the decision I made. I stood up and made my choice. Then I put my arms around my sisters and my brother. And I led us from our mother's room.

Acknowledgements

With grateful thanks to the Authors' Foundation and the Society of Authors, for the John C. Laurence Prize, awarded for writing which improves understanding between races.

With thanks to Imogen Taylor, Clare Alexander and Ayesha Karim, for keeping faith with me on the long journey to delivering this sixth novel, and for the frank and insightful feedback which made it a truer book.

And with thanks to my family, my husband Phil and my children Jaan, Zaki, Zarena and Alia. For knowing who I am, and what I do, and still putting up with me.

Roopa Farooki is the Ambassador for Family for Relate, a registered charity which provides counselling, support and information for all relationships, between children, parents and families.

Visit www.relate.co.uk or follow on Twitter @Relate_charity

BEHIND THE SCENES
AT TINDER PRESS . . .

For more on the worlds of our books and authors
Visit us on Pinterest
Ⓟ TINDER PRESS

For the latest news and views from the team
Follow us on Twitter
🐦 TINDER PRESS

To meet and talk to other fans of our books
Like us on Facebook
f TINDER PRESS

www.tinderpress.co.uk